# JUDE DEVERAUX

## Scarlet Nights

**SIMON &
SCHUSTER**

London · New York · Sydney · Toronto · New Delhi

A CBS COMPANY

First published in the USA by Atria Books, 2010
A division of Simon and Schuster, Inc.
First published in Great Britain by Simon & Schuster UK Ltd, 2010
A CBS COMPANY

This paperback edition first published, 2012

1 3 5 7 9 10 8 6 4 2

Simon & Schuster UK Ltd
1st Floor
222 Gray's Inn Road
London WC1X 8HB

www.simonandschuster.co.uk

Simon & Schuster Australia, Sydney

A CIP catalogue record for this book is available from the British Library.

B Format ISBN 978-1-84983-279-3
Ebook ISBN 978-1-84983-280-9

Printed and bound by CPI Group (UK) Ltd, Croydon, CR0 4YY

# Scarlet Nights

# 1

I THINK WE'VE FOUND her," Captain Erickson said. His voice was forced, showing that he was working hard to control his jubilation.

They were sitting at a picnic table at the Hugh Taylor Birch State Park, just off A1A in Fort Lauderdale. It was a September morning, and South Florida was beginning to cool off. By next month the weather would be divine.

"I guess you mean Mitzi," Mike Newland said, for just yesterday the captain had given him a thick file on the family. Mizelli Vandlo was a woman several police departments, including the fraud squad of Fort Lauderdale, plus the Secret Service—for financial crimes—and the FBI—for violence—had been searching for for years. As far as anyone knew, the only photo of her had been taken in 1973, when she was sixteen and about to marry a fifty-one-year-old man. Even then, she was no beauty and her face was easily remembered for its large nose and lipless mouth.

When the captain didn't answer, Mike knew that a Big Job

was coming, and he worked to keep his temper from rising to the surface. He'd just finished an undercover case that had taken three years, and for a while there had been contracts out on his life.

Although Mike had never worked on the Vandlo case, he'd heard that a few years ago there had been major arrests in the family, all of it happening on one day, but in several cities. But Mitzi, her son Stefan, and some other family members—all of whom they had many photos of—had somehow been tipped off and had quietly slipped away. Until recently, no one had known where they'd gone.

Mike poured green tea from a thermos into a cup and offered it to the captain.

"No thanks," the captain said, shaking his head. "I'll stick with this." He held up a can of something that was full of additives and caffeine.

"So where is she?" Mike asked, his voice even more raspy than usual. He often had to answer questions about his voice, and his standard half-lie was that it was caused by a childhood accident. Sometimes he even elaborated and made up stories about tricycles or car wrecks, whatever appealed to him that day. No matter what the story, Mike's voice was as intimidating as his body was when he went into action.

"Ever hear of . . . ?" As the captain fumbled in his shirt pocket for a piece of paper, Mike could tell that he was excited about something other than finding Mitzi. After all, this was at least the sixth time they'd heard she'd been found. "Ah, here it is." The captain's eyes were dancing about. "Let's see if I can pronounce the name of this place."

"Czechoslovakia no longer exists," Mike said, deadpan.

"No, no, this town is in the U.S. Somewhere up north."

"Jacksonville is 'up north.'"

"Found it," the captain said. "Eddy something. Eddy . . . Lean."

"Eddy Lean is a person's name, not a place."

"Maybe I'm saying it wrong. Say it faster."

A muscle worked in Mike's jaw. He didn't like whatever game the captain was trying to play. "Eddylean. Never heard of it. So where—?" Halting, Mike took in a breath. "Ed-uh-lean," he said softly, his voice so low the captain could hardly hear him. "Edilean."

"That's it." The captain put the paper back into his pocket. "Ever hear of the place?"

Mike's hands began to shake so much he couldn't lift his cup. He willed them to be still—while he tried to relax his face so his panic wouldn't show. He'd told only one man about Edilean, and that had been a long time ago. If that man was involved, there was danger. "I'm sure you've found out that my sister lives there," Mike said quietly.

The captain's face lost its smile. He'd meant to tease Mike, but he didn't like seeing such raw emotion in one of the men under his command. "So I was told, but this case has nothing to do with her. And before you ask, no one but me and the attorney general know about her being there."

Mike worked on controlling his heart rate. Many times before he'd been in situations where he'd had to make people believe he was who he wasn't, so he'd learned to keep calm at all costs. But in those times, it had been his own life in danger. If there was something going on in tiny Edilean, Virginia, then the life of the only person who mattered to him, his sister Tess, was in jeopardy.

"Mike!" the captain said loudly, then lowered his voice. "Come back to earth. No one knows about you or your hometown or your sister, and she's perfectly safe." He hesitated. "I take it you two are close?"

Mike gave a one-shoulder shrug. Experience had taught him to reveal as little about himself as possible.

"Okay, so don't tell me anything. But you do know the place, right?"

"Never been there in my life." Mike forced a grin. He was back to being himself and was glad to see the frown that ran across the captain's face. Mike liked to be the one in charge of a situation. "You want to tell me what this is about? I can't imagine that anything bad has happened in little Edilean." Not since 1941, he thought as about a hundred images ran through his mind—and not one of them was good. While it was true that he'd never actually been to Edilean, the town and its inhabitants had ruled his childhood. He couldn't help it as he put his hand to his throat and remembered *that* day and his angry, hate-filled grandmother.

"Nothing has happened, at least not yet," the captain said, "but we do know that Stefan is there."

"In Edilean? What's he after?"

"We don't know, but he's about to marry some hometown girl." The captain took a drink of his cola. "Poor thing. She grew up in a place that sells tractors, then Stefan comes along with his big-city razzle-dazzle and sweeps her off her feet. She never had a chance."

Mike bent his head to hide a smile. The captain was a native of South Florida where there were stores on every corner. He felt sorry for anyone who'd ever had to shovel snow. "Her name's Susie. Or something with an *S*." He picked up a file folder from beside him on the bench. "It's Sara—"

"Shaw," Mike said. "She's to marry Greg Anders. Although I take it Greg Anders is actually Mitzi's son, Stefan?"

"You sure know a lot about the place for someone who's never been there." The captain paused, giving Mike room to explain himself, but he said nothing. "Yeah, he's Stefan and we have reason to believe that Mitzi is also living in that town."

"And no one would pay attention to a middle-aged woman."

"Right." The captain slid the folder across the table to Mike. "We don't know what's going on or why two major criminals are there, so we need someone to find out. Since you have a connection to the place, you're the winner."

"And here I'd never considered myself a lucky man." When Mike opened the folder, he saw that the first page was from the Decatur, Illinois, police department. He looked at the captain in question.

"It's all in there about how Stefan was found. An off-duty cop was on vacation in Richmond, Virginia, with his wife and he saw Stefan and the girl in a dress shop. The cop found out where they lived. As for you, a guy you worked with a long time ago knew about Edilean and your sister." When Mike frowned at that, the captain couldn't help grinning. Mike's secrecy—or "privacy" as he called it—could be maddening. Everybody in the fraud squad would go out for a few beers and afterward the captain would know whose wife had walked out, who was getting it on with a "badge bunny," and who was having trouble with a case. But not Mike. He'd talk as much as the other guys as he told about his training sessions, his food, and even about his car. It seemed like he'd told a lot about himself, but the next day the captain would realize that he'd learned absolutely nothing personal about Mike.

When the Assistant U.S. Attorney General for the Southern District of Florida called and said they thought one of the most notorious criminals in the United States might be in Edilean, Virginia, and that Mike Newland's sister lived there, the captain nearly choked on his coffee. He would have put money on it that Mike didn't have a relative in the world. In fact, the captain wasn't sure Mike had ever had a girlfriend outside a case. He never brought one to the squad functions, and as far as the captain knew, Mike had never invited anyone to his apartment—which changed every six months. But then, Mike was the best undercover cop they'd ever had. After every assignment, he'd had to hide until all of the people he'd exposed were in prison.

Mike closed the folder. "When do I go and what do I do?"

"We want you to save her."

"Mitzi?" Mike asked in genuine horror. "So she can stand trial?"

"No, not her. The girl. Of course we want you to find Mitzi, but we also want you to save this Sara Shaw. Once the Vandlos get whatever it is they want from her, no one will ever see her again." He paused. "Mike?"

He looked at the captain.

"If your sister really is there and if they find out about you . . ."

"Don't worry," Mike said. "Right now Tess is in Europe on her honeymoon. I'll tell her to keep her new husband out of town until this is solved one way or the other."

The captain opened another folder and withdrew an eight-by-ten glossy of a woman with dark hair and eyes. She was stunningly beautiful. She was standing on a street corner, waiting for the light to change, and a slight wind had blown her clothes close to her body. She had a figure that made a man draw in his breath. "Does your sister really look like this?"

Mike barely glanced at the photo. "Only on her worst days."

The captain blinked a few times. "Okay." He put a picture of Sara Shaw on the table. The young woman had an oval face, light hair, and was wearing a white dress that made her look as sweet as Mike's sister looked, well, tempting. "She's not Vandlo's usual type."

Mike picked up the photo and studied it. He wasn't about to tell the captain that he knew quite a bit about Sara Shaw. She was one of his sister's two best friends, which said a lot, since Tess's sharp tongue didn't win over many people. But from their first meeting Sara had seen past Tess's biting words and extraordinary looks to the person beneath.

"Do you know her?"

"Never met Miss Shaw, but I've heard some about her." He put the picture down. "So no one has any idea what the Vandlos want in Edilean?"

"There's been a lot of research both from a distance and locally, but everybody who tried drew a blank. Whatever it is, Miss Shaw seems to be at the center of it. Is she rich but no one knows about it? Is she about to inherit millions?"

"Not that I've heard. She just opened a shop with . . ." His sister kept him up-to-date on the gossip in Edilean, but it wasn't easy to remember it all. Now it seemed that every word she'd told him was of vital importance. "With her fiancé, Greg Anders. Tess hates the man, says he snubs everyone who isn't buying something from him. But Tess does all of Sara's accounting, so she's made sure Sara hasn't been put into debt by him."

"That sounds like a Vandlo." The captain hesitated. "Your sister manages people's finances?" His tone said that he couldn't believe a woman who looked like Tess could also have a brain.

Mike had no intention of answering that. He well knew the captain's curiosity about his private life and he wasn't going to reveal anything. "So you want me to catch these criminals, but I'm also to get the lovely Miss Shaw away from Stefan Vandlo? Is my assignment to follow and watch? Or am I to do more than that?"

"You have to do whatever you must to keep her alive. We think Stefan will murder Sara the minute he gets what he wants from her—and what he seems to want most is marriage."

"My hunch is that since the dresses in the shop are expensive, Sara must get into a lot of rich houses. Maybe the Vandlos want to see what's in them."

"That's what we thought too, but as her boyfriend, Vandlo already has access to the houses and no robberies have been reported. It's bigger than that and no one has a clue what it is." The captain tapped the folder. "After you read what's in here, I think you'll see that this scam of theirs is much more than just stealing a few necklaces. It's got to be, if both mother and son are there." He lowered his voice. "We think Stefan divorced his wife of nineteen years just so his marriage to Miss Shaw will be legal—which means he'll inherit whatever she owns after she dies in some so-called accident." He looked at Mike expectantly. "You're sure you have no idea what's connected to Miss Shaw that's so valuable that two of the most evil conners in the world have prepared so well for this?"

"None whatever," Mike said honestly. "The McDowells are rich, and Luke Connor lives there, but—"

"The author of the Thomas Canon books? I've read every one of them! Hey! Maybe you can get me an autographed copy."

"Sure. I'll be a tourist who's lost his way."

The captain became serious again. "Too distant. You're going to have to use your connections to your sister, to the town, anything you can find, to get close enough to this girl to talk her out of marrying Stefan. We do *not* want it set up that he can inherit what is hers. And you have to do this right away because the wedding is in three weeks."

Mike looked at him in disbelief. "What am I supposed to do? Seduce her?"

"No one would ask you to do this if we didn't think you could. And, besides, I seem to remember that you've succeeded with several women. There was that girl in Lake Worth. What was her name?"

"Tracy, and she got ten to twenty. This one is a *good* girl. How do I deal with her?"

"I don't know. Treat her like a lady. Cook for her. Pull out her chair. Girls like her fall for gentlemen. I'm sure that's how Vandlo got her. And before you ask, no, you can't kidnap her and you can't shoot Stefan. This young woman, Sara Shaw, has to stay there to help you find out what those two want." The captain grinned in a malicious way. "We've arranged for Stefan to be away for the whole time before the wedding. We gave him some family troubles that he can't ignore."

"Such as?"

"Even though he divorced his wife, we know he's still attached to her, so we arrested her on a DUI charge—which was easy. She's done a lot of drinking since Stefan left her, so we just picked her up one night, and now she's facing jail. We let her call him in the wee hours, and just as we'd hoped, he came immediately. If he gives us any trouble, we'll lock him up until he cools off." The captain smiled. "I wonder what he told his fiancée to explain why he went running off to his ex-wife?"

Mike was closing his thermos, his mind still on how to accomplish this mission. "I doubt if a liar like Vandlo had told her about his ex-wife."

"Eventually, you'll have to tell Miss Shaw the truth, so that should be a point in your favor. Whatever you do, you just have to do it *fast*," the captain said. "And never forget that this young woman would be the fourth one to disappear after she got attached to Stefan Vandlo. He used a fake name and took those girls for everything they had. Then the girls 'disappeared' and the boyfriend, Vandlo, couldn't be found."

"Yeah, I read that," Mike said. "And if it weren't for some vague eyewitness reports, we wouldn't know who he was."

"Right, because Stefan left nothing behind, not so much as a fingerprint. And you know the rule: no evidence, no conviction. Personally, I'd like to arrest the man right now, but the higher-ups want an undercover operation so we can get the mother.

We take away her son, and she'd just start using her nieces and nephews. She's the brains, so we have to get *her* out of action. Permanently."

Mike looked at his watch. "I just need to stop by my apartment to get some things, then I can leave—"

"Uh, Mike," the captain said in a tone of apology, "it looks like you haven't seen the local news in the last couple of hours. There's something else you need to know."

"What happened?"

The captain took the last documents from the bench and handed them to him. "I'm really sorry about this."

When Mike opened the folder, he saw a computer printout of a news story. APARTMENT BURNED, the headline read. CIGARETTES TO BLAME, SAY THE AUTHORITIES.

Mike's anger flared as he looked at the photo. It was his six-story apartment building, and flames were coming out of the corner of the fourth floor—his apartment.

He put the papers with the others before he looked up at the captain. "Who did it?"

"The Feds say it must have been . . . Let me check. I don't want to misquote anyone." His voice was sarcastic as he flipped a paper over. " 'A fortuitous accident' is what they called it. Lucky for them, that is." The captain's eyes were sympathetic. "I'm sorry about this, Mike, but they want you to go there clean. Your story is that your apartment burned down, so you decided to take a much-needed vacation from police work. It makes sense that you'd stay at your sister's apartment since it's empty. It's supposed to be a coincidence that her place is on the same property as Miss Shaw's. We—they—want you to lie as little as possible. Oh, yeah, I nearly forgot." He reached into his pocket, pulled out a new BlackBerry, and handed it to Mike. "Stefan cut his teeth on pickpocketing, so when you do meet with him he'll take your phone. We don't want him to find any numbers on it that would give you away. While you're in Edilean you're to contact us *only* through your sister. Will that be all right with her?"

"Sure," Mike said and renewed his vow to tell Tess to stay away. The case must be really serious if they'd burned his apartment. He'd never tell anyone, but Tess had been sending him baked goods from her friend Sara Shaw for years now, and it was Mike's opinion that anyone who could bake like she could deserved to be saved.

When Mike was silent, the captain said, "Sorry about your clothes." They all knew Mike was a "dresser." "What did you lose?"

"Nothing important. Tess keeps whatever means anything to me in a storage bin in—" He hesitated. "In Edilean."

"My advice is that you don't visit it." The captain wanted to lighten the mood. "Again, too bad about the apartment. I was going to volunteer to look after your goldfish."

Mike snorted as he stood up. He didn't have goldfish or a dog or even a permanent home. He'd lived in furnished, rented apartments since he left his grandparents' home at seventeen.

Mike glanced at the roadway that wound through the park. He'd take a run—he needed it—then go. "I'll leave in two hours," he said. "I should be in Edilean about ten hours after that—if I use the siren now and then, that is."

The captain smiled. "I knew you'd do it."

"Want to go for a run with me?"

The captain grimaced. "I leave that torture to you. Mike?"

"Yeah?"

"Be careful, will you? Stefan has a bit of a conscience—or at least a fear of reprisals—but his mother . . ."

"Yeah, I know. Could you put together more info for me on mother and son?"

"How about if you jog over to my car right now and I give you three boxes full of material?"

Mike gave one of his rare laughs, making the captain look at him in question.

"You have something in mind, don't you?"

"I was thinking of how to introduce myself to Miss Shaw and I remembered a story my sister told me about a very old tunnel. It just happens to open right into the floor of my sister's bedroom. All I have to do is move Miss Shaw in there."

The captain waited, but Mike didn't elaborate. "You've only got three weeks. Think you can entice Miss Shaw away from a big city charmer like Stefan in that time?"

Mike gave a sigh. "Usually, I'd say yes, but now . . ." He shrugged. "In my experience, the only way to get a woman is to find out what she wants, then give it to her. It's just that I have no idea what a woman like Sara Shaw could possibly want." He looked at the captain. "So where are these boxes of info? I need to get out of here." Mike followed him to his car.

Ramsey McDowell was sound asleep when he heard Bonnie Tyler's "Holding Out for a Hero" blasting from his wife's cell phone. Groaning, he put the pillow over his head and tried to shut out the noise—and shut out his feelings. It was her brother calling her, a man Rams had never met, a man more elusive than a ghost, more secretive than a spy. But even though he'd never *seen* the man, Rams had heard more about him than he cared to. According to his bride, her brother was the smartest, most industrious, most heroic and, of course, the best-looking man on the planet.

"She's succeeded in making you jealous, hasn't she?" his cousin Luke had said, laughing. "Don't worry, old man, a few days—or years—in a gym and you might live up to his reputation."

Jealous or not, Ramsey knew that his wife halted everything—meals, arguments, even sex—if her phone emitted that outrageous song.

"He is *not* a hero," Ramsey said the first time Tess had jumped off of him to run to her phone. "He's just a policeman."

"Detective," Tess said over her shoulder. She was nude, and the sight of her beautiful body running was enough to make him forgive her. But that had been weeks ago and he was tired of the daily calls.

Tess said, "He usually only calls me once a week, but he's off now so we can talk all we want."

"All we want" turned out to be *every day*, and with the way the man caught them in the midst of every "activity," Rams thought a camera had been set on them. Even now, on their honeymoon, he still called her.

"Mike!" Tess said as she picked up her phone. Her voice was breathless and a bit frightened. "Is something wrong?"

Rams looked at the clock. On European time, it was the wee hours of the morning. Why couldn't the man get a girlfriend like normal people did?

"All right," Tess said softly into the phone as she sat back down on the bed. "Of course I'll do it."

Rams moved the pillow off his head and looked at her with curiosity. He'd never heard her use that tone before.

"Mike, you'll be careful, won't you? No, I mean it. *Really* careful."

Rams sat up in bed and watched her more closely. There was enough light in the room that he could see tears in her eyes. "What's wrong?"

She held up her hand for him to stop talking. "I understand completely. Luke will do whatever I ask him to."

"Luke will do what?" Ramsey asked.

Tess looked at her husband. "Would you please be quiet? This is important."

Angrily, Rams flung back the covers, pulled on his trousers that were hanging over a chair, and opened the curtain to look at the mountains outside. Behind him, Tess kept talking.

"Yes, I think it's in good condition, and besides me, only Luke knows about it. I'm sure he didn't tell Joce. He was afraid she'd want to explore it, and he's always thought it was too dangerous." Pausing, Tess smiled. "Not yet, but Rams is working on it with enthusiasm and endurance. Yeah, the first one will be named Michael."

In an instant, Ramsey's anger left him and he stretched out on the bed beside his wife. He didn't like the way she'd told intimacies about them to her brother, but he did like that she'd said she planned to have children. They'd not talked about having kids, but he now realized he hadn't done so in fear that she'd say she didn't want any. Tess was a woman of very strong opinions. But once he was over his first pleasure at hearing that she did want children, Ramsey began to imagine a dozen of them, all with a name in some form of Michael: Michaela, Michalia, Mickey, Michelle—

"What an extraordinary call," Tess said as she clicked off her phone.

"I draw the line at Mickey. No mice."

Tess gave him a look of disgust. "Are you going to start on your jealousy again?"

"I'm not—" Rams began but stopped himself. "So why did your brother feel he had to call you in the middle of the night? Or is he playing James Bond in a country where it's now teatime?"

"He just arrived in Edilean."

Rams looked at her. "Your brother is in *our* hometown and you aren't packed yet?"

"No, and I'm not going to. He wants us to go on an extended honeymoon—and stay away from home."

"Not that I object, but why does he want us to do that?"

"It seems that my big brother has been sent to Edilean on a case."

"But he—" Ramsey swallowed. Tess's brother went undercover for big cases. Huge cases. He dealt in crimes that had international repercussions. He infiltrated gangs that were at war with each other—he'd been shot repeatedly.

Rams got off the bed and went to the closet.

"What are you doing?"

"I'm going home; you're staying here. If your brother's been sent to Edilean, then something is very wrong."

"If you go, I'll follow you, and that will put my brother in danger. And Mike said that if I'm there *I* might become a target. Is that what you want?"

Turning, Ramsey looked at her. She wore no makeup or clothing, and she was so beautiful he could hardly stand upright. He still couldn't believe that when he'd asked her to marry him just four weeks ago, she'd said yes. Three weeks later they'd been married in a private ceremony with only a dozen guests. And except that her brother hadn't been able to be there, it was how they'd both wanted it. In fact, Tess had said, "If you think I'm going to make a fool of myself by wearing a hundred yards of white silk and having a bunch of women around me in pink dresses, then you've asked the wrong woman to marry you. Spend the money on a rock. I want a ring big enough to dance on." He'd happily done just what she asked. And he'd added a pair of diamond earrings—all of which she was wearing now. Just the diamonds, her skin and hair.

"What's going on in Edilean?" Rams asked. "Who is in danger?"

"You know Mike can't tell me anything. His cases are top secret. If anyone found out, lives could be lost."

Ramsey gave her a piercing look. As far as he could tell, her brother didn't keep secrets from her.

Tess sighed. "Sara."

Ramsey took a deep breath. "My cousin Sara? Sweet, dear Sara? It's that bastard she wants to marry, isn't it?"

"Yes," Tess said simply. "He's not who he says he is."

"Now there's news! I've disliked him from the moment I first saw him."

"All of us have felt the same way, but he's helped Sara to recover, and their customers love him. Mike wants us to do some things."

"Mike wants *us* . . . ?" Ramsey grimaced. "If he asked *us* for help then he meant for you to tell me about Sara, didn't he?"

Tess smiled. "Do you think I'd tell you anything Mike didn't want me to?"

Ramsey started to, yet again, tell her what he thought of her elusive, secretive brother, but he didn't. "Okay. I'll bite. What does he want us to do?"

"First," Tess said as she lowered her voice and slid down in the bed, "he wants nieces and nephews. He says he's sick of having no kids to buy Christmas presents for."

"Did he now?" Rams said as he slipped off his trousers and slid under the covers. "And what else did your very intelligent brother ask for?"

"To figure out what Sara owns that a thief would want. It seems that Greg is a big-time crook and Sara has something he's gone to a lot of trouble to get." When Rams started to move away, Tess pulled his face down to hers. "And you're to take me to Venice."

"For how long?" he murmured.

"Until Mike says we can return."

Ramsey didn't like the autocratic way his brother-in-law was making decrees, but he would do whatever he must to keep his beloved wife safe. Abruptly, he pulled away from kissing her neck. "What kind of gifts does your brother give to kids?"

"C-4." When Ramsey gave her a look of horror, she laughed. "I don't know. Why don't we wait and see?"

The next morning, while Ramsey was in the shower, Tess called her friend and Ramsey's cousin, Luke Connor, to talk about what Mike needed. He and his wife, Jocelyn, lived in Edilean Manor, a rambling mansion built in 1770. They resided in the two-story main part, while Sara had an apartment in one of the flanking wings on one side. Until her marriage, Tess had had the apartment on the other side.

A few years ago, Luke, a famous best-selling author, had returned to Edilean to recover from a disastrous marriage. As a way of healing, he'd taken over the maintenance of the old house and grounds. After days of heavy rain that nearly flooded the town, he'd discovered an old tunnel. It had been shored up with heavy timbers, and the floors had been laid with handmade brick—and it opened into the floor of Tess's apartment.

Under normal circumstances, he would have told the people of Edilean what he'd found, but at the time he was so miserable he wasn't talking to anyone. In private, with only the help of his grandfather, he'd restored the tunnel—which he figured had been used during the Civil War as part of the Underground Railroad to help slaves escape.

After his grandfather died, no one but Luke knew about the tunnel—until Tess discovered it. She was curious about the big square cut in the boards in the middle of her bedroom floor. Luke had made sure there were no handles on top and that it was locked from the inside, but that didn't stop Tess from using a crowbar to pry up the boards. She went down the ladder Luke had put there and used a flashlight to make her way along the dark, dank corridor. When she tripped over Luke's sleeping body—and found out where he disappeared to when no one could find him—for several long moments they'd both been in a state of panic. After they'd calmed down, they went to Tess's apartment, and Luke ended up telling her his personal problems. And Tess told Luke about her brother and a little of why she'd come to Edilean. She didn't have to tell him that she was madly in love with her boss, Luke's cousin, Ramsey. He said the whole town knew that. But Tess had had to wait a long time before Rams figured that out for himself.

After that first nearly hysterical encounter, Luke and Tess had formed a bond between them, and unknown to the gossipy little town, Luke often entered her apartment through the tunnel and spent the night in her second bedroom. So now she called and told him what her brother needed.

"Let me get this straight," Luke said. "You want me to sabotage Sara's apartment so she has to move into yours because your brother—who I've never met—wants to sneak into your bedroom where Sara will be staying? And this is in the dead of night?"

"That's exactly right. Is the tunnel in good shape?"

"Bugs and cobwebs, but the structure is sound."

"So will you do it?"

"I have one question."

"And that is?"

"Is your brother married?"

"No. Why?"

"Think he could seduce Sara away from Anders?"

"My brother could seduce Jolie away from Pitt."

Luke groaned. "Sometimes I almost feel sorry for my cousin."

"Rams needs competition," Tess said. "How's Joce?"

"Not so good. We just found out that she has to stay in bed for the rest of her pregnancy or risk losing the twins. But I got her started on doing the family genealogy, and she's liking that."

"Tell her that my heart is with her and I'll call her tomorrow. Anything I can do for her?" Tess asked.

"Come home as soon as you can. She misses you. About Sara, if I tell her I have to fumigate her apartment, she'll be out in seconds. Leave it all to me."

"Thank you very much," Tess said and hung up. When Rams got out of the shower, she was sitting on the little sofa in the hotel room, reading a magazine. "So what do they wear in Venice?"

"Exactly what you have on." She was completely naked. "Except they add a mask."

"And where do they put it?"

Ramsey laughed as he walked toward her, his towel dropping to the floor.

# 2

IT WAS LATE at night, and Sara was sewing some adjustments on the bodice of a gown she and Greg had bought on a trip to New York. It had been "one of those," meaning a dress that Sara'd had to bite her tongue about.

"No woman in Virginia is going to wear this," Sara had said. It had cutouts on the hips.

"Marilyn Steward," Greg mumbled as he tossed aside four other dresses.

"Her left thigh is wider than the waist of this dress." She was holding it up and looking at it. "Maybe Carol Wills. She's young enough and thin enough that she—"

Greg snatched the dress from her hands. "Why do you have to give me trouble on every dress I want to buy? Leave the designing to me, will you? I'll buy the dress in a size twelve, put an eight label in it, and Mrs. Wealthy Steward will love it."

"Right." As always, Sara backed down. As she put the dress on the to-buy rack, she thought, And I'll have to completely remake it to fit her. Which is what she was doing now. She had a closet full of dresses, slacks, jackets and even underwear that needed to be remade to fit their exacting customers.

But in spite of what she thought of his methods, Sara had to admit that under Greg's expertise, the shop was making money. As he'd predicted, they had customers coming in from Richmond, and even a few women from D.C. had shown up. Their selection was extensive, and their free alterations were a hit. They had women buying a size six dress and asking if Sara could please "let out the seams a tiny bit." In other words, make it two sizes larger. Every time, Greg said, "Of course she can." His trick was that he kept the larger sizes in the back. After Sara took the big dress apart and shortened sleeves and hems and drew in the shoulders, Greg would—with a flourish and great charm—present the customer with a dress with a size six label in the back.

The only problem with this scheme—besides the deception, which Sara hated—was that she was the only seamstress.

"Just until we get established," Greg said. "Then we'll buy that house in the country you've always wanted. We'll have a dozen kids and you won't even own a sewing machine."

It was a wonderful dream, one that Sara clung to with all her might, especially now when Greg had left town so abruptly and mysteriously, and Sara was stuck with about twenty-five pieces of clothing to rebuild. At least the wedding was all arranged, she thought, thanks to Greg's splendid planning abilities. In fact, she'd had nothing to do but choose her dress—and that was an heirloom. Greg said, "Leave everything to me. I know exactly what you like." Sara'd had so much work to do for the shop that all she could say was, "Thank you."

But the truth was, the possibility of his absence during next week's Scottish Fair was a bit of a relief. That she'd wanted to go and he didn't had been one of their few serious arguments. He'd told her she was welcome to stay in Edilean for it, but he was going to New York and he had tickets for a Broadway play that he knew Sara wanted to see. When she'd said it was almost as though he'd arranged the trip to keep her from going to the yearly event, he got angry.

"Of course I did!" Greg yelled. "I want to be with you all the time, but how can I go to some rural hoedown in this town? All your friends and relatives *hate* me. And you know why? Because I've taken their precious little workhorse away from them!"

"I'm not—" Sara began, but she'd said it all before. Sometimes she felt torn between the man she loved and the town she adored. Which was, of course, absurd. But it was true that in her hometown of Edilean, people didn't like the man she was going to marry. Out of town, people loved him. Their customers asked his advice, laughed at his jokes, and soaked up his compliments like rum on sponge cake. But in Edilean . . .

So Sara had agreed to go to New York with Greg and miss the fair for the first time in her twenty-six years. She wouldn't be sewing the Scottish costumes for her many cousins, wouldn't help her mother bake bannocks and tattie scones. She wouldn't help run Luke's booth full of herbal wreaths, and she wouldn't have a day of laughter at seeing the knees of all the men in town when they wore their kilts. She wouldn't get to—

She broke off her thoughts because to her astonishment, part of the bedroom floor seemed to be lifting upward. She put the dress she was working on down on the bed and rubbed her weary eyes. She was in Tess's apartment, on the opposite side of Edilean Manor from her own apartment, so maybe it was normal for the floor to start to lift. Or maybe she needed a whole lot of sleep.

Silently, Sara got off the bed and stood on bare feet by Tess's dresser. It was dim in the room, with only the light from the floor lamp she'd put by the foot of the bed so she could see to work.

As she stared at the floor, she realized there was a trapdoor under the little rug. She'd not seen it before, but then, until today when her cousin Luke had run her out of her own apartment with his nasty termite spray, she'd never been in Tess's bedroom.

As the door in the floor rose a couple more inches, Sara's first instinct was to get out of the apartment, and grab her cell phone off the kitchen counter as she ran. She'd call the police, then go over to Luke's.

But the bedroom door was facing the front of the trapdoor. Whoever was sneaking into her room would see her—and be able to reach her—before she could get out. She decided to risk it and try to escape. In one quick gesture, she switched off the light and made a leap across the trapdoor, meaning to hit the floor on the other side running.

But to her utter disbelief, a man tossed the lid back just as Sara leaped, and she would have fallen if he hadn't shot up through the floor and caught her. Instinctively, she fought as they went down together. She tried to use her nails on the back of his neck and to bring her knee up between his legs, but he blocked her. She would have pulled his hair, but it was cut so short she couldn't get hold of it.

"Damnation!" he said in a deep, raspy voice that sounded as though it had come off a horror movie.

The voice and the fact that they were now on the floor wrapped about each other made Sara fight harder. He was half on top of her as she twisted and kicked to get him off.

"Would you *stop* it!" he said in his odd voice. "I'm already in pain. You don't need to add to it."

"Get *off* of me!"

"Gladly," the man said and rolled to one side, his back on the floor.

Instantly, Sara stood up. The only way out of the room was to step across him, but she had one foot in the air when he grabbed her ankle, paralyzing her in place.

"Not so fast," he said. "I think you should explain to the police what you're doing in here at this time of night."

What he'd said was so preposterous that Sara stopped moving and stared down at him—even as he was holding her ankle above his chest. It was too dark in the room to see clearly, but he had on a white shirt that she knew cost quite a bit. It was not the normal dress of a thief. "Police?" she whispered. "*You* want to call the police on *me*?"

He let go of her ankle and in an easy move stood up in front of her. "All right then, tell me what you're doing in here."

"Tell *you*?" Sara felt that she'd entered some comedy act. "I *live* here."

The man leaned to one side to switch on the floor lamp, and when Sara started to move toward the bedroom door, he caught her wrist. He didn't hold it tightly, but she knew she couldn't break his grip. "I know that's not the truth," he said as he pulled her forward, then deftly set her in the only chair in the room. "Now, young lady, start talking."

Sara looked up at him. He wasn't an especially large man, certainly not as tall as her cousins Luke and Ramsey, but he was quite handsome—in a street thug sort of way. For all that his hairline was halfway back on his head, he had a heavy growth of very black whiskers. All in all, she did *not* like being alone in a poorly lit room with him.

Her very ordinary life in a small town hadn't prepared her for such an encounter as this, but then she, like everyone else, had seen a lot of movies. She put her shoulders back and took a breath—and wished she weren't wearing a nightgown of semitransparent Irish linen. And it was too bad her hair was down about her shoulders. She would have liked to look more "tough."

"The question," she said as calmly as she could manage, "is who are *you*?"

He bent down to close the open door in the floor, and when Sara shifted in the chair, he looked back at her. "I'm the brother of the renter of this apartment and *you* are trespassing."

Sara's mouth came open in astonishment. "Tess? You're Tess's brother? You don't look like her."

The harsh expression left his face, and when he gave a little smile that showed a dimple in his left cheek, he no longer looked frightening. "She got the beauty, but I got the brains."

Sara had to work not to smile at that. His insinuation was that Tess was a brainless beauty, but Tess was one of the smartest people Sara'd ever met. She wasn't going to let him make her overlook the issues. "Until I see some proof, I don't believe you."

He reached into the pocket of what she could tell were quite expensive trousers, removed a thin wallet, and flipped it open to a driver's license.

Sara didn't look at it. "I would only trust Tess."

"Sure. Let's call her." He pulled a cell phone from his front pocket and pushed a button.

"She won't answer," Sara said. "In case you don't know, she happens to be on her honeymoon with my cousin." If he didn't know that, he couldn't be Tess's brother. Everyone knew that Tess talked to her brother every Sunday afternoon, and she readily admitted that she told him *everything*.

When it rang once with no pickup, Sara glanced toward the doorway. Could she make it? If she screamed really loud, would

Luke hear her through the walls? Could she scream loud enough to wake him up?

She glanced at the man, and he had such a smug look on his face that Sara wanted to hit him.

Tess picked up in the middle of the second ring and with an annoying little smile, he handed the phone to Sara.

"Hey big brother!" Tess's unmistakable voice said, but she was clearly upset. "Are you all right? Has anything happened?"

"Tess, it's me, Sara."

"Sara?" Tess's voice rose. "Why are you on my brother's phone? Oh God! Has he been injured? I'll be there—"

"No!" Sara said. "I just need to know if this man who broke into my . . . I mean, your apartment is actually your brother. It's obvious he has his phone, but he's not how I pictured *your* brother to look."

"Oh?" Tess said, and her usual calm was restored. "What does your intruder look like?"

Sara couldn't stand the man's I-told-you-so look, so she lied. "He's short, skinny, half bald, hasn't shaved in a week, and he has a voice like a toad with a bad attitude."

"Then I take it he has his clothes on," Tess said.

That confusing statement made Sara's fear return. Tess had always been vague about exactly what her brother did for a living. "What do you mean, that he has his clothes on? Tess, I don't think—"

The man took the phone from her. "Baby sister, whatever you said, you're scaring her." He paused. "Why didn't you tell me someone else had moved in here while you were away?" He smiled, again showing that dimple. "I see. You're so busy with your honeymoon duties that you forgot all about me. Yeah, yeah, I understand." He glanced back at Sara. "So what do I do with her?"

Sara glared at him.

He laughed at whatever Tess said. "I'm more than willing, but, somehow, I don't think she would like that. By the way, who is she?" As he looked at Sara, his eyes widened. "Sara Shaw? The one who makes that apple bread you send me? The one who repaired my leather jacket? The girl you said was the best friend you'd ever had in your life? *That* Sara Shaw?"

Sara was flattered by his words, but at the same time, she didn't believe him. She got out of the chair, put on a blue silk robe she'd just repaired, and went to the kitchen. She filled the electric kettle with water and got the box of loose black tea out of the cabinet. Someone had given the tea to Tess for Christmas and now, months later, it hadn't been opened. She could hear the man in the bedroom quietly talking on the phone.

What was his name? she wondered as she tried to remember. Something ordinary. William or James. No. It was Mike. Mostly, Tess called him "my brother." As in: "My brother can run up mountains and lasso the moon whenever he wants to." Or thereabouts. Sara and Joce used to tease her when she'd run to the telephone if she heard Bonnie Tyler's *Holding Out for a Hero*, which was the song she'd set for her brother.

One time when they had a girls' night out, Tess's phone rang and it was Ramsey, her fiancé, but she ignored it. A few minutes later when it was her brother, she took the call. She mostly murmured "yes," then hung up. When Sara and Joce burst out laughing, Tess didn't get the joke.

"What is it about your brother that makes you drop everything when he calls?" Joce asked.

"I wouldn't be here if it weren't for him."

"You mean he sent you to Edilean?" Sara asked.

"No, I mean I wouldn't be alive if it weren't for my brother."

Sara and Joce didn't move so much as an eyelash. Tess *never* talked about her childhood. They held their breaths as they waited for her to tell more, and when she didn't readily share, they kept up a determined stare.

Finally, Tess shrugged. "What can I say? He's a good man, through and through, inside and out. He helps people."

"Doing what?" Sara asked.

Tess seemed about to speak, but then she buried her face in a menu. "So who wants a pizza?"

Another time, they asked her why he never came to visit. She told them that Mike saved all his vacation time to go places and study, and that when she was in college, she went with him. Joce and Sara thought that "study" referred to a university, but that's not what Tess meant. In her freshman year, they went to Japan so Mike could study kendo. Sophomore year it was China for kung fu, then the next year to Thailand for Muay Thai. For her senior graduation, they went to Brazil where they both did a course in jujitsu. "Of course Mike was a bit better than I was," Tess said, her eyes laughing.

So her brother was a jock. That still didn't explain what Tess's mysterious brother did for a living. They tried to get information out of Rams, but he was as closemouthed as the woman he loved. "If she wants you to know about her brother, she'll tell you."

But no matter how hard they tried, they couldn't find out. All they knew was that he was a police detective in Fort Lauderdale and he "traveled a lot."

So, now, Sara was in an apartment alone with Tess's elusive brother.

"I think apologies are due," Mike said from the doorway.

"If you think I'm going to—"

"No, me," Mike said quickly. "I need to apologize to you. My only excuse is that I was driving for ten hours, I'm tired, and all I wanted to do was sleep. I didn't expect anyone to be in Tess's apartment. Here, let me do that." He took the electric kettle from her, poured water into the pretty ceramic teapot—another Christmas gift—sloshed it around to warm the china, then poured it out. He put three heaping scoops of loose black tea in the pot and filled it with boiling water.

Sara watched as he opened cabinet doors until he found the cups and saucers. Since he didn't know where things were, she guessed he'd never been in the apartment before. She knew no one in town had ever met him, but he could have come through the tunnel and secretly visited and—

"Milk?" he asked as he opened the refrigerator and pulled out a carton. Her eyes widened when he poured the milk into a little pitcher that matched the other china, and set it all on the oak table Ramsey had recently bought. Mike put cookies on a plate. When he finished, the table looked ready to entertain a duchess.

He pulled out a chair for her, and when Sara was seated, he sat down across from her and held out the plate of cookies. "I'm sure they're not as good as your apple bread."

Sara knew he meant it as a compliment, but she wasn't appeased. "What are you doing here? And why didn't Tess warn me about you? And how did you know about that . . . Is it a tunnel?"

"Are you saying that you live here but don't know about that tunnel?"

"I know nothing about it."

"Then I doubly apologize. Tess told me about it some time ago. She even drew a map showing where the entrance is. Your cousin Luke found it while he was gardening, and he said it was for the Underground Railroad. Tess told me he's kept it in good repair for years now." He sipped his tea. "I forgot to ask if you wanted sugar."

Sara shook her head. "So where are you planning on spending the night?"

Mike glanced toward the hallway that led to the two little bed-rooms.

"No," Sara said as calmly as she could muster. "You aren't going to spend the night with me."

He looked at her over his cup.

"You know what I mean! I know you're a cop in a big city, but this is a small town, so you can't . . ." She trailed off because he yawned.

"Sorry. Long day. Mind if I take the bathroom first? Unless you . . . uh . . ."

"No," Sara said, "I don't have to 'uh' anything. I was just saying—"

Mike stood up. "I guess I'll see you tomorrow." He put his empty teacup in the sink. "Just leave the dishes and I'll take care of them in the morning. Sleep well, Miss Shaw." With that, he went into the one bathroom, which was between the two bedrooms, and shut the door.

Absolutely not! Sara thought. Under no circumstances was she going to spend the night in the same apartment with him. As she thought of the rampant gossip that would spread if she did, she got up, grabbed her phone off the counter, and started to call her mother. She would spend the rest of the night at her parents' house. If she did that, maybe the town wouldn't even find out she'd been alone with this stranger for the last hour. And if they didn't know, then no one would tell Greg.

It was at the thought of Greg that she quit punching buttons. Yet again, she remembered the abrupt way he'd left her just two nights before. They'd been in her apartment—the lease was up on Greg's place, and he'd said there was no need to pay for two resi-dences, so he'd moved in with her. His cell had rung just before midnight, waking both of them, and Sara had watched him fumble for the phone. When he saw the name in the ID, he sat up straight,

instantly wide awake, and said, "What is it?" He had listened in silence for what had to have been five minutes, then he'd said, "Don't
worry. I'll take care of it," and hung up.

He flung back the covers, got out of bed, and began to dress.

"What's wrong?" Sara asked, blinking sleepily.

"Nothing. I have to go away for a while, that's all. Go back to
sleep."

"A while? How long does that mean? The wedding—"

"Damn it, Sara, you're not going to start nagging me again, are
you? I know when the wedding is. How could I forget when I was
the one who got stuck with all the work for it? Something's come
up and I have to go. I'll be back for the wedding." He grabbed his
wallet and car keys off the dresser and left. Just like that, with no
explanation.

Sara had sat up in bed feeling like she'd just been through a
tornado. She didn't know what had happened, but Greg was gone,
not taking so much as his shaving kit, and she didn't know when
he'd return.

She couldn't go back to sleep and as soon as it was daylight she
began calling Greg, but he didn't answer.

Then, early this afternoon, Luke had run her out of her own
apartment with his cans of noxious bug poison, saying he had to
spray right then and that she could move into Tess's apartment while
he fumigated. Sara started to put her things into the guest room, but
Luke had insisted she take Tess's bedroom. "But why?" Sara'd asked.
"I don't need—"

"The bed in the other room is bad. No springs," Luke said as he
went back outside.

All in all, the whole thing was so odd that for a while Sara had
thought a surprise wedding shower was being planned for her. But,
hard as she looked, she saw no evidence of it.

Sara heard the water running and it now occurred to her that she wouldn't mind if Greg did hear that Tess's brother had stayed in the apartment with her. "What else could I do?" she'd ask Greg, her lashes fluttering helplessly. She'd say, "It was nighttime and he had nowhere else to go. You can see that I didn't have a choice." When she imagined Greg's anger and jealousy, she smiled on the way to the bedroom. Yes, it might be quite good to be able to tell Greg that another man had been alone with her.

As she closed the door, she thought about the tussle she'd had with Tess's brother. He could certainly move quickly! And when she'd been on top of him, she'd felt the man's muscles. But later, he'd handled a teapot in a way that was worthy of a geisha. She was used to men like her father and Luke, who left their dishes where they lay.

Sara was drifting into sleep when she heard him leave the bathroom, and she remembered that he hadn't answered her questions about why he was there and why Tess hadn't warned her he was coming. Tomorrow, she thought, I'll buy a lock for that trapdoor and one of us will leave.

# 3

SARA SLEPT LATE the next morning, and it was several moments before she remembered all that had happened during the night. Rolling onto her stomach, she looked at the floor. There was a small rug by the bed, but one corner of it was folded back, a testament to last night's fiasco. She got up, moved the rug aside, and saw that the square cut in the floorboards was clearly visible.

"I'm going to give Luke Connor a piece of my mind," she said aloud. It angered her that he'd let her move into the apartment without telling her about the trapdoor that led to . . . To what? she wondered. That the man had come up through it meant it must lead down to an underground exit. So why didn't everyone in town know that Edilean Manor had a secret tunnel? She could almost hear her cousin saying, "Then it wouldn't qualify as a 'secret,' would it?" Luke could sometimes be maddening!

Sara took her time dressing and was quiet about it. If the man had driven all the way up from Fort Lauderdale the day before, then he probably wanted to sleep in. And when he did get up, Sara planned to be cordial and polite, but she'd also be firm: He *had* to leave. He could *not* stay in the apartment with her. It was one thing to tell Greg that a man had stayed with her for one night because of an emergency, but it was another to say that he'd spent two nights—or more.

It crossed her mind that she should be the one to get out, but where could she go? If she moved into her parents' spare bedroom, she'd again have to hear her mother's speech that she could "do better" than Greg Anders. Worse, she'd have to see her father looking at her with sad eyes.

Sara had lived in Edilean all her life and she had lots of friends, not to mention relatives, so she could go to one of them, but that would cause too many questions. They'd want to know where Greg went and when he was going to return. Would he be back in time for the wedding? they'd ask. That Sara had no answers for these questions would lead to the one she most hated: Was Sara absolutely *sure* she wanted to marry him?

No, where she was, in Tess's apartment, so near her own place, was where she was going to stay. If she needed a change of clothes or sewing supplies, she could easily get them. She just had to hold her breath against the pesticide fumes when she went into her apartment, but she could do it.

When she was dressed, Sara tiptoed out of the bedroom and made a quick trip to the bathroom, noting that it was spotlessly clean. No whiskers in the sink, no soap scum on the shower door. It was so exactly the way she'd left it that for a moment she thought maybe she'd dreamed that a man had come up through the floor.

As she left the bathroom, she glanced at the closed door to the other bedroom. She'd not heard a sound from him. On the kitchen table was a note. Picking it up, she read it.

"Dear Miss Shaw," it said in what she thought was a very formal manner. His handwriting was even and readable.

*Again, I am very sorry about last night. It wasn't my intention to disturb anyone. I'm going into Williamsburg this morning to go to a gym, then I must run some errands. I'll have lunch at the Williamsburg Inn at one, so if you'd like to take a break from your work and join me, perhaps I can make up somewhat for last night. I should be home at about five and I'll cook dinner tonight. Maybe we can take turns? If there's anything I can pick up for you while I'm in town or if you'd just like to talk, please call me.*

He put his cell number with its 954 area code at the bottom.

Sara tossed the note back on to the table. "Of all the audacious, presumptuous . . . !" she said aloud. Have lunch with him? Surely he must know that she was about to be married. Last night when Tess told him who she was, he'd known several things about Sara, so he probably even knew the time and place of the wedding. And what did he mean by "if you'd just like to talk"? Did he think she had no *friends*? And "take turns" cooking? How long was he planning to stay?

Angry, she glanced about the kitchen and saw that he'd kept his word and cleared away everything from their little tea party of the night before. When she opened the refrigerator, what few items she had inside were neatly arranged.

"Not my kind of man," she said aloud.

In silence, she ate a bowl of cereal, put her dirty items in the dishwasher, then went to the bedroom to start her day's work. But when she looked in the closet at the three boxes of clothes and the dozen or more garments on hangers, she wanted to close the door and leave.

This was all Greg's fault, she thought. A hundred percent of it was caused by him. Why did he have to run off like that? Why couldn't he have told her where he was going and what he had to do that was so important? Why couldn't he have written her a note like the one Tess's brother had left? "My darling Sara," it would say, "I'm very sorry but I had to leave to go—" That's where she always drew a blank. Before two nights ago, she would have said that she knew nearly everything there was to know about the man she planned to marry. The two of them had spent many hours together as he told her about his life before they'd met. She'd heard in detail about the two women who'd treated him so badly that it was a wonder he could ever care for any woman again. But he said that Sara's love had made him forget everything that had happened before.

So if she knew so much about him, who had called and made him go running? Who besides Sara was important enough to make him drop everything and leave like that?

When her cell phone rang, she leaped on it so fast she must have looked like a football player diving for the ball. "Hello?" she asked in a breathless voice.

"Sara, dear, are you all right?"

It was Luke's mother, her cousin by marriage, but since the woman was the age of her mother, in Southern tradition, Sara had always called her "aunt." "I'm fine, Aunt Helen. I just, uh, tripped on the way to the phone. I'm sorry about the costumes for the fair this year, but I have so many things to do for the shop that I couldn't get to them."

"That's all right, dear. My sister is working on them with me.

I was just wondering if there's anything I can do to help with your guest."

"My guest?"

"Yes. Tess's brother, Mike. Such a polite, helpful man, isn't he? When he told me he was staying in Tess's apartment and I remembered that Luke'd had to fumigate yours, I thought how very kind it was of you to let him stay."

Sara glanced at the clock on the bedside table. "Aunt Helen, it's only nine-thirty in the morning. How did you find out all this so fast?"

"The battery on my car gave out again—I'm going to skin my husband if he doesn't get me a new one today—and Mike gave me a lift into town, so I had a chance to ask him a few questions. He is such a pleasant young man and I enjoyed his company so very much."

Sara pulled the phone away from her ear to glare at it. How unsubtle could a person be? she wondered. Her aunt Helen was one of the women who disliked Greg very much. "Yes, he is a nice man, isn't he?" Sara said sweetly. "Why don't you and Uncle James invite him to stay at *your* house? I'm sure he'd love your cooking."

Helen didn't hesitate. Just as pleasantly, she replied, "I do wish I could, but you know how James needs his privacy. I hope to see you in church on Sunday, and why don't you bring Mike? With Tess away, the poor man is all alone."

"Maybe he can go with Luke," Sara shot back. "I may go out with Greg on Sunday."

"Oh? Is he back?"

Sara wasn't going to answer that because if she did, she'd have to deal with more questions about where Greg went and when he'd return. "Uh oh, the pan I have on the stove is boiling over. I have to go."

"You must be starting dinner for Mike. How considerate of you.
He—"

"Bye," Sara said and clicked off. "Of all the—" No, she thought,
she was not going to let herself get upset about this. Tonight she'd
calmly tell Tess's brother that he had to leave and that would be the
end of it. In fact, maybe it was good that her aunt Helen had found
out about Mike. Maybe the town residents could shuffle him back
and forth.

Sara had just picked up the first jacket that needed to be remade
when the phone rang again. This time the ID showed that it was her
aunt Mavis calling. "Wonder what good deed he did for *her*?" Sara
mumbled and let the phone go to voice mail. When it rang again
ten minutes later and the ID showed it was her mother, Sara didn't
take that call either.

She picked up her sewing basket and two dresses, left her cell
phone on the charger, and went outside. She knew she should keep
the phone with her in case Greg called, but at the moment she didn't
want to talk to him or anyone else.

Outside, she sat down at the pretty little iron table and chairs
under a shade tree and began to sew. She had half a dozen seams
to repair in an expensive dress that a woman seemed to have worn
while jogging. In the afternoon, Sara knew she'd have to spend time
on her sewing machine. She planned to turn on HBO and listen to
one movie after another while she worked. Maybe she could find
something scary so it would take her mind off where Greg was—
and off the man who had broken into her apartment last night.

"Good morning."

She looked up at Luke and smiled. She wasn't going to let him
or anyone else see how upset she was. "Why aren't you writing?"

"Need to think," he said as he held up his shovel. It was a family
joke that whenever Luke was upset about anything, he dug holes.

"Is Joce okay?" Sara went to see Luke's wife every day, as she needed some relief from the tedium of being bedridden. For over a year Joce had been working on a biography of her grandmother, a woman prominent in Edilean's history, but she'd reached a standstill in her research and had had to put the book aside.

"Fine. Great. Well, maybe she's not so good right now." He gave a little grin. "She's working on her family's genealogy and . . ." He grinned broader. "Last night she found out that she and I are seventh cousins. I think she's worried that the babies are going to be morons."

"Or hemophiliacs," Sara said, referring to the European royal families who were so interbred that they'd passed the disorder around for centuries.

Luke got the allusion. "Please don't mention that to her or she'll add it to her list of what could go wrong. Are you going to meet Mike in town for lunch?"

Sara groaned. "Don't tell me he got to you too!"

Luke looked surprised. "Got to me? I don't know what you mean. I saw him at about six this morning, he asked me about gyms in the area, and I told him."

"You were outside at six A.M.?"

"I usually am," Luke said, "and if you ever got up before midday, you'd know that."

"I've never slept to noon in my life."

Luke looked at her.

"All right, so maybe I have, but I haven't in years. Too much work to do."

"So how are you coming with all that Greg gave you to do?"

Sara knew exactly what he was up to. After all, he was her cousin and she'd known him all her life. For all that he was eight years older than she was, they'd always been close. "I've already had my share of hassle for today, so don't *you* start on me. I can't understand why this town is taking the side of a man they don't even know. For all any of you know, Mike Newland might be a serial killer."

"He's related to Tess and we know her," Luke said. "And when she married Rams, she became one of us. Mike is her brother."

Sara didn't want to argue with her cousin, and she didn't want to have to discuss her future. She decided to attack. "With all your talk about 'us' why didn't you tell me about that tunnel? This time it was someone we know who used it—know by relationship any way, certainly not by character—but what do I do next time when a stranger comes climbing into my bedroom?"

"Mike said he was sorry about that, but—"

"He told you that he sneaked into my apartment in the middle of the night and nearly scared me to death? Did he also tell you that he wanted to call the police on me?"

"Technically, he had a right to do so. He was entering his sister's apartment, while you're—"

She did *not* want to hear that Mike Newland was right and she was wrong. "How's *my* apartment coming?"

"Fine," Luke said. "I took out the toilet this morning."

"Before or after you met Tess's brother?"

Luke acted as though he had to think about that. "After. In fact, right after I met Mike, I went into your apartment and saw that the old toilet needed to be replaced. It only took me a few minutes to remove it."

"The whole kitchen needs to be remodeled but you haven't done that yet."

"I know it does," Luke said contritely, but then his head came up. "I know. Maybe I'll get Mike to help me put in a new kitchen. He looks like a man who could handle a screwdriver. Will you make lunch for us every day?"

Sara picked up her big pincushion and threw it at him. Luke caught it, tossed it back to her, then, chuckling, he went into the garden, the shovel across his shoulder.

At noon, Sara went inside to make herself lunch. She'd been too busy to go to the grocery since Greg left, so all she had was a loaf of three-day-old bread and some tuna salad her mother had made for her. As she bit into the boring sandwich she couldn't help but glance at the clock. She still had time to change clothes and drive into Williamsburg to have lunch with Mike at the elegant Williamsburg Inn.

But then she thought about all the gossip that would cause, plus the I-told-you-so look that would be on "that man's" face, and she discarded the idea. Getting up, she checked her phone, but Greg still hadn't called. However, she did have three voice mails from people around town. Reluctantly, Sara listened to each one—and they were all about what a great guy Mike Newland was. He'd helped her aunt Mavis unload a car, and he'd put the chain back on Uncle Arnie's saw—then Mike had cut the tree branch for him. The worst one was from her mother. Mike had paid a visit to Sara's mother, and she said she'd be over in the afternoon and they'd "talk about it."

"What did he do this morning?" Sara nearly shouted. "Go from one house to another and introduce himself? Or did he just perform good deeds all day?" For a moment she entertained herself with the thought that he'd spent the night sabotaging people's property, then in the morning he'd gone from one place to the other correcting the bad that he'd done.

Smiling at her little daydream, she put her dirty dishes in the washer, gathered her things, called Greg and texted him, then she went back outside. She should put her sewing machine on Tess's desk, turn on the TV, and work inside, but then she'd have to hear her phone ringing—or explain to people why she'd turned it off.

This way, she could just give the excuse that she was outside working and didn't hear it. As for Greg, if he did call, it might be good for him to reach her voice mail.

At two, she went inside to make herself a pitcher of iced tea and saw that Greg hadn't called. While the water boiled, she looked at the closed door of Mike's bedroom. Correction, Tess's guest room, and Sara seemed to be overwhelmed with curiosity. Quietly, as though she were being watched, she put her hand on the knob. It wouldn't surprise her to find out that the door was locked, but it wasn't. Feeling like a thief, she peeked in. The curtains were open on the one window, the bed was made, and as far as she could tell, it was exactly the same as it had been the day before. Contrary to what Luke had told her, there didn't look to be anything wrong with the bed.

Feeling bolder, she stepped inside and looked around. Nothing. There was no evidence that he'd been there. She went to the closet and opened it. There wasn't so much as a shirt inside, and no suitcase was on the floor. Now that she thought of it, he'd had no luggage with him last night when he'd come up out of the tunnel.

Frowning, Sara opened all three of the drawers in the chest. They were empty, as were the bedside table drawers, and nothing was under the bed. She even pulled the bedcovers back and looked under them, but there was not one thing of his in the room.

As she left, she thought about his note and that he'd said he needed to run errands. What secret assignations did he have in Williamsburg?

Sara had just closed the door behind her when she heard a car drive up and instantly knew it was her mother. It was, no doubt, some primal instinct that told her when her mother was near, and when she looked out, she saw that she was right. Before Sara could think how to escape, her mother was at the front door. When she saw Sara, she said through the glass, "I need some help."

"Don't we all?" Sara muttered as she opened the door. To her surprise, her mother had eight canvas—never plastic—bags of groceries on the little porch. All Sara's bad thoughts and feelings left her. Her mother knew how hard Sara was working to get the alterations done before the wedding, so she'd taken on the job of cooking for her. Armstrong's—Eleanor Shaw's maiden name—Organic Foods had grown since her mother opened it out of her kitchen in 1976. Now she ran three stores, one in Edilean, one in Williamsburg, and in the summer, a big fruit and vegetable stand on the highway to Richmond. She employed nearly a dozen women to cook food that sold out as fast as they could make it, plus another fifteen to handle the stores. That her mother would take the time in her very busy life to care about her daughter's needs made Sara forget any complaints she'd had. She really did have the most wonderful mother in the world.

Sara put her arms around her mother's neck and hugged her tight. "Thank you. You are the best mother . . . the best friend . . . anyone ever had. How did you know I was practically starving?"

When Eleanor was released, she handed Sara two bags of groceries. "Sorry to disappoint you, sweetums, but Mike bought all of this."

Sara's face fell. "Mike? Tess's brother?"

"You have more than one Mike living with you?"

Sara put the groceries on the counter by the refrigerator. "All right, so what heroic deed of monumental importance did he perform for *you* today?"

As Ellie opened the refrigerator door, she raised an eyebrow at her daughter. "What's got you so riled up? The fact that your husband-to-be went off and left you practically at the altar, or that he hasn't called?"

"How did you know—" Sara glared when she realized her

mother wasn't sure Greg hadn't called until Sara's outburst told her. "All right, out with it. Say what you have to, then go. I have work to do."

"You always do." Ellie put a bunch of dark *cavolo nero* in the crisper and adjusted the humidity level. "In fact, it seems that now you have so much work to do that you don't have time to even feed yourself, much less spend time with your friends and family."

Sara had heard it all before. Reaching into the bag, she withdrew a heavy chunk of Parmigiano-Reggiano cheese. "I don't have—"

"A grater for that?" Ellie said. "Don't worry, Mike took care of it. He *bought* one from me. Paid for it with a debit card. You know, the kind of card that takes money out of his bank account instantly?"

Sara didn't have to be told what her mother was referring to. Not long after she introduced Greg to her family, he stopped by the grocery and got a cart full of expensive, premade food—then wheeled it out without paying. When the store manager went after him, Greg said he could have whatever he wanted with no charge because his "girlfriend" owned the store. It took the manager a few minutes to understand that Greg was talking about Sara, not Ellie. Later, it had been Sara who'd had to deal with Greg's anger because his future mother-in-law wouldn't give him everything he wanted from the store for free. Since then, Sara had done the shopping and paid for everything, even though she did get an employee's discount. She didn't tell Greg because she didn't want to spend more hours explaining, but she was given many items without charge.

Now, as Sara unpacked more food—none of it ready-made— she thought about how to get her mother on her side. The praise for Mike Newland was getting out of hand. "Look, Mom, I know he seems like a nice guy and all, and he is Tess's brother, but there's something about him that I don't trust. Wait until you hear how he broke into my apartment in the middle of the night. He—"

"I know. He came up through the old tunnel."

Sara paused, her hand on a small, reusable canvas bag full of chili peppers. "How do you know about that?"

"Aunt Lissie told me about it when I was a kid, but it'd been closed up. Luke rediscovered it the year before he met Joce. You know, that time when he was so depressed he wasn't talking to anyone. He got my father to help him shore it up. Do you think Dad could do something like that and I'd not know about it? I was the one who washed his filthy clothes and rubbed liniment on his sore back."

"Who else knows about the tunnel?"

"Alive or dead?"

Sara shook her head. "Okay, so lots of people of your generation and older know about it, but that doesn't excuse how he—this stranger—used it. I think he *wanted* to scare me."

"I guess he should have knocked on the door of what he thought was an empty apartment."

"If he and Tess are so close, why didn't he know I was staying here? And why is his room empty? He showed up here at night with *nothing*. Don't you think that's a bit odd?"

Ellie looked up from the refrigerator. "Not if your apartment burned down and all you had left was what you were wearing and your car."

Sara stared at her mother, speechless.

Ellie straightened up, her hand on her lower back. She was sixty-two years old and a handsome woman—due, she said, to not eating the poisons that were in commercially grown foods—but she didn't look anything like her daughter. Sara's delicate prettiness came from Ellie's mother's sister, Lissie, a woman of alabaster beauty. "I thought he might not have told you why he showed up during the night and why his room—which it looks like you've been snooping through—is empty. The poor man has nothing. I ordered kilts for him."

"You what?"

"I measured him, called the shop in Edinburgh, and ordered two complete Scottish outfits for him, one for dress and one to wear to participate in the games at the fair."

"Games? At the fair? Are you talking about the *Scottish* games? Throwing a cable? Shot putting? The mock *battles*?! The Fraziers will slaughter him."

Ellie gave her daughter a sharp look. "What, exactly, is it that you have against this man? He's certainly better—"

When her mother seemed on the verge of saying more, Sara gave her a warning look. "If you're planning on saying anything bad about Greg, don't do it."

"I wouldn't dream of it."

"Only because you can't think of anything you haven't already said."

"Think not? Give me three hours and I could fill them up." At Sara's look, Ellie put her hands up in surrender. "All right, no more fighting. It's none of my business. So how's your work going?"

"Fine." Sara wanted to get the subject away from Greg. "What are all these groceries he bought for? Is he planning to open a rival store?"

"It's what Mike needs to be able to cook." Ellie's face took on a look of enchantment. "I've never met a man who wasn't in the business who knew so much about organic foods. We must have spent ten whole minutes talking about the benefits of flaxseed."

"That sounds fascinating."

Ellie ignored the snide remark. "Mike gave me a recipe for parsnip soup that I'm going to try on your father tonight, and they have a golf date this Saturday."

"Who does?"

"Mike and your father."

"My father is going to play golf with a man half his age, someone he doesn't even know? A policeman?"

"I'll tell Mike to leave his guns at home, and Henry can wear his bulletproof vest. You didn't answer my question about what you have against this man, who, by the way, isn't so young. He's thirty-six and he can retire from the police force in under three years. I wonder where he's planning to live?"

"Mother, if you think that this man and I—"

"Never would I dream of interfering in the life of any of my dear daughters. Actually, I was thinking of Mike and Ariel. Wouldn't they make a lovely couple?"

"Ariel?" Sara asked, aghast. "Ariel Frazier? What's *she* doing in town?"

"Sara, dear, did you forget that Ariel *lives* here?"

"She hasn't lived here since high school when she told all of us that she couldn't wait to get away from this backwater town and everyone in it."

"And she did. She went to medical school and now she's finished and she wants to take a break before she begins the grueling work of doing her residency. Then she'll be a doctor—and she wants to open a clinic here in Edilean."

Sara thought her mother was looking at her as though she expected her to say or do something, but Sara had no idea what it was. Ariel was one year older than she was, and her family had been in Edilean for as long as hers had. Since the beginning, the Fraziers had sold whatever moved on wheels, whether it was bicycles, wagons, tractors, or Lamborghinis. It was said—but no one had any proof—that the original Frazier was the best friend of Angus McTern Harcourt, the man who'd settled Edilean. It was also said—

with even less proof—that the first Frazier had actually been the one who drove the wagonload of gold that had been the basis for the founding of the town. When Sara was in the first grade and Ariel in the second, she'd told Sara that her grandfather said that by rights Edilean Manor, even the entire town, should belong to them. That was the first of many fights Sara and Ariel'd had.

"You aren't saying anything," Ellie said. "Don't you think Ariel and Mike would make a great couple?"

"How would I know? I don't know him and I haven't seen her in years."

"Oh! She's just beautiful! Long red hair and dark blue eyes. And of course she's smart. But then she always was. And Mike is quite handsome."

"Yeah, if you like men from a police lineup."

Ellie looked at her daughter with wide eyes. "I think all that sewing Greg makes you do has damaged your eyesight."

"So help me, if you say one more thing against Greg, I'll—"

Ellie walked to the door. "I told you last time we had a discussion about him that I'd keep my nose out of it. Everyone has to make his or her own mistakes. Sorry. I didn't mean that as it sounded. I'm going. But Sara, my dear child, I do think you could cut Mike a little slack. His apartment and everything he owned burned and the only relative he has is his sister. And . . ."

"And what?"

"My mother used to tell me about Mike and Tess's grandmother. After their parents died, she raised them, and my mother said Prudence Farlane was the most angry person she'd ever met in her life, that it was like a volcano of hatred was inside her. That Mike can retire so early means he joined the force when he was still a teenager. A child, really. Sara, I truly think you should have some compassion for the man."

Sara waited a moment before answering. "Good try, Mom, but I'm still going to marry Greg."

Ellie laughed. "I did my best. Let me know what he does with that *cavolo*. I might put his recipe in the store bulletin." She paused at the door. "And you don't think he's handsome?"

"I think he's gay," Sara said, even though she was lying.

Again, Ellie laughed. "I wonder if I was ever as young as you are? Keep me up-to-date with any news. See ya." With that, she left the apartment, and Sara leaned back against the door in relief.

# 4

BY LATE AFTERNOON, Sara had calmed herself somewhat. She knew that most of her nervousness was caused by not having heard from Greg for days now. And too, she was sick of trying to make the people of Edilean like the man she loved. If Greg would just allow her to tell people the truth about his very difficult life, she knew they'd understand. His childhood had been so harrowing that it was true that he was sometimes awkward in public situations. He'd even admitted that he was jealous of the love the people of Edilean gave Sara. "I've tried," he said as he shed tears that made Sara's heart nearly break. "I've tried hard to make them like me. I didn't understand about the grocery store. I thought that since your mother owned the place that she would share what she had with her daughter."

Sara didn't know what to say. The food was free to her, but not to *him*. "It has to do with accounting," Sara said. "And inventory. I'll talk to her and see what—"

"No!" Greg said. "I don't want her to do anything special for me. If your mother doesn't want me to eat her food, so be it. We'll go to a grocery in Williamsburg."

"If you'd just let me explain to her about your past . . ." Sara said, but Greg always forbid it, and she understood why. He said he wanted the people of Edilean to like him on his own merits—as the people outside the town did. Sometimes he said, "Afterward, you and I will leave here."

"After what?" she'd asked, but he would never answer her.

"Am I disturbing you?"

She looked up to see Mike Newland standing by the table, two glasses of iced tea in his hands.

"I saw yours was empty so I . . . Is that all right?"

"Sure," she said and tried to smooth her forehead. If he stayed much longer she was going to get wrinkles from frowning so much.

He set the glasses down and said, "Do you mind?" as he nodded toward the empty chair.

She kept on sewing while he sat down.

"Look," he said in his raspy voice, "I think you and I got off on the wrong foot yesterday." For a moment he didn't seem to know what else to say. "Did you have a nice day?"

"*You* seem to have been busy. Helped about a thousand people, didn't you?" There was hostility in her voice.

"I, uh . . ." He took a deep drink of his tea. "Miss Shaw, I know I offended you last night, but I thought I was entering an empty apartment. I can assure you that you were as much a surprise to me as I was to you."

Sara put her sewing on the table. "You're right. I'm being rude. It's just that—" She waved her hand in dismissal. "It doesn't matter."

"No, tell me. I'm a good listener." When Sara silently drank her tea and looked out over the garden, Mike said, "Does it have anything to do with your missing boyfriend?"

"Fiancé."

"Sorry. I was told so much gossip this morning that I can't keep up with it all. By the way, who is Ariel?"

"A distant cousin of mine. According to my mother, she's the most beautiful, brilliant, talented female ever put on this earth—next to my two perfect sisters, that is."

Mike looked at her for a moment, then stood up. "It sounds like you've had a hard day. Why don't you come inside and let me cook something for you?" When she hesitated, he said, "It's what I've done with Tess since we were kids."

It was so nice to have someone smile at her that Sara picked up her sewing and docilely followed him into the house. She sat at the table while he took over the kitchen. He tied a half apron (newly purchased) around his waist and began to rummage in the refrigerator. He emerged with an avocado, sour cream, and a couple of limes. "Talk to me," he said as he set it all on the countertop and reached for a knife from the wooden holder.

Sara watched him as he moved about the kitchen. He smashed a clove of garlic with the back of the big knife as though he were a professional chef. "I'm sorry about what happened to your apartment."

Mike gave a one-shoulder shrug. "Hazards of the job."

"It was burned because of your job?"

Turning, he gave her a little smile. "The last thing I want to do is talk about my work or me. I'd rather hear about you. Aren't you having a wedding in a few weeks? Is your dress nice?" He was peeling the avocado.

"It's lovely," Sara said as she hid her smile in her iced tea. He certainly wasn't like the men she knew. "It was my great-aunt Lissie's wedding gown."

Mike put a bowl of the avocado dip he'd made in front of her, along with another one of tortilla chips. "So when do I get to meet your fiancé?"

He hadn't taken long to start in on what everyone hassled her about! Sara thought. She was torn between wanting to throw the bowl at him and bursting into tears. But in the next minute he removed a frosty pitcher of margaritas from the refrigerator and poured her a glassful. She drank it in one gulp. He looked at her with wide eyes but quickly poured her another one.

After she'd taken a long sip, he said, "Better?"

Sara nodded and dug into the chips and dip.

"I take it everyone has been asking about him, but you don't know when he'll be back, so you have no answer to give them."

"Exactly," Sara said, feeling relaxed for the first time since Greg left.

"Maybe he went home," Mike said as he put slices of pear on salad greens.

"He lives here. With me."

"No, I mean, maybe he went to the place where his parents live."

"Oh."

Mike sprinkled piñon nuts over the salad and drizzled raspberry vinaigrette on top. "Did you call his parents?" he asked as he put the plate in front of her.

Sara mumbled a reply.

"I'm sorry. I didn't hear what you said."

She waited while she chewed a bite of salad. "I don't know where his parents live—or if they do. He told me about some extremely unpleasant experiences he had while growing up, but he didn't give me details like names and addresses."

"Ah," Mike said as he turned his back to her, and he thought that it was true that Stefan had had some very unpleasant things happen in his childhood. He'd served two years in juvie for stealing a car, six months for attempting to rob a jewelry store, and had been arrested twice for pickpocketing. By the time Stefan was eighteen, he was an experienced criminal and hadn't been arrested since. "So you don't know about his family?"

"No! And don't you start on me too! Everyone has a right to privacy, and besides, I've heard enough complaints about him from my mother, from this whole town. I bet *you* have things you don't want people to know about."

"Ask me anything. I'm an open book." He removed the two Cornish hens he'd ordered that morning and quickly began to stuff them with wild rice and herbs he'd prepared before he went out to see Sara. One of the good things about his life of living undercover was that he'd had to work at a lot of jobs. One of the handiest was the eighteen months he'd spent as a sous chef for a restaurant in Arizona. He could whip out a fajita in ten minutes.

"Where did you grow up?"

"Akron, Ohio."

"Why does Tess refuse to talk about her childhood?"

"I thought this was about me, not my sister."

"She's my friend; you're a stranger."

Mike tied up the hens. He'd once tied up a man in the same way, legs together, arms in the back, cord down his front. "You're right. What's about me is about Tess. Our parents were killed in a car wreck when I was twelve and Tess was five, so we were raised by our maternal grandparents." He put the birds in the oven.

"I've heard of your grandmother."

"I bet you have. They tell you what a bad-tempered woman she was?"

"Yes," Sara said quietly. "Was your grandfather nice?"

Mike looked back at her. "We rarely saw him. Grans said he had to travel for his job, but after he died in '99, I found out that he'd had a second family."

"Good heavens." Sara paused with the fork on the way to her mouth and watched as Mike took the seat across from her.

"Are you beginning to see why Tess doesn't talk about her childhood?"

"Yes," Sara said, looking at him. "Please tell me more. I need something to take my mind off my own problems. My mother said you joined the police force when you were still a teenager."

Mike hesitated. Never in any of his undercover work had he been required to tell the truth about himself. But there were people in this town who'd known his grandmother, so if he lied, Sara would find out about it. "I was older, so I ran interference between little Tess and Grans, but there was only so much I could take. On the night I graduated from high school, I told the old woman that if she so much as touched Tess I'd kill her, then I left town."

"But of course you wouldn't have. Killed her, that is."

Mike looked up from his salad, but he didn't answer.

"What did you do after you left?"

"I'd always wanted to see the ocean, so I . . ." He smiled in memory. "I flipped a coin to see which one I'd go to and the East Coast won—or lost, I guess. I bummed my way to Florida and stopped in Fort Lauderdale." He took another bite. "One thing led to another and I joined the police force." He looked up at her. "And here I am now."

"What about Tess?"

"She's done well, hasn't she?"

"No, I mean, when did you get back with her?"

"When she graduated from high school, I was waiting outside for her. I'd already picked up her bags from where she'd thrown them out her bedroom window. She threw her cap and gown in our grandmother's face, got in my car, and we drove away. "

"I guess you were the one who put her through college."

Mike had told all that he could without giving away any real information, so he shrugged. Miss Sara Hélèna Shaw was certainly a curious young woman. He knew that while he was out she'd gone through his room. Out of habit, he'd marked the drawers and aligned the little throw rug with the floorboards. When he returned, everything had been slightly askew. He was glad he'd left the case files with his weapons in the hidden compartment under the carpet in the trunk of his car.

He got up to look in the oven window. "So who do you know more about now? Me or the man you're planning to marry?"

"What an odd question. Because I've never met my fiancé's parents doesn't mean I don't know everything else about him. I know what he likes to eat, how he drives a car, what he wants in the future, about his last two girlfriends who broke his heart, his——"

"What he wants for the future?" Mike asked sharply. "And what would that be?"

Sara looked down at her hands. "The usual. A home and children." She wasn't about to tell him that birth control pills made her swell, that Greg was scrupulous in using protection, and that he was vague about when he wanted to start having children.

"Is what he wants here in Edilean? Did he tell you that in those exact words? What did he say?" The moment he spoke, Mike cursed the eagerness in his voice and hoped Sara wouldn't pick up on it.

But she did.

"They got Tess to send you here, didn't they?" Sara stood up.

"Tess to send me here? I don't know what you're talking about," he said honestly. "Who is 'they'?"

"This town. They all think they own me. Other people come

and go, but not me." Her voice was rising. "Sweet little Sara Shaw stays at home and *helps* people. Everyone else goes away and *does* things, but *I* stay here and watch other people come back with their careers and their husbands and their adorable little kids. But good ol' Sara is always here."

Putting her hands on the table, she leaned toward him. "You can tell all of them—your sister, Ramsey, Luke, everyone—that they may not like Greg but *I* do. He's made me achieve things. He may be abrupt and rude at times, but at least he gives me hope for the future."

She leaned so far forward her face was inches from his. "As for you, Mr. Newland, you can forget about trying to get information out of me, or seducing me away from Greg, or whatever you have planned, because it won't work. Do you understand me? I'm not interested in you or any other man, so you might as well leave *now*."

With that, she went down the hall to her bedroom and slammed the door.

Mike fell back against the chair in utter bewilderment. He had *no* idea what he'd just been accused of. "Seduce her?" He hadn't come close to her.

Mike ran his hands over his face. His instinct was to knock on her door and try to talk to her, but as he had no idea what to say, that would be useless. Why couldn't she have drawn a nice big gun on him? A revolver. A semiautomatic would have been a good choice. She could have said, "Get near me again and I'll kill you." He'd had that said to him multiple times, and he'd always handled it easily.

The timer went off for the hens, Mike got them out of the oven, then went outside to call Tess.

She answered on the second ring.

"So what do you think of her?" Tess didn't bother with prelimi-naries.

"She's stressed-out. And she knows I'm lying."

That astonished Tess so much she could hardly speak. "But you *always* lie. It's what makes you so good at your job. You lie about . . . about what kind of toothpaste you use, but people never know it."

"Are you sure you're on *my* side?"

Tess didn't laugh. "I don't understand this. Sara believes every word of a guy the whole town knows is a jerk, but she doesn't believe *you*?"

"Who can understand it?" Mike's voice conveyed his puzzlement. "I've treated her like I would a princess, cooked for her, cleaned up after both of us, but she still accuses me of . . . I don't really know why she's so angry at me."

"What about the people of Edilean? Not the newcomers, but the ones who know Sara. What's going on with them?"

Mike took his time in answering. "I talked to some of them this morning, and they're genuinely concerned about her. They don't want her to be hurt."

Tess well knew what he was saying. "That town is astonishing, isn't it? Those people actually *care* about one another. Of course you have to be on the inside to get that caring, but it does happen."

"Not what we were told about this place, is it?"

Tess gave a low laugh. "Not by a long shot. Have you talked to anyone who knew Grans?"

"No, and I don't want to. I'd like to think that mess was buried with her."

"Me too," Tess said. "So, now, I want to hear what *you* think of Sara."

"I think she's . . ."

"She's what?"

"Beautiful."

"How beautiful?"

"She makes me nervous."

"That bad, huh?"

"The strangest things make her furious at me, but it's impossible for me to get angry back at somebody who wears clothes that look like angels made them."

"I know. Sara wears long sleeves even on the hottest days. She orders a lot of the fabric from Ireland, then makes her own clothes. They go with that porcelain skin of hers, don't you think?"

"Yeah, I do," he said in a low, throaty way.

"What about Sara as a woman? Great, huh?"

"I don't think I've seen her as she really is, but I like what I've been told about her. Everyone in town thinks she's practically a saint. She's the one who volunteers to help everybody. She earns so little money that if it weren't for her mother feeding her, she'd starve."

Tess was glad Mike couldn't see her because she was smiling broadly. She knew he had never come close to being serious about a woman, but then his "dating" was always connected to the undercover cases he worked on. He'd once had a torrid affair with the wife of a drug lord so he could get info about her husband. When the arrests were made, she'd slapped Mike so hard—and he let her—that he wore a neck brace for a week. Only Tess knew the despondency Mike went through after that. He'd liked the woman, even liked her two children. It had been Tess who'd taken care of him after that case and seen what he went through over it.

"I made an appointment for you tomorrow," she said.

"For what?"

"For the house closing that I've been nagging you about for an entire *year*. It's at the title company in Williamsburg, and now that you're there, you can do it."

"But I'm here on a case, so maybe another time would be better. I could—"

"No! I am not going to give you more time. I made the appointment and I texted you the address. Show up there at two, sign the papers, and the place is yours."

"A farm! What do *I* want with a farm?"

"We are *not* going through that again," Tess said, her teeth clenched. "Whether you like it or not, I swore to our grandmother that someday our family would own that place, and I'm keeping that promise." Tess would never tell her brother but she'd sworn on *his* life, and Tess superstitiously feared that if she were to break the vow, the horrible old woman would come out of the grave and take her revenge.

Mike interrupted Tess's ugly memories. The truth was, what else was he going to do after he retired but live close to her?

"Tell me again why you and Rams don't live on the place?"

"He has a piece of land that he wants to build on. I've told you all of this. And I've also told you that I think you'll *like* that old farm. You can move around, and fixing it up will give you something to do after you retire."

Mike's voice went back to teasing. "Okay, so what's your plan for me with this farm? Am I supposed to grow corn? Or do you guys up here raise cotton?"

"That would be better than the vile job you have now. But when you visit, just don't forget about the old man who's the caretaker. He greets guests with a shotgun, so you'd better call first."

"You're not talking about old . . . What was his name?"

"Brewster Lang."

"That's right," Mike said. "How could I forget that name? Grans's only true friend in all of Edilean. You don't think he's as mean as she was, do you?"

"I think he may have taught her all she knew."

Mike gave a low whistle. "He couldn't be that bad."

"Tell me when you're going to the farm unannounced and I'll alert the hospital to expect a man with a body full of buckshot."

"Point taken. But he must be nearly a hundred years old now. Is he able to ever leave the place?"

"It's not New York, where everything is delivered, so I assume he has to get food." She paused. "Here comes Rams. I have to go."

Mike laughed. "I forgot to ask: How's the honeymoon?"

Tess's voice dropped to a whisper. "I'm pretty sure I'm pregnant, but I haven't told Rams yet. Buy my kid a pony and keep it on your farm. I love you. Bye." She hung up.

When Mike clicked off the phone, he was surprised at how good Tess's announcement made him feel. A baby? A fat little kid sticky with fruit juice, a soggy diaper, a dimple in his cheek? He could almost see the boy.

"And me living on a farm," Mike said aloud. "A kid, a pony, and a farm. I might as well shoot myself now."

He went back inside, ate dinner by himself, wrapped up the leftovers, and put them in the refrigerator. He went for a run and returned to see that Sara's door was still closed, but there was a light on. After his shower, he slipped a note under her door saying he was going to bed and to please help herself to the food.

When he was in bed, he listened but heard no sound from her. He felt bad that all his questions had made her so angry that she'd gone without dinner.

After his run, he'd stopped at his car to get some of the files the captain had given him, and he stayed up until midnight reading them. Whereas he'd seen the criminal files, he hadn't had time to read the in-depth reports.

He'd never before been involved in the Economic Crimes Unit, so reading about how the Vandlos worked fascinated him. Stefan was ordinary—seduce and take—but Mitzi was more interesting. What she did took cunning and a total disregard for the quality of human life.

Until a few years ago, Mitzi was living in upstate New Jersey and commuting into New York City, where she worked scams on rich women. She lured them to her through a tiny office in the center of Manhattan with PSYCHIC painted on the window. Women in trauma, in grief, whose lives were in chaos, thronged to her, hoping to find answers about what they should do to solve their problems. Mitzi took the ones who were so desperate for relief that they were willing to pay all they had to get out of the turmoil their lives had become.

Mitzi's code, refined through generations, was three part: trust, faith in The Work, and control. First, she spent months gaining the trust of the women. She was an expert at body language and could tell what someone wanted within minutes of meeting her. And she listened to them in a way they had never been listened to before. Mitzi heard what her victims said and remembered it. She understood; she championed the woman, was always on her side. Mitzi was the best friend anyone could imagine.

When she'd gained her victim's trust, Mitzi started on making her believe in "The Work" and that she, Mitzi, was only a vessel being used by spirits/angels/God, whatever appealed to the victim. Believing that she was doing everything for a Higher Power made a person feel that she'd at last found her purpose in life.

Once the victim had faith, Mitzi would start working her way into controlling and completing the isolation that was necessary to pull off a major scam. She would meet the victim, looking red-eyed and haggard, telling her that she'd been up all night with The Work and had seen horrible things. By this time Mitzi knew what the woman's deepest fears were, so she could use them against her. If she was afraid of her ex-husband, then Mitzi said he was plotting with friends against her. It was best to get away from them.

What Mitzi really gave her victims was hope. She promised love, children, fortunes—whatever was wanted—and the frightened women held on to it like a life raft. Hope became everything to them, what they lived and breathed for. And Mitzi made them believe that only *she* could give them what they needed—if she was given the money to create the energy to perform the task. But it was all right to pay because Mitzi swore that when The Work was completed, every penny would be returned.

As in all abusive relationships, there came a time when the good ended. The listening disappeared, the feeling of deep friendship, when you were both dedicated to a purpose, stopped. The victim became so desperate for that time to return that she paid more and more money. By then she had no other friends, just Mitzi, so she worked hard to please her.

But, eventually, the victim would run out of money, and that's when Mitzi would instantly and abruptly stop the relationship. Suddenly, Mitzi's phone would be disconnected, her office empty. If the frantic victim was able to contact Mitzi—sometimes after months of trying—her desperate pleas for help would meet Mitzi's coldness. Crying, devastated, the victim would ask for her money to be returned, as she had been promised. That's when Mitzi would tell her that every penny was "gone," used up by The Work. Without the slightest bit of compassion, Mitzi would hang up.

The victim would be left alone. She was usually nearly bankrupt, and under Mitzi's tutelage, she'd cut herself off from everyone. She had no one to turn to for moral support as she tried to recover, and she was usually too embarrassed to go to the police and tell them how—as she saw it—stupid she'd been.

If the woman did screw up her courage and go to the police, she was usually dismissed. According to them, she'd given the money away of her own free will, so there was no crime. But the Fort Lauderdale Police Department had listened to one victim and after they'd subpoenaed some of Mitzi's many bank accounts, they were shocked at the sheer magnitude of what they saw. Mitzi Vandlo had taken millions of dollars from many women.

Whenever there's lots of money involved in a crime, the federal bureaus step in, and everything changes. It was soon found out that Mitzi was just a small part of what looked to be one of the largest organized crime rings in the world—and no one knew anything about it.

As the investigation went forward, fortunately, it was backed by a recent U.S. Supreme Court ruling that said the gullibility of a person didn't eliminate the fact that a crime had been committed. People who did what Mitzi had done were as guilty as bank robbers.

State criminal law and federal law work in opposite ways. Criminals arrested by state law enforcement are incarcerated, then evidence is found. But the Feds will spend years gathering information before arrests are made. Unfortunately, the first time around, when they were ready to indict Mitzi and twenty-eight of her family members, she'd been told what was coming. She and her son had disappeared where no one could find them.

As Mike straightened the papers, he agreed with the captain that the only reason Stefan *and* his mother would come to a two-bit town like Edilean, Virginia, would be for something really big. And it looked like during the time Mitzi was missing, she'd found another way to extort money, and this time, it involved Miss Sara Shaw.

Mike put the papers in his bedside table drawer, making a mental note to take them out in the morning. He couldn't risk Sara finding them when she snooped through his room.

As he closed the drawer, he couldn't help but think of the irony of the evening. This afternoon, while he'd spent a couple of hours at Williamsburg's outlet mall buying new clothes, he'd envisioned a nice, domestic evening with Sara. They'd have good food and the wine that was never opened. He imagined that after dinner he'd get his new clothes out of his car, and he and Sara would go through them. Since she was in the business, he'd ask her advice about what he should wear. And every scenario that he came up with ended with Sara telling him what it was that the Vandlos wanted. But, somehow, everything had fallen through.

As he turned off the light, Mike thought, Strippers. From now on, he was going to deal *only* with strippers. No more good girls who made no sense whatsoever.

# 5

THE NEXT MORNING, Sara awoke with what she knew was a hangover. Two margaritas wouldn't be enough to make most people drunk, but Sara'd never been able to tolerate much alcohol.

As she splashed cold water on her face, she began to remember what she'd said to Mike the night before. Her excuse was that he'd asked too many questions about Greg, made too many insinuations, and added to all the other things going on now, it had been more than she could take.

She would, of course, have to apologize to him. Last night, it had seemed clear that . . . well, it was almost as though people were plotting against her—but that couldn't be true. However, the idea stayed with her and began to grow.

As the day wore on and she worked constantly on the pile of sewing, she told herself that it couldn't be possible that Tess had worked with the whole town to bring in Mike to get Sara away from Greg.

But there was an old murder mystery on TV, and as she sewed and listened, she seemed to see conspiracy in every second of the last few days. Greg abruptly called away; Luke taking over her apartment; Sara having to move into Tess's place where the trapdoor was. Then Tess's mysterious brother just "happens" to show up—and now he was living in the small apartment with her.

At one, Sara went to the kitchen to get lunch and saw that the refrigerator was full of the food Mike had cooked. What had he been planning last night with that delicious meal? She vaguely remembered accusing him of trying to seduce her.

Maybe she'd watched too many black-and-white movies, but she had an image of herself drunk and winding up in bed with Mike. Then two men with cameras with huge round flashbulb holders would burst in and take their photo.

Would they give the lurid pictures to Greg? For a sickening moment Sara imagined Greg's rage if he saw photos of her in bed with another man. He went ballistic when she so much as laughed at a salesman's joke. "It's just because I love you so very much," Greg'd said many times.

She got a plate from Tess's cabinet, filled it with the food Mike had cooked, put a paper towel over the top, and microwaved it. She poured herself a big glass of iced tea and sat down to a feast.

As Mike left the title office with the fat portfolio in his hand, the closing complete, he was still shaking his head about Sara. He hadn't been able to figure out what he'd done to make her so angry. Sure, maybe his arrival through her bedroom floor was a bit crude, but he still saw no other way to get close to her as fast as he did. If he'd knocked on the door and introduced himself, she would have been polite, but he would have been sent to a hotel and he wouldn't have seen her again.

Truthfully, he thought the way the townspeople were ganging up on her against the man she wanted to marry was too much. While it was true that he knew Vandlo was a criminal, *they* didn't. Where was all this "support" that women talked about all the time? TV from four until six was what Mike called the "Support Hours." One time when Tess was staying with him—he was recovering from a bullet wound (his fourth)—and he was bored with being still, and sick of pain, he took his frustration out on the TV. He tossed a pillow at it and said, "If I hear the word *support* one more time, I'm throwing the thing out the window. No matter how stupid a person is, how bad a decision, all you women care about is that you 'support' each other."

"So now I'm one of 'you women'?" Tess asked calmly, not even looking up from her magazine. "I can assure you that never in my life have I supported a woman when *she* made a decision so stupid that *she* got shot."

In an instant, Mike's bad temper left him and he managed to get off the couch and cook a decent dinner for Tess. Two days later, she went home to Edilean.

As Mike drove away from Williamsburg, he wondered if he should bother cooking. He was bending over backward to impress Sara, but no matter what he did, he made her furious. Never before had he had trouble with women. In fact, one of his big problems in life had been that women liked him too much. They flirted with him and teased him. In fact, he'd never had to do any work to get a woman he wanted.

But that wasn't the case with Miss Sara Shaw. She had disliked him from the moment she saw him, and her animosity toward him had increased rapidly since then. But then, as he'd told the captain, women like Sara were a complete and total mystery to him.

When he got back to Edilean Manor, he almost expected the

door to the apartment to be bolted, but it was unlocked. The detective in him came to the fore. Maybe he'd conduct classes on home safety in Edilean and talk to them about the importance of keeping their doors locked. He saw Luke at Sara's apartment, carrying out what looked to be the kitchen sink, and again Mike felt sorry for her. The entire town was against her, and he thought that if he were in her shoes, he might marry a person just to spite them.

Inside Tess's apartment, he glanced down the hall to the bedroom Sara was using, but it was empty. As he put the folio from the title company on the table, he thought that maybe later he would talk to her about what the town was doing to her. Maybe that would loosen things up between them. Or he could talk to her about becoming the owner of a farm. She might help him relax about taking on such a heavy responsibility.

When he looked out the window, he saw Sara outside, sitting under a big tree, her cell in her hand, with her never-ending sewing on the table beside her. This morning the captain had sent him information through Tess. Just as they'd hoped would happen, Stefan's temper had erupted when he'd talked to the police about his wife's arrest. Within minutes, he was handcuffed and put in a holding cell. The captain had gleefully told Tess of the accusations and threats that Vandlo had shouted at the police as he was put into jail. And Stefan kept saying that he "had to get back," which was taken to mean that he had to return to Sara and the scam he had going with her.

When he'd been taken into custody, his phone had been confiscated, so they saw all the e-mails and text messages that Sara had sent Stefan Vandlo since he'd left Edilean in such a hurry.

Sara's messages to him were a mixture of anger and pleading. She kept asking him where he was and when he'd be back. She'd only alluded to Mike by saying that she'd had some "problems" at home that she needed Greg's help with.

Mike was told that Vandlo had never answered her, even when he'd had his phone returned to him.

After he'd made some iced tea, Mike took it outside to Sara. He was prepared for more anger, but when she smiled at him, he was relieved.

"About last night . . ." she began, but Mike cut her off.

"I didn't mean to upset you and you're right that I ask too many questions. Another hazard of my job. Did anybody tell you that I did good deeds today?"

"Not one," Sara said, smiling and sipping her tea. "Did you put your crusader cape in mothballs?"

"It's not the cape I want to get rid of. Did your mother tell you she ordered me a couple of *skirts*?" When Sara laughed, he liked the sound and wanted to hear more of it. "No, really. I saw Luke and asked where the best place in town to buy organic food was and he—"

"Sent you to my mother. I know. She told me."

"I thought she wouldn't want customers at that time of morning, but she was there, unloading boxes of cauliflower."

"My father says the best time of day is the two hours after Mother leaves the house and before he has to get up." She looked at Mike in speculation. "So what did she say to get you to agree to participate in the games?"

"You mean I had a choice? As far as I could tell, she'd already decided before I got there. Tess has always told me how fast news flies around this town, but I was shocked that she already knew so much."

Sara nodded. "You told Tess, who told Rams, who called Luke, who told Joce, and she called my mother."

Mike laughed. "If only our government worked so efficiently."

"The government isn't as nosy as this town is. So what about the kilts?"

"Your mother——" Mike looked at his glass.

"You aren't blushing, are you?" Sara leaned toward him. He'd shaved, and without his black whiskers, he looked less like a pirate. "I'm afraid to ask what she did."

"Took off my jacket, pulled up my shirt, and put her arms around me."

"I assume she was holding a tape measure."

Mike nodded.

"In case you don't know, putting you in the fair is her way of making you part of Edilean. She'd had a few hours of knowing that another man was near me, and that's all it took for her to decide that you were better for me than the man I'm going to marry."

"About that——" Mike began, but Sara interrupted.

"It's all right. I know what they think, since most of them have told me. It's almost as though Greg works to annoy the people in this town."

Mike took a deep drink of his tea. "Why would he do that?"

"I don't know. Sometimes I think that what Greg really wants is for the two of us to move to some remote island and live there all alone."

Mike didn't say anything. The first rule of control is to isolate your victim. It looked as though Vandlo had already started to put it into Sara's pretty head that they would be better off away from people who knew her. It was Mike's guess that Sara was right and Stefan was purposefully making the people of Edilean dislike him. After he and Sara were married, Mike figured Vandlo would increase the animosity until he got Sara to move away. When they were living among strangers, Sara would meet with a fatal accident, and as her husband, Stefan would inherit whatever she owned.

He didn't want Sara to see the seriousness in his face. "So what's for dinner?"

She didn't hesitate but held up the stack of clothing. "Let's see . . . There's cotton for an appetizer, wool for the main course, and silk for dessert."

"Sounds perfect. Would you mind if I put a few scallops and asparagus with them?"

"I think that's the best idea I've heard all day. But only on one condition."

"And that is?"

"More tequila."

Smiling, Mike stood up, picked up her sewing for her, and they began walking back to the house. "Maybe tomorrow you'll show me your shop. By the way, who's running it now?"

Sara gave a loud sigh. "Greg hired a woman from D.C. She has a degree in . . ." She waved her hand. "I don't know. She wears suits and she's so brilliant at business that she scares me. I think that when Tess gets back I'm going to sic her on the woman."

"Are you referring to *my* baby sister? My sweet-tempered, gentle little Tess?"

"The one and only. Did you ever hear the story about the red dress?"

"I heard it from Tess, but she told it only from her point of view." Tess had told him that Ramsey, who at that time was her boss, had called her into his office for an evaluation. He had no complaint with the job Tess was doing, but he said she should stop wearing her skin-tight jeans. "After all, this is a place of work," he'd said pompously. Mike could have told him that ordering Tess not to do something was a guarantee that she'd do it. The next day she'd shown up in a red silk dress so tiny it could have been used as a handkerchief. Since some people he was trying to impress had been there that day, Rams was properly chastised. Never again did Rams complain about anything Tess did.

"Were the men in the office also put into their place?" Mike asked.

"Ha! My cousin Ken wanted to declare a Red Dress Day in Edilean, but his wife vetoed it."

They were at the door of the house, and Mike held it open for her. As they had yesterday, she sat down at the table while he moved about the kitchen, and Sara glanced down at her phone. The red light wasn't on.

All day, every time her cell buzzed, her heart had leaped. Maybe it was Greg at last calling her. But it never was. It was either someone in town asking her some asinine question about whether she was going to be in church on Sunday or if she was going to the fair—or whatever he/she could come up with to find out if Greg had called her. Sometimes they asked about the wedding. The planner—whom Sara'd met only once—called to say that she was having trouble getting carnations the exact color of yellow that she, Sara, wanted. Listlessly, Sara'd said that whatever she had would be fine. If it had been left up to Sara, she would have ordered flowering, fragrant herbs and big roses that dropped their petals, and she would have asked her mother's employees to decorate the church. Sara had grown up around most of them, and she knew they'd love to make garlands and wreaths. But when Sara had suggested that to Greg, he'd said that her mother hated him so much she'd probably fill the church with poison ivy.

By that afternoon, when Mike arrived with a glass of iced tea, Sara was near to tears. There'd been no call from Greg, and he'd not so much as acknowledged her e-mails or texts. Was it over between them but he just hadn't told her? She'd never felt so alone in her life.

But Mike's dimpled smile diminished her unhappiness. He too was alone since he knew no one in town—and he didn't even have a home to return to. When she'd thought of him during the long day, she'd vowed to be nicer to him. Even if Tess and the town had conspired to introduce Mike to her, Sara didn't think he was part of it.

Last night he'd seemed to be genuinely puzzled by the accusations she'd hurled at him. In fact, today she'd thought of telling him the truth about what was going on. She even thought of telling him about her fears with Greg. It hurt that she had no one to confide in. If she told anyone in Edilean that she was worried that he was dumping her, they'd probably raise a banner of celebration in the town square. But Mike was an outsider, so maybe they could be friends.

"What's that look for?" Mike asked.

"I've just been thinking, that's all. I'm looking forward to another scrumptious meal."

"You sound like you're in a good mood. Something happen?"

"If you're asking if Greg called, no, he didn't. But that's all right. I'm sure he has a reason."

Mike had to turn away to keep from saying, Yeah, iron bars. He looked back at her. "I didn't ask if you like scallops."

"Love them." Sara watched him move about the kitchen. Like yesterday, he was beautifully dressed. He wore dark slacks of a lightweight wool and a perfectly pressed blue cotton shirt with the sleeves carefully folded to the elbows. His shoes were polished, and she knew from her retail experience that they had cost several hundred dollars. "Do you always dress like this?"

"Sometimes the only real thing in a person's life is his body, so I do what I can with it."

Since his arrival, she'd been too agitated to give much thought to his looks and, now, how she'd described him to Tess rang in her head. When she looked at him, he wasn't as bad as she'd first thought. Actually, Mike wasn't exactly short. He was more average height. And her seamstress eyes calculated that he had a waist that was no more than thirty inches. Some of her female customers would kill for a waist as small as his.

"You're looking at me awfully hard," he said as he pulled packages from the refrigerator.

"I still don't see that you look like Tess."

"You'd see the resemblance if we were together. You like asparagus?"

"Only if it isn't covered in that awful pink sauce."

"A girl after my own heart." When Mike smiled like that, he almost looked handsome.

Turning away, Sara saw the big folder on the table with a title company's name on the front. "What's this? Did you go to a closing today?"

"Yes, and it's a gift from my sister." Mike was washing the scallops.

"She gave you land, or is it a house?" Sara's voice was astonished.

"Both, I guess. The place's been owned by the McDowell family for years, and now it's mine as long as I or my descendants *live* there. If I so much as try to rent it out, it goes back to my new brother-in-law."

"That sounds like Rams. So which place is it? The family owns about a dozen houses."

Mike was mixing the salad dressing. "It has some odd name." Which he'd heard all his life, but he didn't want to tell her that. He'd said too much about himself already. "Like something out of Harry Potter."

Sara was opening the package. "Maybe it's Castle Heights, but I didn't know the McDowells owned anything over there." She pulled the deed from the package and began to read it. At last she whispered, "Merlin's Farm."

"That's it," Mike said as he put the scallops in a hot skillet. "Merlin, Potter. I knew it was something to do with wizardry." He bent to look at the flame and turn it down. When he straightened, Sara was standing beside him—and her face was red with anger.

"You bastard!" she said under her breath.

"What?"

"You lying, sneaking bastard." Her voice was rising. "You *are* in on this. You're working with them to destroy what I want in life. I was ready to believe you were innocent, but you're the worst one. You—"

For the second time in Mike's life, he allowed a woman to slap him. He made no effort to stop her or to protect himself, because he knew that every word she was saying was true. But how had she found out about his undercover work?

When he saw tears in her eyes, he fought the urge to pull her into his arms. He wanted to apologize to her and to all the women he'd hurt in his life. Right now there were four women in prison because of his testimony. They all deserved to be there, but he still didn't like that *he* had put them there.

As the tears filled Sara's eyes, she seemed unable to say anymore. She swept past Mike, and as she'd done the night before, she slammed her bedroom door.

For a moment, Mike stood there, his cheek burning, and tried to figure out what had happened. She'd found him out, but how? He turned off the burner on the stove, went to the table, picked up the portfolio, and looked in it. Sara had taken out only the top paper.

He read it, but it was just the usual legalese stating the longitude and latitude of a piece of property commonly known as Merlin's Farm, and deeding it to Michael Farlane Newland.

When Sara spoke, he nearly jumped because he hadn't heard her come into the kitchen. "I want you to leave," she said softly.

Turning, he looked at her. Her eyes were red from crying and she looked so lost and forlorn in her pretty white dress that he just wanted to protect her—which he was trying to do. For a moment the photos he'd seen of the women they were fairly sure had been murdered by Stefan Vandlo flashed before his eyes. If Mike moved out and gave up watching over her, would he soon see pretty, delicate little Sara Shaw in a shallow grave?

"I want you to leave now. I'm sorry your apartment was destroyed, but you have to find somewhere else to stay. If you can't find a hotel, I'm sure my mother will take you in. Or maybe *I* will leave." There was an old land line telephone on the wall, and when Sara reached for it, he saw that her hands were shaking.

If he weren't on such an important mission, he would have done as she asked and left. He didn't like being the cause of any woman's tears. But he couldn't leave.

When he went to her, he couldn't help himself as he put his arm around her shoulders. She didn't push him away, so when she started crying again, he pulled her against his chest. "I'm sorry," he whispered. "Whatever I did, I didn't mean to. Please tell me what's wrong."

She was crying hard, her whole slight body trembling against his, and her tears were wetting his shirt. He could feel the damp and the warmth of them on his skin.

Carefully, he led her into the living room, sat her down on the couch beside him, grabbed a handful of tissues, and began to blot her face.

She took the tissues from him and blew her nose, and he handed her fresh ones.

"Will you talk to me? Please?"

"Merlin's Farm," she managed to get out.

"Is that the problem?" he asked gently. "Did *you* want the place?"

She gave a hiccup and blew her nose again as she nodded. "And Greg wants it very much, even more than I do."

It was as though an electrical current passed through Mike. Stefan Vandlo wanted an old farm that according to Tess was rotting to the ground? Mike took a couple of breaths to calm himself. He knew that he had to be cautious in what he said now so he wouldn't set Sara off again.

"Rams wouldn't sell the farm to Greg," Sara said, sniffing.

"That's because Ramsey promised it to Tess nearly two years ago."

"Two years? But they weren't even lovers then."

"No," Mike said slowly, cautiously, doing all he could not to further upset her. "But Tess took care of Ramsey's life and his office, didn't she?"

"Yes, but . . ." Sara trailed off, seeming not to know what else to say.

From his end there was no secrecy involved in the farm, so Mike decided to be honest with her. "At the end of the third year she'd worked for him, Ramsey asked Tess what she thought would be an appropriate bonus, and she said she wanted Merlin's Farm."

"And he gave it to her? Just like that? He *gave* her a farm that's been in his family for over two hundred years?"

"No. Tess didn't ask that of him. She wanted him to draw up a contract that gave her a lifetime lease on it, but only after she'd managed to save twenty percent of its value as a down payment."

Sara wiped at her teary eyes. "That sounds like Tess. And I guess she wanted the place for *you*." There was bitterness in her voice.

Mike was dying to ask what the farm had to do with Vandlo, but he knew he had to hold back. "The truth is, she hopes it will entice me to retire here."

"And what you want most in the world is a broken-down old farm?" Sara looked him up and down, at his pristine clothes. "You don't look much like a farmer. Wouldn't you rather have some sleek apartment in Williamsburg?"

When Sara kept looking at him in expectation, Mike knew he was going to have to tell the whole truth, which meant that he would have to reveal a great deal more about himself than he'd told anyone since he was a kid. As an adult, he'd worked hard at avoiding telling anything about his personal life, but then, secrecy was ingrained in him. But ever since he'd arrived in this town, it seemed that everything he'd tried to achieve was being knocked down. The first time someone had mentioned his grandmother to him, he'd wanted to leave.

"That's all right," Sara said as she started to get up. "You don't have to tell me."

He caught her arm and she sat back down.

As she waited for him to answer, he thought that being shot was easier than having to confess the truth. "Remember that I told you I picked Tess up when she graduated from high school?"

"Yes."

"What I didn't add was that Tess was underage then—but I wasn't. Our grandmother said she'd raise a stink with the police if Tess didn't agree to do what she wanted her to. If the old woman had reported me, I probably wouldn't have been prosecuted, but since I was new to the force, she could have halted my career."

"What did she want Tess to do?"

Mike leaned back against the sofa. "She wanted Tess to—somehow—obtain Merlin's Farm."

"But why?" Sara asked. "Did your grandmother want to be a farmer?"

Mike shook his head. "Far from it. She had our backyard covered in concrete because she didn't like the dirt."

"So, then, why . . . ?"

It was difficult for Mike to keep calm. One time after he'd had too many beers, he'd made a joke that nothing in his undercover jobs frightened him because no one he'd ever met was as treacherous as the woman who'd raised him. The men he was drinking with had wanted to know more, but Mike hadn't said a word—and he'd stopped drinking.

Sara put her hand on his arm. "Is this hard for you to talk about?"

"Naw," he said with as much bravado as he could muster. "The old woman hated Edilean and everyone in it, but she used to say that her only good memory of it was the afternoons she spent at Merlin's Farm with a boy named Lang."

"Not *Brewster* Lang?" Sara asked, her eyes wide.

Mike grinned. "I heard he's the crankiest man in Edilean."

"Try in all of Virginia. Forget him, what about the farm?"

"Grans used to rhapsodize about it. I think that over the years she made it into a sort of Valhalla, a heaven, where only good could happen. I think she meant to die there."

"It was her 'happy place.'"

"It sure wasn't with us kids!" Mike said with feeling. "So, anyway, she threatened to report me for kidnapping an underage child if Tess didn't swear that after she finished college, she'd go back to Edilean and do anything she could to own Merlin's Farm. At the time, I tried to get Tess to say no, but . . ." He shrugged. "You know Tess." He didn't embellish his story by telling how Tess had kept in touch with the old woman for the rest of her life. Nor did he tell her that after their grandfather's death, it had been financially difficult for him and Tess to keep their grandmother in a retirement home. She had demanded a place that was known for its luxurious accommodations and caring staff.

Sara stared at him in silence for a few moments. "Everyone wondered why Tess agreed to work here as Ramsey's secretary. We knew she had an MBA, but she came here to this little town to take dictation."

"She swore to our grandmother that she'd do what she could, and the old woman was still alive when Tess graduated, so she felt she had to keep her vow." Mike smiled.

"What?"

"I was just remembering one of the fights Tess and I had while she was still in school. I didn't want her to go to Edilean, but she wouldn't listen to me. You know what she said?"

"Tell me," Sara said eagerly.

"She said she'd get Merlin's Farm no matter what she had to do. I said, 'And how will you do that?' Tess said, 'I plan to get a job with the McDowell law firm, and if I have to, I'll marry whoever owns that damned farm.'"

Sara looked at Mike in astonishment. "And that's exactly what happened. Tess came to Edilean and took a job from my cousin just to get an old farm from him."

"It started that way." Mike was afraid he'd made her think Tess had falsely enticed Ramsey into marriage.

"I know," Sara said, and her eyes softened. "Tess fell in love with Rams, then waited for years for him to realize he was in love with her."

"Yeah, she did." His voice showed his relief, and he thought that it was a good thing Grans was dead by that time or the old woman would have shown up with a machine gun. Her granddaughter marrying a McDowell! That's the worst thing she could have imagined.

"So now, to Rams's old-fashioned mind, you're family, so the farm could be given to you."

"With lots of limitations," Mike added, with the thought that finally, at last, he could get back to what he wanted to talk about: Stefan Vandlo. All in all, he thought, criminals were much easier than "good" people. If he wanted information from a crook, Mike just paid him money. To get information from sweet little Sara he had to bare his soul. Oh yes, criminals were much easier. "Uh, Sara," he said cautiously. "You mentioned that your fiancé wanted the farm."

She gave him a look of apology. "I don't know what it is about you, but you bring out the anger in me. You'd never believe me, but I rarely show anyone else when I'm angry. You can ask Greg and he'd say I don't even have a temper."

Mike had to resist the urge to kiss her hand in gratitude because he knew that Vandlo liked to hit women who thwarted him. But Mike sat still. "It's your turn for confessions. Why does he want that old farm?"

"I'm not sure," Sara said, but she shifted her eyes sideways, making Mike think she wasn't telling the truth, or not all of it, anyway. "Greg talked about a lot of things, from remodeling it and opening it to the public, to starting our own organic stores. Whatever Greg plans to do with it, I know he deeply and desperately wants that farm."

Mike swallowed, trying hard not to show his excitement. This was a real breakthrough in the case! "But Rams wouldn't sell it to him?"

"No."

"But you're part of Ramsey's family and you're to marry Greg, so isn't that the same thing as with Tess and me?"

Sara tightened her lips. "That's the way I saw it, but Rams said no. It was the biggest fight Ramsey and I ever had. The biggest fight I've ever had with any human being—at least until I met you. He went on and on about how that place had been in his family since the eighteenth century, handed down from oldest son to the next. His father's two older brothers died young, so that's why it went to his father, Benjamin. Oh! When I think of the sob story he gave me! He even whined about how the Langs, father and son, had been caretakers of the place for . . ." She threw up her hands. "Since it was built for all I know. And to think that the real reason was that he'd promised to lease it to Tess—and probably because Rams doesn't *like* the man I love. I could just *hit* Ramsey!"

Mike frowned in his best imitation of sympathy. "But you have *no* idea why Greg wants an old farm?"

Sara's pretty face turned blush pink as she looked down at her hands. "Greg's never said so, but he may want it for me. When I told him that I'd always liked the farm, he said he'd buy it for me."

"Did he mention the place first or did you?" Mike knew he sounded like an interrogator, but he couldn't help it.

Sara didn't seem to notice. "I don't remember. No. Wait. One time he told me he'd heard of it from somewhere else, before he even came to Edilean."

"Tess didn't say anything to me about your asking Rams for the farm."

"If I know my cousin, he didn't tell her. Do you have any idea how many people have asked the McDowell family to sell that farm to them?"

"Why, no." Mike was surprised. "I don't know anything about it except that it's falling down. Why would anybody want it?"

"The farmhouse was remodeled around the original cabin, so it's still there. And the McDowell family has made sure every outbuilding has been kept up just enough to keep it standing."

Mike knew his face was blank because he had no idea what she was talking about. Not a word of it made sense.

Sara's voice slowed as she further explained. "The house was built in 1674, and when it was added on to, the old house was left inside, intact. The outbuildings are the same as they were when they were built."

Mike was staring at her. "Are you saying that that farm has been left alone since 1674?"

"Pretty much."

"Through the Revolutionary War and the Civil War?"

"And two world wars. My mother says it even survived the hippies in the '70s, and that they were more invasive than Sherman."

Mike was hardly listening to her. He didn't know what the Vandlos were after, but his gut told him it had something to do with Merlin's Farm. There was no other reason Stefan would want a farm. He wasn't about to open a house to the public, that's for sure—unless he and his family could pick the pockets of the visitors.

"So when do we go see it?" Sara asked.

"What?" Mike came out of his reverie.

"When do you and I go see your new home?"

"I don't think it's safe for you to go. Tess said old Brewster Lang carried a shotgun." Mike didn't want Sara near a piece of property the Vandlos wanted.

"He makes his living selling vegetables—especially heirloom tomatoes—to my mother. I'll get her to make him leave on the day we want to visit."

"And what excuse will you give her?"

"All I have to do is tell her I want to go with *you* and she'll drive us there." She gave Mike a hard look. "So you *didn't* come here to break Greg and me up?"

This is where Mike was good: bald-faced lies. More than once he'd fooled lie detectors. "My sister nagged me into coming here to Edilean to sign papers—and she made me swear I'd use her apartment. My plan was to sneak in here, sign the papers the next day, then leave. Your being in this apartment was a surprise. You don't think Tess set it up between you and me, do you?" He hated selling out his sister, but right now it was necessary to make Sara trust him.

"Yes," she said firmly, "I do. I think Tess called Luke, and the two of them arranged it all."

"Now that I think about it, Tess was the one who told me to use the old tunnel instead of the front door." He vowed to send his sister flowers—or maybe a few sapphires.

"Now I'm sure I'm going with you," Sara said brightly. "Mr. Lang comes into town on Thursdays, day after tomorrow, for the Farmers' Market, so that's when we'll go."

"No, you can't possibly go with me. I need to—"

Sara got off the couch. "Do you think those scallops were burned? I could eat a dozen of them. What can I do to help make dinner?" Turning, she left the living room to go back to the kitchen.

As Mike watched her leave, there was one thing he was sure of: Sara was *not* going with him. Until he found out a great deal more about this Merlin's Farm, she wasn't getting near the place. Of that, he was absolutely, totally *certain*.

# 6

ON THE DRIVE to Merlin's Farm, Mike couldn't help being pleased with himself. All through dinner last night, Sara had given him multiple reasons why she should join him on Thursday while Mr. Lang—as she called him—was at the Farmers' Market. Mike had been polite, had even pretended to consider what she was saying, but the truth was, he'd never come close to wavering in his decision to not allow her to go.

However, to ensure that nothing went wrong, he decided to go a day early. That night, after the kitchen was cleaned up, he went outside to call Tess. He asked her to do whatever she needed to in order to secretly get Lang off the property the next day so Mike could make a thorough inspection without Sara knowing.

"I'll call Luke," she said. "He's the only one who can manage the old man."

"Luke seems to run this town."

"I think it comes with owning the Big House. But then, knowing Edilean, it's probably some leftover from medieval times. So you've been thinking of the farm?"

"Yeah," Mike said, but he didn't tell her about Sara's fiancé's interest in it. Maybe it was a coincidence, but it could be the break they needed.

Tess said she'd arrange it, and ten minutes later she called back to say that Luke would take great delight in causing Brewster Lang enough problems that he'd have to stay away all day. Over the last few years, whenever Luke tried to repair anything at Merlin's Farm, the old man had followed him around, complaining so much that Luke had wanted to strangle him.

After Mike hung up, he went back inside the apartment. Sara's light was off, and he was glad. He didn't want to hear any more reasons of why she should go with him. On Thursday he planned to tell her he'd already seen the farm and that would be the end of the discussion.

This morning when Mike left early to go to the gym, Luke was outside, filling the bed of a red Kawasaki Mule with tools. "I'm preparing for my day with ol' Brewster," he said as he threw in a posthole digger. "Are you sure you want to take on something like that old place?"

"The last thing on earth I want is to own a farm. This is purely my sister's idea."

Luke grinned. "Wants to tie you down, does she? So how many blind dates have they tried to set you up on?"

"So far, two. There's—"

"Let me guess. Ariel Frazier and Kimberly Aldredge."

"Those are the names. Tell me, does anyone in this town have any secrets?"

"You seem to have more than a few," Luke said quickly.

Mike didn't reply, just got in his car and put down the window. "Why don't you go to the gym with me tomorrow?"

"I was there yesterday, remember? And I caught the last of your routine. Forty-six minutes of hell. I don't think I could stand working out with you."

Mike continued to look at him. Luke was a big guy with quite a bit of muscle on him.

"I'll be ready at six tomorrow," Luke said.

As Mike drove away, he wished he didn't have to go all the way into Williamsburg to a gym. He wondered what kind of zoning Merlin's Farm had. Could he put in a mixed martial arts studio there? Maybe he could have a few paying clients. After he retired, he'd have his pension from the police force, and he had savings, but it would be good to have a supplemental income.

He ran his hand over his unshaved jaw. His sister and the whole town of Edilean were poisoning his mind. He had nearly three years before he left the force and moved to . . . probably to Edilean, since Tess and her—he smiled—kid would be living there. But he still couldn't see that he'd ever *like* living on a farm.

As Mike pulled into the gym's parking lot, he thought about what to do with old man Lang. He'd lived at Merlin's Farm his entire eighty-five years, so it wasn't going to be easy to get rid of him. Maybe they should put him into the same nursing home in Ohio where Mike and Tess's grandmother had spent the last years of her life. The people there had dealt with cantankerous clients like her before and knew just how to keep smiling and not let her hurt their feelings. Without people to terrorize, Mike's grandmother had deteriorated quickly, until one morning they'd found her in bed, dead, her eyes open and angry.

An hour later, Mike left the gym and drove to Merlin's Farm. It was northwest of Edilean, through the same deep wilderness that surrounded the little town and made it seem more isolated from the world than it actually was. He drove past McTern Road, which led into the town, and kept on. Twice, he passed trucks hauling motorboats as they went into the surrounding nature preserve for recreation.

As he checked the directions Tess had texted him, he remembered what she'd told him. The farm had once been on a thousand acres, with a huge race track just half a mile from the house. But now all that was left was twenty-five acres, with pretty little K Creek running through the center of it.

His first sight of the farm was a big NO TRESPASSING sign. Mike pulled his car well off the road to park it under a huge oak tree. Even though he'd been assured Lang was gone for the day, he didn't want to drive in and leave his car to the mercy of an angry man. Mike noted that there was an old, falling-down fence hidden in the tall weeds, and beyond it he could see the top of a chimney.

He had on a pair of Levi's, a tan T-shirt, and a cotton jacket. He checked in his jacket pocket to make sure the plastic bag was there. He'd laced some ground beef with a common tranquilizer—one of several drugs he kept in his car—and was ready to confront Lang's dogs. Tess had warned him about them, saying Lang trained them to alert him to anyone who stepped on the property. The dogs were yet another reason he'd not wanted Sara with him.

Mike decided not to walk down the driveway, but to go through the weeds to the side of the house. Quietly, he made his way through a field of chest-high Queen Anne's lace, seedy grasses, and wild daisies while doing his best not to leave a path. "I guess this is where I'm supposed to grow a crop," he said under his breath and couldn't help chuckling at the absurdity of the idea.

As he walked, he listened, but he heard nothing but the birds. When the tall grasses abruptly ended, he saw that in the distance was one end of the house. For all the fanfare he'd heard about it, it looked quite ordinary, just an old two-story house that needed paint and repair. There was a brick chimney that went from the ground to above the roofline, and as he'd had some experience with carpentry, he guessed that the fireplace drew well.

There were four windows in the end, two on each floor, and he could see a long porch jutting out from what he guessed was the back of the house. From this angle, he couldn't see the front.

If he hadn't been told about the house, he would never have guessed it was extraordinary, as there looked to be nothing to distinguish it from thousands of other Virginia farmhouses. Except for one thing. Between him and the house were four buildings that looked like something out of a movie that took place in George Washington's time. There was one to his right that was perfectly square, with a pitched roof, but no windows or even a door that he could see. To the left was a larger building, shorter but wider, with an addition on the side, and several windows. In between them was an odd wooden structure that looked to be just a roof set on the ground. He couldn't imagine what it had ever been used for. And set back from the other three was what was unmistakably an outhouse.

Mike stood still, staring at all of it. There were some huge trees around the house, shading the whole area. As he looked from one building to another, he began to understand what Sara was talking about. This was an untouched plantation, still the same as it had been hundreds of years ago, and he had a sense of how unusual this place was.

Turning, Mike saw a small fence—the only wood that looked as though it had been painted in the last fifty years—around a garden that was set out in big squares, with paths laid with white gravel. For all that the garden looked like something out of a history book, it was also very much in this century. An old table standing at the side of a path was covered with balls of strings, hand tools, and plastic markers. In one corner was an old metal cabinet with a door hanging open, and he could see wooden-handled tools inside.

As for the garden itself, it held the most magnificent vegetables he'd ever seen; they looked like an advertisement for fertility. Whatever else was said about old man Lang, he was certainly good at making plants grow.

Cautiously, while looking around for the dogs, Mike left cover and went into the vegetable patch. Everything was in perfectly straight lines, with not a weed in sight.

The whole place was so unusual to Mike—and so beautiful—that he couldn't help walking along the rows. In the center was what he guessed was an herb bed, a square crisscrossed with paths, a small tree at each corner.

It was while he was looking at the herbs that he got his first idea that something was wrong. He was startled to see that smack in the middle of each triangle was what looked to be a tall, thriving marijuana plant.

When Mike took a step toward the closest plant, he heard a faint click. It was a sound that, had there been any noise of, say, dogs barking, he wouldn't have noticed. But Mike had heard the sound once before—and seconds later a friend of his had been blown up.

Mike stood absolutely still, not moving except to look down at what he'd stepped on. It didn't appear to be a land mine, but he could see a circle of something hidden under the dirt.

Keeping his foot in place, he slowly pulled his knife from his jeans pocket and used the long blade to move the dirt away. It looked to be an old iron trap with teeth on it. Had it sprung, it would have cut deeply into his ankle.

Carefully, Mike put his hands on the two iron half circles and held them down while he lifted his foot. The nasty little trap sprang shut the second he let go. It was like a lethal Venus flytrap—and it was meant to hurt anyone who tried to get near the marijuana plant.

Okay, so the old man was making some money through illegal

drugs. In Mike's life, that was nothing, but he wondered if more traps had been set around the other plants to protect them. Or was it the other way around and the cannabis was being used as a lure?

As cautiously as he'd ever worked in his life, Mike began to closely inspect the vegetable garden. Each of the marijuana plants had a trap near it, and each one was concealed under the dirt.

At the gate Mike saw four holes in the ground, and the grasses were flattened in the center. He realized a tent had been placed there, and Mike thought that made sense. If the old man was growing weed, the local boys were probably trying to steal it, so Lang had been sleeping outside to protect it.

It was a plausible explanation, but, still, Mike didn't believe it. Something wasn't right. For one thing, there was no way Lang could so openly grow those plants and not have everyone in Edilean know about it. Mike had been told that Luke repaired the buildings and often cut the grass around the house. He would have seen the plants, and Mike didn't think he'd tolerate them.

If, by some long shot, Luke didn't tear out the plants, Mike was sure that Sara's mother wouldn't allow them. He'd spent less than an hour with the woman, but it was enough to know that she'd refuse to buy vegetables from a man who was growing marijuana.

Mike stepped over half a dozen spiny, smelly herbs to reach one of the cannabis plants. When he brushed away the dirt, he saw that it was inside a pot. It looked like Lang was growing them somewhere else, then when he went away, he put them in the ground. Mike was even more sure that the old man was using them to entice someone into the garden.

Mike reset the trap he'd triggered, removed all trace that he'd been there, and left to continue his exploration.

He went away from the house, toward the large lawn. There was another garden directly in front of the main house, with tall box-wood hedges encasing geometric beds.

In the second square, he saw a net hidden in a tree branch that hung over the garden below. When Mike moved a stick on the ground, he found a trip wire. If he'd walked across it, the net would have come down on him.

"It's a damned Tarzan movie," he muttered as he moved out of what he thought of as the flower garden.

At the far end was about a half acre of mown lawn, and he didn't want to run across it, but at the other side was another fenced area that he wanted to see. In the middle of the lawn was a gravel drive-way, narrow, but it had recently been used for a car, so obviously, it was trap free. It looked like Lang just didn't want anyone sneaking about where he couldn't see them.

Mike jogged down the drive to what looked to be an old or-chard, and when he got there, he stood at one end and couldn't help admiring it. The trees looked to have originally been planted in five neat, long rows, but now there were many gaps from missing trees, and half of the remainder looked too old to produce fruit.

For the first time, Mike thought of this property as being his. He'd like to take out the dying trees and replace them. He thought it would be nice to pull an apricot or a plum off his own trees. He glanced at the big lawn and envisioned playing catch with Tess's kid. And when she wasn't around, he'd show the boy—or girl—a bit of kickboxing. Maybe he could put some weight machines in one of those old buildings and—

He made himself get back to business. The fenced area near the orchard was a cemetery. He wasn't surprised to see the name MCDOWELL on a dozen old markers, but when he got to the gate, he saw something that drew his attention away. A few yards from the cemetery was a line of small, handmade concrete stones with names and dates drawn into them. They were obviously pet graves, and they started in the 1920s. The most recent graves were for animals named King, Queen, Prince, Princess, Duke, Duchess, Marquess, Marchioness, Earl, Countess, Viscount, and Viscountess. The last two were freshly dug and dated this year.

As Mike looked at the dates, he realized that each of the dogs seemed to have lived very long lives—except for the last two. They were no more than three years old when they died. Maybe it was Mike's cynicism from what he'd seen in his life, but he wondered if the dogs had been murdered. Losing his dogs would explain why Lang had made traps that were lethal.

Mike wasn't sure yet, but he thought there was a war going on here, and it was probable that the dogs had been casualties of it. It was his guess that someone had been attacking the old man and Lang was trying to protect himself. But at the same time, like a spider and a fly, Lang had been trying to lure his enemy into a trap. When someone tried to get the marijuana, he'd have his foot nearly torn off. When the enemy sneaked through the old flower garden, he'd find a net falling on top of him.

Of course the first thing Mike wanted to know was *who* was after old Brewster Lang. But if he couldn't find that out—and he felt sure he already knew—then he was going to figure out the cause of this war.

# 7

SARA WALKED DOWN the long driveway of Merlin's Farm and marveled that there had been so few changes since she first saw it when she was just eight years old. At dinner the night before that visit, her mother had excitedly told her family that Brewster Lang had contacted her to say that he wanted to sell some of his vegetables to Armstrong's Organic Foods. That he grew the most succulent and beautiful produce in the county, maybe in the state, was well known.

"And how did he contact you?" her husband, Dr. Henry Shaw, asked. "Smoke signals? Or did he use two cans and a string?" He hadn't grown up in Edilean and often let his wife know how backward he thought the town was.

Only Sara giggled at the joke, but then she'd always been a "daddy's girl." Her two older sisters were as perfectly conventional as Sara was a dreamer.

"Telephone," Eleanor said as she passed the bowl of carrot and raisin salad to Taylor who, at twelve, was the eldest of their three daughters. "I'm going out there to see him tomorrow, and, Sara, you're going with me."

Everyone at the table paused, frozen, as they looked at Sara in surprise. Whereas the two older daughters were as organized and determined as their mother—but without the hippie undertones—Sara was content to play with her many dolls and sew endless dresses for them.

Sara looked as though she didn't know if she was being punished or honored. "Me?" she whispered. She'd gone to work with her father many times. Of course it was always on a Saturday, when he had more paperwork to do than patients to see, but she liked the old hospital in Williamsburg where he worked, was fascinated by his office, and most of all, she loved being with her father. But, unlike her sisters, she'd never been to work with her mother.

"Yes, you," Ellie said. "Merlin's Farm is old and mysterious. It's right up your alley. You'll stay outside while I negotiate terms with Mr. Lang, but that shouldn't take more than half an hour."

But it had taken over four hours, and during that time, Sara had wandered about in her little pink dress—given to her by her aunt Lissie—and had fallen in love with the old farm. She'd made friends with Mr. Lang's two dogs, had mingled with a flock of geese that were nearly as big as she was, and had explored every old building on the property.

When her mother was ready to leave, it seemed to Sara that she'd spent only minutes there. But not so her mother. She was the most angry Sara had ever seen her.

Behind her came a short, heavy man whose back bent forward so much he reminded Sara of a storybook character: the Hunchback of Notre Dame. He was trailing behind Sara's angry mother and smiling as though he'd won a prize.

But when he saw Sara standing by the car, he stopped and stared at the little girl, and his round face recomposed into a look of menace.

"She looks just like her," he said in a deep, wiggly voice that, to Sara's mind, was funny. If he hadn't been scowling at her so hard, she would have giggled.

Ellie was opening the car door, and in her agitated state, she dropped the keys. As she picked them up, the old man removed the sneer from his face so that when Ellie turned, he was merely gazing at the child. "You mean my aunt Lissie. Yes, Sara looks like her and *is* like her." She flung open the back door of the car and waited for Sara to get in. Ellie got in the driver's seat and started the engine.

In the back, Sara looked out the window at Mr. Lang, and she knew her mother didn't see the way he glared, and certainly didn't see the way he pointed his finger at her. Just as her mother sped away, the old man made his hand into a gun and pulled the trigger.

Sara slid down in the seat in sheer terror and listened to her mother complain all the way home about what a "pirate" Brewster Lang was. "He might as well have held a gun to my head," her mother said—and her words made Sara slide down farther.

Sara never told anyone what Mr. Lang had done, with his hand firing a shot at her. Over the ensuing years, she was able to separate the beautiful old farm with its butterflies flitting about from the scary old man who seemed to hate her because she looked like her aunt Lissie. One day Sara asked her great-aunt about the old man, but all Lissie would say was that Sara should stay away from him. "Remember, dear, you must never believe anything Brewster Lang says."

After that, Lissie refused to say another word about Mr. Lang. Aunt Lissie had believed in the power of positive thinking so deeply that she absolutely refused to allow bad words to cross her lips. It had always amused Sara that some people in Edilean remembered this trait with great fondness, while others said Lissie made them insane.

So now, it was afternoon, and Sara was once again visiting Merlin's Farm. This had come about because at two she'd been outside sewing when she saw Luke walking about Edilean Manor garden with a little man. She didn't think about it until she felt a chill go through her. She gave a little shudder, rubbed the goose bumps on her arms, and looked up. Standing just a few yards away from her, glaring at her in what she could only describe as hatred, was the boogeyman of all her dreams: Mr. Lang. She hadn't seen him up close since she was a child—she'd made sure of that—but he hadn't changed much. He was still ugly, his head as large and round as a pumpkin. Maybe he was a bit shorter and his face had a few more wrinkles, but he was essentially the same.

And yet again, just as he had before, he made a motion as though he was shooting her. But this time, Sara wasn't a little girl. She gave him her sweetest smile, then lifted her second finger at him. He smiled back at her in a way that made the goose bumps return to her arms, then he turned away and trotted after Luke.

After that, try as she might, Sara couldn't continue sewing. She gathered her things, went back into the apartment, and locked all the doors and windows. When she'd finished, she remembered that Mike was staying with her and he'd not be able to get in.

With the thought of Mike, everything fell into place. Last night at dinner he'd been so nice, listening hard to her reasons of why she should go with him to see the old farm. She'd gone to bed confident that she'd persuaded him. Since she'd first seen Merlin's Farm, she'd dreamed of going back, but only if "he" wasn't there. When she'd had the idea of going with Mike, a detective who probably carried a gun, it had seemed like the perfect opportunity. She'd even thought about what she'd wear and the food she'd pack for a picnic.

But it looked like Mike had never had any intention of letting her go with him. "After all I've done for him!" she muttered in anger. That she couldn't think of anything she'd done for him didn't stop her anger. She knew Mike had arranged for Luke to babysit old Mr. Lang while he, Mike, went to see the farm. Alone.

"Two can play at this game," she murmured, then called her mother's store manager and asked that they make a picnic lunch for two. Sara knew the news that she'd ordered a basket full of food would spread all over town within minutes, but that was fine with her. She was truly sick of men treating her like she was too delicate to hear the truth. Greg refused to tell her what had happened that was so urgent that he'd had to leave immediately. And now Mike had made it clear he thought she couldn't handle visiting a *farm*! With the help of *her* relatives, he'd gone there a day before he said he was going.

Twenty minutes later, Sara had the picnic basket in her car and she was on her way to Merlin's Farm. When she saw Mike's car partially concealed under the big oak tree, it made her even more sure she was doing the right thing.

For herself, she refused to sneak about. She drove in through the gate, parked her car in front of the farmhouse, and got out. If she saw Mike fine, if she didn't, that was all right too.

As she picked up her handbag, she felt her phone buzz. Her mother had sent her an e-mail saying she had the dried molokhia

Mike wanted, and Joce had texted to ask her to come over and tell her all about the dreadful little man who was following Luke around the garden. And Tess had left a voice mail asking how she and Mike were getting along. And there were four e-mails from clients asking when their clothes would be ready. Sara put her bag back on the seat, took her cell, and as she walked, she rapidly pushed buttons to answer everyone.

# 8

MIKE WAS IN the loft of the old barn using a pitchfork to search through the dried-up hay. He'd already found two leg traps in the barn, one homemade and one that was probably old in the Civil War. The tine of the fork caught on something by the overhead door, and he bent to look at it. There was a long, ragged tear from the hem of his jeans where he'd nearly been caught by a snare that sent steel darts flying. The only warning he'd had was the sound the lethal projectiles made as they came toward him. He'd dropped and rolled and the darts had whizzed over his head and embedded themselves in a nearby tree.

Mike had cursed as he pulled the darts from the branches and reset the trap. As much as he hated doing it, he was keeping with his decision to not let ol' man Lang know anyone had been there.

Now, it was late afternoon and Mike was almost ready to leave. He'd found traps and snares everywhere. He hadn't visited any building or garden that hadn't been rigged to hurt an intruder, to maim, and even, sometimes, to kill.

He had only the barn left to go through and he'd be finished. Mike didn't flatter himself that he'd found all of the contraptions, but he'd certainly made a dent in the number of them. And during the hours that he'd been searching, he'd learned a great deal more than just how to rig a homemade killing device. He'd seen that Lang was a clever—and strong—old man who had no conscience at all. In his blind obsession with protecting what he saw as his, he was ruthless—and without any concern for the consequences. If a child had sneaked into the orchard . . . Mike didn't want to think what could have happened.

It was obvious that Lang cared only about keeping out whomever was trespassing.

Mike heard a noise below, inside the barn, and caught a movement out of the corner of his eye. Instantly, without a sound, he went flat onto his stomach and looked down to the floor below, but he saw nothing. Damn! Luke said he'd keep Lang away until four.

Mike lay absolutely still, thinking how he could get out without Lang seeing him. Behind him, above the open window, was a big post with a rope suspended from it. He didn't know much about barns but he figured it was there to help haul bales of hay up to the loft. Turning only his head, he studied the rope and the beam. They looked to be sound, but after what he'd seen today, he wouldn't be surprised that if he swung out on it, it would break.

He looked back down through the cracks in the floorboards, and what he saw shocked him. Sara was blithely walking into the barn with her head down as she concentrated on the keyboard of her BlackBerry.

Mike's first instinct was to shout at her to stay where she was, but he didn't know who had come with her and might hear.

"Sara!" he hissed down at her.

She kept typing.

He couldn't figure out how she'd entered the barn without being hit. Just in front of the doorway was a thin piece of nearly invisible nylon fishing line, and hovering about it, ready to fall, was an old horse collar made of wood, leather, and iron. Mike didn't want to think what such a thing would do to pretty little Sara Shaw if it dropped on her.

"Sara!" he said again.

She hesitated on her keyboard, then, to his horror, she started walking out of the barn. She may have missed the trap on the way in, but she'd certainly trigger it on the way out.

Mike didn't think about what he did. Many years of training had made him react without thought. He jumped up and leaped out the big window, clutching the rope as he flew past it. The rope, attached to the pole above, kept swinging. It burned Mike's hands, but he slid down enough that when Sara stepped through the doorway, just as her foot was about to set down on the fishing line, Mike grabbed her with his right arm and kept swinging.

They landed on the grass at the side of the barn just as about fifty pounds of old horse harness came tumbling down in the exact spot where Sara had been.

She was lying on top of him, the breath half out of her, and her face inches from his. "We really must stop meeting like this."

Mike didn't laugh but rolled out from under her to stand up and bend over her. "What the hell are you doing here?! I *told* you to stay away. I told you—"

"Actually, you didn't tell me anything and I'm beginning to think that whatever you have told me is a lie." She looked him up and down. "You're a mess. Would you like to tell me the *truth* about what's going on?"

Mike was torn between wanting to angrily shake her—or kiss her in relief that she wasn't hurt. She was so pretty in her little yellow dress with the pink flowers on the big collar that he just sat down on the grass beside her. "You could have been killed."

"I can see that," she said as she looked at the pile of leather and wood. "I wonder where Mr. Lang found that and what century it came from?"

Mike's mind was working at warp speed as he tried to figure out how much he could tell her and what had to be hidden.

"What's going on here?" she repeated.

She was so calm that the last of Mike's anger left him. "All I wanted to do was to look at the property my sister gave me."

Sara looked from him to the barn and back again. "You didn't want me to go with you because you thought there might be something like this here, didn't you?"

Mike gave a half smile. He wasn't going to be able to lie his way out of this. "Smart women are a real nuisance in my business."

"So you *are* here in Edilean on a case?"

"You didn't happen to bring any food, did you? I'm starving."

"I did. A whole basket full of it."

Mike stood and held out his hand to help her up, but she ignored it. She kept looking at the pile of horse harness. "I'm not going to let you stay in my apartment a minute longer if you don't tell me what you've been doing here today."

"I can't," he said.

"Fine. My mother has a spare room. If you think I'm a snoop, you haven't experienced anything until you've spent a day around her. My dad says she can squeeze secrets out of a pineapple."

Mike sat down again. Maybe it was better to tell her at least some of the truth. "A major criminal lives in or near this town."

"Who?"

"If we knew that we'd arrest her, but we don't even know what she looks like. The only picture we have of Mitzi Vandlo was taken in '73 when she was sixteen years old."

"So she'd be fifty-three now?"

"Right." He admired her arithmetic abilities.

"And you know for sure that she's here in Edilean?"

"There's no mistaking the name of this town."

"What's she done?"

Mike hated having to tell this, but then, it was better than hitting her with the truth about Stefan. "You name it, she's done it. Murdered her husband, for one. Not that he didn't deserve it, but it's still illegal."

"She's come to Edilean to *kill* someone?" Sara's hand was on her throat.

"Honestly? We don't know why she's here, and a lot of what we know about her has come to us second- and third-hand." He wanted to lighten the moment. "There's a rumor that she's so ugly that to trick Marko Vandlo into marrying her, she had to wear a veil over the bottom half of her face. The story's even more remarkable when you know that she was sixteen and he was fifty-one."

Sara didn't let him take her off the main subject. "If she killed her old husband, why wasn't she put in prison?"

Mike shrugged. "The family keeps what they do to themselves. The agents working on the case were told by an informer that the story was that he fell down some stairs and died. However, when his body was exhumed recently, he had three depressions in his skull that exactly fit a golf club." Mike lowered his voice. "She specializes in duping people out of their life savings, and we really want to get her off the streets."

"If she was doing something like that in Edilean, we'd all know about it."

"Why she'd be in this little town is a big puzzle to everyone. She usually works out of cities, the bigger the better, so what's in Edilean that she wants?" He waited a moment to give Sara a chance to answer, but she said nothing. "You haven't heard anything, have you?"

"Not that I remember, but I've been so busy with the new store and Greg that I might not have noticed. My mother might know—"

"No! The fewer people who know about this, the better."

"I understand," Sara said, but she didn't meet his eyes.

"What about the rich women who go to your shop? What do you know about their lives?"

She looked at him in speculation. "If you're interested in them, then I'm your best bet as a contact. You *did* plan all of this, didn't you? Luke ran me out of my apartment so you could come up through the tunnel and move yourself in."

Before Mike could think how to answer that, Sara got up and started quickly walking down the path to her car.

Mike caught her before she'd gone three feet and held her by her upper arms. "Yes! You have been lied to and used shamelessly. But you don't know how many lives have been ruined by this woman. There were some young girls who—"

"Greg! Did *you* take him away just before my wedding?"

There was no time to consider his answer. "Yes." When she tried to twist away from him, he held on. "And they burned my apartment and everything in it just to give me a good cover. Sara, I'm sorry you were pulled in to this, but you have access to places and people that no one else in Edilean does. For all we know, Mitzi could be one of your clients."

"You took the groom away before my wedding!" Sara said. "That isn't fair."

"I know," he said softly. "But what Mitzi does to people is a great deal more than unfair."

"Where is Greg?"

"Safe."

"What does that mean? That you put him in jail somewhere?"

Mike knew that at the moment Greg was still being held in custody, but his lawyer was about to get him out. That was too bad, because the man in the cell with him was an undercover agent. But Mike couldn't tell Sara any of that. "I was told so little about this case that there's still a lot I don't know. My captain told me about it, then when I said I needed to go home and pack, I was shown a newspaper photo of my apartment on fire." When he saw the sympathy in her eyes, Mike relaxed his grip on her shoulders, but he didn't release her.

"I'm sorry for all this," he said again. "Some guy I knew way back in training remembered that I'd said my grandmother was from Edilean. That was when I was too young to know not to tell much about myself. When the name of the town came up, he remembered it and me, and the Feds contacted my boss, so here I am."

Sara was frowning, but in a way that made Mike relax more, and he removed his hands from her shoulders. "It looks like I got blood on your dress."

Sara glanced at the stains, then took his hands in hers and turned them palm up to look at the torn skin. "You did that on the rope?"

"Yeah." He was watching her.

"I think that was the only time I'll ever get to play Jane."

Mike's eyes lightened. "We could always go to the flower garden and have a net fall on you. I could put a knife between my teeth and cut you out."

"Out of the net or my dress?" Sara asked seriously.

"Dress. I'd leave the net alone."

The look he gave her was so lascivious, so naughty, that she laughed. "All right. Here's what we're going to do. We're going back to my car and I—not you—am going to drive us to your car. We're then going to walk down to K Creek—you may carry the picnic basket—and we're going to eat and talk. And you're going to explain to me what's going on."

"As much as I can."

She glared at him.

"Okay. All of it." They started walking. "So how do you know where my car is?"

"Puh-lease. It's where everyone trying to hide on this road parks. Half the girls in Edilean lost their virginity under that tree."

"Did you?"

She opened the door on the driver's side. "Who said I've given it away yet?"

Laughing, Mike got in the other side and closed the door.

# 9

"So you're saying I own *that* tree?" Mike asked. He was stretched out on a red-and-white-checked tablecloth, the basket of food was between them, and Sara was sitting on the other side. At the bottom of the gentle slope was pretty little K Creek.

"Every inch of it."

"The Virgin Tree. That thought is going to keep me awake at night."

"You also own some of the creek and all those old buildings. What are you going to do with all of it?"

"Move into the house and let Lang be my butler. He'll serve me sliced tomatoes with a marijuana dressing—all from his garden." He gave her a sideways look to see if she'd be shocked, but except for a flicker of her lashes, she didn't react. Good, he thought. Cool in the face of surprise.

"If Luke finds out about illegal plants, he'll skin the old man."

"That's just what I thought, but what your mother would do scares me more than Luke."

"Me too," Sara said and smiled at him.

He put his hands behind his head and looked up at the sky. "I've never owned any property before."

"Not even a condo on the beach in Fort Lauderdale?"

"Especially not a condo."

"So are you ready to tell me what's going on?"

"Couldn't we just enjoy the day?"

"No," Sara said. "I want to find this woman so I can get the groom back for my wedding. How do we go about finding her?"

"DNA." He moved on to his side and looked at her. "We have to collect DNA from every woman in this town who is around fifty-three years old and send it to a lab. We don't have anything from Mitzi, but we do have DNA from her son and other relatives, so we can match them."

"And you're sure she's here?"

"No, but with this woman even a possibility is worth whatever it takes to get her." Mike picked up a bunch of tiny, sweet, champagne grapes, turned on his back, held them above his head, and began to eat them.

"You look like a disciple of Bacchus. You aren't actually as civilized as you've been pretending to be, are you?"

"If by that you're asking if I cook four-course dinners every night, the answer is no. I've been trying to impress you. Have I?"

She wasn't going to answer that. "So what's the plan?"

"I had one all worked out, but you changed it today when you refused to stay home. I think it's your turn to come up with a plan."

"Okay," Sara said. "First, we have to decide what you and I are to each other."

"That sounds good. So what are we?"

"Friends," she said quickly. "That's all we can be, since I'm about to be married. You *are* going to release my fiancé for our wedding, aren't you?"

"Unless your mother finds out where he is and won't let us." He looked at her. "Has your mother hated all your boyfriends?"

"There's only been one other boyfriend, and no, she didn't hate him. She's saved all her anger for Greg. Could we please get back on the subject?"

"Sure. You're going to marry a man the town hates and live here in the middle of all that animosity."

She narrowed her eyes at him. "If you want my help, you have to be nice about Greg."

"That should be easy, since I've never met him. You think I'd like him?"

"I have no idea, since I know little about you that's truthful. I think maybe you've lied to me about everything."

"Haz—"

"Don't say it again! Hazards of the job, ha! Could you please stay on the subject?"

"I thought Greg was the subject." When she glared at him, he put his hand up. "All right. We'll tell the town you and I are friends. Will that make you relax around me and stop treating me like your enemy?"

"Maybe."

Mike put the grapes down. "I guess the idea of there being anything between you and me is out of the question."

"Completely."

"Are you sure?"

Sara refused to look at him. "If you're going to try using that voice on me, then you'll have to leave my apartment. I'm not going to stay with you—or help you—if you try to . . . to proposition me."

"All right," Mike said and moved onto his back. "We'll be the best of friends. Chums. Roommates."

"Like brother and sister. Like you and Tess."

"No. Not like Tess and me. We *are* brother and sister."

"What does that mean?"

"She runs around in her underwear. She has me adjust her, you know, straps. I couldn't do that with you because you're the prettiest, most desirable woman I've seen in years. Sara, I've been working undercover almost since I joined the force, and that means that the women I've been around are usually on some drug. Most of them are married, and when it comes to clothes they think that less is more. Except for jewelry and makeup, then more is better. But you . . ."

He turned to look at her. "You're like no other woman I've ever seen in my life. You look like you just stepped out of a spring breeze. I find that your clothes that cover up nearly all of you are about as sexy as anything I've ever seen in my life. The way you move, the way you talk, I like all of it. I promise that I will do my best to keep my hands off of you, but it's not going to be easy. Are there any more of those little sandwiches left?"

Sara sat there blinking at him. "Well, uh . . ."

"Sandwiches?"

"In the basket," she finally managed to murmur. "I didn't know you felt that way about me."

"How could I not?" He was rummaging inside the basket. "I can't find them."

"Let me," she said, and as she brushed his hands away, their faces were close together. For a moment, Sara almost bent forward, but then she drew back. "I guess it would make your job easier if you and I were sleeping together."

"Oh, so very, very much easier," he said. "In fact, I truly believe that our being together would help our country become greater."

Sara shook her head at him. "It's not going to happen."

Mike gave a big sigh. "Can't blame a man for trying. Okay, so what's the rest of your plan?"

"To do what you said and collect DNA from the women who come to our shop. But . . ."

"But what?"

"Erica."

"And she is?" Mike had his mouth full of tuna salad sandwich.

"The woman Greg got to run the shop. She won't let me—"

"Don't you own that place?"

"I'm a partner only on paper. Greg and Erica make the decisions."

"I'll make a call and have someone come and break her legs."

"How about her arms too?" Sara said eagerly.

Mike grinned. "You're not as innocent as you look, are you?"

"Make up your mind. Do I look like a vestal virgin or am I killer sexy?"

"Both. Is there any more coleslaw?"

"You eat a lot, don't you?"

"I've been crawling all over that farm all day, sometimes barely escaping with my life, and now I'm sitting with a gorgeous dame who says I can't touch her. Yeah, I'm starving."

"If you tell me everything you saw today, I'll tell you about my two bad encounters with Mr. Lang."

Mike's face lost the teasing look. "You must tell me everything you know."

"Not until you tell me at least half of what you know."

"About what?"

She threw a piece of bread at him—and Mike caught it in his left hand.

"Sara, my lovely, I honestly and truly don't know what's going on. I know one of the biggest criminals in American history is or has been living in this pretty little town. Maybe Merlin's Farm has nothing to do with her, but something has been going on there." Mike couldn't tell her that he felt sure Stefan's wanting the farm connected the Vandlos with either Brewster Lang or the old plantation.

When Mike looked at Sara, he saw she was waiting in quiet anticipation for him to explain. "This morning when I went to see the farm I expected a derelict old ruin, just as I'd been told it was. What I found was a war zone."

"What do you mean?"

He related, in detail, what he'd seen. He elaborated about the traps and how he believed the marijuana plants had been used as a lure. When he got to the recent graves of the dogs, Sara frowned.

"What about the geese?"

"I didn't see any."

"Mr. Lang and his father always kept geese. They're a rare breed called Sebastopol, and they have curly feathers and the sweetest tempers in the world. My mother says that those geese are the secret to Mr. Lang's great vegetables."

Mike looked at her in question.

"Geese eat bugs and weeds, and they produce manure."

"Oh. You know a lot about farming, don't you?"

"Hazards of being my mother's daughter."

Mike chuckled at her play on his words. "So what did Lang do to you?"

Sara told him about Brewster Lang twice making his hand into a gun at her—and Mike grinned at her retaliating hand gesture at the second encounter.

"And you think he did that because you look like your great-aunt Lissie?" Mike wasn't about to tell her that he knew a great deal about that particular hatred.

"I guess so. Unless he despises all children. With him, who knows? One thing I do know is that when I was little the farm wasn't booby-trapped. That day when I visited, I went inside every building."

"Surrounded by geese and dogs," Mike said. "You must have looked like something out of a storybook."

She glanced at him, stretched out full length on the cloth. Already, his black beard had grown back. He really did have nice lips, she thought. As for his short hair and high forehead, she was growing used to it. What she hadn't accustomed herself to yet was the fact that Merlin's Farm was never going to be hers. Her children weren't going to grow up there.

Mike didn't look at her, but he could feel her staring at him. "So, tell me, Sara, where do you see yourself in five years?"

"Mother of two kids," she said instantly.

"No husband?"

"Sure. Of course. I've imagined that I'd be with Greg and I'd stay home with the kids, and—"

"And what?"

"I'd make Merlin's Farm glorious again." She didn't want to talk about the end of her dream, so she changed the subject. "I didn't get to see much before you came swinging down on top of me." She looked at him in speculation.

"What's that look for?"

"Not many men can hold on to a rope with one hand and lift a full-grown woman with the other."

Mike shrugged. "You're not what I'd call fully grown. What do you weigh? Ninety?"

"You're sweet. Greg says I need to lose ten pounds."

So her body will more easily fit in the trunk of his car? Mike wondered. "If Greg can't lift you, he needs to go to the gym more often."

"Where do you see yourself in five years?" she asked.

"I haven't thought about it. I leave my future to Tess."

"And she wants you to marry, have kids, and live on Merlin's Farm."

"I'm stealing your future," Mike said softly, and when he saw sadness in her eyes, he wanted to take it away. "Want to know a secret?"

"Sure." She was gazing at the creek, a faraway look in her eyes.

"It's a good secret."

"Oh?" She sounded distracted.

"It's the kind women love."

Sara turned to look at him. "What do you know about girl secrets?"

"Tess is going to have a baby."

When Sara's eyes widened, Mike was glad to think that he'd cheered her up. But then, in the next second, to his utter disbelief, she burst into tears.

Mike sat up, grabbed napkins, and handed them to her as he put his hand on her back. "I'm sorry. I didn't mean to upset you. Please don't cry."

"These are happy tears," she said as she wiped at her face with the napkins. "Really, I'm just so very happy for them. Except . . . Except . . ." She looked at him. "My two best friends are pregnant, and I'm not even married!"

Mike was learning that Sara had a good sense of humor. "I'd be willing to help you out with one of those predicaments. I'd certainly give it my very best try."

For a moment she didn't know what he meant. "You're horrible," she said, but she was smiling.

"No, really," he said with a look of concern. "I'm serious. It's a creed of mine that I always try to help out a lady in distress."

Sara was sniffing. "Thank you. You made me feel better." She blew her nose and began to start packing the dishes away. "I think we should go. It's getting late. What fabulous things are you going to cook for dinner?"

"Tonight's your turn. I'll make the salad."

"That should go well with McDonald's."

"You aren't serious, are you? All that grease and—"

"You and my mother! You can relax; I was just kidding. Let's go raid the storage area of my mom's grocery." She leaned toward him. "Want to hear a secret from me?"

Mike held his breath. "Yes."

Sara held up her ring of keys. "I have a key to the back door of Armstrong's Organic Foods."

At first Mike didn't understand why she thought that was a secret, then he remembered that one of the stories he'd been told about Stefan was that he'd demanded free groceries from Sara's mom. If Mike understood her correctly, she was offering him something she'd denied the man she was going to marry. He didn't want her to see how much this pleased him. "A key to all that organic food? Forget sex, give me tree-ripened peaches."

Sara laughed. "So when are you going to tell Mr. Lang that you own the farm that he considers his? His mother gave birth to him in the front parlor."

"Sure it wasn't in the barn?"

Before Sara could reply, her cell phone buzzed and she looked at it. "Oh no! You made me forget that I promised to visit Joce this afternoon. This is awful of me! Poor Joce is stuck in bed, trying to keep the babies from wanting to come out too early. Her father died a few months ago, Luke works all day, and Tess is away, so Joce is mostly alone."

"And you visit her to keep her company. Hey! I have an idea. Why don't we make dinner for them tonight? Didn't Tess tell me Luke put a new kitchen in the main house?"

"Yes and no. Luke wanted to gut the old kitchen, but his dad and Joce vetoed him. He ended up repairing the old cabinets and repainting them, and Joce finally agreed to put in"—she sighed—"white marble countertops."

"Did you just make a speech of love about a *kitchen*? Between the Virgin Tree and the way you said 'white marble countertops' I'm definitely not going to sleep tonight."

"You almost make me think you're serious. But yes, I like the idea of making dinner for them. Poor Joce is at the mercy of Luke's ability to buy take-out and the kindness of the townspeople." Standing up, Sara looked down at Mike. A dinner party, she thought. How very ordinary, but at the same time how utterly divine. Greg always found fault with every social event they'd been to in Edilean.

At that thought, she frowned. It was far too late to start comparing the man she was going to marry to someone else.

When Mike picked up the picnic basket and offered her his arm, she smiled at him. It had been quite nice having a man swing on a rope, grab her about the waist, and rescue her.

# 10

So what's he really like?" Jocelyn asked. "Other than being gorgeous, that is."

"I don't think of him that way, but then I'm in love with someone else." Sara enunciated her words carefully to make sure Joce heard them. Earlier, she and Mike had raided her mother's huge storage room at the grocery, then they'd gone directly home. Sara had already called Joce, who'd said that Luke might burst into tears at the thought of a home-cooked meal.

"Then he can join me," Sara muttered, but she didn't explain her meaning. "So it's all right if Mike and I make dinner in your kitchen tonight?"

"Sara, you can move in and make three meals a day if you want to."

"Mike is the cook, not me."

"He can cook too?"

Sara knew she was being pushed toward another man, but

she'd made her decision about Greg, and she was going to stick with it.

As soon as they went in the main house, Luke took Mike outside where a charcoal grill had already been lit. A bed had been set up downstairs for Joce, and she lay on it, her big belly pushing up the light covers. Sara stood beside her and looked out the window at the two men, who were talking and laughing.

"They seem awfully chummy," Sara said.

"Mike finally got Luke to agree to go to the gym with him tomorrow, and I'm so glad. Luke hovers over me like I'm going to kick off at any second. Promise me that you'll stay with us in the delivery room. I'm afraid Luke will collapse."

"I promise," Sara said. "And I hope you'll be there with Tess and me."

"You're—?"

"No," Sara said quickly. "Tess is, but I'm not sure Ramsey knows about it yet."

"So you and Mike have advanced to the point where you share secrets about his sister?"

"We don't—"

"Is he easy to live with?"

"I don't actually—"

"Does he have a girlfriend?"

"Stop it!" Sara said, then quietened. "Look, before this whole thing gets out of hand, you should know that Mike is here on a case. And that's not to leave this room."

Joce gave a quick nod. "What's the case?"

"Some woman, a big-time criminal, is living in Edilean and Mike came here to find her."

"How does he know she's here?"

Sara shrugged. "I don't know. He tells me little pieces here and there, but I can never get a full story out of him. Did you know that your husband ran me out of my own apartment so Mike could go through some secret tunnel and come up in my—Tess's—bedroom?"

Joce's eyebrows rose. "I knew something was going on because he didn't use any pesticide in your apartment. But he did remove your toilet and kitchen sink."

Sara looked out the window and glared at her cousin, who was drinking beer from a can, turning steaks on the grill, and laughing at whatever Mike was saying. She looked back at Joce. "Want to help me find out what's going on?"

"Since my husband has been keeping secrets from me too, I'd love to help."

The two women looked at each other in conspiracy.

Thirty minutes later, the meal was done and they were sitting around Joce's bed, each with a tray full of steak, salad, and grilled vegetables.

Mike and Luke were dominating the conversation with their endless talk of working out. "I've seen what this guy does at the gym and he wants *me* to go with him," Luke said.

"I know he can play Tarzan," Sara said, and she and Mike smiled at each other.

"What does that mean?" Luke asked as he looked from one to the other.

Before Mike could reply, Joce spoke up. "So how did you find out this woman you're hunting is living in Edilean?"

Luke had no idea what his wife was talking about, but he saw that Mike looked like he was about to explode.

"Mike," Joce said, "don't worry about it. No one will tell your secret. We want to help you."

Mike was glaring at Sara, but she was smiling back.

"What's going on?" Luke asked.

"Mike's here on a case," Joce said. "He's after some criminal, a woman."

"Yeah?" Luke asked.

"I think we should go," Mike said as he looked at Sara. His teeth were clenched.

"No," Sara said. "I don't want to be alone with you right now." She wasn't the least bit afraid of Mike, but she didn't want to hear his lecture—even though she knew she deserved it. But then, he didn't know Joce and Luke as she did.

"Whatever's going on, you can tell us about it," Luke said. "I can assure you that whatever is said to us will be kept in confidence."

"That's not what I've seen of the gossip in this town." Mike was still looking at Sara—who was eating and didn't seem in the least perturbed by his glare.

"Mike," Joce said softly, "I know how you feel. I'm new to this town too, and I'm still not used to it, but they *can* keep secrets. When I first came here, everyone in town conspired to keep me from knowing something about the man I was falling in love with, and—"

"Were you?" Luke asked. "I didn't know that. I thought you and Ramsey—"

"You and Ramsey were a couple?" Mike asked. "But Tess wanted him from the first. She told me—"

"Mitzi!" Sara interrupted loudly. "Remember her? Criminal extraordinaire?"

Mike looked down at his plate. He wasn't used to sharing his life with anyone but Tess, and even she didn't know half of what he did.

"Is that the woman's name?" Joce asked.

Everyone sat in silence as they waited for Mike to speak. They could see he was in a dilemma, but there was no way he could re-move what they'd already been told. He decided that bringing the Vandlos to justice was more important than his own dislike of re-vealing things about himself.

"Tarot cards," he said at last.

"What about them?" Sara asked.

Mike took a bite. "You asked how she was found and the answer is 'tarot cards.'"

Everyone sat there staring at him, but Mike didn't seem inclined to say more.

"See what I have to put up with?" Sara said as she waved her fork about. "He does this all the time. He'll tell some intriguing little sentence, then not say a word more."

"I know how you feel," Joce said. "You mentioned a tunnel, but I've never been told about a tunnel under *my* house." She gave Luke a look that said he had some explaining to do.

"Mike," Luke said, "you wanta help me out here before I get put in the dog house for the next year?"

Mike had to take a few deep breaths before he could speak. "Ev-erybody has weaknesses."

"Even you?" Sara asked, blinking innocently.

"Mine seems to be a pretty young woman who runs around sur-rounded by a gaggle of geese."

As Sara looked down at her food, her face turned a lovely shade of pink. She didn't see the way Joce and Luke looked at each other with hope in their eyes.

Quickly, Mike told them the same story he'd given Sara, again being careful to leave out the part about Sara's fiancé being Mitzi Vandlo's son.

"So we come back to my first question," Joce said. "Why do you think she's here? Other than that she wanted her fortune told, that is. And by the way, no one in Edilean reads tarot cards. At least not for money. We'd know if they did."

"We have informants, people who try to save their own skins by ratting out their friends and relatives. One of them told us Mitzi's great weakness."

The three others leaned forward in anticipation.

"She collects gypsy tarot cards."

One by one, they leaned back.

"That's it?" Sara asked. "All of this because of a bunch of cards with gypsy pictures on them?"

"That's all of it," Mike said in a way that didn't allow for more questions. "Anybody want some more tea? Or a beer?"

"I'd like a margarita with lots of salt," Joce said as she rubbed her belly.

"Don't make jokes to him about food," Sara said. "He's more of a fanatic than my mother."

Joce and Luke looked at him in awe.

When Mike stood up to go to the kitchen, Joce said, "If you don't tell us the rest of this story I may give birth here and now and *you* will do the delivery. Sit! Talk!"

With a smile that showed the dimple in his cheek, Mike sat back down and told them what he'd read in the files the captain had given him. Through an informant, they'd found out that Mitzi Vandlo had what was probably the best—and maybe only—collection of gypsy-inspired tarot cards in the world. In an attempt to trap her, the Feds had obtained a deck that had once been in a museum. "As far as anyone knows, it was the only set in the world, and I can guess how they got them. They put them up for sale on eBay."

"On eBay?" Sara asked.

"Plain, ol' eBay?" Joce asked.

"Yes. The Feds made a bidding frenzy, but when it hit $75,000, they all dropped out. Except for one. He stayed until the unknown bidder won at $82,500."

"And that was Mitzi?" Sara asked.

"They think so. It took six weeks to trace the buyer. There were shell corporations that owned other corporations until they came down to a P.O. box in Richmond. It was owned by a woman who had a driver's license with an Edilean address."

Mike was lying at the last, but he was careful not to show it. The truth was that the box had been rented by a man with a Pennsylvania license. The Feds had watched the box, but it had never been opened. Then, one day, a car in the parking lot had exploded, and the post office was evacuated. When everyone returned, the cards were gone.

They had found out about Edilean through Stefan. After years of silence, when they didn't know where he was, he'd suddenly reappeared long enough to divorce his wife of almost twenty years, then go underground again. The next time he'd been seen was by an off-duty policeman in Richmond, and he was engaged to Miss Sara Shaw and living in Edilean. Put the odd actions of Stefan with the delivery of the tarot cards to nearby Richmond, and the Feds thought they might have found Mitzi. It was a dream come true when they were told that an undercover detective had a sister living in Edilean.

But Mike couldn't tell any of that. He'd soon have to tell Sara the truth, but not yet.

"Maybe she knew she was being watched, so maybe by now she's left town," Joce said.

"We don't think so. We think she came to Edilean to get something, but we have no idea what she wants. You guys know of any hidden treasure buried around here?"

Sara spoke into the ensuing silence. "Tell them what you saw at Merlin's Farm."

Mike had to work to keep from frowning. He was going to have to talk to her about not blabbing what he'd told her in confidence. On the other hand, maybe he should keep his mouth shut and tell her less.

When Mike hesitated, Sara said, "All right, I'll tell them." She then proceeded to give an accurate recounting of all Mike had told her of his day on the farm. "Did I miss anything?"

"No," Mike said cautiously, "but remembering where traps are set doesn't mean you can go there by yourself. Tomorrow I'm going to go talk to Lang and tell him that I now own the farm and—"

"Mike only gets to keep it if he lives there with Ariel and produces umpteen kids," Sara said with a fake sigh.

Mike put up his hand before anyone could speak. "I've never even met the woman. But my brother-in-law did put quite a few restrictions on the deed."

"I can imagine," Luke said. "My cousin is a born lawyer."

"Harsh," Joce said.

"Way too harsh," Sara echoed.

"So how can we help?" Joce asked, but she was looking at her husband.

Mike saw that Luke seemed to be in a trance. His eyes were glazed over, and he was staring at the wall. Mike looked at the two women in question.

"It's his writer's face," Joce said. "He has a book idea, and it's no use talking to him until he returns to earth."

"Oh," Mike said. "I've never been around a writer before."

"Joce is a writer too," Sara said.

"But I write biographies. I dig and find out about people. It's not the same as making up plots. Luke starts with a blank piece of paper and—"

"The fair," Luke said.

"What about it?" Mike asked. "By the way, where's it to be held?"

"Nate's Field," Joce and Sara said in unison.

"Merlin's Farm, K Creek, Nate's Field," Mike said. "Where do all these names come from?"

"No idea," Joce said, her eyes on Luke.

He turned to Mike. "How do you plan to draw this woman out?"

Mike couldn't very well say that he intended to use Sara's fiancé to get the woman to show herself. "You have any ideas?"

"My publishing house has a fantastic in-house art department with state-of-the-art equipment."

"Great," Mike said, but he didn't see the connection.

"What if we create a set of tarot cards with gypsy pictures on them, my pub house prints them, then we get someone to tell fortunes at the fair? That way this . . ."

"Mitzi," Sara said.

"Mitzi—if she's here—will see them."

"And want them," Joce added.

Mike sat there blinking at them as he thought about the idea. It was either brilliant or could get someone killed. "I . . . I don't know if it would work. Where do we get an artist on such short notice?"

"Shamus," Luke, Jocelyn, and Sara said in unison.

"Don't believe I've met him," Mike said, smiling at the assurance on all three faces. "Who is he?"

"He's the youngest of the Fraziers," Luke said.

"The afterthought," Sara added. "The surprise to his parents."

"He's only fifteen, but he is a Frazier," Joce said.

"What does that mean?" Mike asked.

The other three looked at one another but didn't reply.

"So I get to be the fortune-teller, right?" Joce said. "I can lie on a chaise lounge and turn over the cards Shamus makes."

"Absolutely not." Luke's tone said it was a done deal. He had spoken.

"Oh?" Joce asked, her eyebrows raised. "I guess you mean for me to stay here in this house during the fair. Lie in bed taking care of *your* babies, looking after *your* house, seeing to *your* food, and—"

"It was your house when the tunnel was mentioned, and now it's *my* house?" Luke was calm, and his voice was firm.

"I think we'll be going," Mike said as he held out his hand to Sara.

She scooted off the bed, took Mike's hand, and after making their farewells, they left the house. When they were outside in the evening air, they looked at each other and started laughing.

Mike didn't release Sara's hand. "So who do you think will win?"

"I'll put twenty on Joce calling me tomorrow and asking me to make her some outfit for fortune-telling."

"I never take a bet I know I'll lose. Doesn't Tess have some big, round earrings?"

"I know which ones you mean. Small children could use them as swings."

Smiling, Mike kissed the back of her hand.

"Hey!" Sara said as she jerked out of his grasp. "Married woman, remember?"

"You're not even close to being married." It was dark and cool outside and the crickets sounded good. "Want to take a walk?"

Sara was familiar with the big garden, so he followed her. There were no outdoor lights, but the moonlight was bright. "Are you looking forward to getting this case done and going home to Florida?"

"I just got here. You want to get rid of me already?"

"No, but when your case is solved, you'll be free."

Mike was glad the darkness covered his smile. Sara seemed to think Mitzi Vandlo would fall for the ruse of the fake tarot cards. Did Sara imagine policemen throwing back the tent flaps and putting handcuffs on the woman?

"You're laughing at me, aren't you?" she asked.

"Of course not."

"Yes, you are. I can feel it."

"Women's intuition?"

"If you don't stop making fun of me, I'll—"

"You'll what?" His voice lowered. When she turned to look at him, the moonlight on her face made him want to pull her into his arms. Most of the women he'd met in his adult life let him know they were willing, so why did Sara look at him like he was her . . . her *friend*?

"I'll get you back by setting you up with a second date with Ariel."

"You really hate her, don't you?"

Sara started walking again. "I can assure you that it's mutual. Want to hear what she did to me in the fourth grade?"

That was the last thing Mike wanted to hear about. "What's that smell?"

"Probably my mom's perfume. When's your first date with Ariel?"

"Saturday. Is your mother here and hiding in the bushes and that's why I smell her?"

"That's not what I meant and you know it. I'm wearing her perfume."

Reaching out, Mike caught her arm and looked at her in the silvery light. "Do you mind if I smell it at a closer range?"

Sara lifted her chin to give him access to her neck, but then she abruptly straightened. "Wait! You're not a vampire, are you?"

"What in the world goes on in that head of yours?"

"I've been watching teen movies. Who would have thought that teenagers liked sex?"

"Every counselor of teen pregnancy," Mike said. "So what about the perfume?"

"Oh, sure." Sara turned her head, and Mike leaned forward, his face on her neck.

When his lips touched her skin, she jumped away from him, frowning. "Don't do that. I'm only human."

Mike stepped back until he felt a tree. "Sara, you're going to drive me insane."

"That's nice to hear, but I don't believe you."

He was trying to get himself under control. A warm evening, darkness, beautiful, desirable Sara in a white dress that seemed to be made of moonlight, and an erotic, enticing smell that surrounded them. "Where did your mother get that perfume?" he managed to ask, his voice low and throaty.

She was looking at him in speculation, and what she wanted to do most in the world was put her hands on his chest. "She . . ." Sara had to take a couple of breaths to calm herself. Greg, Greg, Greg, she silently chanted—and tried to forget that it had been months since they'd made love. It had been even longer since they'd kissed more than a parting peck.

"You're looking at me oddly," Mike said as he held out his hand to her.

Sara took a step back. "My mother."

"What about her?" Mike took a step forward.

"She dabbles with making products, shampoos and such. But this is the only perfume she's ever made. It's called—"

"What?" Mike took another step toward her.

"Scarlet Nights."

"Sara . . ." Mike held out both hands to her.

She started walking backward down the path she knew well, facing him, and she was talking fast. "My sisters and I have always been embarrassed by the name. About eight years ago my parents went away for a long weekend and they came back . . . well, giggling. Two days later, my mother made a perfume and named it Scarlet Nights."

"I like it," Mike said softly. "I like that scent, and I like the name."

"My sisters and I said she couldn't possibly call it that, but she just laughed at us and said . . ."

"Said what?"

"That every generation loves sex. I think we should go inside. It's getting cold out here." Before he could reply, Sara ran past him toward the house.

As for Mike, he needed to stay outside until he was fit to be seen in public. He knew he needed to get himself under control—*all* of him, mind and body.

At the moment, the situation he was in confused him. In the past, he'd made love to women for the sole purpose of getting information from them. Later, some of the women had been taken off to prison. But except for one time, Mike had been able to disassociate himself from them because he'd known that they'd be all right after he left. They'd all had money, children, and homes. They might tell Mike he'd broken their hearts, but he knew they'd recover.

But Sara was a whole different case. What would happen to

her after Mike left? Especially if they did become intimate? He hoped the two Vandlos, mother and son, would be handcuffed and put in squad cars, but what then? Would Mike also get in his car and leave?

He visualized the scene. Would he wave good-bye to the people of Edilean? Luke and Joce? Tess and Ramsey, the brother-in-law he'd never met?

If he later returned to visit his sister and her kid, would the townspeople hate him for having deserted Sara?

And what about Merlin's Farm? Could Mike live there after his retirement? Would Sara be married by then? To some local guy who smoked cigarettes and watched football all weekend? Some man who fried a turkey and set the house on fire? Or would she fall for another out-of-towner who'd slick-talked her into . . .

Mike ran his hand over his face. Long ago he'd trained himself not to get emotionally involved with his undercover subjects. He'd not always succeeded, but no matter what his feelings, in the end, he'd left them behind and gone on to another job. The thought of doing that to Sara made him feel queasy. Whereas he usually dealt with criminals, Sara was a true innocent.

Maybe it was this town that was bothering him. Or maybe it was the fact that he was facing retirement and didn't have a clue what he was going to do with the rest of his life. He remembered standing in that old orchard at Merlin's Farm and seeing a future that didn't involve shooting people, or even betraying them. Maybe, just possibly, his sister knew what she was doing when she'd given Mike that old farm.

Turning, he looked back at the house. If catching the Vandlos weren't so important, he'd leave now before anyone—especially Sara—got hurt.

But he couldn't do that.

He walked back to the apartment and smiled when he smelled popcorn. Inside, Sara was bent over the DVD player.

"Want to see a movie?" she asked.

"Only if it's a romantic comedy. They're my favorite."

"That's odd. I would have pegged you for a Jason Statham fan." She held up a copy of *Shank*. "But if you don't like it, I have a couple of Katherine Heigl films around here somewhere."

"I'll suffer through another action film if I have to." He walked toward the couch, where a huge bowl of popcorn was on the coffee table. "How's your neck?"

"Washed, so you can draw in your fangs."

"Fangs aren't the part of me that needs drawing in," he said as he sat on one end of the couch and patted the seat beside him.

Sara picked up the bowl of popcorn and put it next to him.

With a grimace, he said, "Give me that" as he held out his hand for the remote.

Sara suppressed her laughter and sat down as far from Mike as the couch allowed.

In the main house next door, Jocelyn sent a text message to Tess:

> DID YOU KNOW YOUR BROTHER IS FALLING IN LOVE WITH
> SARA?

Immediately, Tess wrote back:

> I'M GOING TO SPEND TOMORROW AT ONE OF THE CATHE-
> DRALS HERE PRAYING IN THANKS. WHAT ABOUT SARA?
> SHE TREATS HIM LIKE HE'S ANOTHER COUSIN.
> CONTRIVE TO GET HIM UNDRESSED.

Joce looked up at Luke. "You said you saw Mike at the gym. Did you happen to see him with his clothes off?"

"Not something I would pay attention to, is it?"

"So what's he look like naked?"

"Fat. Big belly. Scrawny legs. Not a muscle on his body."

Joce texted back to Tess:

WILL DO. YOU REALLY ARE MY BEST FRIEND.

# 11

MIKE LOOKED FOR Sara across what he'd been told was Nate's Field, but he didn't see her. "Maybe I should look for a woman so angry her hair is on fire," he muttered as he remembered what she'd seen that morning, of his sitting on the edge of Erica's desk and openly flirting with her.

Across the open field were about a dozen men wearing leather tool belts as they built the pavilions for the coming fair. If he weren't going to spend a second day searching Merlin's Farm he'd be helping them. Maybe he'd be able to tomorrow, he thought. Jocelyn had sketched some designs for the fortune-telling tent, and she'd given them to Sara to replicate. Mike and Sara laughed that Joce had won the argument over her participation in the fair.

"She won't be in any danger, will she?" Sara'd asked. "I mean this Mitzi person won't bash Joce on the head to get the cards?"

"And miss out on what she really wants—whatever that is?" Mike asked. "No, I don't think she will."

Mike didn't say so, but he didn't want Sara in direct contact
with Mitzi. But he did want to obtain as much DNA as he could.
His new plan—which he didn't tell Sara—was to get the notorious
Erica to help out. She would call as many women of the appropriate
age as possible to come into the shop, fit them with dresses, and get
them to drink the free wine from a paper cup. She would write the
name of the woman on the cup and bag it. It wasn't much, but it
was a start.

Mike had asked a couple of people about Erica, and if she was
half as sexually voracious as he'd heard, he knew how to deal with
her. He'd persuaded a lot of women like her into doing what he
wanted.

Earlier that morning, on the way to the gym where he was
to meet Luke, Mike had stopped to talk to Sara's mom and got
her to agree to keep both Sara and Brewster Lang busy all day
so Mike could search the farm in peace. Ellie said she'd give Sara
the job of making wreaths for Luke's booth for the fair, but that
Lang was about as easy to trap as a greased eel. She promised to
do her best.

Mike had gone from there to the store that Sara owned with
Stefan. Mike had left the quaint little town center of Edilean,
where people felt as though they'd stepped back in time, to the
inside of a store of all chrome and glass. He couldn't help it as he
glanced back through the front windows to reassure himself that
he was still in Edilean. The town's building codes hadn't allowed
the outside to be changed, but the inside was utterly modern.
Mirrors were everywhere, as were gold fixtures and silk-uphol-
stered seats. Mike glanced at a price tag: $1,200 for a simple
white blouse.

No wonder the town of Edilean hated Vandlo. The clientele this
type of store would bring in weren't the ones who'd contribute to

the town. No, they'd just park their expensive cars, get what they wanted, then leave.

As Mike looked around he saw what people like the Vandlos would think was high class, but he didn't see anything that reminded him of Sara. He hadn't seen her apartment yet, but he doubted if it was like this place.

"May I help you?" a young woman asked.

Mike looked her up and down. Her all-black attire was more appropriate for New York than Edilean. "I need to see Erica," he said.

An hour later, he was leaving the store. Everything with Erica had gone just as he'd planned, and he'd managed to coax her—forty-ish and desperate—into taking over the job with the women. The problem came when Sara, carrying a load of clothes, had walked into the store before he was finished.

Out of the corner of his eye, he saw Sara leave, and he could tell from her quick step that she was angry. He'd wanted to go to her, but at that moment he couldn't stop what he was doing with Erica. In fact, he'd had to spend extra time soothing her to get her back in the correct mood after Sara's unexpected appearance. He knew that what he was doing with Erica might not look like business to Sara, but it was, and he had to continue.

So now, everything was arranged with Erica. At the end of the day an agent would pick up the bags containing the cups and take them to a lab. Their great hope was that one of the samples would be a relative of Stefan's.

With Lang being kept busy at the Farmers' Market, all Mike had left to do was calm Sara down.

"My salary ought to be doubled for this job," he muttered as he walked across the fairgrounds. A few people raised their hands to acknowledge him, but Luke knew what Mike wanted. He pointed to the shade trees along one edge. Mike saw Sara's golden head bent over what looked to be a few tons of weeds.

She glanced up, saw Mike, started to smile, then her face changed and she looked down again.

Around him, men he didn't know looked at him with curiosity, and Luke slapped him on the shoulder in sympathy.

"Good luck," Luke said, laughter in his voice.

Mike went to where Sara was sitting, her lap full of wire and long stalks of purple-flowered stems. He wondered if she'd speak to him.

He shouldn't have worried.

"You were disgusting," Sara said, her upper lip curled into a sneer. "You were sitting on the corner of Erica's desk like some 1950s secretary. And you were leaning over her and using that weird voice of yours to . . . to flirt with her."

"Yeah. So? What's your complaint?"

"That's no way to conduct business, that's what. You know how this town gossips. If you didn't care about how people see *you*, you should have thought of Tess. She's going to be living here. *With* her children."

"So how should I have done it?"

Sara couldn't contain her anger. "In a businesslike way. Sit in a *chair* in *front* of the desk and talk to her in a respectful way."

"You wanted me to *politely* ask her to do your work? To spy on her own clients? And to gather information for a federal investigation but keep her mouth shut about it?"

Sara was aghast. "You told her about Mitzi?"

"Of course not. I told her I'm from the U.S. Bureau of Health and Disease—which doesn't exist—and I'm investigating an STD outbreak. It seems that everyone in Edilean is sleeping with everyone else."

"You didn't say that!"

"I did."

"Do you have any idea what people are going to say when they hear such a lie?"

"Who's going to believe what an outsider like Erica says? And for that matter, I'm not sure she'll tell anybody. Besides, Erica strikes me as a person who'd like to know that other people have some sexually transmitted disease. Wanta put money on it that she'll be at her doctor's this afternoon?"

"The point isn't *what* you said but *how* you said it. Don't you have any pride?"

"Enough to believe that most women—except for you—like me."

"That's because I think on a higher plane than just physical attraction. And for your information, there's more to being in love than just sex."

"You sound like a woman whose well is dry."

"That's absurd—and vulgar." Looking away, Sara busied herself with the wreaths. "Not that it's any of your business, but Greg and I have a fulfilling relationship in every possible way."

When Mike said nothing, she looked up and saw that he was smiling as though he didn't believe her.

"So how long's it been?" he asked.

"He's only been gone a few days."

Mike kept his smug smile.

Sara narrowed her eyes at him. "So how long has it been since *you* have been with someone?"

"Years. Centuries. It's been so long the crack of dawn is in danger."

Sara tried not to laugh, not even to smile, but she couldn't help herself. She looked back down at the wreaths.

"Are things settled between us now?" When she didn't answer, he said softly, "Sara, I do what I have to in order to get criminals off the streets. In normal life I wouldn't come on to some woman the first time I met her, but I needed something done, and that was the fastest way to achieve it."

"You do know, don't you, that now Erica's going to expect you to go to bed with her?"

"I don't think so," he said solemnly.

Sara gave a sigh. "All right, what did you learn from her?"

"I think she has a boyfriend."

"Erica? She never leaves town."

"So it must be someone in Edilean."

"I'd know about it if she did. Everyone would, and I've not heard a word. She's a workaholic, and she's with Greg twelve hours a day."

When Mike made a little sound as though to say "ah ha!" she glared at him. "Don't even think it. Whatever complaint people have against Greg, he's a hard worker. And no one says he isn't. Well, except for Joce, that is, but she . . ."

"She what?"

"Nothing. What are you going to do today? My mother stuck me with making wreaths for Luke's booth for the fair."

"Do you need some help?"

"Sure. If both of us work together we can get these done in half the time."

"Sara, uh, I meant that maybe someone here could help you. Don't you have some female cousins?" He took a step back.

"Okay, I can take a hint. This is a girl thing and you want to get away. Going to visit Erica?" She was being facetious, but when she glanced at Mike there was a dull shine in his eyes that she was beginning to recognize.

"I thought I'd go to the gym in Williamsburg for some cardio, then to the outlet mall," he said. "I still need some more clothes."

There was something so awkward about the way he'd said that, she knew it wasn't true. "You're lying," she said calmly. "You are flat out, going-to-hell lying."

"That's ridiculous. I need to go."

Sara looked at the wreath in her hand for a moment, then back up at him and smiled. "I hope you have an enjoyable day, and I bet I get at least a hundred of these made. I'm sure they'll sell really well."

Her change from anger to sweet agreeability puzzled him.

She kept smiling. "How about if I make dinner tonight?"

"Tuna casserole?" he asked in a teasing voice.

"Tuna surprise."

"Sounds great," he said, but he was frowning. "Are you sure you're all right?"

"Couldn't be better. Go on. Get your new clothes. You can show them to me tonight. Maybe even model them for me, and I'll save my best wreath to show you."

He was walking backward. "That sounds great. See you about five?"

"Perfect."

Still frowning, Mike turned away and went to his car. Why had she given in so easily? he wondered. One second she was saying he was going to hell for lying and the next she was wishing him well.

It hit him in an instant. She knew where he was going and why. When he'd driven into the lot at Nate's Field, he'd noticed Sara's car parked under a big tree. It took him about two minutes to get there, and he wasn't surprised to see her leaning against the tree, her handbag on her shoulder.

"Took you long enough to figure it out," she said. "Are you *sure* you're a cop? My car or yours?"

"Sara . . ."

"Yes?"

Visions of tying her up, putting her in the trunk of his car, and taking her someplace safe ran through his mind. But she was at the center of everything, and he had to keep her nearby. "Mine. That thing you drive is a piece of garbage."

"Aren't you a snob? We can't all have five-liter V10s with five hundred horsepower that do zero to sixty in four-point-six seconds."

He looked at her in astonishment.

"I looked it up on the Internet."

"You snooped through my room *and* researched my car? What other devious things have you done?"

"Wouldn't be much of a secret if I told you, would it? Have you ever considered that it would save a lot of time if you just told me the truth about what you're trying to find?"

"If I swear on Tess's life that I don't know, will you believe me?"

"Yes," she said seriously. "But I am the key, aren't I?"

When they reached his car, he looked at her sharply.

"You don't have to tell me," she said. "I'm not stupid. I know I'm one of the women you flirt with to find out things. Is it because I own the dress shop and have access to people?"

It wasn't yet time to tell her about Stefan. "Yes." He unlocked the doors and they got in. "Sara, I really can't tell you everything, but you must trust me. The truth is that you *are* the center of this case. It may be about the dress shop, but we aren't sure. I can't tell you why or how, partly because I don't know, but we believe you have something or know something that Mitzi wants."

He could see that she was trying to be calm, and to act as though he hadn't just hit her with a thunderbolt.

"My aunt Lissie left me some jewelry in her will," she said at last. "Maybe it's valuable."

Mike wanted to put his arms around Sara, but they were in an area that was too public. Instead, he made himself think of the list of jewelry Mitzi Vandlo had accumulated over the years. Her clients gave it to her in gratitude for what they thought she'd done for them. "Maybe."

"You are truly the *worst* liar in the world. This case is bigger than some pieces of jewelry, isn't it?"

"Unless she left you the Hope diamond, the answer is yes."

As he started the car, she could see a muscle in his jaw working. "Did you talk my mother into piling those wreaths on me?"

"Yes."

"And I guess you told her she was to keep Mr. Lang away from Merlin's Farm today."

"Until four."

"You and my mother have become thick, haven't you?"

"Whisper a few words about enzymes to her and she's mine. What's Luke going to think when his wreaths aren't done?"

"It's okay. I have two older sisters who are super achievers. They love to excel at everything."

"What does that mean?"

"When they find out that I walked away from all those wreaths and left poor Luke in the lurch, they'll trample over each other to show me up. I learned long ago to just look helpless and I'd get out of a lot of work."

Mike shook his head at her. "Who in this world besides me knows what you're really like?"

"My dad—and Tess a little bit."

"Not your mother?"

"She thinks I'm a wimp."

"How about the boyfriend?"

"I assume you mean Greg, my fiancé. No, he thinks I'm sweet and quiet and agreeable to his every idea."

"Is a lie like that a good basis for a marriage?"

"Maybe *you* could teach me about honesty in a relationship."

They looked at each other for a moment, then laughed together.

# 12

I THINK YOU SHOULD be more cautious when you snoop around Merlin's Farm," Sara said from beside Mike as he drove along the curving road. "I know you hide evidence that you've been there, but if Mr. Lang found out . . . Well, he's notorious for his retaliations."

"Such as?"

Sara was watching Mike drive. He never took his eyes off the road, and the way he sat, with both hands on the wheel, looked like he was prepared for something bad to happen. "No one can prove anything, but we know in Edilean that if you cross Mr. Lang, you get punished. It's something we're all told from childhood up, and I was told that his father was just like him."

Mike glanced in all three mirrors.

"Are you expecting someone to follow us?"

"With this case, I never know what I'll have to do."

"I guess that includes oozing all over someone as sex-starved as Erica."

Mike gave her a quick glance out of the corner of his eye.

"All right." Obviously, Erica was not something he was going to discuss further. "Let's see. Where do I begin? I've heard these stories all my life. When I was about twelve, a man who worked in Williamsburg moved here with his family and he prided himself on his plum jam. I remember my mother telling him that Mr. Lang would be his competition at the local fair and that he usually won."

"Lang has to win or else?"

"Oh, no. He's lost before, but his produce is so good that it's rare for him not to win. But when he lost that time, he went to my mother, who was a judge, and told her the man had cheated. I remember my mother being angry and saying Mr. Lang was a sore loser, so, unfortunately, she didn't investigate the matter."

"What did he do?" Mike asked.

"You have to understand that Mr. Lang is a very keen observer of people." Sara paused. "The truth is that he's a Peeping Tom. No one's been able to prove it, but we all know it's true. If you cross him, he tells you secrets about yourself and what you're doing that you don't want people to know about."

"So what did he do about the plum man?"

"I didn't see it but I was told that at the next class assembly at a high school in Williamsburg, they were treated to a slide show of the man kissing the principal's wife. And they were wearing very little clothing."

Mike couldn't help chuckling. "Let me guess. Your mother investigated the jam."

"Oh, yes! It contained white rum, which was against the rules. Mr. Lang also said the fruit had been stolen from his trees, but that couldn't be proven."

"It would be interesting to know if when Lang was sneaking

around whether he was looking at pretty girls or spying in general." Mike thought that if the old man was snooping, he might have seen something useful.

"I've never heard it said that he watches girls dressing. I think he does as much listening as he does looking. Mother says he has no life of his own, so he watches other people's lives."

"And no one in this town has done anything about him?"

"The Langs are part of the place and we know to keep our curtains drawn."

"Doors left unlocked but windows covered," Mike said, shaking his head. "What else has he done?"

"One time some man was determined to get the McDowells to lease Merlin's Farm to him. Ramsey's dad said he could have it if he could get Mr. Lang out. The poor man didn't know that Uncle Benjamin was joking. My mother refused to tell me the details of what Mr. Lang exposed about the man, but he resigned his position at William and Mary, and moved to Maine."

Sara paused. "But, to be fair, Mr. Lang's done some good too. When I was a teenager, a little girl ran away from home, and Mr. Lang not only knew where she was but why she'd run away. After she was found and was able to talk, a neighbor was put in jail."

"Interesting," Mike said. "Has no one tried to spy on *him*?"

"Sure. Luke and Ramsey dedicated a lot of their childhood to trying to see what Mr. Lang was up to. They used to hide in the bushes around Merlin's Farm and try to watch him, but except for one time, he always found them."

"Lang didn't hurt anyone, did he?" Mike asked sharply, thinking about the traps.

"He knew better than to do that. He shouted at everybody who came near—and his dogs were great at guarding. All the kids said Mr. Lang was part bat, that he could hear and see in the dark."

"His senses probably are better, since he spends so much time alone."

"Are all the things you know about him from your grandmother?" When Mike nodded, she added, "Since she loved the farm and Brewster Lang lived there, maybe they were sweet on each other."

Mike snorted. "Grans said she used to laugh about the way he looked at her when he thought she wasn't looking. But she told Tess and me that if she owned the place, he would be her servant boy."

"Boy? Are you sure she called him that? Weren't they the same age?"

Mike was pulling under what he'd dubbed the Virgin Tree, only this time he made sure his car couldn't be seen from the road. "My grandmother told the same stories over and over, so there are some things I know for sure. Tess and I grew up hearing of the ingratitude and conniving of every person in this town. Lang was just fifteen when my grandmother left Edilean; she was twenty-two. She liked to tell Tess and me that she'd someday return to Merlin's Farm and Lang would wait on her, that he'd be her butler. She always thought of him as a boy and not of her class. In her mind, he never grew older than fifteen. You think you can walk through fields in that getup?"

He was referring to Sara's pale yellow cotton dress and her strappy Italian sandals.

"You would have been disappointed if I'd worn a pair of jeans and a T-shirt."

"They would have been more suitable for traipsing about an old farm."

She looked at him.

"Okay," he said at last. "I would have been weeping with regret."

He didn't smile but the dimple in his cheek showed. "Follow me and do whatever I tell you to."

"Always do," she murmured, and laughed at Mike's groan.

He went the same way he had the first time he'd seen the farm and was doubly careful not to make a path. Once, he put his arms under Sara's and swung her over a muddy place. But when she was on a dry surface, he kept his arm around her.

"I can walk the rest of the way," she said.

"Sure?"

"Of course I am. I can—" She realized he was teasing her. "Tell me, do I come before or after Erica in your list of women you flirt with to get information?"

He started walking again. "I'll have to think about that. I'll bet Erica knows some tricks you don't."

"I'm sure she does," Sara said as she followed him. "But then I am oh, so teachable."

"Don't start something you don't mean to finish," he said over his shoulder.

Sara couldn't repress her grin. Sometimes Mike made her feel like the most desirable woman on the planet. Of course she knew that what he was doing was just part of his job, but it still felt good. She and Greg had long ago passed the point where he told her she was beautiful and sexy. In fact, in the last months they seemed to have stopped saying anything that didn't have to do with the business.

She looked at the back of Mike as he made his way through the weeds. He deftly jumped from one flat place to another, and when he landed, he'd turn and hold out his hand to take hers to steady her for the short leap. She realized that she'd come to depend on him whenever she needed help.

"What's that look for?" Mike asked.

"Nothing. Just thinking, that's all."

"About what you have that Mitzi wants?"

"Oh, right. That. Yes, that's exactly what I was thinking about."

"Now who's lying?"

"I learned how from you."

Chuckling, Mike stepped into the clearing and halted as he looked around.

"If my mother said she'd keep Mr. Lang busy today, she'll do it." Sara was beside him. "Did they give you a key to the house at the closing?"

"Yes, but I have no intention of using it."

"Then how—?"

He gave her a look up and down. "I'm going to love pushing you through a window."

"And I'm going to enjoy—" She broke off from saying that she looked forward to being pushed, and reminded herself that she was engaged to be married. Just yesterday she'd spent three hours with the wedding planner—and Sara had changed several things. The carnations were gone and roses were in. She knew Greg would be angry, but right now she couldn't make herself worry about that.

"We're going in through a window because Lang might have set traps in the doors. And once we get inside, you're not to touch anything, you understand me? He may have rigged some pretty box with a bear claw—and I don't mean a pastry."

"I doubt if—" At Mike's look, she cut off. "I will touch nothing."

"Except me," Mike said without a hint of a smile.

"Right. Got it. Hands only on Mike." She wasn't smiling. "Any particular places I'm to touch?"

"Knees would be nice. Start there and work your way up. Slowly."

Sara laughed. "Go on. You lead, I'll follow."

"I've always wanted to hear a woman say that." Turning, he walked across the open area so fast that Sara could hardly keep up with him. Once they were at the house, he made quick work of pushing up a window, then he grabbed the sill and hoisted himself inside. He's a gymnast, Sara thought. A Tarzan and a gymnast.

When Mike leaned out the window and put his hands out for hers, she didn't hesitate, and it again occurred to her how much she'd grown to trust him in their short time together.

As he pulled her up, he made what she was sure were several unnecessary touches on her body. When his hand went down her leg, she wanted to make herself glare at him, to remind him that she was engaged to be married. But she couldn't. She liked the feeling, and especially liked being touched by a man who had desire in his eyes.

Love and marriage aren't only about fantastic sex, she reminded herself as Mike released her and began to look about the old farmhouse. There are other things in marriage that are just as important, such as friendship and—She didn't want to think about that because she and Greg weren't what she'd call friends, certainly not like she and Mike were. Greg and she were—Mike was staring at her, waiting for her to put her mind back on the current task.

She'd never been inside the house before but she knew as much about it as was possible to find out. "Do you want me to give you a tour?" Sara needed the distraction of words to keep her from thinking about Mike. It seemed that lately all she did was compare him to Greg. Everyone who met Mike liked him. She couldn't see that he was making an effort with anyone, but was just being himself. Greg worked hard to make anyone he sold things to like him, but with her family and friends, he didn't conceal his contempt. "Country

morons" is what he called the people of Edilean. Greg especially
ridiculed Luke. "The man must make a fortune with those books he
writes. So why doesn't he hire someone to mow his lawn for him?"
Sara had tried to explain that being a success was no reason to become a King Midas. That Sara'd mentioned a name Greg had never
heard of made him furious.

"Sara?" Mike was looking at her in curiosity.

"Oh, sorry. My mind was elsewhere. What did you say?"

"I asked when you'd seen this place that you hadn't told me
about."

"I have *not* withheld any information!" she snapped, then apolo-
gized. Her annoyance was from her memories of Greg, not from
Mike. "I know about the interior of the house through HABS."

"Why don't you tell me what you know while we look around?"
he asked gently, as though he knew something had upset her.

Sara turned away so he wouldn't see more than she wanted him
to. Why was it that Mike, who she'd known for only days, was becoming more clear to her than Greg, who she'd known for over a
year? Greg was a man she'd been through a lot with. They'd set up
the store together. Well, maybe Greg had made all the decisions and
Sara had done the bulk of the actual work, but it had been *together*.
Hadn't it?

"Are you going to tell me about that haves?" Mike asked.

"HABS, all caps. Historic American Buildings Survey." He was
looking at her hard, as though trying to ascertain what she was thinking. Again, she compared him to Greg. Greg would *never* ask her
to tell him what she knew about something. Sometimes it seemed
that Greg believed Sara should only think and do what he told her
to. Or worse, lately, starting about the same time as sex between
them stopped, Greg had begun to say that if Sara truly loved him,
she'd *know* what he wanted. She'd somehow intuit all his needs. One

night he told her that if she loved him as much as she should, she'd have known that he didn't want chicken for dinner because he'd had it for lunch. She said, "If you'd called and told me that, I could have—" Greg interrupted. "Do you have any idea how busy I am all day? You expect me to tell you what I ate for *lunch*? Next you'll be telling me I have to tell you *who* I had lunch with. Is that what this is all about? Jealousy?"

Sometimes arguing with Greg made her head spin around until she had no idea what they'd been talking about in the first place.

"Are you okay?" Mike asked.

"Yes, I'm fine."

"Maybe you should wait in the car."

"And miss seeing my dream house?" Sara asked, then launched into talking about the house.

Mike didn't know what had happened to Sara as soon as they entered the old house, but something about the way she looked pleased him.

He half listened to her telling a story about how HABS had begun, with President Franklin Roosevelt setting it up to provide jobs during the Depression. What he heard was that there were old photos and even floor plans for the house somewhere on the Internet—and he planned to look at them ASAP. But for right now he just wanted to see the house his grandmother—and Sara—had so rhapsodized about. And he wanted to try to find a reason why the Vandlos might be interested in the place.

As Mike searched, running his hands along walls, looking inside everything, Sara talked nonstop. "Crown moldings" and "original" seemed to be her every other word. She spoke of paneled doors and said something about there being a cross on them.

"To ward off evil," she said.

They went through the four big rooms and the wide hallway

downstairs. The house wasn't grand or majestic like Edilean Manor, but Mike could see that with paint and repair, it could be quite livable. He imagined Tess's child riding a tricycle inside the big dining room. But then, Sara probably wouldn't allow that, for fear the old wood paneling would be damaged.

Quickly, he glanced at her, thinking that she might have read his thoughts, as she sometimes seemed to do that. But she was still talking about proportion and the height of the rooms. He'd never thought of himself as the marriage-and-kids type, but when he imagined living in this old house, Sara was in every picture.

He watched her as she gestured at the ceiling and kept on talking, and he was astonished at how much time she must have spent studying this house.

He turned back to his search. It couldn't be possible that Vandlo had wanted the house because Sara did, could it? No other reason except to please her—to help persuade her to marry him? But Mike couldn't make himself believe that.

As Mike was more interested in the present, he noted what Lang had done to it. The house was clean and tidy—and sparsely furnished. In the big living room the couch had a block under one leg and was covered by a well-worn canvas. The chairs were cheap to begin with and had been patched repeatedly.

There was little of a personal nature in the rooms. No photographs, no books, just a stack of well-thumbed catalogs from seed and plant companies that were on the old coffee table.

As Mike followed Sara through the rooms, he saw that if Brewster Lang was living there now, he hadn't always done so. They were in what had probably once been the library, and he could see that there used to be books in the built-in shelves. He saw light squares on the walls from where pictures had hung.

He turned to Sara. "I know Lang and his family were caretakers of this house in 1941, and he lives here now, but who lived in it in between?"

Sara looked surprised. "You are observant, aren't you? An historian from Williamsburg and his family lived here for ten or twelve years."

"So why doesn't one of the McDowells live here?"

Sara shrugged. "They don't like the place. Ramsey can't stand it, and neither can his sister."

"Then why don't they sell it?"

"Until recently, they couldn't because it was entailed until the twenty-first century. Some McDowell a couple hundred years ago made out a will saying the farm couldn't be sold until—"

"The year 2000," Mike finished for her. "So where does the historian come into this?"

"I don't know all the story, but I think Mr. Lang's mother ran off with someone when he was just a boy." Sara shrugged. "After she left, Mr. Lang's father quit taking care of the buildings, so Uncle Alex moved the two men—I think Mr. Lang was seventeen or eighteen then—into another house, and that's when he rented the farm to the historian. The man had just been married and they raised a family here. But all that was a long time ago. By the time I was born, Mr. Lang's father was dead and he, the son, was living alone in this house."

"Are you saying that Lang has another house somewhere? Someplace he can go?"

"You *are* thinking of moving here, aren't you?"

"Maybe. What with Tess and her kid and—"

"Don't forget Ramsey."

"Oh right. Him."

"Do you want your sister all to yourself?"

"I think," he said softly, "that I'd like *someone* all to myself."

For a moment, their eyes locked. Sara was the first to turn away. "Ready to go upstairs?"

"I'll follow you wherever you go," he said.

"Then I'm going back to the barn."

"Over my—" Mike grinned. "Okay, so you got me. Lead on."

They wandered about upstairs to see the four bedrooms and the one big bath. It was tiled in perfect 1930s fashion, all black and white. "I'd leave it just as it is," Sara said.

"I know, because it's 'original.'"

Sara's voice was prim. "When I use that term concerning this house, I mean original to when it was built in 1674. For your information, that bathroom is quite modern."

Mike looked at the old pedestal sink and the unusually high toilet. "That room is new?"

"Yes." She went on talking about moldings and paneling, but when she again said "original" he laughed at her.

"You do *not* appreciate the significance of this house!" she said, but she was smiling.

"As long as I have you to take care of it, I'll be fine. You can do anything you—" When he realized what he was saying, he broke off. "Does this place have a kitchen?"

Sara practically ran down the stairs, while Mike took his time. It still astonished him to think of the house as belonging to him. As he stood at the head of the stairs and looked down, he thought of screen doors slamming and kids running in and out—and Sara calling to all of them.

"Come on, slow poke," she said as she looked up the staircase. "The kitchen is horrible. Wait until you see the floor."

He went down, then out to the addition that she said had been stuck onto the house sometime in the 1930s. "Probably when the bathroom was put in," she said.

For all that the bath had charm, the kitchen didn't. The old linoleum floor was worn through to the boards below. The appliances were 1970s avocado, and the cabinet doors were barely hanging on.

"This room could be redone," Sara said.

"I know, with white marble countertops. Please let me hear you say those words again."

"Ask Ariel on Saturday. She's the one who'll be living here with you. Unless Erica gets you first."

Maybe it was the mention of reality or maybe it was the sound of a squirrel in the chimney, but it brought them both back to the present. For a minute they stared at each other.

Mike broke the silence. "Is the old summerhouse still standing? I didn't see it on the day I was dodging Lang's weapons."

Sara's face brightened. "You know about that place? I remember seeing it when I was a child. It's truly lovely; the walls are made of lattice."

"Grans told us she used to go there when this town got to be too much for her."

"That sounds sad."

"If I know her, whatever chaos she was in, she caused it. Think you can find it again?"

She pulled a piece of paper that looked to be a map from her pocket. "Another advantage of dresses is that you can have pockets. Jeans don't."

"Jeans have lots of pockets."

"And they're all packed full of the body parts women want to show off."

Mike laughed. "That is wonderfully true. So where's the summerhouse?"

When Mike reached for the map she pulled it away. "No, you don't. I like it when you follow me."

"I certainly do like the view."

Ten minutes later they were at the old summerhouse, and it was prettier than Sara remembered. Mike hadn't seen it on his earlier trip because it was set behind shrubs that had been allowed to grow eight feet tall. From the side of the path, the area looked to be impenetrable, but Sara knew just where to look for the hidden opening.

Inside, they didn't have to worry about trampling weeds because Mr. Lang had trimmed around the old place until it looked like something on a garden tour. Overhead was a beautiful copper beech tree with low-hanging branches, the ground under it carpeted with moss.

The summerhouse was an octagon, only big enough inside for two people, and its latticework walls had been recently painted a greenish blue. The building and the setting were as secluded and as romantic as Mike's grandmother had described.

While Mike explored the little building, Sara sat under the big shade tree and watched him. He climbed onto the bell-shaped roof and when he finished with that, he checked every inch of the concrete foundation. She guessed that Mike's interest in the pretty little building was more than just about the case, but she also knew he'd not tell her directly. She'd have to wheedle it out of him, or do something devious to find out. It was a sport she was beginning to enjoy.

When Mike finished his inspection, she was sure he'd say they had to leave—no doubt for her "safety"—but he surprised her by stretching out beside her on the soft, fragrant undergrowth of the tree and putting his hands behind his head. His elbow was inches from her hip, almost touching but not quite.

She leaned back against the tree. She didn't want to leave this place. Ever.

"The house needs a complete overhaul," he said into the silence.

"Mmmm, that it does."

"You sound like that makes you happy."

"I helped Luke remodel Edilean Manor and I had a good time."

"And you'd like to tear into this place. I'll tell you what, you design and I'll saw the boards."

Sara wanted to laugh but she couldn't. She still hadn't come to terms with the fact that Merlin's Farm would never be hers. "Your wife will want to do that."

"I'm a long way from marriage. With my job, I might not live until tomorrow."

"From what I hear, I could go with you," Sara said lightly.

"Not if I have any breath left," Mike said softly.

There was an awkward silence between them, so Sara got them back on the house. "At least most of the paneling put in by the first Merlin is still there."

"And who was that?"

"My guess is Alexander McDowell." She was smiling. "Sorry, that's an inside joke. All first McDowell sons are named Alexander. The family line goes back to Scotland and Angus McTern Harcourt. He's the man who settled our little town and named it after his wife."

"Yet another name I've heard often."

She looked at him in question.

"Grans said that in Edilean only the descendants of Angus Harcourt got a fair shake."

"That's probably true," Sara said, "but then it is *our* town."

Mike groaned. "Spoken like a true aristocrat."

"I don't think that being descended from a Scotsman who quite possibly was a thief and a kidnapper qualifies me as an aristocrat. Ariel said the man stowed away on a ship—and it wasn't the *Mayflower*."

Mike rolled onto his side to gaze at her. "You look like a lady to me." He thought she was so beautiful sitting on the ground under the big old tree. He could see her with a wide-brimmed hat and her sewing. "This place suits you." He rolled onto his back. He had to quit looking at her or he'd reach out to touch her. He made himself remember the case and Stefan Vandlo. Vandlo would *never* live in an old house, especially one as small as this one, Mike thought. From the look of the store, Vandlo was more of the gold-faucets-in-the-guest-bath sort of guy.

They were silent for a while, then Sara couldn't help herself when she asked, "Have you ever been in love?"

"No." Mike paused. "But I came close to it once."

"What happened?"

"When she found out I wasn't who I'd told her I was and they took her husband off to prison because of me, she fell out of love with me. Instantly."

"Imagine that."

"Later I heard she bailed his mistress out and they moved in together. But she never forgave *me*."

Sara couldn't help laughing. "What a very strange life you've led."

"I guess it's all in how you look at it. So what would you do with this place if it was yours?"

She didn't hesitate. "First, I'd replenish the orchard."

"Not the house first? No white marble in the kitchen?"

"Trees need time to grow. That marble is waiting for me in a warehouse somewhere."

"You think Anders would agree to all that?"

"Anders? What happened to calling him 'Greg'?"

"Sara," he said slowly, "I've never met this man you're engaged to, but from all I've heard, I don't think he's worthy of you. Are you *sure* you want to marry him? Wouldn't you rather—"

"Don't even say it." She didn't want his words to strengthen the doubt that was beginning to come into her mind. "Everything for the wedding has been arranged. I've been having meetings with the planner."

"How are you going to get Merlin's Farm if *I* own it?"

"I don't know." Sara could hear the frustration in her voice. "Since I met you, it's like everything in my life has changed. Before you, I knew exactly where I was going, but now I . . . I don't know. I can't seem to think clearly."

"That's the best thing I've heard in months, maybe years."

"Maybe for you, but not for me," she mumbled.

Mike got up and held out his hands to her. When she was standing in front of him, he kept holding her hands. "Sara"—his voice was soft—"sometimes it seems like I've known you forever." He leaned forward to kiss her and when she didn't move, he was encouraged.

When he was half an inch from her lips, she said, "Did you say that to the woman whose husband you arrested?"

Mike pulled back. "What?"

"Your women, the ones you've wooed then betrayed. Did you say the same things to them that you do to me? You know, about how I'm the most beautiful, the most—"

He dropped her hands. Yes, he *had* said a lot of the same things to them as he did to Sara, but . . . He turned away. The difference was that this time he meant what he was saying—and that revelation shocked him. "You ready to go?"

"So now you're angry at me?"

He turned on her. "I've done what I had to, whatever was necessary to bring about justice. And for your information, I have never put anyone in prison who didn't deserve it. And many of the women who should have been indicted, I let go."

Sara was unperturbed by Mike's anger. When Greg got angry at her, she felt a sense of panic—and often, bewilderment. Rarely was she sure about what she'd done to cause his rage. All she knew was that she *had* to calm him down, make him forgive her, and get things back to the way they were in the first months they were together.

But she didn't feel that confusion with Mike. His anger always had a reason, and something that had caused it. It was Greg's irrational fury, that had no known cause, that made her crazy.

She reminded herself that no matter how much she came to like Mike, he was temporary. He was here for a job, and when it was done, he'd leave and she'd never see him again—except maybe as Tess's brother. But she even doubted that. Tess had lived in Edilean for years, and Mike had never visited.

As for Merlin's Farm, Mike had made it clear that that was Tess's idea, not his. After his retirement, Mike would probably stay in sunny Florida and the farm would go back to the McDowells.

"Why are you looking at me like that?" he asked.

"I was just thinking about how different you and I are. I want permanence, someone to share my life with. I want children and fruit trees. But you want—" She paused. "What *do* you want? Do you even know?"

No woman had ever before asked him those questions and he didn't know how to answer them. His whole life had been spent getting away from something, not moving toward anything. But Sara wasn't like other women, and she made him question himself.

"Is now when you tell me that I'm different from all the other women you've sweet-talked in the name of duty?"

She was so right on that Mike couldn't help laughing. "I was thinking about it." He looked up at the sky. "It looks like it might rain. I think we should go."

Sara started in the direction of the car, but Mike caught her arm and pulled her back to him. For a moment, she thought he was going to kiss her. Instead he put his finger over his lips. Sara listened, but heard nothing.

As Mike kept hold of her hand, he looked around. There were only two ways out. One was through high weeds at the back of the summerhouse, but that would leave a path. The other was to go into an open area and try to get to the barn—but whoever was approaching would see them.

Mike glanced up at the old tree, then looked at Sara in question. She nodded.

Behind them was a faint sound of gravel crunching and Mr. Lang's unmistakable voice muttering. When she was a child, her sisters made fun of her because when Mr. Lang walked by at the Farmers' Market, Sara dove under the counter. Even today, the sound of his approaching scared her.

Mike pointed to her feet, then patted his shoulders. It took her a moment to understand what he meant, then she nodded.

He went to the tree, squatted down, and looked at Sara over his shoulder. If silence and speed hadn't been so important, she would have argued that he couldn't lift her from his crouching position. But there was no time for discussion. Quickly, she slipped off her sandals, put the straps over her wrist, and stepped onto Mike's shoulders. Instantly, he stood up and Sara nearly gasped at the quickness of it. Her hands were on the tree to steady herself and she easily reached a branch. It was harder to swing herself up, and for once she wished she'd worn one of her two pairs of jeans. But she didn't have time to think about propriety or tearing her dress. She swung a leg over and sat up on the fork of the heavy branch.

Below her, Mike was looking up at her in question. She nodded, and seconds later Mike made a leap, caught the branch and swung himself up.

Sara could hear Mr. Lang more clearly now and saw movement through the shrubs. He was getting closer.

Mike touched her arm and when she looked at him, he nodded upward. He wanted them to climb up. He made a motion for her to stay seated, while he stood up on the branch. When he leaned forward, his hands out to another branch, Sara gasped aloud in fear.

Turning, Mike frowned at her, but when he saw that she was afraid for him, he gave a cocky little grin. In the next second, he grabbed a higher branch and swung himself up onto it. Leaning down, he held out both arms to Sara.

She didn't hesitate. She reached up to Mike just as she'd done at the window, except that this time if she fell, she'd be seriously hurt.

Grasping her wrists, Mike pulled her upward. It was an awkward movement, and for all that he'd told her she was light, she could see that he was straining.

The second branch was smaller than the first one, with little room on it. Mike leaned back against the tree, his legs hanging down, and pulled Sara into his arms, her back to his front.

She knew he'd set up the position, and had the circumstances been different, she would have moved out of his grasp. Maybe, she thought. Maybe she would have moved, but she had to admit that her body fit well against his. Mike's chin rested at the top of Sara's head. Perfect.

She was thinking so hard that she forgot why she and Mike were up in a tree, so when she heard Mr. Lang in the clearing below, she almost spoke. But Mike's arms tightened about her, and she leaned back against him. When she felt his whiskery cheek against her neck, she closed her eyes. His breath was soft and she could smell the sweetness of it.

His hands came up to the side of her head and she felt his strong fingers in her hair, against her scalp. She put her head back, her eyes closed, and tipped her head to one side to give him access to her neck.

But the kiss she anticipated didn't come. Instead, she felt Mike's body tense up and his hands freeze in place.

Reluctantly, she opened her eyes. Mike's cheek was against hers and he was looking down at Mr. Lang below. Sara shifted a bit so she could see the man more clearly. He had brought two big plastic buckets with him, and they were both full, but she couldn't see what was in them. He was muttering in his guttural voice. She couldn't hear what he was saying, but he sounded angry.

She was much more interested in the fact that she was backed up against Mike than she was in whatever odious thing Mr. Lang was doing. Probably building another trap, she thought.

When Sara moved her cheek against Mike's, he pulled away, and she repressed a sigh. Of course it wasn't true, but her first thought was that yet another man had lost interest in her. In her lifetime, many men had come on to her, but only two of them—and Mike— had interested her. But then, she couldn't really count Mike as one of the men in her life, could she?

It was while she was contemplating this that she heard Mr. Lang say the word *Anders*. She heard it clearly enough that, before she thought, she gasped.

Instantly, Mike's hand went over her mouth. Below them, Mr. Lang stopped what he was doing and looked around.

Mike removed his hand and Sara held her breath. If Mr. Lang saw them hiding in the tree above him, they'd never find out why he was muttering Greg's name.

Mike pointed to the lower tree branch and she knew that he meant to go there so he could hear better. Quickly, and with great agility, Mike moved away from Sara, grabbed an overhead branch, and swung down to the one below. He stretched out on his stomach, flattening himself, as he listened.

Sara wasn't sure she wanted to hear what the old man was saying. Wouldn't it be better not to know if the man she was going to marry was somehow involved in what Mike had called a war? Surely Greg couldn't have—wouldn't have—done something that caused Mr. Lang to set traps all around the property.

It was when she heard the word *dogs* that she sat up straighter. Below her, to her right, Mike was looking up at her. He'd heard the word too.

Sara's instinct was to put her palms over her ears. If Greg was doing something he shouldn't, she didn't want to know of it.

On the other hand, if she didn't listen, she knew she would be postponing the inevitable.

With a defiant gesture, Sara secured her sandals on her arm, then stretched out on the tree branch just as Mike was, and gave her attention to the old man below. It was easy to see that he was constructing another trap. He put almost invisible nylon fishing line across the bottom of the doorway to the summerhouse, and attached something inside, but she couldn't see what it was.

Minutes later, she heard him chuckle—an ugly little sound— and he stepped away to admire his handiwork. He picked up a small rock and tossed it, hitting the line with one shot.

To Sara's horror, four big, steel-tipped arrows flew across the doorway and landed in the wood at the other side.

Sara had to put her hand to her mouth to keep from shouting in protest. She glanced at Mike and he mouthed, "Okay?" She nodded, but it wasn't easy to do. If she and Mike had come later or tomorrow, there was a chance the metal spears would have hit him, for it was Mike who always went first.

When Mike smiled at her, the calm of him restored her equilibrium. He turned back as Lang began to mutter again, but this time it was louder.

"That'll teach you, Greg Anders," Brewster Lang said as he pulled the arrows out of the wood and reset the trap. "You can't murder my dogs and get away with it. I hope these arrows kill *you!*"

Angrily, he picked up his tools, put them in the buckets, and made his way back to the path to the house.

Mike looked at Sara across the space between the branches and waited for at least ten minutes before he stood up on the heavy branch.

"Can you step across to me?" he asked.

She was distracted by what she'd heard. "Sure." Mike took her hand, and Sara made the long step, but her mind wasn't on it and she slipped.

But Mike caught her. He was holding on to a branch above his head with one hand and to Sara with the other. As fast as she could, she scrambled up and leaned against him. They were standing on the branch, Mike with his back against the big tree, with both arms around Sara.

She stood there, her arms folded against his chest, and was glad for the security of him. When had Greg done this? she wondered. He was always at the shop, so when had he had time to go to Merlin's Farm?

And *why?* Just because he wanted the place? Did Greg think that Mr. Lang was the reason Rams wouldn't sell it to him? Or was the reason because Sara, the woman he loved, wanted it?

Mike put his hand under her chin and lifted her face up to his. "Are you sure you're all right?"

"Yes," she said. "Shocked, but I'm all right. What about you?"

"Not shocked," he said quickly and looked around them. "Even though I'd like to stay here all day, just like this, I think we should get down and go."

Sara didn't want to leave either. Besides, she knew that when they were back on the ground she'd have to face the truth about the man she was to marry.

"Sara?"

"I know," she said as she reached up to hold on to a branch.

Mike started to move away, but then turned back and sweetly kissed her cheek. "It'll be okay. I promise."

"Yeah, sure," she said and tried to smile but couldn't quite manage it.

Mike jumped down from the low branch, and got Sara to fall into his arms. He tried to make a joke about her nearly knocking him down, but when he looked at her expression, he stopped.

He quickly led her around the hedge and back past the house to get to his car. He unlocked it and held the door open for her. When he saw that her hands were shaking, he fastened her seat belt for her, then got in the driver's side.

They were halfway back to Sara's apartment before either of them spoke. Mike wanted to give Sara as much time as she needed to digest what she'd heard. For him, he wanted to call Lang and thank him. From here on, Mike would start the process that would end in his telling Sara the truth, that the man she planned to marry only wanted her because . . . He hadn't yet figured that out.

He glanced at her, sitting silently in the seat next to him. Her pretty dress was covered with leaves and twigs, and there was a tear at the shoulder.

"Sorry about your dress," he said.

"Do you think Greg was trying to get Merlin's Farm for me?"

"You can answer that better than I can."

"Greg might have done what he could to get Mr. Lang to leave, but he wouldn't kill the dogs. I think that must have been a coincidence of timing and Mr. Lang put them together without any evidence."

It was too soon for Mike to tell her what he knew. When he was younger, he'd learned the hard way not to tell too much too soon. On his first undercover case, right away, he'd gleefully told a woman her husband was an arms dealer and that he had two mistresses. In his naïveté, he'd thought the woman would be grateful for the information. But she'd had the opposite reaction. She'd called Mike a liar and had stood by her husband to the very end. When she was being led off to prison, she spit on Mike. Yes, he'd learned to be cautious. "Are you sure you know him well enough to be able to say that?"

"Greg may not be the most honorable person on earth, but he is a good man." Sara was silent for a moment. "I know Greg does some things I don't like, but—"

"Like what?"

She told him about Greg switching the dress sizes. "But that was just to make the women feel good. It's a far cry from poisoning dogs."

"I didn't say they were poisoned, and I don't know that they were. What made you say that?"

She hesitated for a full minute. "The owner of Edilean Drugs told me to remind Greg to be careful with the rat poison he bought."

Mike gritted his teeth, as this was something she hadn't told him. "I take it you don't have a rat problem?"

"When I asked him about it he said there was a nest of them in the back wall of the store. It made sense that he'd buy poison." She took a breath. "Even though I still don't think Greg would do something like that, I wish I could replace Mr. Lang's dogs."

Mike grinned at her. "Now there's where you're lucky."

"Why?"

"On this case, I'm working for the federal government, and you know why we put up with their delusions of their own grandeur?"

"No."

"Money. They have lots and lots of greenbacks. Tell me what kind of dogs Lang had and we'll replace them."

"I was only a child when I saw them so I don't know what breed they were. But I thought they were beautiful. My mother once said that they were Irish."

"Would you recognize them if you saw a picture of them?"

"Maybe."

He handed her his phone. "Text Tess to send you photos of Irish dogs."

"You always remember your sister but you forget that she's married to my cousin. How about if I text Rams to tell me what kind of dogs Mr. Lang had?"

"Even better." He smiled at her.

"What's that look for?"

"I was thinking how much you're like all the other women I've worked with."

His sarcasm made her feel good. "They didn't hide with you in trees?"

"No, and they missed a lot. I liked holding you." When Sara kept looking straight ahead, he added, "And they didn't want to replace the dogs of some old man they disliked." Mike had to look away to hide his pleasure at the way the day had gone—and at the way Sara was sitting there frowning. It was the first real dent that had been made in the myth of Greg Anders.

"How about if we take the night off from the case?" he said.

Sara's eyes brightened. "Watch more movies together?"

"I was thinking that maybe we could go to your apartment and fix dinner over there. You haven't even shown me your place yet."

"I guess you forgot that I have no kitchen sink." She narrowed her eyes at him. "You want to search through everything I own, don't you?"

"Yeah," he said, but in such a lascivious way that she laughed.

"Fine with me. You can not only look at the jewelry Aunt Lissie left me, you can try it on."

"I'd rather you model it for me."

"After what I heard today about my fiancé, I just might do that." Mike's grin almost cracked his face.

# 13

EVERYTHING ABOUT SARA'S apartment said "family." Whereas Tess's place was like Mike's, with furniture that had come from stores—preferably in preplanned rooms—he didn't think Sara owned so much as a dish that hadn't come through her friends and relatives. And what she'd bought had been carefully chosen because it looked old and worn in that romantic way that women liked.

As soon as she opened the door—unlocked, of course—she ran to her bedroom. But Mike stood in the doorway and stared.

Even though Sara's living room was shaped like Tess's, they couldn't be more different. Sara's room looked like something off the History Channel titled "Furniture Through the Ages."

She had a big peach-colored couch with huge rolled arms. Mike wasn't much of a historian, but he could imagine ladies in long dresses taking tea on that sofa. The chair next to it was nearly as plush and was covered in a flowered fabric. On the other side was a big chair upholstered in old brown leather, and he was sure he'd seen one just like it in some World War II movie.

Around the room were little tables and knickknacks that ran the gamut of years from Thomas Jefferson's time to the 1980s. Nothing he saw was new.

And everywhere, there were photos in frames. They ranged from so old it looked like Matthew Brady had taken them, to one of Tess on her wedding day. Mike smiled when he saw she was dressed in a dark blue suit that she'd probably later wear to work. He and Tess had been taught frugality and recycling long before it became fashionable. He remembered how hard he'd tried to be there that day, but he'd been tied up—literally.

"So who gave you all of this?" he called to Sara.

"Everybody," she answered. "There's a saying in town that if you don't want it, give it to poor Sara."

Mike snorted at that. Nothing could be further from the truth because every item had been carefully selected. He ran his hand over a small table that had extensions on the sides. He didn't know much about antiques, but he'd spent a lot of time in rich houses, and he knew Sara's little table was worth some money. If he'd been dealing with a different criminal he would have said that whatever treasure was being sought was somewhere in this room. But Stefan had lived here with Sara, so he must have seen all this—and known that there was something more valuable elsewhere.

Sara came into the room. She'd showered and changed into a dress of pale blue cotton, and he thought she'd never looked prettier.

Sara walked to Mike and turned her back. "Could you please button me?"

There were about thirty little white buttons down the back of her dress, and he started from the bottom up. Her skin was covered by an old-fashioned slip, and he wondered if she'd also inherited her clothes. "You couldn't get out of this dress very quickly," he said, joking, and working very slowly.

"But then that's the point, isn't it?"

Mike chuckled. "I guess it is. There. Done. So tell me about your home. Have you ever bought a piece of furniture in your life?"

"No. Just knickknacks. In fact, my dad pays the rent on a big storage unit in Williamsburg that's full of old furniture and photos that relatives have given me. They like Ikea; I like Edwardian."

"It sounds like a giant hope chest."

"At one time I thought it was."

"And you showed what's in storage to Anders?"

"I don't want to know how you guessed that, but yes, Greg and I spent three days going through everything. He wanted to see what we could use when we have our own home. I'd planned to take it all with me with Brian, but . . ."

"Who's he?" Mike asked. He was looking at a photo of two pretty young women with their equally cute kids. It was his guess they were Sara's older sisters.

"First serious boyfriend." She didn't say that she'd been so sure they were going to marry that six months after they met, she'd turned down an excellent job as a conservator at a Boston museum. Her life with Brian would have taken her in a different direction, and that's what she'd wanted so very much.

When Mike looked at Sara in question, she shrugged. "Dumped me. Boo hoo. Feel sorry for Sara."

He knew she meant it as a joke, but he could feel the hurt in her voice. "Stupidest man I ever heard of," he said and was pleased to see her smile. "So what does the fiancé think of all this?" He motioned about the room.

Sara laughed. "That it would make a good bonfire. He likes chrome and glass."

Mike turned away so she wouldn't see his frown. If Vandlo had been so honest about his likes and dislikes, and Sara's were so different, why the hell was she marrying him? He sat down in the big leather chair. "I like what you have here. No chrome, and I hate glass-topped tables. They break during fights and can cut a man. I once saw a severed artery that—" He broke off with a shrug.

Sara remained standing and staring down at him.

"Did I grow horns?" he asked.

"You look at home in that chair. You look like some World War I pilot. I can almost see you in a bomber's jacket."

"You mean one of those guys who died before he was twenty-three? Fought the Red Baron and went down in flames?"

"Yes, that's just what I mean." She sat down on the edge of her couch and kept looking at him. "Greg—"

"What about him?" Mike tried not to sound keenly interested.

"Nothing. You look good in this room. Most men are awkward in here, but you look like you've read a book and been places and done things in your life."

"Sara," he said softly, but she got up before he could say more.

"I'll get the jewelry." She hurried down the little hall to her bedroom.

Mike wandered around the rest of the apartment. The kitchen needed remodeling, and there was a big hole where the sink had been. He couldn't help smiling at the way Luke had disabled the whole place.

"Was there *anything* Anders liked?" he called to Sara. "So much as a chair or even a photo?" His voice lowered when she came back into the living room.

"Not really." She handed Mike a small wooden box.

Opening it, he saw six pieces of jewelry. They were old-fashioned, and he didn't doubt that the stones were real, but even if they were, none was big enough to be worth much. Certainly not enough to tempt a Vandlo. He closed the box. "I don't think . . ."

"I know. The good stuff went to her daughters-in-law. Ram's mother has some big clunkers that she never wears. I got the pretty things."

"Sara, you could wear jewelry made of iron and make it look good."

"I . . ." she began, and he could see the blush coming into her cheeks. But then her eyes went to the wall behind him. "The CAY painting."

"What?"

She stepped around him and went to the far wall. "One time Greg said that the only thing of mine he actually liked was this painting. He wanted me to give it to him." She removed from the wall a frame, about ten by twelve, and handed it to him.

For a moment his heart raced, but when he saw the picture he was disappointed. It looked like a child's drawing of a pond with ducks on it—except that the sky was green, the pond pink, and the poor ducks were purple.

The watercolor looked old, but he couldn't see it as being valuable. Maybe Vandlo wanted it for his future grandchildren. According to his family's tradition, his teenage daughter would soon be married off to some old man.

Mike looked in the corner of the painting at the three initials: *CAY.* "One of your ancestors?"

"I don't know. Aunt Lissie didn't know who he was. She said the picture had been in the McDowell family forever, but she and I were the only ones who liked it. We figured it was Victorian."

"No chance it's a Beatrix Potter, is there?"

"I wish. No, it's a castoff, like everything else in here. Even me," she added as she turned away.

Frowning, Mike put the picture back on the wall, and when he looked at Sara there was a slump in her shoulders that he didn't like. It seemed that she'd been tossed aside by her first boyfriend, and he knew that it was going to be exposed that the second one only wanted her for what he could get.

Mike didn't think about what he did, he just reached out, took her arm, and pulled her to him. He put his lips on hers and kissed her with all the longing he'd felt since the first moment he saw her.

He half expected her to pull away, but instead, her arms went around his neck and she tilted her head. Her lips were sweet, and her body against his fit more perfectly than any other woman's ever had.

It was all Mike could do to keep from making the kiss deeper, and from leading to much more.

He was the one to break away. He held her, his lips on her neck. "Sara," he whispered. "I want—"

She pushed him away. "I know. I'm part of your job. And you want—" Breaking off, she hurried to the door. "Meet me at Joce's in an hour. I need time to think about all this."

In the next second she left the apartment and Mike sat down heavily on the leather chair. His assignment had been to do whatever was necessary to get Sara away from Vandlo.

"Hell!" Mike mumbled. "I'm being lured into this town with the bait of an old farm, comfortable furniture, and the prettiest, sweetest little temptress who ever walked the earth." He ran his hand over his face. "If anyone is being seduced, it's *me*."

# 14

JOCE WAS IN her bed, surrounded by genealogy charts; a printer was on the bedside table. "Want to know who your third cousin six times removed is?"

"Not especially," Sara said. "I have enough cousins here and now."

Joce looked at her friend—and seventh cousin, she'd just found out—and said, "What's wrong?"

"Mike kissed me."

"Oh. Well. I know that's terrible, since you're engaged to another man, but before the lamentations begin, what was the kiss like?"

"Great. But then he's had a lot of experience."

Joce wasn't going to comment on the last remark. "So how does he compare to Greg?"

Sara sat down heavily on the chair by the bed. "Did you ever know for absolutely *sure* that what you were doing was right, then something happened that made you doubt everything you knew?"

"If you're referring to men, yes. In college I had a boyfriend I adored. I was sure he was The One. Then I went home—meaning to Miss Edi—and spent a week with her. One morning, we were sitting at breakfast and I imagined what it would be like if he were there. Instantly, I knew I'd spend every moment dealing with his jealousy. If you'd asked me the day before if he was a jealous man, I would have said no. But he was. He was jealous of my job, of my girlfriends, even of my awful stepsisters. Is that what you mean?"

"Pretty much. I'm beginning to see and remember things that a week ago I wasn't aware of." Sara sighed. "When Greg and I were first together it was so wonderful I would have walked through fire for him."

"And from what Tess and I heard through the walls, you did a few times."

Sara nodded. "Everything was great. It hadn't been long since Brian left me and . . ."

Joce had never met Sara's other boyfriend, but she'd heard about him. He was a young archaeologist from England, and he and Sara had been inseparable for over four years. Everyone, including Sara, thought they were going to get married. When he told her he was going to marry his childhood girlfriend, Sara had been devastated.

"The worst thing," Tess told Joce, "was that everyone in town treated Sara like she was on the point of insanity."

"Was she?" Joce asked, for she knew some about being close to breaking.

"Yeah," Tess said. "She was."

So now, Joce reached out to take Sara's hand. "Greg made you feel desirable, that someone *wanted* you."

"Yes, and that the town disliked him made me feel like I was fighting against . . . I don't know. Maybe I felt like Shakespeare's

Juliet and I was struggling to retain True Love. Now I think maybe I just wanted to show people . . . I don't know what."

"I know about rebellion," Joce said seriously. "In that backwoods family of mine I caused a lot of anger because I absolutely refused to get a tattoo."

Sara laughed. "Not even one?"

"Not even a butterfly on my left ankle."

"You *are* a rebel."

Joce waited a moment before she spoke. "So what about the wedding?"

Sara put her hands over her face. "I don't know. I mean, I really and truly don't know!" She looked back at Joce. "Just days after I met Greg, we were in business together and traveling and—"

"Working."

"Oh, yes," Sara said. "Masses of work. Great mountain loads of things that I had to do that kept me busy seven days a week."

"And sex."

"At first, yes. I so very much wanted to prove that I was at least as desirable as Brian's . . . as the woman he wanted to marry, that I was insatiable."

"What about now?"

"Now I'm remembering Greg the man. He's not easy to live with, and he's impossible to please. But I didn't have time to think about anything after I met him. We went from a blind date to marriage plans in what seems like minutes."

"So where does Mike fit into all this?"

"Nowhere. Mike has nothing to do with anything."

"Oh," Joce said.

"What does that mean?"

"Nothing. I just thought that you and he were—"

"Friends. That's all we are to each other." When Joce said nothing, Sara gave in. "Okay, so maybe Mike has reminded me what it's like to enjoy a man's company. He and I do things together."

"Like what?"

"Swing through trees." Sara lifted her hand. "That doesn't matter."

"Are you sure? That I liked the things Luke and I did together made me choose him over Ramsey."

"Joce, get real. You had the hots for Luke from the day he dumped mustard down the front of you. Ramsey never had a chance. Besides, he was in love with Tess but was too dumb to know it."

"You're right," Joce said. "I know it's a cliché, but I think you should follow your heart."

"If I did that, then I'd marry Merlin's Farm. It's what I *really* love."

Joce laughed so hard the babies started kicking.

# 15

MIKE WAS DRESSED for the gym, it was still dark outside, and there was no light from under Sara's bedroom door. The night before, as soon as Mike had pulled up in his car, Luke had stepped outside to speak to him in private.

Quietly, Luke had asked how the case was going and if he needed any help.

Mike felt his usual sense of caution, but with each day that was fading. "I can't find what Sara has that the Vandlo family wants."

Luke showed his shock at Mike's word of "family." "There are more people here than just Mitzi?" When Mike just looked at him, Luke drew in his breath. "It's Greg, isn't it? How is he involved?"

"He's Mitzi's son."

Luke gave a low whistle. "Does Sara know?"

"No. I want her to trust me more before I tell her."

"From what I've seen, she couldn't trust you more than she does now."

"Yeah?" Mike couldn't stop his grin.

Luke arched an eyebrow at him. "You are aware, aren't you, that if you hurt our Sara we'll murder you?"

"And what happens if *my* heart is broken?" Mike asked.

"I have a staple gun in the truck."

Mike laughed. "At least tell me it's a *big* staple gun."

"A pocket-size mini."

As they got to the door they were laughing, and an adolescent young man came out. He was as tall as Luke, but outweighed him by about a hundred pounds—and all of it looked to be muscle.

The boy didn't say anything, but when he saw Mike, he stopped and stared. He took Mike's chin in his hand, turned his face to the side, and ran his finger down Mike's nose. It had been broken several times but rarely repaired. As a result, he had a slight hook at the top of it that he'd been told looked like an axe blade.

The young man said nothing, just removed his hand, and kept walking. Waiting by the big pillars into Edilean Manor was a sleek little Mercedes convertible. Sitting at the wheel was a slim, extraordinarily pretty young woman with an abundance of dark red hair. She waved at Luke, stared at Mike, and waited while the boy got into the passenger seat, then spun away in a flurry of gravel.

"Who the hell—?" Mike began.

"Fraziers." Luke went into the house.

"The big kid . . . ?"

"Shamus. He's drawing the gypsy cards."

"Why was he looking at *me*?"

"He likes faces, but who knows what a Frazier is thinking?"

"The girl's a looker."

"That's Ariel, and she's a terror. She has the Frazier temper."

"I guess I'm better off with Sara," Mike said.

"Oh, yeah."

"Does everyone in this town work at matchmaking?"

"Not Mr. Lang," Luke said instantly.

As Mike laughed, they heard the voices of the women and went into the drawing room, where Joce and Sara were.

As before, the evening was very pleasant. Mike could almost forget the case as they talked about food and Luke's trip to the gym that morning.

"Forty-six minutes of hell," Luke was saying. "Who would have thought you could do so much damage in so short a time?" He put a hand on his shoulder. "My delts will be sore tomorrow."

"You have strong lats. I'm going to have to work to keep up with you."

"Right," Luke said in sarcasm. "This from a man who cools down on a trampoline." He looked at the two women. "You should see what this guy does in the gym. I swear half the people there stopped their own workouts just to watch him."

From there they went to talking about Merlin's Farm. As Sara spoke of seeing the inside of the old house, Mike marveled at the rapture in her voice. He'd never thought about loving an in-animate object as she seemed to care for that place. But then, he thought Sara would probably say he loved his car that much. She'd already teased him for keeping it so clean, but he saw nothing wrong with daily washing and vacuuming, and people really shouldn't eat inside a car. And what was wrong with keeping the tires oiled?

"Then Mr. Lang returned and ruined it all," she finished with a quick glance at Mike.

She'd left out the part where she and Mike had sat in a tree, snuggled together like baby birds in a nest.

After they'd finished eating, Sara and Luke went to the kitchen, while Mike sat on a chair beside Joce and went through her genealogy charts. They were incredibly detailed, and he told her what a great job she was doing.

"Sara likes you," Joce said quietly. "And you're pulling her away from that horrible Greg."

"You're one of the people who doesn't like him?"

"He works to make everyone feel bad. Unless you have money. He fawns over the women who go to the shop." She leaned closer to Mike and lowered her voice. "If you can stop the wedding—"

Mike picked up her hand and kissed the back of it. "That's why I'm here."

"Really?" Joce's eyes widened. "I thought your concern was catching the bad guys."

"It's all part of it. Say nothing to Sara."

Joce looked at him with gratitude in her eyes.

"Are you making a pass at my wife?" Luke asked from the doorway.

"He couldn't control his lust." Joce put her hands on her big belly.

"I understand and I forgive," Luke said. "So who wants some cake?"

"How many pounds of it am I allowed?" Joce asked, and they all laughed.

So now, it was early morning, and Mike was about to leave for the gym, but Sara's voice stopped him. He went to her bedroom door and opened it. She was sitting in bed wearing a white nightgown that looked like something from a BBC production.

"Off to the gym?" she asked.

"Want to go with me?"

Sara grimaced. "So what's on for today?"

He stepped into the room. "I thought I'd help with the building for the fair today."

"Do you know how to do that?"

"I learned some about construction on one of my first cases." She was gazing at him with wide eyes, as though his stories were truly exciting; it was an irresistible look. "I went undercover to find out about some contractor who was taking kickbacks from manufacturers. His buildings tended to collapse on top of people."

"Did you have an affair with his wife?"

"No," he said solemnly. "I did *not*." His eyes began to sparkle. "It was with his twenty-two-year-old daughter. She taught me a thing or two. Wait! That was the case where I beat up half a dozen men at once and saved the girl. She was twelve, I think. Or was that the time—?"

Sara laughed. "You'd better go. I doubt if they can open the gym without you there."

"They manage. What do you plan to do today?"

"Oh, this and that."

"You aren't going to glue yourself to a sewing machine, are you? I told Erica to get someone else to do all that, that you're a boss, not a wage slave."

"Thank you," she said.

"I guess I won't see you until this evening." When Sara smiled but made no reply, he left her bedroom.

As soon as Sara heard Mike's car pull away, she texted Joce.

MIND IF I USE YOUR KITCHEN TODAY?

ONLY IF I CAN HELP.

YOU CAN SIT AND PEEL FRUIT. IS SHAMUS THERE?

YES. I GOT HIM OUT OF SCHOOL. THE CHILD LOVES ME.

Ten minutes later, Sara was dressed and on the way to her mother's grocery.

As soon as Mike left the gym, he checked his phone. Tess had called, so he rang her back.

As always, she didn't bother with preliminaries. "If you make Sara fall in love with you, then drop her for one of your bimbos, so help me, I'll never speak to you again. I will completely and totally disown you."

"There's no danger of that," Mike said. "Sara wants nothing to do with me except as her"—he nearly choked—"friend. We share bowls of popcorn and watch movies together. I've made lots of passes at her, but she doesn't seem to be interested."

Tess was silent for a moment, and when she spoke, her voice was barely a whisper. "Women have liked you since you hit puberty, but you're saying that Sara doesn't want you?"

"Are you laughing at me?"

"I'm trying not to, but it's not easy. So how are you going to keep her from marrying that jerk?"

"Tie her up, I guess."

"Then do delicious things to her?"

"Whatever happened to that support you women talk about so much? You act like you *want* me to handcuff your friend."

"You very well know that I want you to marry Sara and live happily ever after at Merlin's Farm. Who's my kid going to play with if you don't get busy with her?"

"I didn't sign on to this for *marriage*. I think—"

"I have to go. Rams is here."

Twenty minutes later, Mike was at Nate's Field. He wanted to help with the fair, but he also wanted to hear more gossip. Although

Sara said she'd told him all she knew, he kept discovering new information.

There were permanent bleachers in the big, open lot, and several trees, but nothing else. When Mike walked up, everyone grew quiet, and he knew what was going on. They were men and they were waiting to see if he knew which end of a hammer to use. No doubt they'd heard from Sara's mother that Mike knew about organic foods and how to cook them—all of which he'd learned on undercover assignments. A couple of times he'd had to go into training for months before taking on an assignment. Over the years, Mike had done a lot of construction, so he felt at home with a tool belt on.

After a couple of hours of watching Mike, the other men loosened up and began to include him in their talk. But he and Luke worked best together. With Luke on one end and Mike on the other, they hoisted studs into place and nailed them down.

"Ever use one of these?" Luke asked as he held up an electric nail gun.

"On a person or a piece of lumber?" Mike asked so only Luke heard him.

"When your case is done, I want you to help me with my murder mysteries."

"By the way, my captain wants an autographed copy of your latest."

"Gladly," Luke said as he picked up a hand saw. "Know how to use one of these?"

"Want to hear about the time I was forced to build my own coffin with hand tools and no electricity?"

"With all my heart and soul," Luke said sincerely.

"They were bored, so while they waited, they came up with this plan that I should—"

"Who are 'they'?"

"Can't tell you that, but they were bad."

Nodding, Luke began to listen as he slipped his hammer into the strap of his tool belt.

About 10 A.M., three young men showed up, and they were as big as professional wrestlers. "So who's the beef?" Mike asked Luke.

"Frazier brothers. And our competition at the games at the fair."

Mike was looking at the three of them and wondering, if it came to a fight, whether he could take them. He reminded himself that such a thing would never happen, but he couldn't break a habit. For all the size and muscle of the three Fraziers, they didn't move quickly—but then they didn't have to. "I have a date with their sister tomorrow. I guess I better be good to her."

"Ariel can take care of herself." When Mike looked at him in question, Luke smiled. "Don't worry. You saw that she's not as big as her four brothers."

"Right, I can't forget young Shamus. How's he doing?"

"He's at home with my wife, bent over a drawing table, and making pictures of gypsies. He won't show them to anyone, so Joce is planning a big reveal."

"Good," Mike said, smiling.

At ten-thirty, they took a break and Luke introduced Mike to his cousin Kimberly Aldredge, who was one of the women manning the drinks table. She was about Sara's age and quite pretty, and she'd been repeatedly suggested to Mike as a good choice for dating.

"Kim designs jewelry and sells it in Sara's shop, among other places. She made Tess's engagement ring." Luke's tone told that he was proud of her. Moments later, he excused himself to see a man about some plants he wanted.

"You're all the town talks about," Kim said as she handed Mike a paper cup full of lemonade.

"That's bad." He drained the cup and held it out for more.

Kim leaned toward him and lowered her voice. "Can I be honest with you?"

"Please do."

"We all love Sara, but she's been cutting off her friends and family. She and Greg have time for their customers but not for us. Every family picnic, birthday party, whatever, she's too busy, or she has to go somewhere with Greg. I don't think Sara has any idea what he's doing to her. The scuttlebutt around town is that you're bringing her home to us."

"I'm not making much progress with her," he said modestly. "She believes in being faithful."

Kim studied him for a moment. "You look like you have it bad for her."

"No, I'm . . ." He didn't know quite what to say.

She smiled. "That's okay. I won't tell. Sara deserves some good things to happen to her. The last few years have been difficult for her."

At twelve-thirty, Sara showed up with her mother and a van full of sandwiches and salads. In the back were homemade pies. Men started slapping Mike on the shoulder and saying "thanks, man," and "we owe you one."

"What's this all about?" he asked Luke.

"Sara hasn't baked in a long time. When she was growing up, there wasn't a town function that didn't include Sara's . . . her fruit things. What she can do with a piece of fruit is legendary. But she hasn't baked anything since—"

"Let me guess. Since Anders came to town."

"Actually, she quit before then. I guess you've heard about her first boyfriend. The downturn in Sara's life started when he dropped her in a way that still makes me angry. I wanted to go to England

and shove a few teeth down his throat, but Rams talked me out of it." Luke's head came up, and he yelled to his cousin, "Ken, if you take all of that peach pie, I'll show you what a nail gun is really used for. Sorry, I have to go," he said to Mike, then left.

Mike saw Sara standing by the van, holding aloft a paper bag and a red pie plate. He couldn't help smiling as it looked like she'd saved a lunch just for him.

That night they again had dinner with Joce and Luke, and they talked of the fair. When they got back to her apartment, Sara was yawning. "Sorry," she said, "but I've been on my feet all day and I'm worn out."

"I had no idea you could bake like that. What was in that apricot one?"

"I used Moscato d'Asti in the zabaglione," she said over her shoulder as she went to her bedroom. "See you in the morning."

Mike stood there blinking. She'd used an Italian dessert wine to make the creamy sauce. Since he'd met her, he'd had the impression that Sara knew little about cooking. True, Tess had sent him her apple bread, but that could have been the only thing she knew how to make. But from what he'd seen and tasted today, Sara could give the pastry chef at the five-star hotel where he'd worked undercover a run for his money.

The more he learned about Sara Shaw, the more he liked.

# 16

M IKE SPENT SATURDAY at a golf course in Williamsburg with
Sara's father, a retired doctor who was as laid-back as his wife
was hyper. He spoke of Sara with love in his voice, and Mike often
felt the man watching him.

It went against Mike's grain to throw any sports match, but he
didn't want to make Sara's father look bad. At the first tee, Mike
didn't make his best effort and the ball fell far short of the hole.

Dr. Henry Shaw looked at Mike in speculation. "The lower
your score, the better I'll speak about you to my youngest daughter."

Mike looked at the man for a moment, mumbled "another
matchmaker," then made a hole in one.

By the time they got back to the clubhouse, half a dozen men
were asking for games with him.

"What they need are lessons," Dr. Shaw said under his breath
and slapped Mike on the shoulder.

"So what about our deal?" Mike asked.

"I would have done that anyway. Luke said you were a natural athlete, and I wanted to see if it was true."

"Now I see where Sara got her love of conniving."

Dr. Shaw laughed heartily. "Don't tell her mother that. Ellie thinks Sara is the 'weak' one."

The two men had lunch together, and Mike was introduced to everyone as "Sara's friend." Not one person mentioned that Sara's wedding date—to another man—was soon approaching.

That night, Mike was to go on his date with Ariel Frazier.

"I'll cancel it if you want," he told Sara when he got back to the apartment.

"Why would I want that? Ariel is intelligent, well traveled, and she's beautiful. I'm sure you'll have a great time."

It was, of course, absurd, but Mike was disappointed when Sara didn't mind that he had a date with another woman. During the last few days, they'd come to . . . well, almost live together. They shared most meals, went nearly everywhere together, and people in Edilean seemed to consider them a couple.

"Are you sure?" Mike asked.

"Go on. Have a good time. I'll see what Joce is doing. Luke said he'd be busy writing, so Joce will be alone."

"If you're sure it's all right . . ."

"Go! Enjoy yourself."

As soon as Mike was out the door, Sara texted Joce:

DID I EVER MENTION THAT I HATE ARIEL FRAZIER?

Jocelyn replied with

MIKE WON'T LIKE HER. COME OVER AND WE'LL TALK ABOUT IT.

As Sara clicked off her phone, she tried to remember Greg's face. She could, but not clearly. And she had no pictures of him to remind her. One of Greg's former girlfriends had been a professional photographer, and he said she'd been so horrible to him that she'd turned him against ever again having his picture taken. When Sara thought of that now, she wondered if it was a true story.

Over the last few days not only Greg's face had faded from her mind but also the . . . well, the essence of him. All she seemed able to remember now was the work he piled on her and how he made her feel confused and inadequate.

Where was he? she wondered. And what was he doing? She still sent him messages now and then, but they no longer had the urgency they once did.

She knew it was all Mike's fault. He was easy, pleasant to be with—and when they weren't together, like tonight, she missed him.

She didn't want to think about it, but she did *not* miss Greg.

Sara left the apartment and went to see Joce to talk about the man who'd taken over her life.

From the first moment Mike had seen Ariel Frazier in her car at Edilean Manor, he knew he wasn't interested in her. Her diamond earrings and three gold bracelets had reminded him too much of the women in his past. Besides, in that first glance, he'd recognized Ariel's aggression and her self-sufficiency.

Now, she was sitting at the bar of what posed for a country club in Edilean, wearing black trousers, a green top, and high heels that probably cost as much as his last month's salary. There were at least four men eyeing her and trying to decide when to make a move.

In other circumstances, meaning before he'd met Sara, Mike would have been pleased to see such a woman waiting for him. But now, he thought she looked gaudy and overly made up.

When he looked at her eyes, he saw amusement in them and understood that she knew what he was thinking. He went to stand beside her at the bar and gave two of the men watching her looks to get lost. Only then did he turn back to Ariel. She really was quite beautiful. There was no need to introduce themselves, so they didn't.

When the maître d' told them their table was waiting, Mike stepped back to allow Ariel to go ahead of him. When they were seated, she didn't open her menu. "I'll have the ceviche, then the trout," she told the waiter.

"Same here," Mike said, and their menus were taken away.

As soon as they were alone, Ariel said, "You've fallen under Sara's spell, haven't you?"

"I'm not sure what that means, but, yes, I do like her."

The waiter poured white wine into Mike's glass. After he'd tasted it and nodded, the waiter filled Ariel's glass.

When they were alone, Mike said, "So you're about to become a doctor?"

"Now why is it that I think you have no interest in what *I* do? My guess is that you accepted this date so you could find out more about Sara. Am I right?"

She was correct; Mike did want to know what she knew, but he said nothing. It was his experience that people always filled up silence.

"Everyone in town knows what you're doing," Ariel said, then paused to take a sip of wine. "You're trying to win Sara away from her fiancé."

Mike didn't show it when he let out a breath of relief. For a moment he'd thought she—and maybe the entire town—knew about the case.

"Did Sara tell you that in school she and I were rivals?" Ariel didn't wait for him to answer. "She was always surrounded by boys asking her out, wanting to study with her, whatever, but she wouldn't let them get near. It drove the boys mad. As for me, it was always 'Hey, Ariel, wanta play baseball?' or 'Ariel, grab the other end of the picnic table and help me carry it.'

"I couldn't wait to get out of this town and away from my over-protective father and brothers. I wanted to go someplace where men saw me as female, not as 'one of the Fraziers.'"

Mike felt a sense of déjà vu, that he was back on one of his cases. Ariel Frazier had everything going for her, but she was still whining about what had happened to her in high school.

"It's not working, is it?"

"And what's that?" Mike's voice was cool.

"The 'poor little me' act."

"Not at all."

"Well, good," she said as she reached into the bread basket. "If I can't impress you, then we'll have to be friends. And that means I don't have to play the dainty lady. How about some butter?"

Mike's smile was genuine. "Good idea."

"So what do you want to know about dear little Sara?"

Mike gave her a look that said "cut it out" and Ariel laughed.

"Tell me about her first boyfriend," Mike said as their food was served. "Brian something."

"Never met him." Ariel bit into a piece of heavily buttered bread.

"It's my guess that you remember every word you've ever heard about Sara. Right?"

Ariel smiled. "You got me there. His name is Brian Tolworthy, and he's an archaeologist. Just like in some fairy tale, Sara went to Williamsburg and came home with a gorgeous Englishman. And of course he was to inherit the obligatory Big House and a fortune with it. Sara would have been Lady Tolworthy. I remember the name because when I came home at Christmas it's all my mother could talk about. I was entering med school, but all she wanted was for me to get married and have babies like perfect little Sara was going to do. Sorry. Sara Shaw is a sore point with me."

"So why didn't she marry him?"

"This town is saying that Tess and Luke conspired to get you and Sara together. Is that true?"

"This town talks too much. Why didn't Sara marry the English guy?"

Ariel's face changed to more serious. "I wasn't here, but my mother wrote me that he received a call in the middle of the night. Someone said his parents had been killed in a car crash. Sara drove him to the airport and—" Ariel shrugged. "I heard that she never saw him again. My mother wrote me a couple of months later that Sara had received a letter saying he was marrying his childhood sweetheart back in England." She looked at him. "If you're living with Sara, why aren't you asking her about all this?"

Mike was experienced at ignoring questions he didn't want to answer. "So then what happened?"

"What happens to all the Princess Saras of the world? Another man showed up right away."

"Anders."

"Yeah. Greg Anders." Ariel gave a little smile. "Do you know him?"

"Never met him, but I've heard a lot about him."

"He likes to cause problems." Her smile broadened and she gave a little laugh under her breath.

"It sounds like *you* know him."

"Every half-decent-looking woman in this town—who isn't likely to tell Sara, that is—has had an encounter with him. My brother Colin told me that Sara couldn't be getting much in bed in the last few months because he's been too busy jumping on Erica at the store—and with two of his clients. He seems to like older women."

Mike thought about what he'd read in the files. Stefan's marriage was one of those arranged deals so favored by his family. When he was sixteen, he was married off to a thirty-four-year-old widow. Stefan's son was now eighteen and his daughter seventeen—and he had a stepson born the same year he was. But for all the age discrepancy, the marriage had worked. Everyone knew that Stefan genuinely loved his wife, who was a year older than his mother, but that didn't make him stay faithful to her. And, yes, their records showed that Stefan liked older women for his many affairs.

Ariel looked down at her plate for a moment. "I can't imagine how I must sound to you, but those old school yard rivalries die hard. In high school I had to work night and day to be included with the other kids. I was on the cheerleading squad and I put the yearbook together. You name it, I did it. But you know who won Best Liked? Sara. I don't think she had even one extracurricular activity."

Ariel was quiet for a moment. "So do you plan to take her away from Anders then go back to . . . Where is it you live?"

"South Florida."

"So you two will live in a condo on a beach and deal with hurricanes every summer?"

"Only people who don't live there worry about hurricanes."

"That was a good nonanswer."

"And the best one I have. You ready to go?"

"In a hurry to get back to Sara?"

Mike started to make a noncommital reply, but instead, the truth came out. "Yes."

"I envy her."

Mike paid, and they left the restaurant. Mike made sure Ariel got into her car safely, then he called Tess and asked her to find out anything she could about Brian Tolworthy of England.

"Can I send him hate mail?"

"You knew him?"

"Of course. We all thought he was going to marry Sara, but then he dropped her in a really rotten way. I wanted to go to England and kick him, or better yet, to send you to beat him up. I wrote you all about it."

"Did you? I can't remember every dumped-on girl you wrote me about. Could you find out everything you can about him now? Tell the captain to send me any stats he can find and to call the police in England. Tell them to send someone out to talk to Tolworthy—and take a tape recorder. I want to hear the bastard's side of what he did to Sara."

Tess was silent for a moment. "You think Greg had something to do with this, don't you? I can hear it in your voice. Do you think maybe he threatened Brian and made him leave? I know Greg showed up in town not long after Brian left, and we've all thought Sara latched on to Greg on the rebound. She seemed to want to prove to us, and herself, that she could get a man and keep him."

"And you didn't think to tell me all this?"

"I *did* tell you!" Tess yelled. "I told you every word of it!"

"You probably did," Mike said calmly, "but I forgot. Find out everything, will you?"

Tess regained her calm. "How are the tarot cards coming?"

"I haven't seen them. Can you get it spread around town that Joce is going to tell fortunes with a very unusual deck of gypsy cards?"

"Sure. Easy. I'll call one person, and three hours later, everyone in town will know. Mike, Joce won't be in any danger, will she?"

"No, but I hope a deck or two of cards disappears. We're making a curtain that can be drawn, so Joce can look away when customers of the right age show up. If Mitzi is here, we hope she'll pocket an unopened deck. And one of Luke's cousins is installing a camera system so we can record everything that goes on in the tent."

"Which one?" Tess asked.

"The cameras are made by—"

"No, you idiot! Which cousin is setting up the camera system?"

"How the hell would I know? Everyone I've met is a cousin or aunt or whatever to Sara."

"So how'd you like Ariel? Too much of a good thing, right?"

His sister didn't fool him; he knew exactly what she wanted to know. "She's a hag compared to you."

"Yeah?"

"Good night, baby sister."

"Good morning, big bro."

When Mike got back to the apartment, he was glad Sara was in bed. He'd again brought in some files to go over, searching to see what he'd missed.

Hours later, Mike closed the files and tucked them under the mattress. No matter how many times he read about what Mitzi had done, it still shocked him. That such crimes could go undetected and unpunished for so very long—generations—made him sick.

It was six A.M. when he turned off the light and for all that he'd found out, he still had no idea why the Vandlos were after Sara.

# 17

ON SUNDAY MORNING, Sara told Mike through his closed bedroom door that he *had* to get out of bed and get dressed to go to church.

"Go away," he said, sounding like he had a pillow over his head.

"I'm not leaving without you. You get up every morning before daylight to go to the gym. It's after nine A.M. now, so you can get out of bed to go to *church*." She waited but heard nothing. Quietly, she turned the knob and went into the room. It was so dark that Sara guessed Tess had had a thick interlining put in the curtains. In anticipation of her brother visiting? Sara wondered.

Tiptoeing, she went to the window, threw back the curtains, and sunlight flooded the room. She turned at Mike's groan. All she could see of him was one bare arm holding the pillow over his head.

"Get up, Mr. Sleepy. It's time to go."

"Edilean . . ."

She couldn't understand what he'd said, so she lifted the corner of the pillow, but Mike pulled it back down. "Did you say a naughty word on the Lord's Day?"

Mike turned his head away and didn't release the pillow.

"Michael Newland!" Sara said, her hands at her waist. "You *must* get out of bed. I'm not facing church alone. Everyone will drive me insane with questions about you. You can—Oh!" she squealed as Mike's hand shot out and pulled her off balance. She fell forward, her hands out. When they touched the bed, Mike swiped his hand across her wrists so she landed facedown on the bed, her feet still on the floor.

"Good. Quiet," he said, sounding more like Tarzan than ever.

Sara pulled herself upright. "Brute strength will get you nowhere. I said get up and I mean it!" She grabbed the quilt and threw it back. Mike didn't move so much as a muscle—which was unusual, since it seemed that he slept in the nude.

For a long moment Sara stood there looking at him, her eyes wide. *"Then I take it he has his clothes on,"* Tess had said that first night, and now she knew what his sister meant.

Mike's body was magnificent. He could have modeled for a Grecian statue of an athlete. His wide shoulders tapered down to a narrow waist, and even lying absolutely still as he was, she could see the deep muscles on his back. There were mounds and valleys that she very much wanted to touch.

Below his waist, his round, firm buttocks were perfectly shaped above legs that curved down to the back of his knees.

"Cold," he murmured.

"Wh . . . what?" Sara asked but the word came out in a croak. "What?"

"I'm cold. If you're through examining me, doc, put the cover back."

Sara swallowed and took a breath. Heaven help her but she

wanted to skip church, forget about her promise of marriage, and climb into bed with this Adonis.

Instead, she got herself under control. "Inspect you, ha! I've seen the Frazier boys stark naked, and you're not even a close second." As she went to his closet to pull out his only suit, she didn't add that the boys had been in preschool and she was little more than a baby. "If you can stop showing off, you have thirty minutes to shave and dress."

When she heard movement behind her, she didn't look back because she knew Mike had turned over. She'd resisted him once this morning but she didn't think she could do it a second time. Besides, she didn't know if he'd pulled the cover over the lower front of him.

"Thirty minutes," she repeated as she left the room, shutting the door behind her.

A minute later, she was running out the back door to go to her own apartment. She was dressed for church, but once she was inside, she began to remove her clothing and toss it on the floor. She was happy to see that Luke had put in a new toilet, but that wasn't her objective. She quickly got into the shower and turned the cold water on full blast. If she'd had time, she would have filled the tub with ice and jumped in.

She ran the shower as long as her ecologically minded conscience could stand, then turned it off. She was covered in goose bumps, but they didn't remove the images in her mind. Mike naked, facedown on the bed. His muscular arms, legs . . . his *back*! The valleys of muscles in his back were deep enough to plant seeds in.

Sara stood there, dripping, and put her hands over her face. She did *not* want to be one of Mike's women who he took to bed in order to win a case. She didn't want—

"The hell I don't!" she muttered as she wrapped a towel around her bare body.

She looked in the mirror at her red cheeks, and her lips were nearly blue from the cold shower. She'd been to bed with only two men in her life. All through school she'd saved herself for love, and ten minutes after she met Brian, she knew they were going to get married. She'd had no idea of his aristocratic origins or the money and property he was to inherit, she just knew that he was perfect for her.

But he had left her, and Greg had taken his place. Greg was as different as it was possible to be from Brian. Brian was gentle and sweet and loved to sit back and let Sara run their lives. His interest was in archaeology, so Sara made it possible for him to study and write. She took care of his food and clothes and their social life. The first time Sara met his parents, she saw that they were just like her and Brian. His mother ran everything, while Brian's father piddled on a book he hadn't completed in twenty-three years.

To Sara, she and Brian had been perfectly suited, but when she'd received the letter from him saying sorry, I'm marrying someone else, it was as though her entire foundation was destroyed. In one typed letter, the future she'd been so sure of had disappeared. For weeks, she couldn't see clearly. If it hadn't been for her mother forcing her to work at the grocery, Sara would have stayed in bed and cried.

She'd started getting her life back together and was doing a great job of pretending that she'd never been in love and that her heart hadn't been broken, when Joce arrived in town. Soon afterward Sara'd been introduced to Greg. That he was wildly different from Brian pleased her. Maybe if she followed a man rather than led, she'd do better. Sometimes, she was glad that the townspeople of Edilean disliked Greg. It repaid them for all the looks of pity they'd given her after Brian had so coldly left her. "She gave up everything," she'd heard two women in the drugstore say. "She even gave up her career for that young man and he dropped her flat."

Sara pulled a garment from her closet and realized how good it felt to be in her own home. She took out a freshly ironed dress of dotted Swiss—her mother'd said, "Sara, you're the only female on earth who still wears that fabric"—and put it on.

After a couple of deep breaths to regain her courage, she went outside. Mike, wearing a suit and tie—and marvel of all, shaved clean—was sitting at the iron table, reading the Sunday newspaper and drinking coffee.

"Where have you been?" he asked without looking up. "Church is probably over by now."

"They don't start until I get there. It's in the bylaws."

Chuckling, Mike folded the paper, put it on the table, and looked at her. "So why did you change clothes?"

"You had a pillow over your head. How did you see what I was wearing?"

"I saw everything." The dimple in his cheek showed.

Sara refused to let him know how the sight of him naked had affected her; she stared right back at him. "My car or yours?"

Mike snorted at the question, and they walked together to his car where he opened the door for her. "I like that thing you have on."

She slid onto a cream-colored leather seat. "I like your clothes too."

"Just so I have on something, right?"

"Either way, it makes no difference to me." She looked out the window to conceal her red face. Were lies told on a Sunday worse than other fibs?

When they got to Edilean Baptist Church, they were over-whelmed by people. The few in town who hadn't met Mike were clamoring to talk to him. When Sara was nearly pulled away, Mike reached out and took her hand, and she heard about five women draw in their breaths. In a short time Sara was to be married in this very church, but not to the man whose fingers were entwined with hers.

Sara knew she should let go, but she didn't. Mike's skin was warm and it made her feel safe. And, besides, his hand was attached to *that* body. Again, the images of him nude on the bed, the sunlight on his skin, flooded her mind.

As though he could read her thoughts, Mike looked away from her uncle James for a moment and their eyes held. Sara felt such a rush of lust run through her that she made a silent prayer for forgiveness. She should not be thinking such thoughts while in church.

She and Mike sat next to each other, and she was pleased to see that he knew all the words to the songs. As the sermon started, she looked at him in question.

"Never missed a service when I was a kid," he whispered. "Gramps saw to that."

Smiling, she turned her attention to the pastor.

# 18

AFTER A LAZY afternoon with Sara, it seemed like a perfect ending to the day when Mike's cell rang at four and he saw that it was Tess. He went outside to the big tree to take the call, hoping she'd found out something about Brian Tolworthy.

"Hey, little sis," Mike said. "Told the old man about the baby yet?"

"No, she hasn't." It was Ramsey, and his voice sounded as though something horrible had happened.

Instantly, Mike was so full of fear that his knees gave way under him and he collapsed onto the little iron chair. "How bad is it? Is she still alive?"

"Tess is fine. She's under sedation, but she's all right."

"The baby?"

"It's doing well. She hasn't told me about it yet, but I've spent too much time near my ever-pregnant sister not to know why Tess has been so tired. That isn't the problem. It's Sara."

"But she's here with me. And how would you know if—?"

"I wouldn't," Rams said in dismissal. "Tess remembered that she had Brian's number in her phone, so she called him at home in England."

"Yeah? So how's the bastard doing?"

"He's dead—but his parents are alive and well."

Mike felt his fear for the safety of the two women in his life leave him and he became professional again. "Tell me all of it."

"It looks like the call Brian received saying his parents had been killed was a lie. When he got back to England, the rental car he was driving from the airport was hit by a train. It was stalled on the track with no lights on. Tolworthy died instantly. His parents say they called Sara several times to tell her what happened, but there was no answer. They assumed Brian was coming home unexpectedly because he and Sara'd broken up and she didn't want to hear anything about him. They've always blamed her for his agitated state that probably caused the wreck."

When Ramsey stopped, there wasn't a sound from Mike. "Are you still there?"

"Yes. Tess took the news hard?"

"Very hard. She's scared for Sara and for you. Whoever's doing this means business, and it's obviously been a long time in planning."

"I'll take care of it."

"Can you get Sara away from this?"

"No," Mike said. "Wherever I take her, they'll follow."

"Couldn't you hide her?"

"For the rest of her life?" Mike said angrily. "If you want to help, figure out what she has that people are willing to kill to get."

"Greg—"

"If he marries her and she dies, he'll inherit whatever it is that she has. Sara's coming; I have to go. Fax what you have to Luke and think hard. And take care of Tess."

"I will. She—" Rams didn't say any more because Mike had hung up.

"Wow!" Sara said as she looked at Mike sitting on the iron chair. "You don't look well at all. Is Tess all right? Is the baby—?" She broke off at his look, then sat down across from him. "What's happened?"

"Nothing," he managed to say, his eyes searching her face. He had no doubt that the Vandlos had killed the man Sara was to marry. Then Stefan had shown up in town, and as Captain Erickson had said, Vandlo had used his "big-city razzle-dazzle" to woo a girl whose heart had been broken. It couldn't have been difficult, Mike thought. Sara still had no idea why the man she loved had dropped her, and Mike had seen enough of Edilean to know that the pity from everyone would have been enough to drive her mad. The Vandlos specialized in people, especially women, who were in pain.

"Mike," Sara said softly, "you're beginning to scare me."

His mind was racing. There was only one way to protect Sara and that was to take the focus off of her and put it on him. "Does Edilean have a mayor?"

"Yes, but what does that—?"

"Who is it?"

"Actually, it's my mother. She—"

Mike stood up. "Sara, I—" He didn't know what to say. "You have to trust me. Understand?"

"Sure. You're Tess's brother and—"

"No! Trust *me!* You have to know that I have your best interests in mind."

"Now I am frightened. Please tell me what's upset you so much."

"I don't have time now, but I'll tell you everything as soon as I can." As he hurried toward his car, he stopped and turned back. Sara was standing by the little table and looking after him in puzzlement—with fear in her eyes.

Turning, he went back to her, took her in his arms, and kissed her. It was a quick, hard kiss, and for a moment he held her so tightly she couldn't breathe. He put both hands on the side of her head, his nose to hers. "Trust me," he whispered. "You must trust me with your life."

He pulled away from her and smiled. "Put on something pretty," he said, then he ran to his car and quickly drove away.

Sara wasn't surprised when her cell rang less than a minute later. It was Joce.

"What in the world was *that* all about? I saw you guys out the window. I thought you two weren't . . . you know."

"We aren't, haven't," Sara said. "And I have no idea what's going on."

"Want to come in and talk about it?"

"Yeah, sure, but . . . No," Sara said. "I think I'm going to take a long bath and use some of that super expensive shampoo and conditioner you gave me for my birthday."

"Now I'm intrigued. What did Mike say to cause this reaction?"

"It wasn't what he said but how he said it. I have to go."

"Keep me informed," Joce said and hung up.

Four hours later when Mike returned, Sara was clean and fresh, wearing a dress of white eyelet, and nervously looking through a magazine she'd already read.

"Sara?" Mike called, and she felt her heart give a little jump of pleasure.

When did that start happening? she wondered. "In here," she answered.

Mike came in and nearly fell onto the chair across from the couch where she was sitting. Sara thought he looked as though he'd aged ten years. When she started to get up, he said, "I need to tell you some things."

"I know. But first I'm getting you something to drink." She'd learned that Mike's workouts made him drink twice as much liquid as other people. "Replacing the sweat," he'd said.

He looked at her in gratitude, and minutes later, she returned with a tray she'd already prepared for him. There was a big glass of red currant iced tea and a large piece of raspberry crumble she'd made the day before. Mike emptied the glass in one long drink but set the pie aside.

"How bad is it?" she asked as she sat down across from him on the couch.

"I guess that's all in how you look at it. I have some . . . some truly awful things to tell you."

Sara's hand went to her throat. "Someone's been hurt."

"No," Mike said. "At least not recently."

With a sigh of relief, Sara fell back against the couch. "You have something to tell me about Greg, don't you?"

"Yes."

"It's okay. I've already decided to call the wedding off."

"And when did you decide that?"

She wanted to say "this minute," but didn't. Instead, she shrugged. "When I realized I was hoping he'd never return, I knew I couldn't go through with it. My life is much more pleasant when he's not here." Sara was hoping Mike would be glad of that, but his face didn't lose its look of worry. "You can tell me," she said. "Whatever it is, I can take it."

He wished he had the time to tell her everything slowly, but it had all become urgent. He took a deep breath. "Brian Tolworthy didn't marry someone else. He died right after he got to England."

In the hours she'd been waiting for Mike's return, she'd imagined a lot of things, but this was not one of them. "Brian is dead?" she whispered. "But his parents . . ."

"Are still alive. And they've wondered why you never responded to their attempts to contact you to tell you about Brian." That was as kind as he could put it.

"But I didn't receive anything, not a call, nothing! And I called Brian a hundred times, but he never picked up." When Mike was silent, Sara let out her breath.

"There's more, isn't there?"

"We don't think his death was an accident."

"Not an accident? It wasn't suicide, was it?" The look on Mike's face answered that question. "Are you talking about *murder*?"

"Yes," Mike said softly, his eyes boring into hers.

For a moment, Sara could do nothing but look at him, and when what he was trying to tell her hit her, she almost couldn't breathe. "You think he was murdered because of me, don't you?" she whispered.

Mike said nothing, just kept looking at her, and his eyes confirmed what she'd said.

"I don't understand." Tears began to roll down her cheeks. She wasn't sobbing, her face wasn't wrinkled, but tears were gliding down her cheeks. "His poor parents. They loved Brian so much, and he was to inherit and—"

Mike left the chair to sit on the couch and pull her into his arms. As they had before, her tears wet the front of his shirt. He handed her tissues.

After a while, she pulled away and blew her nose. "I'm always crying on you. How did you find out about Brian?"

"I asked Tess to do some research on him and she called his home in England. Brian's mother answered the phone."

"Oh, Brian," she said. "He was such a sweet man. I thought—"

"That you two were going to get married and live in England."

"Yes, I did." She wiped her eyes.

"Sara, I have more to tell you."

She saw the seriousness on his face. "This is the part about Greg?"

"Yes. He's Mitzi Vandlo's son."

For a moment Sara's head seemed to reel. "The son of the criminal? The one so many people are searching for?" Her voice was rising. "Did he . . . Do you think Greg . . . that Greg murdered Brian to get to *me?*"

Mike took Sara's hand and held it firmly in his own. "Sara, you must stay calm. You can't panic."

"My second boyfriend probably killed my first boyfriend and you want me to be *calm?*"

"Yes," Mike said firmly.

Sara jerked her hand from his and stood up. "That bastard! Do you have any idea how much I put up with from him? He flirted with every woman who had a dollar in her hand. Platinum American Express cards nearly gave him an orgasm."

Mike had to bite his lips to keep from smiling, and the dimple in his cheek was an inch deep.

"One time a woman had one of those black AmEx cards, and I thought I was going to have to call an ambulance." She glared at Mike. "And you know *why* I put up with his crap?"

"I truly have no idea."

"That's because *you* have never been thrown onto the rubbish heap by anyone."

"Well, actually—"

"Women going to jail don't count. But *I* was dropped flat by a man I genuinely loved. I had saved myself all through high school. Boys were groping me, sweaty hands were all over me, but I held out for 'true love.'"

Mike watched her as she paced the room, her anger making her face bright—and he was glad of it. Anger was easier to cope with than grief.

Suddenly, her anger left her and she sat down hard on Tess's armchair. "Brian, Brian, Brian," she whispered. "Why didn't I believe in you more?"

For a moment she put her hands over her face, and even though Mike saw her shoulders heaving as she cried, he didn't go to her. He had more to tell her, and he was dreading doing so.

She looked back at him. "It was that movie, the one with Meg Ryan making a fool of herself."

He looked at her blankly.

"When Meg Ryan's fiancé dropped her, she ran after him to France and made a laughingstock of herself. After I received that hideous letter from Brian telling me he was going to marry someone else, I decided I had more pride than that. I wasn't going after him. And I wouldn't let him and his family see how much I'd been hurt. It was bad enough being the pathetic loser here in Edilean, but to go to another country . . ."

She looked back at Mike. "If only I had gone. If only—"

"You can't do that," Mike said sternly. "You can't even think of blaming yourself. You're innocent in all this."

Sara fell back in the chair, her hands gripping the arms. "You have something else to tell me, don't you?"

"Yes, but . . ."

"It couldn't be worse than what you've already said."

"Depends on how you look at it."

She waited, but he said nothing. "Mike?"

"Yeah, okay, I'm getting around to it. Just give me time." He took a breath. "Look, Sara, what I'd like to do is send you into hiding, but I can't do that. You're at the center of whatever the Vandlos want. We think Stefan—"

"That's Greg?"

"Yes. We think he divorced his wife so his marriage to you would be legal."

"Wife?" Sara said. "Does he have children?" She held up her hand before Mike could speak. "No, don't tell me. I don't want to hear the extent of my blind stupidity."

"You aren't stupid. The Vandlos have been cheating people for centuries."

"Great. I'm historically dumb."

Mike's eyes showed his amusement.

"I take it they planned to do away with me after the marriage."

"We think so," Mike said. It was too late to sugarcoat the truth. "And Stefan would inherit whatever you have that only he knows about. *We* certainly don't."

Sara's face lit up. "That's why he made the people of Edilean hate him. He planned to use their dislike of him as an excuse to take me away from here so he could . . . so he could murder me."

"Yes," Mike said softly, "that's just what we think he aimed to do."

Sara was quiet for a moment, her hand at her throat. "So why did he want Merlin's Farm?"

"Good question," Mike said. "But it could be as simple as Vandlo getting angry at Lang about something, then wanting revenge."

"Greg did kill the dogs, didn't he?"

"Probably. Sara, there's more. I've spent the last hours doing a lot of planning. I talked with my captain and I also made some arrangements with your parents."

"My parents?" Again, she waved her hand. "Don't let me interrupt you. Tell me what your plan is."

"I need to do whatever is necessary to take the Vandlos' attention off of you and put it on me."

"What does that mean? You go in shooting?"

"That was my first choice." He was watching her intently. "But they have relatives, so if I shoot them, more Vandlos will come after you in their place. Sara," he said slowly, then stopped.

"You're frightening me again. What horrible thing do you want me to do?"

"Marry me," he said simply.

"What?"

"If you marry me, then the Vandlos will have to kill *me* before they can get to you."

"Oh," Sara said. "Oh."

Mike felt his ego deflate by half, but then he wondered what he'd expected, that she'd run to him and say she *wanted* to marry him? He got himself back under control.

"I want you to marry me in secret. Now. Tonight. Tomorrow morning I have to return to Fort Lauderdale, and until Vandlo gets back I don't want anyone here to know we're married. I'll return for the fair, then I plan to let everyone know that you're no longer free to marry someone else."

When she said nothing, just sat there and stared at him, he continued. "Sara, don't worry. You don't have to stay married to me, and in the meantime, we can keep living separately just as we've done. We can arrange living any way you want, but I want it legal between us. If Vandlo gets whatever you have, he'll have to take me out first."

"I . . ." She didn't know what to say.

"It'll be all right, I promise. As for the marriage ceremony itself, it's all been set up with your parents."

"My parents? I think I'm old enough—"

"That's not what I meant. Your mother is the mayor, and people owe her favors. Tonight she called them in and got a license for us on a Sunday night. Are you ready to go?"

Sara couldn't think of anything to say. There was too much in her mind for her to comprehend. Brian, sweet, dear Brian killed because of *her*. And Greg—The truth was that she wasn't surprised to hear that he was a criminal. Over the months they'd known each other, she'd looked away from the many underhanded things he did.

Silently, she followed Mike to the car. It was the early evening on an ordinary Sunday night and she couldn't make herself realize that she was on the way to her wedding.

When Mike got in beside her, she looked at him. She'd known him for only eight days, but it didn't feel that way. She thought of when they'd hidden in a tree together, of baking for him, of watching him walk along the top of a pavilion. He'd walked across rafters like he was a circus performer and Sara's heart had pounded in fear. She thought of his date with Ariel. When she'd seen Ariel in church, she'd wanted to throw spitballs into her glossy red hair, as she'd done when they were children.

Mike pulled out of the driveway. "Sara, I'm sorry about this. I know you wanted your wedding to be in front of the whole town and—"

"No, I didn't. That was Greg's idea. I wanted it to be in Edilean Manor with Luke and Rams, and Joce and Tess there. And my parents. I didn't even want my sisters to come. It was Greg who wanted a big wedding and he insisted that *all* the shop clients be invited."

"And one of them probably would have been his mother," Mike said.

"I guess so . . ."

Mike pulled his cell phone out of his pocket and handed it to her. "Call Luke, wake them up, and tell them we're on our way to get married in their old house."

Sara couldn't help the little wave of joy that ran through her. "Really?"

He smiled at her. "I can't give you everything you want—and deserve—but I can give you the wedding you'd like to have. Minus the correct groom, of course."

Sara didn't reply to his last remark. There were too many other things on her mind. "Did you tell Tess?"

"Yes." He didn't want to burden Sara with more than she'd had piled on her tonight, but Mike had spent twenty minutes calming Tess down. She was nearly hysterical with fear that both Mike and Sara were going to be killed.

"What did Tess say?"

"That if she were here, she'd have Rams draw up a contract saying that if you and I divorce, you get Merlin's Farm."

Sara managed a smile. And she remembered the way Tess had protected her from Greg's greed. How she missed her friend! But Sara's mind was too full to feel much else. On top of the horror of finding out the truth about Brian and about the man she'd almost married, was how close she'd come to being murdered. And now she was at last getting married, not because of love, but to save her own life. Mike's marriage proposal had talked of secrecy and living separately, and of not staying married. She'd never imagined words so cold.

When they reached her parents' house, Dr. Shaw was outside,

waiting for them. He put his arm around his daughter's shoulders and led her inside.

Mike stood outside in the dark. "Okay, Newland," he said aloud. "Straighten up and be strong. You're about to get *married.*"

Mike waited for the shudder to come, but it didn't. The truth was, he wanted to get this done with before Sara came to her senses and told him to get lost.

# 19

BY THE TIME they got into the house, Sara's sober mood began to leave her. By rights she knew she should be miserable. She'd just found out about Brian's death and that Greg wanted to murder her. To further complicate things, she was marrying a man she'd known for only a few days and the marriage would probably end in divorce.

All in all, she knew she should be sad, but she wasn't. Instead, she looked at Mike and felt warmth spread through her. It didn't make sense, but what she was doing felt *right*.

"Where's Mom?" Sara asked her father.

"Already at Edilean Manor. After Mike's call, she went into action—and you know what that means."

"Orders," Sara said.

"Exactly. She said you're to put on Lissie's dress here and I'm to drive you to Luke's house."

When Sara and her father turned to look at Mike, he didn't know what they wanted. "Oh. Right. I'll meet you there. Sara—"

She couldn't bear hearing another apology. "Go! Get your suit on and meet me at the house. And remember . . ."

"What?"

"If you chicken out I'll be obliged to marry Greg."

Mike smiled at her. "Yeah. Good. Okay." He couldn't seem to make a complete sentence. He went to his car, and minutes later he was outside Edilean Manor. The house was ablaze with light and he could hear voices inside.

Luke threw open the front door, a glass of champagne in his hand. "I have a houseful of excited women. Well, really only two women, but they're making enough noise that it sounds like New Year's Eve."

"Luke!" Sara's mother called. "We need you."

"I suggest you slip over to Tess's house to change. I'll come and get you when it's time. Okay if I'm your best man?" When Mike nodded, Luke said, "If you come in here, they'll put you to work."

"Doing what?" he asked, but Luke had already shut the door.

Mike went to his sister's apartment, showered, shaved, and dressed.

In his pocket were two new platinum wedding bands that Sara's mother had given him when he'd gone to them to arrange the marriage. He'd thought they would protest his outrageous plan, but they hadn't. Mike had told them that Greg was a criminal and he wanted something from Sara that he could only get by marrying her. To Mike's surprise, neither of them had questioned his story. Ellie said, "What can we do to help?" When Mike told them *he* wanted to marry Sara that night, he'd hardly finished the sentence before Ellie went into action. As for Dr. Shaw, for a second there were tears in his eyes, then he jumped up and went to work helping his wife make arrangements.

"From Kimberly?" Mike had asked when she'd handed the rings to her. "No questions asked?"

Ellie smiled. "You fit into Edilean very well," she said as she left the room.

"You've done it now, boy," Dr. Shaw said. "Once they accept you, they don't ever let you leave this town." He made sounds of eerie music.

"I heard that," Ellie called from down the hall.

Now, in Tess's apartment and dressing for his wedding, surprisingly, Mike felt good. As he waited for Luke to come and get him, he again called Tess. Her pills hadn't worn off, and combined with the hormones of pregnancy and having just told Rams about the baby, she did little but cry.

"I wish I were there," she kept saying. "I wanted to see you get married. And Sara . . ."

Rams took the phone and asked Mike to let Tess listen to the ceremony.

"Of course," Mike said, then looked up to see Luke in the doorway. It was time. He followed Luke to the main part of the big, old house.

Mike was shocked at the sheer quantity of flowers that draped the entrance of the house.

"They're for a wedding that's to happen tomorrow," Luke said from beside him. "We figure no one will know if the flowers spend a few hours here." They were standing in front of the big parlor fireplace, which had been made into an altar, with an archway of roses and ferns. Big bouquets of white roses with blue ribbons dangling from them made a pathway through the room.

"Nervous?" Luke asked.

Mike nodded. "I was calmer that time I faced two men with automatic rifles."

"We really need to talk about your life. How'd you get out of that one?"

"Knives. I always carry—" He stopped talking because music began to play over a stereo system, and Luke hurried back down the aisle. Moments later he reappeared with his hugely pregnant wife in a wheelchair.

There were only three couples there, just six people, but the music and the flowers and the beautiful house made it feel like a true ceremony.

When the wedding march began to play and Sara appeared in the doorway on the arm of her father, Mike knew he'd never seen anyone so beautiful in his life. Her dress was of lace over satin, very old-fashioned-looking, and fit her perfectly, smoothing down over her hips to flow out gently into a skirt. She had on a traditional veil that covered her face, and Mike couldn't help feeling pleased that he'd get to lift it. It almost made the wedding seem real.

When she reached the little altar, Dr. Shaw gave Sara's hand to Mike and he squeezed it. Under the veil, he could see her smile.

Beside them, Luke dialed Tess and Rams to let them hear everything over the speakerphone.

Mike and Sara turned to her mother, who stood there in a long white robe, a Bible in her hands. When she'd told Mike she was ordained to conduct wedding ceremonies, he hadn't been surprised.

Now, Ellie's eyes were red, and her nose swollen from crying.

"Dearly beloved," she began, then had to stop to blow her nose. "We are gathered here today—" She stopped again because her tears were dripping.

"Daddy!" Sara hissed at her father, who was standing behind Joce in her wheelchair.

Chuckling, Dr. Shaw went to help his wife get through the ceremony.

When Mike slipped a ring on her finger, Sara looked at him in surprise, and when he handed her a ring for him, there was a smile of gratitude on her face.

Given his background, Mike had thought he'd hesitate over the promises he was to make to Sara. But he didn't. He answered the questions and made the vows without so much as a pause.

Sara said everything with so much happiness in her voice that he could almost believe what she was saying.

"I now pronounce you—" Ellie began, but dissolved into tears so copious that she couldn't speak.

"Really, Mother!" Sara said.

Dr. Shaw pronounced them man and wife, and Ellie nodded in agreement. "You may kiss her now, son," he said to Mike.

Smiling, Mike lifted Sara's veil and looked at her beautiful face. Gently, he took her in his arms and kissed her—and flashbulbs went off.

Laughing, blinking, they broke apart and smiled for all four cameras that were aimed at them.

"Cake," Dr. Shaw said. "I demand cake and champagne."

In the dining room were more flowers and in the center was a three-tiered wedding cake with white icing and about a hundred roses in different shades of pink. It was an extraordinary creation.

Dr. Shaw raised his glass. "To the Whitley-Cooper wedding in gratitude for the flowers and cake that they gave us." He lowered his voice. "And may the Lord be with us tomorrow when the bride is told that her cake was eaten during the night."

Luke was the first to laugh, and the others joined him—but they all knew that Ellie would spend the rest of the night remaking the cake. She would never let a bride under her care go without.

They insisted that Mike and Sara feed each other while they snapped more pictures.

Thirty minutes later, Luke told Mike that Joce was exhausted. "And if we're to keep this wedding a secret, we have to clear all this stuff out before dawn."

"Yeah, sure," Mike said and glanced at Sara. She was dancing with her father, her head on his shoulder, and he didn't want to break them up.

But minutes later, the music stopped and Sara looked at Mike. He nodded. It was time to leave.

As Mike and Sara stood in the doorway, Ellie started crying again as she kissed her daughter and slipped something into her hand.

"She thought I'd never catch a man," Sara said under her breath to Mike as they kissed everyone good-bye, but Mike knew that Ellie's tears were from relief that her daughter wasn't going to marry Greg. She'd always felt there was more wrong with the man than just a bad temper.

Once they were outside, the cool night air felt good. He was glad when the others stayed inside and left them alone. Mike started to go to Tess's apartment, but Sara turned toward her own and he followed her.

"So what did your mother give you?"

Sara held up a small bottle to the moonlight. "Scarlet Nights perfume. I told her you liked it."

"Wasted on us," Mike said as he opened the door to Sara's apartment.

"What does that mean?" She went in ahead of him, and he shut the door behind them.

"Nothing." He yawned. "I need to leave as early as possible in the morning." He looked at his watch, then smiled at Sara. "It's been a long day." Bending, he kissed her cheek and turned toward the guest bedroom.

From behind him, Sara said, "I don't get a wedding night?"

Mike stopped in the hallway, but he didn't turn around.

"What is it about me that men don't like?"

Mike turned to look at her. "Men like you too much."

Sara lifted her hands in frustration as she went into the kitchen. "Do you know how long I knew Brian before he made love to me? Six months. We dated for four whole years, but he didn't ask me to marry him. Then Greg came along and he talked about nothing but marriage and our fabulous future together. Today I found out that he was actually plotting my death.

"So now I'm *married* to some gorgeous hunk who seems to have slept with half the universe but he won't touch *me*." She glared at Mike. "What happened to real *men*?" Angry, she turned to go to her bedroom.

Mike caught her arm before she took a step and for a moment he looked into her eyes.

Sara tried to jerk away from him, but he held fast and pulled her to him with a jolt that almost knocked the breath out of her.

Mike had kissed her before, but they'd always been sedate kisses, chaste and pure. But not now. His mouth opened over hers and his tongue assaulted hers with a force that nearly made Sara collapse. Her mind was full of the sight of his body and she wanted to touch it, to run her mouth over every inch of it.

Mike seemed to be thinking the same thing as he reached for the shoulder of her wedding gown.

"Tear it and I'll never forgive you," she murmured, her lips on his cheek.

"You've dealt with too many boys," Mike said and two minutes later her dress fell to her feet. She couldn't imagine how he'd so quickly and deftly unfastened all the satin buttons down the back.

When Mike saw her without the dress, he drew in his breath. Joce had overseen Sara's undergarments, so she wore a pale pink corset of silk and lace, and a garter belt with pink hose that reached to midthigh. Her white heels were at least four inches tall.

"Sara," he whispered, and for the first time she saw his face without its guarded expression. He wore a look of desire so strong that Sara felt her body grow weak.

In the next second, Mike waved his arm across the little kitchen table and everything on it went flying. He lifted Sara up onto it, her long, slim legs, still in the stockings, hanging down, while Mike ripped off his own clothes. As his skin was exposed, Sara's eyes widened. She'd seen his nude back, but the front of him was even better. He had strong pecs above a stomach that looked like a terrain map.

Reaching out, she put her hand on his warm skin and felt the rock hard contours while he removed his trousers and her underpants.

A moment later she saw that his chest wasn't the only part of him that was "rock hard." He entered her with all the pent-up desire he'd felt since he met her. And Sara clung to him, her mouth on his, searching, exploring. Her hands roamed over his body as she felt all the incredible muscle on him. She'd rarely seen bodies like his and certainly never touched one.

His low voice turned husky, and he told her how good she felt to him, how much he'd wanted her since the first. His voice and his lips excited her—all while he was sliding into her with long, deep, gentle strokes that gradually increased in strength and speed.

Sara's arms went back against the wall, her hands made into claws, as Mike moved harder and faster. Faster and harder.

"Okay, baby?" he asked, his lips on her ear.

All Sara could do was moan.

When Mike slipped his hands under her bottom and lifted her so he could go deeper, Sara would have screamed if he hadn't put his mouth over hers.

When she came, it was as though lava erupted from the center of her and flowed into her veins. Her whole body shook, and Mike held her to him, his arms around her as he also shuddered.

For Sara, she didn't think she could have walked if her life depended on it, so Mike slid her forward on the table, keeping them attached in their most vital areas, and wrapped her legs around his hips. She clung to him, their sweaty skin pressed together. He carried her to Sara's bedroom, where he dropped her onto her bed.

When he turned his back to her she came up on her elbows. "You aren't leaving, are you?"

Turning, he smiled at her. "I was thinking of filling your tub with hot, soapy water and a generous dose of Scarlet Nights. Suit you?"

"Oh, yes," Sara said. She lay back on the bed and listened to the water running and thought—She sat up. This was her wedding night, and the last thing she wanted to do was *think*.

She went to the bathroom and saw a naked Mike standing by the tub. His body was so beautiful that she just stood there and stared at him. She slowly looked from his toes, to his stomach, to his neck, to his lips. And when she got through she saw great evidence that he was ready for her again.

"What do you look like under all those clothes?" he asked in a voice that was little more than a growl.

"The best you've ever seen," she said with a smile.

"Yeah? Well, let's see."

When she stood near him, he sat on the edge of the tub and slowly, expertly, began to undress her. He unsnapped the garters and with kisses began to unroll her stockings. When he got to her foot, he lifted it, put it on his thigh, and massaged it. His hand went up her leg, and after a few caresses in the center, his hand moved to her other leg and removed that stocking.

She started to turn around so he could reach the back clasps of her corset but he pulled her onto his lap and entered her. Sara wanted to move her hips, but he held her down as his hands reached around the back of her, and in seconds the corset was on the floor.

He kissed her, still not letting her move her hips, while his hands caressed the sides of her breasts, his thumbs moving inward to stroke her nipples.

By the time he released her so she could move up and down, she was groaning. She put one foot in the tub with its warm water, the other on the floor. Again Mike's strong hands cupped her bottom as he helped her with her movements.

When she was near to peaking, he pulled her up, never breaking contact, and lay her down on the rug on the bathroom floor.

His thrusts were hard and fast, and went deep, deep within her. This time, she felt his climax as strong as her own.

Minutes later, they were in the tub together. Mike's back was against the far end, and Sara was leaning against him. She kept glancing at her ring and looking at what she could see of Mike. Two weeks ago all she'd known of him was that he was Tess's "mysterious brother." When she'd first seen him, he'd been coming up through her bedroom floor, and she'd been terrified.

Now she was married to this man. There'd been no mention of love, and if it hadn't been for her, she wouldn't even have had a wedding night.

What she wanted now was a honeymoon.

"Are you looking forward to going home for a week?"

Mike was soaping Sara's arms. He'd already poured perfume into her freshly washed hair and the scent was intoxicating. "No," he said absently.

"But you must want to see your friends."

"Yeah, I guess. Gym buddies and guys on the force."

"What about other people you don't work with? Just friend friends?"

Mike chuckled. "My life isn't like yours. I go away on undercover assignments that last for years. I've worked in LA twice and once in Iowa and—"

"Iowa?" She turned to look at him. "Surely they don't have crime in *Iowa*!"

Mike laughed at her joke. "Evil is everywhere, even in sweet little Edilean, Virginia."

Relaxing, she leaned back against him. "No friends, no place to live. It doesn't sound like a true home."

Mike kissed her earlobe. "I make do with eighty-degree winters and palm trees blowing in the breeze."

"And nightclubs with gorgeous Cuban girls?"

Mike nuzzled her neck. "I never noticed them."

"Mike, I was thinking. Maybe—"

"No."

"No to what?"

"No, you can't go with me to Fort Lauderdale."

"I didn't ask you if I could, but now that you mention it . . ."

"I have to work. I'll be at the office at seven and won't leave until ten at night. You don't realize how big this case is. The Feds are—"

"Did you tell them to get dogs for Mr. Lang?"

"Yes. I'll probably bring them back with me. They're Airedales."

"So you found a breeder?"

"It's Florida, so of course we found a breeder."

"Did I ever tell you I've never been to Florida? Joce grew up in Boca Raton and she's told me wonderful things about the place."

"No, you can't go," Mike repeated. "When I get back I need to let everyone in this town know that we're married. Luke said there are games at the fair, so I'll need to win them. That'll draw lots of attention to us. Then—"

"Ha!" Sara wasn't happy about being left behind. "The Fraziers always win the games. There's the cable toss, where you have to throw a telephone pole. I've seen Ariel's oldest brother, Colin, lift the front end of a pickup truck."

"Yeah? So where does he work out?"

"I don't know. Gyms have never been of interest to me."

Mike held up her arm, which was slim but had no discernible muscle. "I can see that."

"Are you saying that I'm—"

Mike kissed her to silence, his hand on her breast.

Sara leaned back against him.

"Are there any contests for skills of agility?" he asked.

"Like the rope jumping?" She was teasing him.

"I can do that," Mike said.

"You're outclassed there too. Anna Aldredge, Kim's little sister, will win that. She placed third in the national championships."

"Does she need a partner?"

"She's twelve and a brat."

"I like bratty females."

"I need time to tell you about all the events so maybe I should—"

"No," Mike said yet again.

"What if Greg shows up here while you're gone?"

"He can't, because he's under lock and key, and his cell mate is an FBI agent. Vandlo will be let out this coming weekend and we're sure he'll run here to Edilean—straight to you. By the time he gets here, everyone will know who I am, thanks to the games. I think we should wait until Vandlo is here to announce the marriage. How do you feel about kissing in public?"

"With whom?"

Mike was nuzzling the back of her neck. "Who do you want to kiss?"

Turning, she put her arms around his neck. "Mike, we're married but we hardly know each other. I'd like to see where you've spent most of your life and to meet your friends."

"And to go to the gym with me?"

She was kissing his eyelids, her breasts just touching his chest. "Luke said you do squats with so many forty-five-pound plates that the bar bends. Is that true?"

"I guess so. I never thought about it. I'll start you on just a couple of light plates and—"

Sara didn't want to argue but she was *not* going to lift weights. She moved her hand under the water to between his legs. "Remember when I said I was teachable?"

He didn't smile but the dimple appeared in his cheek. "I'm willing to learn whatever you're teaching."

She was kissing him while her hand fondled him below. "I'll do my best."

She heard the tub begin to drain. Mike had released the valve with his foot.

"I'm up for it," he said.

"I can see that you are."

He put his arm around her waist, and when he stood up he lifted her with him. "You won't win at the cable toss," she said, but Mike just grunted as he stepped out of the tub.

He carried her, both of them wet and dripping, to the bedroom. "I am your pupil," Mike said, and Sara smiled.

An hour later, Sara had been Mike's student. As they were falling asleep in each other's arms, Mike said softly, "Sara, I just remembered that I didn't use birth control. It was all unexpected and I forgot. I'm sorry."

Sara snuggled closer to him. "That's all right. I forgot too, and besides, it's the wrong time of the month."

They were both lying.

# 20

WHEN SARA AWOKE the next day, it was nearly 11 A.M. and Mike was gone. It was her guess that he'd waited for her to doze off then left. Which meant that he was driving with no sleep.

"And I let him go," Sara said aloud. Her first day of marriage and she'd already failed as a wife. If anything happened to Mike on the drive, especially if he fell asleep at the wheel, it would be her fault. "I should have let him sleep last night. It's what he wanted to do. What he *needed*."

She put her hands behind her head, stared at the ceiling, and thought about her wedding night. She wasn't ready to make such a revelation to Mike, but he was far and away the best lover she'd ever had. Not that she was especially experienced—she and Brian had bought a book so they could learn things—but Greg had been. Now Sara saw that for all the sex she and Greg—Stefan—had had, it lacked the cuddling, the snuggling, the lying in the bathtub wrapped in each other's arms and talking.

Sara looked about the room. As always, Mike had picked up his clothes, and now there was no sign that he'd been there. If she weren't wearing her new wedding band she would have thought the whole thing was a dream.

But as she began to remember the reason behind the wedding, she grew agitated. Dear, lovable Brian, as unaggressive a human as ever existed, had been murdered because of something to do with Sara.

"What is it that Greg wants?" Sara half shouted as she got out of bed and began to dress. "What does Stefan Vandlo want from me?" She was sure that if she knew, and if Greg walked in the door right now, whatever it was, she'd gladly, freely *give* it to him.

But then what? Would Greg take what Sara gave him and leave town with his murderous mother? Would Mike then return to Fort Lauderdale to his job? Would she receive divorce papers a few weeks later? Maybe when he retired he'd come back to Edilean because of his sister and the farm he now owned. But he wouldn't return for Sara.

She reminded herself that when he'd told her she had to marry him, it had been with the understanding that after the case was done, they'd separate.

"Married and divorced," she whispered, and tears came to her eyes.

Her cell phone on the bedside table started buzzing. It was a text from Joce.

> YOU'RE NOT GOING TO BELIEVE WHAT SHAMUS DREW ON THE CARDS. LUKE MADE PANCAKES. WANT TO COME OVER?

Sara pulled on one of her oldest dresses—no need to bother with her appearance if Mike wasn't there—stuck her feet into flip-flops and went next door.

"You look happy and miserable," Joce said. "How can that be?"

"Easy. Marry one day, smile. Get left behind the next, frown. So where are the cards?"

Joce hesitated. "I think you need to sit down."

"What did Shamus do now?" Last year he'd seen a high school girl crying, and when he asked her what was wrong, she'd told him about a teacher who'd demanded kisses for good grades. That night Shamus and his brothers broke into the school and Shamus painted a twelve-foot-tall picture of the teacher—naked—running after some frightened girls. There'd been a lot of turmoil, but in the end the teacher was fired, the Fraziers gave a six-figure donation to the school, and Shamus painted a respectable mural on the gym wall. Since then he'd been the hero of every girl in the school.

Sara sat on the end of the bed and Joce handed her a stack of tarot cards. The backs were beautiful, with one of Luke's weedlike plants that he loved so much on a cream background.

She turned them over and gasped at the first card. It was the Gypsy King, and it was a portrait of Shamus's father. His mother was the Queen.

Sara looked at Joce.

"Go on," Joce said. "Look at the rest of them."

Sara fanned through them, and everyone in Edilean whose family had been there for generations, plus some new people, was on the cards. When she came to the Lovers, there she and Mike were.

And everything that anyone had ever heard about gypsies was there too. Shamus had used photos Joce had downloaded off the Internet to put all the people in the garb of gypsies. There were round-roofed caravans, voluptuous women with gold coin earrings, and men with clay pipes holding on to beautiful horses.

The Hanged One was Greg, hanging upside down, his single gold earring dangling. "This is . . ." She looked at Joce. "I don't know if this is good or bad. Mike will either love these or throw them on a fire."

"I saved these for last." Joce handed her a stack of fourteen cards.

On the Cards of Coins, Shamus had drawn the faces of women—all middle-aged—who came to the dress shop. Since he often spent afternoons sitting in the town square drawing, he'd seen them all. On each card was a wheel with spokes leading outward to the face of a woman, the number depending on the card. The Nine of Coins had the pictures of nine women.

In the center of each wheel was Greg's face—and Shamus had distorted it on each one so he looked greedy, angry, menacing. The portraits ran the gamut of the emotions of evil.

"It looks like Shamus heard us talking," Sara said.

"You think?"

Sara shook her head. "This isn't good." Her mother was on the Card of Judgment, her father on the Hermit. "Who is this woman on the Devil Card?"

"Luke's mother said it was Mike's grandmother."

Sara's head came up. "Do you know what the big mystery is about that woman?"

"Don't get me started. I've tried everything to find out that story, but no one will tell me. I can't finish my book about Miss Edi until I know what happened, but I can't get it out of anyone. Maybe Mike would . . ."

"You mean the Mike who spent the night making fabulous love to me—at my request—then ran off this morning? Some bride *I* am."

Joce was silent as she gathered the cards. "I think Mike really and truly *needs* to see these cards." She was looking hard at Sara.

"We could scan them into a computer and e-mail the whole deck to him."

"That's not the same as holding them in his hands, is it? And who's going to tell him who each person is?"

Sara was puzzled. "We could write notes on all of them."

Her voice rose. "Don't you think it would be better for Mike to actually *see* them?"

Sara finally understood. She stood up, still looking at Joce.

Luke came into the room. "Did you see those cards?" he asked, then when he saw the women's faces, he said, "What's going on?"

Joce and Sara were still staring at each other. Joce spoke first. "The keys to my car are on the table by the front door. It's faster and safer than yours. Get on 95 and head south. I'll text you the rest of the directions. You'll have to stop for the night on the way down. Don't try to do what Mike does and drive it all in one day."

Nodding, Sara ran toward the door. She had to pack.

"Sara!" Luke said. "Mike told me to watch over you. You can't—"

She turned back to him, and everything she'd been through— Brian, Greg, and now Mike—was in her eyes.

Luke loved her too much to say no. "Be careful," he said and Sara ran out the door.

# 21

CAPTAIN ERICKSON LOOKED at Mike and regretted asking him to take on the Vandlo case. In the eleven years they'd worked together, Mike had always kept his distance from his victims. While it was true that Mike sometimes got more involved than he should, and there were a few times when some of the women should have been prosecuted but weren't, in the end, Mike had always been able to disassociate himself.

But this case seemed to have taken something out of him. That he'd *married* a victim, while not unheard of, was certainly outside the requirements for the job.

On Sunday evening when Mike called and told the captain his plan, he'd tried to talk Mike out of it. "I know I told you to do whatever you had to in order to protect her, but you need to come up with another way to deal with this."

"I don't see one," Mike said and proceeded to tell the captain about Brian Tolworthy. "And right after that, Stefan Vandlo appeared in town and went after Sara with a vengeance."

"But now you're planning to marry this girl just to keep her safe?"

"Yes," Mike said.

"And what about later? After the case is over?" The captain wanted to ask whether this marriage was Mike's idea or the girl's, but he didn't.

Instead, he insisted that Mike return to Fort Lauderdale ASAP so they could set up their plans concerning the fair. They were going to fill the grounds with armed men and women, all of them in disguise as locals. Stefan would be released, and when he got to Edilean, his every move would be watched.

To the captain, this was enough. Mike had done a good job in finding out information and setting up a time and place where they could possibly see the Vandlos together. The girl, Sara Shaw, would be protected. And best of all, from what Mike had said, she wouldn't be running back to Vandlo out of some misplaced sense of loyalty.

The idea of using the tarot cards as bait was excellent, and he said so.

"You can thank your favorite author for that," Mike had said. "It was his idea."

"We need for you to come here right away to brief us and draw some maps," the captain replied. What he was really thinking was that it was Sunday night and it wouldn't be possible for Mike to marry his little country girl before he left. Maybe a week in Fort Lauderdale would make him see that the case could be solved without the drastic action of marrying the victim.

But Mike had reported to work this morning wearing a wedding ring.

"So you did it," the captain said.

"Couldn't see any other way. If Vandlo wants whatever it is he thinks Sara has, he won't be able to get it by marrying her."

"Unless he kills you," the captain said.

Mike gave a half smile. "That's the idea, and I plan to make myself highly visible at the fair. I think I'm going to enter a rope jumping contest with a twelve-year-old national champion."

Mike's physical skills were well known—and treated with awe. "I'm sure you'll win."

"Maybe. This kid is supposed to be good."

The captain smiled, but it didn't go to his eyes. He knew Mike was evading the issue. "I want to know about this girl you married. What's she like?"

"She . . ." Mike hesitated. He wasn't about to embarrass himself by talking about how much he enjoyed being with Sara, how she made him laugh, how much he already missed her. He shrugged. "Church on Sunday, good at baking, makes her own clothes. That sort of thing." He had an image of Sara climbing the tree branch over his head. He remembered her tears and her smiles. And then there had been their wedding night. No, he was going to keep his thoughts to himself. "Small town girl."

The captain wasn't like Mike; what he felt showed on his face. "When the case is over we can help you get out of this. We'll make sure your pension won't be in jeopardy. You can—"

Mike stood up. "Is that all? I've got a lot of people to talk to and things to do."

"Yeah, sure," the captain said. "There's a general meeting at two. See you then."

Mike left the office to go back to his own desk.

The captain left his door open, and all day he heard men and women coming by to say hello to Mike. He was popular, and since they rarely saw him, when he was there, everyone wanted to visit. Mike's workouts were legendary so anyone who'd been in a gym in the last six months wanted to show him their biceps. All day there was talk of quads and delts, glutes and triceps. But after that lead-in, what they actually wanted to know was if the rumor that Mike had married a victim was true.

The captain heard the same questions over and over. "Drugs?" they'd ask, meaning was his new wife a user. "Any convictions?"

Mike politely answered their questions but gave no real answers. As usual, he kept his thoughts to himself.

The women teased Mike a lot. One said she would have paid some con artist to cheat her if it meant Mike would rescue her with a marriage.

"Help me! Help me!" one very pretty rookie cried, her hand to her forehead. "Save me with a wedding ring."

Mike bore it all good-naturedly, but as the day wore on, the captain saw that his smile diminished. But the captain didn't think it was the teasing that was getting Mike down. There was something else bothering him, but the captain couldn't figure out what it was. His guess was that Mike was realizing that he'd made a big mistake.

Mike's actions had been noble as all hell, but the reality was that he was now facing a divorce. If the girl wanted to fight him and say that Mike had tricked her into the marriage, he stood to lose a lot financially.

At two, there was a meeting in the big conference room. As soon as they were seated, a Secret Service agent took over and began outlining the plan to infiltrate the Edilean Fair.

Mike was leaning back in his chair and turning his new wedding ring around and around on his finger. And with every turn, the captain's frown deepened. Maybe it would be better if Mike didn't return to Virginia, he thought. It was enough that he'd married the girl. Mike was right when he said that since she was married to someone else, Vandlo couldn't get to her. Now all they had to do was assign someone to stay at her side, and when Vandlo tried anything, they'd step in. This way, Mike's life wouldn't be in jeopardy.

When the Secret Service guy had asked a question, the captain was so distracted he'd asked the man to repeat it. It was obvious that no one else was worried about Mike's safety, but the captain was.

The door opened, the captain's secretary came in and handed him a note. What now? he thought as he opened it.

Mike Newland's wife is downstairs and she says she has the tarot cards.

Captain Erickson had to read it twice before he believed it. His first impulse was to slip out and see the girl for himself. Maybe he'd take her into an empty room and talk to her about what Mike had done for her, "above and beyond" what he needed to do.

But as the captain sat there thinking about what he should do, he knew that what he most wanted was to see how Mike felt about the girl. Today Mike had been moody, even morose. Was it because he knew he'd put himself in an impossible situation?

The captain turned to his secretary who was waiting with her usual impatience. "Go get her and bring her up here," he whispered.

"Here? To this room?"

"Yeah," the captain said. "In here."

He moved to the other side of the table, across from Mike, so he could see out the glass doors. It took a while for his secretary to get down the stairs and lead the girl up through the rabbit warren of doors and long hallways of the Fort Lauderdale Police Department.

When the captain first saw Miss Sara Shaw coming toward them, he sat up straighter. He'd seen a photo of her, but she was prettier than that, with her blonde hair neatly about her shoulders. In a state where women constantly wore tank tops and frayed blue jeans, Miss Shaw's prim yellow dress was a throwback in time.

The detective next to the captain saw her, and he too stopped listening and stared. He punched the guy next to him, and soon they were all watching Sara walk toward them.

By the time she got to the door, the only person not looking at her was Mike. He seemed to be in his own world as he toyed with his ring and stared into space.

The speaker opened the door for Sara. "Can I help you?" he asked, smiling broadly.

Sara only had eyes for Mike. Taking the few steps to his chair, she stood there watching.

It was a while before Mike heard the silence in the room. When he looked up, he saw Sara standing in front of him.

"Shamus and Luke finished these and I brought them to you," Sara said, holding out the stack of tarot cards.

Mike just sat there, looking at her.

"I think we should—" the captain began.

He stopped talking when Mike abruptly stood up, grabbed Sara in his arms, and twirled her around. The cards went flying about the room.

"You're here!" Mike was saying as he kept hugging his wife. No one had ever seen Mike so happy. "You're really here!"

When he started to kiss her, Sara pushed at his chest. "Maybe you should introduce me." Her face radiated happiness.

The men who weren't regulars were on their knees picking up the cards, but the men and women Mike worked with were behind him, all of them eager to meet his wife.

"Yeah, sure," Mike said as he put her down but kept firm hold of her hand. "This is Sara Sh—" He looked at her. "Newland. Sara Newland, my wife."

His coworkers stood there staring in silence. They're in shock, Sara thought, and knew she needed to break the ice. "Notice that the word 'wife' nearly choked him," Sara said. "It'll take a while for him to adjust to the concept that he's no longer a free man."

Everyone, including the captain, laughed. But more important than laughter was that he realized Mike's moodiness that day had been caused by his missing this pretty young woman. Maybe Mike's main reason for marrying her was to protect her, but there was more to it than that.

"Speaking of husbands," Mike said, "I told you you couldn't come here."

Sara looked at the captain. "He's worried that I'll be lonely in this big, bad city while he's at work. Is there a possibility that he could have some time off for a three-day honeymoon?"

"Sara, this isn't the time—" Mike began.

"I think that can be arranged," the captain said. "Oh, yeah, Mike, I forgot to tell you." He tossed two keys on a ring to him. "I raised a bit of a ruckus about what had been done to your apartment, and I managed to get you a new one. There is now an FBI agent who's after my scalp because *he* was supposed to get this place." The captain looked at Sara. "Let me know if you like it or not."

"What about the cards?" the Secret Service agent asked as he held them up.

"Mike will tell us everything tomorrow. You kids go on. Mike, show her some of our beautiful city," the captain said.

Sara smiled. "I have a friend who grew up in Boca Raton and she gave me a list of places to see. Mizner Park, Town Center, a place called Las Olas?"

When Mike groaned, the others laughed.

"What did I say?" Sara asked in false innocence.

Mike kept his arm around her as he led her down the hall to his department. "You and Joce are a real comedy routine. Mizner Park!" The places she'd mentioned were high-end shopping, but he was smiling as he stopped at his desk, which was neat and clean, with not one personal item on it.

"You have on a gun," she said.

"Usually do."

"Not at home you don't." She looked around, but the rest of the room was empty of people, just full of desks and heavily laden bookshelves. Now that she was here, she was nervous about how he was going to react. He'd seemed glad to see her at first, but that could have been an act.

"Don't chicken out now," he said. "Be brave and take the consequences of your actions."

"What does *that* mean?"

He kissed her cheek. "You missed me, didn't you?"

"Not at all. I just thought you needed to see those cards right away, so I—" He kissed her on the mouth. "Maybe I did miss you a tiny bit, but not much."

"How'd you get here? That thing you drive couldn't have made the trip."

"Joce's Mini Cooper."

"So she conspired with you to disobey me?"

"Completely. You want to write her a thank-you note?"

"I'll answer that after tonight." He kissed her again, only this time the kiss was more serious.

"Hey Newland!" a man said from the doorway. "Take it outside."

"You're just jealous, Ferguson," Mike answered back. He locked his desk drawer, put his arm firmly around Sara's waist, and led her to the hallway.

"So where's your new apartment?" Sara asked.

"I have no idea." He handed her the keys.

She looked at the tag on the ring. "It's on Ala Street."

They were going down the stairs. "Never heard of it. They probably put me in some hole down an alley. Are you sure you read that right?"

"416 Ala Street. All caps." She gave the keys back to him.

Looking at them, Mike chuckled. "The middle is a number, not a letter. The apartment is on A1A."

"And where is that?"

"On the ocean, baby. Private beaches. Shall we go see it?"

"I'd love to!"

Sara drove Joce's car and followed Mike through downtown Fort Lauderdale on to a street called Sunrise. They passed fabulous-looking stores and restaurants, and finally came to a hill that she realized was actually a bridge that sometimes opened to let ships through. It was probably ordinary to the residents but fascinating to Sara. On the other side of the bridge, straight ahead, she could see the ocean. When they got near it, Mike took a left, and she followed him down a narrow street. On the right, the ocean side, were large houses hidden behind high walls and enormous trees. Brilliant-colored flowers cascaded over the walls. On the other side of the street were ordinary-looking motels and apartment buildings, and she assumed Mike would turn in to one of them.

But he didn't. Just a few blocks down, he turned into a driveway with a high gate set in the walls. At the call box he pushed a button, the gate opened, and Sara followed him inside and parked beside his car. To the left were two other cars.

"Wow!" she said as she looked around. The house was large

and two stories—and it looked like something from Old World Hollywood.

"It's a Mizner repro," Mike said as though that explained everything and led the way to the front door.

The porch was tile floored, deep and long. "Do you know this house?"

"Quite well," he said as he unlocked one of the big double front doors. "It used to belong to a money launderer who washed a lot of dirty cash. He got twenty to life, but since he was already eighty-one, I don't think he's going to live out his sentence."

Mike opened the door to a spectacular room. There was an envelope with his name on it on a little table by the door, and while he read it, Sara looked around.

There was one huge room, with a big kitchen in the back to the left, and a living room with a few pieces of white-upholstered furniture. In front of her the whole wall of the house was glass doors that led out to a garden that looked like paradise. Opening a door, she stepped out. To the left, almost hidden behind trees and shrubs that Sara had only seen growing as houseplants, was a swimming pool and a barbecue area. Straight ahead was an opening with a few steps down that she assumed led to a private area of beach.

Mike came out and stood beside her, but he didn't touch her.

"What did your letter say?" she asked.

"Just explaining things. The upstairs has been divided into two apartments. In the north one lives a motorcycle patrolman and his pregnant wife. The south one contains one of the most successful counterfeiters who ever lived. He's out on parole now but we keep watch over him. Did you see the rest of the inside?"

She followed him back into the house. Past the kitchen with its granite countertops were two bedroom suites, one of them quite large.

"This used to be Benny the Launderer's office," Mike said.

"And you know that because . . . ?"

"I'm the one who brought him down. For an old guy, he put up one hell of a fight."

Sara walked to the bed. It had a mattress on it, but no sheets or pillows. She ran her hand over the big mahogany headboard, her back to Mike, and wondered if she'd ever see the place after this trip. For all she knew, when the case was finished, Mike would kiss her cheek good-bye. Two weeks later, she'd receive papers for a divorce.

She turned back to him, fully intending to ask about their future together, but when she saw Mike's eyes, all thoughts left her mind.

She took a step toward him, and the next second he made a running leap as he grabbed her about the waist and they landed on the bed together. Laughing, Sara didn't have time to catch her breath as Mike began to kiss her. She pushed against him, trying to get closer. They'd only been apart a day and a half, but she'd missed him terribly.

When her skirt came up and she felt Mike's hand on her bare thigh, her passion was ignited. Seconds later, their clothes were in a heap on the floor and her hands were braced against the headboard. Mike's thrusts were as deep and as frantic as she felt.

They came together and, as before, he put his mouth over hers to keep her from crying out.

When their shudders had calmed, he pulled her down onto the bed beside him, her head against his bare chest.

Sara lay snuggled against him, her hand stroking his magnificent chest, her fingers feeling the contours of his muscles.

Mike picked up her hand and kissed her fingertips.

"So some FBI agent was to get this apartment?" she asked.

"Yeah." Mike was grinning.

"Does that mean the rent is affordable?"

"This house was confiscated and now belongs to the U.S. government, and I'm to act as jailer to ol' Henry the counterfeiter. As I have to make sure he doesn't create any more fake hundred-dollar bills, the rent is minimum. And as an apology for burning all my stuff, they gave me a check for fifteen grand. Want to help me buy some essentials?"

"Great!" she said. "Sheets, pillowcases, food. Is there any cookware?"

"I'll go see," he said and headed toward the kitchen.

Sara had the enormous pleasure of watching him walk out of the room nude, and when he returned, the sight of the naked front of him made her slide down on the bed.

"Every kitchen cabinet and drawer is empty," he said as he went into the bathroom. "And if you don't stop looking at me like that the stores will be closed by the time we get out of here."

"Really?" she said.

He stuck his head around the door. "Last one in the shower has to cook dinner."

Sara was off the bed in a flash, and she slid under his arm as she got into the shower first.

"You cheated," he said as he got in after her and pulled the glass door shut.

"It's the influence of this house. There must be some leftover evil lurking about."

He turned on the water, his arm about her, as they waited for it to warm up. "I don't think so," he said. "I think the blood I shed in here took care of that." When she looked at him in question, he pointed to a scar on his shoulder. "I got shot on this case."

Sara kissed the place. "You poor baby. I'm so sorry."

He moved them under the warm water. "Actually, it was this

wound." He touched a place lower on his side, and Sara bent to kiss that.

He said, "I think—"

"Let me guess. You were wounded even lower," Sara said as she went to her knees.

"Any injuries here?" she asked.

But Mike didn't say anything.

It was nearly an hour before they got out of the house, and Mike drove them directly to a Best Buy.

"I thought you wanted essentials."

"Music is necessary to life," he said so seriously that Sara laughed.

They bought what Mike said were the most important things a house needed. She stood back as he chose the components of a stereo, but together they picked out a flat-screen TV that was much too big.

As Mike paid for it all, it was on the tip of her tongue to ask if she was going to be watching and listening with him, but she didn't.

In the CD department they separated. She liked what she considered to be "modern" music but what Mike called "soulless rubbish." He went to Andrea Bocelli. To Sara's amazement, he was an opera buff. But when their hands met as they reached for an Eric Clapton CD, they laughed together.

"Classic," he said, and she agreed.

To reach the next store, Mike whipped across a couple of expressways, got off what he called "the turnpike," and they ended up in a divine shopping center with a huge Barnes & Noble. Like a piece of iron drawn by a magnet, Sara started for it, but Mike caught her arm. Instead, he pulled her into a Sur la Table.

Sara'd seen the catalogs but never one of their stores. For a moment she just stared at the shelves full of beautiful cookware. Mike lifted her hands, put a basket in them, and said, "Think pie making." When she came out of her trance, he directed her toward the back, where she filled her basket three times. An obliging saleswoman took everything to the counter.

They packed the trunk of Mike's car, then went to a restaurant called Brio for dinner.

"You still owe me a home-cooked meal," Sara said, "because I made it into the shower first."

"For a shower like that, I owe you a thousand meals. Here, taste this." He held out a forkful of sea bass marinated in lime juice.

After dinner they went to a Bed Bath & Beyond.

"No flowers and no pink," Mike decreed as soon as they walked through the door.

"And no brown plaid. Or racing cars or men kicking each other."

"Agreed," he said, and they set off.

They settled on off-white sheets and had fun putting their heads on the pillows and trying them out. But when they started kissing, they almost fell to the floor. If it hadn't been for a curious little boy rounding the corner, they might not have stopped.

Laughing, they took their two big carts to the checkout. They had to stuff the backseat with the linens, as the trunk was full.

"No room for groceries," Sara said. "And there's nothing for breakfast."

"That's all right. I never eat before I work out."

"If you tell me where to go, I'll get groceries while you're at the gym, and we'll have breakfast when you return."

Mike gave her a look that she couldn't read and said they'd go to the store together.

Turning away, Sara hid her smile. It seemed that he liked shopping with her.

When they got back to the apartment, they hauled in all

their purchases. Mike put the stereo together—the TV was being delivered—and Sara put the linens through the washer. They both opened the cookware bags and stored things away to the music of Eric Clapton. As they danced around each other, Sara was pleased to see what a good dancer he was.

"Learn undercover?" she asked.

He pulled her into a classic waltz pose and began leading her around the room in graceful moves. "Drug lord's wife. Lessons." As he held her in a dip, he said, "I helped her practice."

He pulled Sara up and went into a tango to the sounds of "Cocaine." "I persuaded her to testify against her husband."

"All because you helped her dance?"

Mike turned them toward the other end of the room. "And because I accidently let her find her husband in bed with their kids' two nannies."

Sara laughed as he lifted her arm and spun her around.

When the song was over, he turned off the stereo. "I have to get up early. What do you say we go to bed?" The look he gave her made her knees weak.

"Uh, sheets," she managed to say. "Dryer."

If there were an Olympic event for speed of dressing a bed, they would have won. Mattress pad went on, then bottom sheet. Mike didn't like the way Sara tucked in the corner of the top sheet, so he quickly redid it.

"Something else you learned undercover?" she asked.

"No. Hot little nurse."

She threw a pillow at him. He dodged it, grabbed it midair, then tackled Sara on the bed.

When he started kissing her neck, she said, "It seems a shame to make a wet spot on our new linens."

Mike picked her up and put her on the floor on the blue and

gold rug. "I happen to know," he said in his deep voice, "that this rug cost eighty thousand dollars."

"Really?"

"The rug importer wanted a favor." Mike kept kissing. "And this was his gift to the launderer."

"Twenty to life?" Sara put her head back, so he could get to all of her neck.

"No, just life."

She pulled back to look at him and at Mike's shrug she knew the man was dead. She wasn't about to ask who killed him for fear Mike would say he had. "It's a very nice rug."

"Yes, quite pleasant," he said as he moved on top of her. "And oh, so very useful."

Afterward, as they lay together, Mike started laughing.

"What's that about?" she asked as she slipped her nightgown on.

"I was just remembering that I told the captain I didn't know how to please a 'good girl.' I had no idea that all of you want the same thing."

"And I told my mother you were gay."

Smiling, they fell asleep, entangled in each other's arms.

In the morning, Sara was sound asleep when Mike threw back the cover. She didn't stir.

"You have to get up," he said.

Vaguely, she heard him, but she didn't move.

"Sara, my dear, you're going to the gym with me."

She buried her head under the four pillows they'd bought.

"Up!"

She didn't budge.

Mike put his hands on her waist and pulled her out of bed. When Sara made no effort to wake up, he hung her over his arm like a wet towel and carried her to the bathroom where he set her on the side of the tub.

He held up a plastic shopping bag. "These are for you. Put them on. You have ten minutes."

"I don't want—"

Mike left the bathroom.

"I hate exercise," she muttered as she picked up the bag. It was full of workout clothes, including sneakers, all in her size.

Sara grimaced. It seemed that yesterday while she'd been happily enjoying their time together, Mike had been deviously, underhandedly, and sneakily planning to make her go to the gym with him.

When she left the bathroom, her hair was pulled back, and she was wearing dreadful black leggings and a blue tank top with a ghastly sports bra under it.

When Mike blinked a couple of times in appreciation of the shape of her, she was sure she had him. "Are you telling me that I have to go to a gym because you don't like the way I look?"

"You look great today, but four years from now you'll hit thirty, and things will start falling. Think of it as prevention." He handed her a bottle filled with water and put his arm around her shoulders. "Look, if you hate it, tomorrow you can stay home and turn into mush. But today we're going to the gym. And who knows? Maybe you'll like it."

Sara started to reply but then he opened the front door and she saw that it was still dark outside. She turned back toward the bedroom but he caught her. Chuckling, he got her to the car.

Sara was *not* laughing. "So when did you connive to buy all this?"

"Yesterday while you were lusting over those expensive cake pans, I called a friend of mine. She got everything and left it outside the front door. She's going to meet us at the gym."

"*She?* You're introducing your *wife* to one of your former lovers?"

"You can try to start all the fights you want but you're still going to the gym. She's a yoga instructor."

"Yoga? Why would you think I'd want to do that?"

"I happen to know that you can put your knees in your ears and your ankles in my ears at the same time—and that's when we're standing up. I don't know why, but I thought yoga and you seemed to be a perfect match."

Sara had to look out the window to hide her smile.

"That's better," he said. "Her name's Megan, and for the record, I've never been to bed with her."

"I'd rather go to bed with her than exercise with her," Sara mumbled unhappily.

"Yeah?" Mike asked, eyebrows raised.

"Don't get your hopes up."

He laughed, and minutes later they pulled into a big parking lot full of cars.

"Who in the world goes to the gym this early in the morning?"

"Us," Mike said, and Sara groaned.

Once they were inside, she followed Mike and saw that he knew nearly everyone. Men—with arms the size of truck tires—shook his hand and leaned toward him in what she assumed was a masculine greeting in South Florida. Women—who had behinds hard enough to repel buckshot—kissed his cheeks and stood much, much too close to him.

Mike introduced her as his wife to all the men, but in Sara's opinion he reacted too slowly with the women, so she introduced herself.

When a pretty, young woman, Megan, came in, Sara was reluctant to leave him alone. But Mike sent Sara off with the yoga instructor and they went into the big wooden-floored court.

"So let's see what you can do," Megan said.

An hour later, Sara was released, and Mike, showered and freshly dressed, met her by the door.

"Well?" he said to Megan.

"Exactly as you said."

"Thanks a lot," Mike said and kissed Megan's cheek. He opened the door for Sara, and they went outside where it was just barely daylight.

"What was that all about?" Sara asked when they got in the car.

"It was Megan's report and she agreed with my assessment of you. You have no muscles to speak of, but you're flexible as all hell. She thinks that if you work really hard, in a year or two you could be good enough to become a real student of yoga. From Megan that's high praise."

"Yeah?" she asked, pleased. Not that she wanted to do that, but it was nice to hear.

"But you need some muscle. I'll take care of that."

"Does that mean I'm to get on top more often? Good for the ol' legs."

"Don't start tempting me. I have to go to work."

"And what am I supposed to do all day?"

"You can—" He broke off because his cell phone rang. He checked the ID before answering. "I'll be there—Oh. All right. I have no idea." He looked at Sara. "Can you type?"

"Yes."

Mike listened at the phone, then turned back to Sara. "Can you take dictation?"

"Luke dictated his first book to me."

Mike looked impressed. "She writes Luke Adams's books for him," he said into the phone.

"I do no such—" Sara began before she realized he was teasing. Mike said a few more words then hung up. "That was the captain. He said I needed to write down everything I'd done and learned in Edilean, and since I'm the world's worst typist, he suggested I dictate it all to you. And what's the mystery about the tarot cards?"

Sara wanted to jump up and down in happiness that she and Mike would get to spend the day together. If her body hadn't just been twisted into several unnatural positions, she might have done so.

They'd reached the house, and Sara waited until they got out before answering. "Shamus made portraits of the people of Edilean."

"He did what?"

"He painted everyone on the cards."

"I guess 'everyone' means the people from the founding families, not the newcomers like me."

"Don't get snobby on me. Your picture and Tess's are on there, and Shamus included a lot of clients from the dress shop."

Mike's eyes widened. "Are you saying that Mitzi Vandlo's picture could be on those cards?"

"I hadn't thought of that, but possibly. I have another set in my suitcase. You can go through them while I take a shower—unless you'd like to join me, that is." She fluttered her lashes at him.

"I want to see the cards now. You should have told me what was on them last night."

Sara gave a melodramatic sigh. "And ruin my twelve-hour honeymoon? How could I have been so selfish?"

Mike didn't smile but his dimple showed. "Take your shower then we'll go get bagels."

"With or without flaxseeds?"

"Go!" he ordered.

Sara was in the shower when Mike came in with the cards.

"You're going to have to tell me who most of these people are."

He held up a card, but she couldn't see it through the foggy glass. He stepped closer to the shower and she moved nearer the glass.

"That's Mr. Frazier, Shamus's father. Mrs. Frazier," she said to the next one.

"And I know these three oxen are Shamus and Ariel's brothers."

"Your beloved Ariel. Think she'll like this apartment?" Sara had her eyes closed as she washed her hair. When she turned around, he was naked and in the shower with her.

"Need some help?" he asked as he put his hands in her soapy hair and massaged her scalp.

"Always," she replied.

# 22

WHILE THEY WERE having bagels and orange juice Mike began to have second thoughts about letting Sara hear all that he'd found out in Edilean. For one thing, all the DNA samples they'd taken had come back negative, so they were no closer to identifying Mitzi than they had been. He was concerned that telling Sara this might frighten her.

"What's made you so quiet?" she asked.

"I'm a very quiet person."

"Unless you're making me do something I don't want to do, then you have a lot to say."

"You liked the gym and you were good at yoga," he said.

"I most certainly did not! All those girls were drooling over you. What fun was that?"

"I saw you in there with Megan, and I could tell that you enjoyed it, and you got into every position perfectly."

Sara looked at him over her juice. "You didn't answer my question about what's bothering you. I'm beginning to learn that when you don't want to answer something, you digress."

"Digress, do I? Maybe you could explain the meaning of that word to me. I didn't have the advantage of a college education, as you and Tess did, so forgive me if I have trouble keeping up with you two."

"College doesn't change a person's intelligence." She narrowed her eyes at him. "You're thinking about something really hard and I want to know what it is."

"No more digressions?" he said, showing that he very well knew the word.

"None!"

He put down his bagel. "I found out some things while I was in Edilean that I don't think you should know."

"Why shouldn't I know? Because the knowledge will put me in danger or my feelings will be hurt?"

"Feelings," he said.

"I can take it."

"Sure?"

"Haven't you learned yet that I'm very strong?"

Mike put his hand on his lower back. "This morning in the shower I thought you were going to break me."

Sara didn't smile. "I want you to pretend I'm some woman who works in your office and tell me what you've found out. I'll type it and I promise not to have palpitations."

"Not even for kisses on the back of the neck?"

"That is altogether different. Can you treat me as though I'm just a regular person?"

"No," he answered quickly.

"Good!" Sara said just as fast.

When they stopped at an office supply store to buy a printer, Mike asked why she wasn't still typing Luke's books.

"My mother. I was only fifteen when he wrote his first novel, and I spent an entire summer with a computer on my lap. When he finished it, Luke had half a dozen ideas for more books. I was going to help him, but my mother gave him a copy of Mavis Beacon—the typing software—and told him to let her daughter have a life."

"Think you'll someday be just like your mother?"

"I pray nightly not to be."

Once they were back at the apartment, Sara turned on Mike's laptop. After he told her to quit trying to access his personal files, he began to dictate.

He told of making contact with the "victim" and taking up residence with her. Mike glanced at Sara to see how she was taking this admission, but her face was stoic. She was concentrating on recording what he said.

It wasn't until he got to the part about Merlin's Farm that she interrupted. "I think you should mention your grandmother's attachment to the farm."

"That has nothing to do with this case. Now, as I was saying—"

"I think there is a connection. Your grandmother wanted the place and so does Greg . . . Stefan."

"My grandmother left Edilean in 1941. What's going on now has nothing to do with then."

"I'm sure you know better than I do," she said in a way that let him know he was wrong. She put her hands back on the keyboard.

Mike turned away. The truth was, he agreed with her. Even though he couldn't see how the two events were related, he planned to work on it. But he wasn't going to worry Sara with that now. He went on with his story, and she didn't interrupt again until he got to his conversation with Ariel.

"Ariel *knew* Greg was fornicating with other women but she didn't tell me?"

"I thought you were going to disassociate yourself from this."

"I'm not angry at Greg. He's the snake that doesn't change character no matter how nice you are to him, but Ariel . . . What in the world can she imagine that I've done to her that she'd let me *marry* a man she knew was that bad?"

"If she'd told you about him, would you have believed her?"

"Not a word of it."

Mike looked at her in astonishment. "Maybe she knew that and that's why she didn't tell you. Would you have told her if she was marrying a philanderer?"

"Oh, yes!" Sara said with a smile. "I would have run so fast my feet wouldn't have touched the ground."

Mike shook his head at her.

"And Colin!" Sara said. "I can't believe *he* didn't tell me about Greg. Colin and I have always been friends! When we get home I'm going to have a talk with the Fraziers."

"That should scare them," Mike said, deadpan. "You ready to get this done? The faster we send this off, the sooner we'll be free. You want to return to Edilean and say you didn't even see the ocean?"

Sara put her hands back on the keyboard. "Lead on, oh fearless leader, and tell me who else has betrayed me."

Smiling, Mike continued. He told what he'd learned, but he also outlined the plan for the next week. For the first time, Sara heard what the police and Federal agents were hoping would happen.

After they finished the document at noon, Mike started to draw a map of the fairgrounds, but Sara took over.

"The booths and rides and the game field are in the same place every year, so I know what goes where."

"Except for Joce's fortune-telling tent."

"Luke's putting it right next to where he sells his weeds, which is beside my kissing booth."

"Your what?!" Mike said.

Sara smiled smugly. "Just seeing if you were listening."

By one, the maps and reports were done. They printed them out on the new printer—which Sara had set up while Mike dealt with the TV delivery—and put it all in a big envelope.

Mike turned to look at Sara. In the next second they had their clothes off and were making love on the big white couch.

Later, Sara lay in his arms and said, "It's odd but I won't even be thinking about sex, then I'll look at you and it's all I *can* think of."

He kissed her forehead. "My virgin princess. Want to go for a swim?"

"Love to. I brought a blue bikini."

"I bet Henry the counterfeiter will enjoy that! You just might see yourself on a thousand-dollar bill."

"When do I get to meet the neighbors?"

Mike was heading to the bathroom and he didn't look at her. "We have to leave tomorrow afternoon."

"Which is no answer to my question," Sara said under her breath as she reached for her clothes. Mike hadn't given even the slightest hint that she'd ever return to Fort Lauderdale, that she'd ever again see this beautiful apartment.

He looked around the bathroom door. "Showering alone wastes water."

"I'm all for green." Sara ran to the bathroom to join him.

"It's been a wonderful day," Sara said as she snuggled against Mike in bed. It was nearly ten P.M. and they had to get up early, but she wasn't sleepy.

"It's been great," he said.

She could tell he was in a mellow mood. "I've enjoyed my honeymoon."

"Me too. I'm not sure but I think the captain had me return here to keep me from marrying you."

She turned to look at him. "That's good. He was looking out for you, but when he saw that I wasn't your usual, uh . . . victim, he let us have time off. He's a nice man."

"You bring out the niceness in people."

"What a sweet thing to say."

They lay quietly together as Mike slowly ran his fingers up and down her back. She took a deep breath to give herself courage. What she wanted to ask him could cause offense. "What were your parents like?"

He didn't hesitate. "Kind, loving, fun."

She snuggled closer against him, her head on his shoulder. "Do you remember them?"

"Very well. But Tess doesn't, so whenever we're together I tell her stories about them."

"I'd like to hear anything you want to tell me about them."

Mike took a moment before answering. "My mother was very pretty."

"Like Tess."

"Yes, but different. Tess is dark like our father, while Mom was blonde, with deep blue eyes. Like you." He kissed the top of her head.

"What kind of things did she like to do?"

"She used to say she was the most unmodern woman in the world because she had no ambition at all. She finished two years of college, then met Dad, and . . ." He shrugged.

"Marriage and children. Sounds good to me."

"You two would have liked each other. You're a lot alike. She used to make us lunches with happy faces on the bread. When I got home from school, she always had something homemade for me to eat."

"What did your dad do?"

"He made himself spend forty hours a week managing a big printing company, but in his real life he cared about two things: his family and sports."

"You must have loved that," Sara said.

"With all my might. My first memory is of being in a seat on the back of my dad's bike—and we were going up a mountain."

"That sounds dangerous. You wouldn't—" She stopped herself. "Did your mom like sports?"

Mike chuckled. "Hated them. She wanted to stay home and watch old movies."

"Oh, yes! We would have definitely been friends. I wish I could have known her." When Mike was quiet, she knew he was thinking about what happened later, with his parents dying so young, and he and Tess being put into their angry grandmother's custody.

"I never understood it," he said softly as he stopped caressing her back. "My mother adored her mother, and Grans practically worshiped Mom. Grans was so good to her. They talked on the phone nearly every day."

"How did she treat you and Tess while your parents were alive?"

"No one existed for Grans except my mother. Grans didn't pay any attention to Tess or me or her husband. It was all about her daughter."

"The accident . . ."

"Nearly made her insane," Mike said. "That horrible day when everything changed, Mom had asked Grans to babysit, something she rarely did, while she and Dad went Christmas shopping for us kids."

"Oh, dear," Sara said.

"Yeah, exactly. The streets were icy, and their car slid, hit an embankment, and crashed into a concrete wall. They were killed instantly. Grans nearly lost her mind, and she blamed Tess and me for the accident. She said that if we hadn't been born, her daughter would still be alive."

While Mike was telling this—and Sara felt sure he'd never told anyone before—he kept rubbing his throat. Gently, she brushed his hand away and kissed his neck. "Tell me what happened."

Mike took a breath. "A couple of weeks after the funeral I asked Grans for three dollars for some school thing. She was sweeping the kitchen floor. She didn't say anything, but I'll always remember the look of hatred she gave me. She glanced down at the broom, then in the next second she hit me across the throat with the handle."

Sara drew in her breath, horrified that someone could do that to a child, but she said nothing, just let him talk.

Mike told her that when his grandmother hit him in the throat, his grandfather had been away, so Mike wasn't taken to a doctor. By the time his grandfather returned a week later, Mike's voice was irreversibly damaged. It never fully recovered.

After that, Pru began to take all her anger and hostility out on Mike. And he soon learned to make sure that she did. Whenever she so much as looked at Tess, just five years old, as though she might take her wrath out on the little girl, Mike drew her attention onto himself.

In school, Mike did little but cause trouble. The coach tried to get him to try out for sports, but Mike was too angry to be a team player. Instead, he fought and made enemies of everyone.

After he finally graduated and went to the East Coast, he sauntered into a boxing gym, and that's where he met Frank Thiessen, who was twenty-three and thinking of joining the police force. They trained together and became such good friends that Frank waited until Mike turned nineteen so they could enlist together. On the force, they were a good team, both of them athletic, both from bad childhoods, but they had at last found a way to channel the anger in them. On their time off, they trained hard and entered matches that they nearly always won.

When they took on undercover assignments, they had to separate, and Frank moved to California.

"I'd like to meet him," Sara said as she tried her best not to let Mike know of her horror at what he'd just told her. She was ashamed that she'd ever complained about her own family.

"Hey!" Mike said. "I'll take anything but pity."

"Good thing, because you won't get any from me. Besides, you've always had Tess, who adores you. Why didn't you ever come to Edilean to visit?"

"Uh oh. This is turning into a question session. I've found out that there's only one way to stop that." Rolling over, he began to kiss her neck.

Sara wasn't sure what had happened, but it felt as though they'd taken a big step forward. She thought she should be despondent, if not depressed, at what he'd told her, but instead she felt almost good because he'd confided in her. No wonder Tess was so secretive about her life.

"Are you going to keep thinking or help me out with this?"

She didn't laugh. "Mike . . . I'm sorry about what was done to you."

"Thank you," he said quietly, and she could tell he meant it.

They didn't make love. Instead, Mike pulled her to him and held her tightly—and it was the closest she'd ever felt to him.

"We'd better go to sleep," he said. "Gym is in the morning."

Sara tried to groan but couldn't do it. The truth was that he was right and she'd rather enjoyed her workout. She'd especially liked spending time in a place where Mike was so well known. In Edilean, she knew everyone, but here it was her husband who knew people.

Smiling at the word *husband* she drifted off to sleep.

The next morning, Mike had to wake Sara, but he didn't have to ask her to get dressed. "Want to try to make some muscles today?"

"So I can get arms like yours?"

He flexed a bicep. "I don't think you need to worry about that."

"You are too vain!"

"Have to be about something. With this face, no hair, and this voice I need to work on the rest of me."

Sara didn't laugh at what she was sure he'd meant as a joke. "I think your face is beautiful."

"That's not what you said the first time you saw me, but . . . thanks. Are you ready?"

"Is Megan waiting for us?"

"No. Today you're all mine!" When he leered at her and Sara gave a fake squeal of fear, Mike grimaced. "If we don't leave now you'll drag me back into that bed and I'm already worn out from what you've done to me these last two days."

"Poor you!" Sara said as she scurried to the door. "How about if I drive?"

"Do two people fit inside that toy car you brought?"

"No, I meant that I'd drive *your* car."

"What a sense of humor you have." He opened the passenger door for her.

They argued all the way to the gym, but Sara didn't make a dent in his refusal to let her drive his car.

At the gym, he spent thirty minutes with her, showing her the perfect form for doing a few rudimentary lifts. She thought it was a bore, but she loved his hands on her elbows and shoulders.

Afterward, she went swimming, and as she put her arms on the side of the pool, her legs lazily kicking, she watched him do his intense forty-six minute workout. He was a mass of sweat that made his pumped-up muscles gleam. By the time he was ready to leave, she could have torn his clothes off on the gym floor.

He looked at her, made no comment, but when they were in the car, he said, "Think you can wait until we get home?"

"Can you?"

Instantly, he pulled the car into the parking lot of a store that was still closed, opened his door, and got out.

"What in the world . . . ?" Sara watched him open the rear door. He got in the backseat and began to unbutton his shirt.

Sara leaped between the front seats, her arms going around his neck and her mouth on his. She was glad his car windows were so dark that no one could see inside. He never did finish removing his shirt.

They spent the morning driving around Fort Lauderdale, where Mike showed her the sights, especially all the magnificent yachts and waterways, which gave the city the nickname "the Venice of America." Sara could hardly listen because she knew that this afternoon they'd start the journey back to Edilean—and she dreaded it. She'd be in Joce's car and Mike in his, so they wouldn't even be together.

Worse, when they got back, all the horror would begin. Greg would be released from wherever they were holding him and at last he'd find out that his fiancée had married Tess's brother. Sara would love to tell him that she knew about his mother, his wife, and how he wanted her, Sara, because . . . No one had yet been able to figure that out.

But she'd been told she couldn't tell him that until Greg's mother was found. The hope was that Greg would be so angry about Sara's marriage that he'd make mistakes. Since his mother was the brains in the family, they all hoped Stefan/Greg's rage at Sara would make him run to Mitzi—and he would be followed.

All this was why Mike planned to compete in the games and draw attention to himself. "You want to become a target, don't you?" Sara'd said when he told her. "*You* will be standing in the way of whatever Greg wants."

"It's either you or me, baby, and I think I'm more used to being a target than you are."

Sara didn't say anything to that because she'd seen the scars on his body. She'd seen enough TV and movies to know bullet wounds when she saw them.

As the last day wore on, she got more nervous. She was worried about Mike. As her husband, he might as well have painted a bull's-eye on his forehead.

"I forgot to tell you that an agent will be driving Joce's Mini back to Edilean," Mike said.

"Then I'll be riding with you?"

"Of course. Did you think you were going to have to drive back alone?"

"No," she said. "I thought I was going to drive your fancy car and you could ride in the trunk."

"Wouldn't be the first time. I think we should leave about one. That way we'll get there around midnight. We'll get a few hours sleep and be ready for the fair tomorrow."

"It doesn't start until noon."

Mike smiled at her. "You aren't getting cold feet, are you?"

When she looked at him, there was fear in her eyes. "Mike, this is serious. If you're out there in public in those games someone could hide somewhere and shoot you."

"Hazards of—" Her look cut him off. He sat down on the couch by her and pulled her into his arms. "I've done this kind of thing a hundred times and I haven't lost yet."

"It only takes once, and I think it's time you stopped!" she said fiercely. "You're thirty-six years old, you're about to retire, you own property now, and I think you should stop risking your life every day."

"Keeping my wife's desires satisfied is more likely to kill me."

She glared at him.

"All right," he said. "I promise that once this case is done I'll think about taking a desk job. Does that make you feel better?"

"I want you to stay away from the fair. You need to stay in a locked room with three armed guards who are so big they make the Fraziers look small. You should—"

Mike kissed her. "How about we walk down to the beach? Maybe we'll see some big turtle laying eggs."

When she just looked at him, he kissed her again. "I'll be as careful as I can be. I promise. Come on. We need to go outside. Want me to carry you down to the beach?"

"No, I don't—" When Mike picked her up and slung her across his shoulder, she couldn't help laughing, and for a while she forgot about her fears.

At one-thirty they were in Mike's car, heading north on I-95, and going faster than the speed limit.

"Are you going to sulk all the way back?" he asked.

"I'm not sulking, I'm worried."

"That's my job. You're the victim, remember? You people innocently get yourselves in trouble and we rescue you."

"If you're still alive, that is."

"You sound like Tess."

"Smart woman!"

"How about some music?" he asked. "Will that cheer you up?"

"Am I supposed to think about what they'll play at your funeral?"

Mike reached across the console and squeezed her hand. "You

need to distract yourself. Tell me about what you did in high school. Did you get good grades? What did you study in college? William and Mary, wasn't it?"

"I'm sure you know every course I took and all my grades. Why don't you tell me what made your grandmother leave Edilean and why she hated the McDowells so much?" She said it as a joke and never for a moment thought he'd tell her. It was the Big Secret among the Oldies in Edilean.

"She claimed she was raped by Alexander McDowell."

Sara looked at him in astonishment. "Aunt Lissie's husband? Rape?!"

"That's the story Grans told. And, yes, it was that Alex McDowell."

"He wasn't prosecuted or I'd have heard about it. But then, the Oldies love to keep secrets."

"Oldies?" Mike asked. "From the way you talk of retirement and me, I think I'm one of them."

"All four times we made love this morning I thought, Mike sure is an old man."

He grinned. "Yeah?"

"I heard a lot of complaints about Uncle Alex's grumpiness, but I never heard of any violence against women."

"I don't think it existed. After Tess moved there and got to know some townspeople, she started asking questions."

Sara waited for more, but Mike was silent. It wasn't easy hearing that all this time Tess had known the full story. "Tell it to me from the beginning," Sara said.

Mike hesitated for a moment. "My grandmother told us that one afternoon in 1941, she was riding on her bicycle down the old road by Merlin's Farm. Someone threw something at her wheels and she fell, hit her head on a rock, and was knocked out. When she woke up, Alex McDowell was raping her. She lost consciousness again, and when she came to, she made her way to the farm, and Brewster Lang called the police."

"And she identified Uncle Alex as her rapist?"

"Yes, but Edi Harcourt swore that Alex was at her house that day, so the charges were dropped."

"That must have been hard on your grandmother. To have reported a rape but nothing was done about it must have been awful. Do you think Miss Edi lied?"

"Probably, but then my grandmother never had a firm grip on honesty."

"Are you saying she wasn't attacked?"

"I don't know. But I do think it was wishful thinking on her part that Alex McDowell was the culprit."

"She liked him?"

"When Tess and I were kids, we were told that Alex adored her, sent her flowers, wrote her poems. It made sense that when she turned him down he got angry enough to commit a crime of violence against her. But when Tess came here, she was told it was the other way around. Grans pursued Alex. Wherever the poor guy went, there she was. She used to tell people she was meeting him when he was actually trying to get away from her. She told us that even though back then he was really poor, she saw potential in him."

"She was right; Uncle Alex made millions," Sara said. "So when she was . . . had sex that night, she *wanted* it to be Alex?"

"That's what Tess and I think. But whatever the truth is, every year we were all subjected to a period of deathly mourning centered around the fourteenth of November."

"The fourteenth of November?" Sara asked in surprise.

"Is that date important to you?"

"Oh, dear. I forgot to tell you something."

"Sara, if Vandlo—"

"No, not him. Did . . . Was there any chance that her molester was wearing a kilt?"

Mike turned his head so abruptly, the car swerved. "Yes! That's how she identified him. She said that only the McDowells wore that blue and gray plaid, but how do *you* know that?"

"Brewster Lang did it."

"What?"

"He was the one with your grandmother."

"Tell me what you know." There was a muscle working in his jaw.

"Don't you *dare* get angry at me! If you'd told me this story a week ago I could have told you about Mr. Lang."

"Sara . . ." he said in warning.

"When Luke and Ramsey were teenagers, one night they sneaked onto Merlin's Farm. They said it was because they saw a fire, but I happen to know that they often sneaked around there."

"What did they see?" Mike asked.

"Mr. Lang was wearing an old kilt and a big white shirt, and he and his dogs were dancing around a huge bonfire. Luke and Rams said it was all wild and primitive-looking. It was the fourteenth of November."

"You're sure of that?"

"Yes. That's my father's birthday."

"Lang didn't see them?"

"No, but the next day he must have seen the weeds knocked down because after that he was worse about trespassers."

"It could have been a coincidence," Mike said. "That was a long time after 1941, and—"

"He does it every year on the same day."

Mike glanced at her.

"The next year on my father's birthday, Luke and Rams went back, and they could see the firelight. They tried to get near, but the dogs were guarding the area. Mike," she said softly, "you don't think Mr. Lang celebrates raping a woman, do you? He couldn't be that . . . that horrible."

"You want the truth? I'm not sure she was assaulted. Her facts changed constantly, and that Lang wears a McDowell kilt makes me doubt her even more. And he was in the vicinity and Grans always said he was her friend. Maybe . . ."

"What?"

"I wonder if she and Lang had sex that night and she used it as a chance to blame your uncle Alex?"

"Wow! Not very PC of her, was it?" Sara was silent for a moment. "And now Mr. Lang celebrates that night every year."

Mike shrugged. "People do a lot of strange things in the privacy of their own homes. And even if it happened the way my grandmother said, I doubt if Lang sees it as a rape. Remember that my grandmother was only semiconscious, and the kilt made her think it was the man she believed she loved. I doubt that she made much of a protest."

"If she welcomed him, Mr. Lang might not have realized she thought he was someone else."

For a while, Mike was silent as he thought about all the hatred and anger that had emanated from his grandmother—but it had been directed toward the wrong people. "You know what Grans tried to get the police to do? Make Alex McDowell marry her. She even told the pastor and the church members what had happened and tried to get them to force the marriage."

"Poor Uncle Alex. No wonder he was so bad tempered. No one could understand why sweet Aunt Lissie married him."

"Miss Edi did it," Mike said. "That's why Grans hated her so much. Lissie's family was about to marry her off to some aspiring young politician, but then Miss Edi stepped in and arranged an elopement."

"I can't imagine anyone less suited for the campaign trail than my aunt Lissie."

"She was like you," Mike said. "You'd hate dealing with strangers."

"I wouldn't. I *like* to meet people. I—" She saw Mike's look. "Okay, so I like family better. So Miss Edi saved Alex from going to jail *and* gave him the beautiful Lissie for a wife? I guess that's why he was so grateful to Miss Edi after she retired."

"I would imagine so. It took Tess years of digging to ferret out all the information. But from what I heard, Alex and Lissie were a good match. Alex was a poor man from a good family, while Lissie's family was newly wealthy and from redneck stock."

"That explains a lot," Sara said. "I always wondered about them because Aunt Lissie was careful to be very proper, while Uncle Alex belched at the table."

"The right of kings," Mike said.

Sara was thinking about all he'd told her. "Your grandmother was filled with hatred because she believed she'd been raped by Uncle Alex, but he wasn't punished in any way."

"Grans hated the people of Edilean because they wouldn't help her in her attempt to force him to marry her."

"Do you think people knew that Miss Edi lied when she gave Alex an alibi?" Sara asked.

"You grew up here, so what do you think?"

"They knew," Sara said. "But they must have also known that Alex wouldn't attack a woman. And Miss Edi certainly believed in him." She was marveling at how many secrets the people of Edilean had held on to.

"She did," Mike said. "But the elopement she set up made a lot of people angry. Lissie's family disinherited her, but the joke turned out to be on them. After Alex made himself rich, he supported Lissie's parents in their old age." Mike looked at Sara. "And until today no one knew who raped Grans." He patted Sara's shoulder. "Good detective work."

"I'm so good at this that I think you should let *me* handle Greg while you spend next week in a cabin in Montana."

Mike chuckled. "You know, don't you, that all this, as interesting as it is, has nothing to do with the Vandlo case?"

"I wonder if that was the only sex Mr. Lang had in his whole life? I never heard even a rumor that he'd ever had a girlfriend." She gave Mike a sharp look. "If they used no protection . . ." Her eyes widened. "Is Mr. Lang your grandfather?"

"No! My mother was born five years after that night." He shook his head. "Grans used to tell us how she staggered to the farm after the attack. Lang called the police and made her tea and served her little cookies."

Sara looked at the road in front of them and thought about what Mike had told her. When she got back, she'd have to tell Joce so she could put this in her biography of her grandmother, Edilean "Miss Edi" Harcourt.

"Hungry?" Mike asked. "I think we should stop, get something to eat, then you and I should talk about *your* life."

Sara groaned. "This is why you wanted me to ride with you, isn't it?"

"Sara, you hurt me to the core," he said with so much feeling that for a moment she believed him. She hit him on the shoulder.

"Ow! I put too much muscle on you this morning."

"I think you should tell me more about *your* life."

"No one is trying to marry me to get whatever it is I have that I don't know belongs to me."

Sara smiled. "That is so convoluted it almost makes sense."

"So start talking."

"Food first."

"What kind and where do you want it served?" he asked with the leer of a dirty old man, and Sara laughed.

Later, at a little after seven, while Mike was driving, Sara sent a text to Joce to tell her they'd be home late. She didn't want the noise to disturb them.

Joce sent back a message that Sara had to read twice to understand. She looked at Mike with wide eyes.

"What is it?"

"You didn't tell me your grandmother had a younger sister."

"First I've heard of it."

"She never mentioned her?" Sara asked.

"I was never told of a . . . what would she be? A great-aunt? Or is it a grandaunt?"

Sara called Joce and asked questions. "Joce says that with aunts and uncles the 'great' or 'grand' depends on where you're from, but they mean the same thing."

As Sara listened to Joce, she looked at Mike and shook her head. After she hung up, she said, "You're not going to believe this. Joce found out that after your grandmother left Edilean, her younger sister stayed behind and got married."

"I'm afraid to ask who she married. You and I aren't first cousins, are we?"

"Noooo," Sara said, drawing out her news. "She married—get ready—a Frazier."

"You mean those giants are my relatives?"

"Second cousins."

Mike groaned. "Now *I'm* related to Edilean."

"You are now one of us." Her voice was gleeful. "Your great-aunt had a baby boy who grew up to be Ariel's father. Right after she gave birth, she ran off to LA to try to become a movie star. Her husband divorced her and remarried six months later. The second wife is the woman the Fraziers know as their grandmother."

"What happened to my great-aunt?"

"Joce said she died in LA, but she doesn't know where or when."

Mike was having difficulty taking the information in, but he knew Sara was watching him. He was thinking that Tess probably had known about this but had chosen not to tell him. No doubt she thought that the idea of having relatives would keep Mike away forever. "I guess this means Ariel and I can't get married."

"You're already married." There wasn't the slightest humor in Sara's voice.

"That's right," he said, smiling. "Are you sure you and I aren't related? Seventh cousins, maybe?"

"Joce says no. Luke and I are vaguely related to the Fraziers through the male line. You're attached by the females."

"Ah, yes, females. That reminds me. Get my jacket from the backseat and look in the pocket."

Sara reached back, got his jacket, and felt inside. When she came to a hard little square, she stopped. Every woman knew what that was. Slowly, she removed the package, put the jacket back, then sat there holding it. She didn't open the little blue velvet ring box.

"You don't want to see what's inside?"

Sara shook her head no. An engagement ring almost made their marriage seem real. But she knew it was all make-believe. She and Mike had married under false pretenses, and they'd never talked about the future. Once the Vandlos were caught—or even if they escaped capture—Mike would return to Fort Lauderdale and his pretty apartment. In a few years when he left the police force, he'd possibly return to Edilean, but for now . . .

"Hey!" Mike said gently. "Are you okay? I thought a ring would make you happy. A diamond will make Vandlo more sure you and I are actually married."

"Yeah, sure," she said listlessly. "That makes sense."

"You want to tell me what's wrong?"

"Nothing. It's all very logical." She opened the box—and gasped. It wasn't just a ring from a jewelry store. It was one of Kim's designs, a one-of-a-kind ring, the only one like it in the world.

"You don't like it?"

"It's . . . When . . . ?"

"On Sunday, when I was at your parents' house planning the wedding, I asked your mother about Kim and her jewelry. Kim had said some nice things about you, so I thought you two were friends."

"We are," Sara said softly as she held the ring up to the fading daylight. Mike flipped a switch so a map light came on. The ring was exquisite, with a large white diamond in the center and flanked by two smaller pear-shaped diamonds. The unique setting made the small ones swirl around the larger stone.

"Your mother showed me Kim's Web site and I chose it off there, but it had to be sized. It came to the office this morning. If you don't like it I can return it."

"No!" Sara nearly shouted. "I mean, yes, I like it very, very much. Kim's creations are wonderful, beautiful. They . . ." She was holding it in her hand tightly.

Sara started to put the ring on, but then she handed it to Mike.

Smiling, the steering wheel in one hand, he slipped the ring on Sara's finger.

When he saw how she couldn't take her eyes off of it, he was pleased. He looked back out the windshield at the road. "Do you think I should change my name to Frazier?"

"I think that you can no longer be a snob about Edilean. Ariel says the Fraziers are descended from English royalty."

"You know, I've always thought maybe I was." When she made no comment, he looked at her. She was still gazing at the ring. "Think you should curtsey to me from now on?"

"No, but I was thinking of kissing some of your royal body parts."

Mike smiled. "I like the way your mind works."

# 23

I DON'T WANT TO go," Mike said, sounding like a sullen child. "You take the dogs and give them to him. I'll meet you at Nate's Field. By the way, did Joce find out why it's called that? You have any ancestors named Nathaniel?"

Sara had her hands on her hips and was glaring at him. Last night they'd arrived in Edilean hours later than Mike said they would because she wouldn't let him go as fast as he wanted to. Without consulting each other, they'd gone to Sara's apartment, not Tess's. But when Mike tried to open the door, it wouldn't budge.

"Who the hell locked this door?" he muttered.

Sara showed him how to pull it forward and lift up to make it open.

"Needs a hand plane taken to it," he said as he carried their bags in.

They were both so tired that they just pulled off their clothes and fell into bed. At 5 A.M. they awoke to find themselves naked, and seconds later they were making love.

At six Mike left for the gym, but he let Sara sleep. When he returned at eight, Sara had made pancakes and cut up fruit. The sound of dogs barking had awakened her and she'd looked out the window to see a couple of very cute young dogs tied to a tree. She knew they were the ones to be given to Mr. Lang.

She'd tried to go back to sleep, but the knowledge that she was going to have to see Mr. Lang—face-to-face, no hiding—almost made her ill.

The only way she could overcome her dread was to remember that Mike would be there with her. Mike was afraid of nothing. He was a man who walked into hailstorms of bullets with no fear, and he would be there to protect her.

But at the mention of going to Merlin's Farm to give the dogs to Mr. Lang, Mike said no.

"What does that mean?" Sara asked.

"No, I can't go. I'm busy. I have things for the case that must be done. You can go by yourself."

"Yes, you do have things to do for the case. You have to protect *me*. Remember? A few days ago my safety was so important that you made the ultimate sacrifice and married me."

"Oh, well, that's not been so bad," he said as he wiggled his eyebrows at her.

"Not so bad?" she said quietly. "I've been waiting on you hand and foot since I said 'I do.' How do you think your laundry is getting done? Who cleans the blade on that machine you use to keep your hair short? Who unpacked your suitcase?"

"Maybe we should hire—"

"You're going with me," she said. "*I* am the one who is afraid of that odious old man and *you* are supposed to protect *me*."

Mike kept his head down over his pancakes. "From bullets, yeah, but not from . . ."

She sat down across from him. "What's going on that I don't know about? You weren't afraid of Mr. Lang the other times we talked about meeting him."

"Mmmm, uh, hmmm grandfather," Mike said.

She stared at him a moment, then picked up her BlackBerry. "I'm going to call Tess and ask her."

Looking up, Mike gave a big sigh. "Tess won't know anything because this is your fault."

She cut off the call. "What's my fault?"

"I didn't tell you that Grans used to correspond with Lang. Not often but once or twice a year."

"So?"

"She loved sympathy, so she told him she'd had a baby from the rape."

"She didn't have one, did she?"

"No. Although now that I've heard she had a sister she never mentioned, maybe she did. I'll get someone to look into that." He picked up his phone, but at Sara's look, he put it down and stared at her.

She had no idea what he was silently telling her, but after a moment she began to understand. This was yet another bit of information that Mike hadn't told her. "If Mr. Lang was with your grandmother, then he'll think *you* are his grandson."

Mike went back to his pancakes.

"That's rather funny, isn't it?" she said.

"Maybe to you but not to me."

"My goodness." She couldn't repress her laughter. "When you came to this town, your only relative was your sister, and now look at you. You're a property owner, you have a wife, and you have cousins. So why not add a grandfather?"

"I'm really not seeing the humor in any of this."

In the end, Sara won. Mike suggested that Luke deliver the dogs, but Sara pointed out that it took Mike's background and knowledge to ask Mr. Lang the correct questions.

"Questions about what?" Mike growled.

"About why Greg and Mr. Lang have been at war," Sara said. "Did you forget that?"

"I haven't forgotten anything in spite of my great age that you keep reminding me of."

She ignored his remark. "Okay, I'll go alone."

Mike looked at her with almost a smile.

"But I tried the big collapsible dog crate, and it won't fit in my car or Joce's, so I'll have to use yours. I'll drive it with the trunk lid up. That's all right, isn't it?" She blinked innocently at him.

"Luke's truck," he said with his teeth clenched.

"In the shop."

As he picked up his car keys, he said, "I remember when I used to be in charge of everything."

By the time they got to Merlin's Farm and saw Mr. Lang's old truck there, Sara was having to work to keep her courage up. When Mike turned off the ignition, she was tempted to say she couldn't do it—but he didn't give her a chance.

"I'll wait for you here," he said.

"No you won't." From the backseat, the dogs yipped, but Mike turned and gave them a look that made them sit down in their cage.

They heard a door slam and Mr. Lang came out with a shotgun in his hands, but when he saw Mike's car, he put the gun to his side. His round face twisted into an expression that could be taken for a smile.

"Will you call him Gramps?" Sara asked.

"Wait until the next time I get you in the gym," he said under his breath as he got out of the car.

"You're Prudie's grandson," Mr. Lang rasped out.

"That I am," Mike murmured as he opened the back door of the car. He was careful when he removed the big crate; he didn't want to hurt the leather of his seats.

Sara had walked around the car to stand behind him, and the look on Mr. Lang's old face when he saw the dogs almost made her forgive him everything. She tried to forget the fear she'd felt since she was a child—and she wanted to forget about his retaliations on people who crossed him.

Mike unzipped the cage, clipped on leashes, and let the dogs out. They were young and energetic and wanted to run. "This is Baron and Baroness," Mike said, "and they're an unrelated pair, so their breeding will be healthy. They've had shots and microchips saying they belong to you put in their necks."

Mr. Lang went down on his old knees to put his arms around the dogs. "Thank you," he said.

Sara was looking at him with sympathy. Everyone in town always worked to stay away from the vindictive old man, so she'd never considered how lonely he must be.

"What happened to your other dogs?" she asked before she thought. The moment it was out, she expected Mike to give her a look to be quiet, but he didn't so much as turn around. He was still holding the leashes of the dogs and his eyes were on Brewster Lang.

Mr. Lang looked up at Sara, and the happiness on his face was replaced with a sneer.

Mike put his body between her and the old man. "She's my wife and you will treat her with respect. Her name is Mrs. Newland." Mike's voice was low.

"Wife? You married a—"

"I know what you did, so you can drop the fake hatred of the McDowells."

Sara peeped around Mike to watch Mr. Lang's face. It went from confusion to shock to fear, and finally, to delight.

"You know?" His voice was so low she could hardly hear him. "You know that your grandmother and I were . . . were sweethearts? And that you are—?"

It looked as though Mike was right and Mr. Lang remembered what happened that night as a love story.

Mike interrupted him. "There are things that shouldn't be said out loud. I'm a policeman and I'd be duty bound to report what I hear."

Sara knew that the statute of limitations for rape was about seven years, but from the fear that ran across his face, Mr. Lang didn't seem to know that. Come to think of it, she hadn't seen a TV in the house, and she doubted if he had Internet service. It looked like he wasn't much in touch with the outside world.

Standing up, Mr. Lang nodded. The dogs were at his feet, and they already seemed to knew who their owner was.

"I have questions to ask you," Mike said as he handed him the leashes and took the shotgun from where it rested on the gravel.

Mr. Lang took the dogs' straps, wrapped them around his hands, and started toward the house. As the leader, he was in the front, not the dogs.

When they reached the house, Mr. Lang opened the door for Mike, but he stood where he was and glared at Lang. Reluctantly, the old man stepped back and let Sara go in first, then Mike, while he stayed outside to take care of the dogs.

Sara and Mike went into the living room and sat down on

the old couch. "You forgot to tell me what not to talk about," she whispered.

"Say anything you want. That old man would die before he gave out any information. He won't spread the news that we're married."

Minutes later, Mr. Lang came into the room carrying a tray full of matching cups and saucers, a teapot, and cookies on a plate. Sara's eyes widened as she recognized the china pattern as one she'd seen in a museum. He poured tea into what had to be a hundred-year-old cup, as fragile as a butterfly's wing, and held it out to Mike.

He nodded toward Sara and with a grimace—a step up from his sneer—Lang handed her the cup.

She took a sip. "Jasmine?"

Mr. Lang just shrugged at her. He looked only at Mike, and his big eyes seemed ready to melt.

"My wife asked you a question."

"Yeah, it's jasmine. I grow it."

"My mother would like to sell this. I've never tasted better."

"She'd sell me if she could," Mr. Lang mumbled. "Your mother turns everything into money."

When Mike started to speak, Sara gently elbowed him. "Actually, that's true. I guess, Mr. Lang, that's why you and I are two of the poorest people in town."

He looked at Sara with blank eyes. "You'll make money on that shop of yours."

"Not if Greg gets what he deserves," Sara said as she picked up a cookie. There were dark flecks in them.

"If those are full of marijuana," Mike said, "I'll—"

"They're lavender!" Sara said. "I can taste it and smell it. If my mother knew you made these—"

"She'd come for my recipes," he said, glaring at Sara.

"Don't worry. I won't tell her. Did you know that Mike now owns Merlin's Farm?"

Mike was looking around the room with a carpenter's eye. The first thing that needed to be done was to inspect it for dry rot and termites, but maybe Ramsey'd had that done. Any wood that needed replacing would have to come from an architectural salvage company. And where would they put a TV in this room? The fireplace was off center, with a built-in cabinet next to it. Could it be wired for cable and a stereo? "What?" he asked when he felt Sara staring at him.

"I was telling Mr. Lang that you now own this farm."

The old man's face showed his astonishment. "You will live here? With me?" He looked as though he'd seen heaven on earth.

"No. I have years before I can retire, so I'll be in South Florida until then. Tell me everything you know about Greg Anders and don't leave out a word."

"He is a very bad man." Lang cut his eyes at Sara, then back to Mike. "Anders likes women."

"We know all that." Mike's voice was harsh and quick, and Sara imagined it was how he usually spoke to criminals. But Mr. Lang didn't seem to mind. He looked at Mike with admiration—and Sara was sure the old man thought he was looking at his own grandson.

"Tell us what we don't know. Why all the traps?"

Mr. Lang blinked in surprise at Mike. "You know about them?"

Mike scowled. "I almost got hit by a couple of your darts and that horse harness you tied up in the barn almost fell on my wife."

Mr. Lang's round little mouth dropped open. "You're like me. I go places and no one knows I've been there."

"I'm not at all like you. What I want to know is why Greg Anders wants Merlin's Farm." There was a flicker in the old man's eyes.

It was for only a microsecond, but Mike saw it. The old man was hiding something. "What did you see in your spying?"

Lang leaned toward Mike, across the tea tray on the coffee table, and whispered—as though Sara, just a foot away, couldn't hear him. "When he's with the women, he steals from them, but they don't know it."

"And how does he manage that?"

"He goes through their purses and their cars." Lang gave a sigh. "None of them live in Edilean, so I don't know what he does in their houses."

"But a woman would notice something missing from her handbag and no one said anything to us at the shop," Sara said.

"Vandlo wanted information, not goods," Mike said over his shoulder. "Did he ever see you watching him?"

Lang frowned. "I'm not as good as I used to be. Can't move as fast."

"So you were spying on him, saw him searching the women's property, and he caught you. Then what?"

Lang's little mouth tightened. "He came here, said he'd kill my dogs if I told. I said I never told anyone anything."

"That's true," Sara said. "You have an extraordinary ability to keep secrets."

Lang looked at her as though trying to decide if she was giving him a compliment or being snide.

Sara smiled at him. "Do you have any more cookies?"

Lang looked at her for a long moment, as though trying to figure her out. "I have some with nasties in them."

"I don't like—" Mike began, but Sara put her hand on his arm. "Nasturtiums? Flowers or seed pods?"

"Flowers, of course." He didn't seem to think much of her gardening skills. "I pickle the pods."

"You wouldn't have made any of those, would you?"

Mr. Lang got up and went to the kitchen.

"You got rid of him," Mike said, "so what do you want to tell me?"

"Did you really *look* at that tea set? It's eighteenth century if it's a day. And these are old recipes. We went through this house thoroughly but I didn't see these dishes, did you?"

Smiling, Mike kissed her cheek. "You *are* a good detective. Maybe there's something here, after all. I'll tell Vandlo I own the farm. It's another thing he'll have to come through me to get." As he said it, he took Sara's hand in reassurance.

"Mike!" Sara said in exasperation. "That wasn't my point. I thought you and I together could search and—"

"Shhhh. He's coming."

Lang sat down, a red metal box in his hands, and she recognized it from having seen it in magazines. It was a candy box from the 1920s, in pristine condition and valuable to a collector. Inside were fresh cookies with pretty nasturtium flowers put into them while they were still warm.

Sara took one but Mike passed. She took a bite. Delicious. "If you sell these at Luke's booth at the fair I'll see that you get a hundred percent of the money."

"No rent, no commission?"

"Nothing," Sara said. "In fact, if you want to use Luke's wife's new kitchen to do the baking, Joce will help you."

"Don't you think you should ask her first?" Mike asked.

Sara shrugged. "She's so bored she'd work with the devil. Sorry, no offense, Mr. Lang."

The old man and Mike were looking at her with identical stares of consternation.

"So, uh, back to Greg," Sara said as she leaned back on the

old sofa, two cookies in her hands. She'd had an ulterior motive in sending Mr. Lang to Joce's house. If he was going to be hanging around the fair, then she wanted him bonded to Joce. Mike said there was no danger to Joce even though she was holding the tarot cards as bait, but Sara wasn't so sure. Besides, Mr. Lang was more experienced in spying than all of Mike's fancy Federal agents put together.

She took another bite. "Oh wait! Did you use stevia?"

"Grow it myself."

Sara nodded. "My mother's erotic dreams have come true. Okay, I'm done."

Rolling his eyes, Mike looked back at Lang. "Did you ever see Anders with an older woman, early fifties? She has a prominent nose."

Lang smirked like a dirty little boy. "I saw him with two at once. An old one and a young one. Together." He looked at Sara, but she studiously kept her eyes on the cookie.

"Look at me," Mike said, "not my wife. Are you saying that Anders killed your dogs just to keep you from telling what you know?"

When Mr. Lang said nothing, Sara spoke. "I don't mean to butt in, but my guess is that the dogs were Greg's way of punishing you because you told the sheriff, didn't you?"

Lang looked down at his hands.

Mike fell back against the couch, his face a study in exasperation. "Are you saying there's a *sheriff* in this one-horse town? And you told him about Anders's thievery?"

Lang shrugged, but he didn't look up.

Mike turned to Sara. "Why wasn't I told about a police force in this little town? I figured this place was in Williamsburg's jurisdiction."

"It is, more or less, and there's the county sheriff," Sara said, "but we have our own, sort of, caretakers. They don't get paid, so outsiders don't consider them real."

Mike waited but neither Lang nor Sara said anything else. "Might I be told *who* handles this 'sort of' police force?"

Sara smiled. "Guess."

"Sara, I don't—" He sighed. "My cousins, the Fraziers."

"You are such a clever man!"

Mike ran his hand over his face, then looked at Lang. "You told the . . . the honorary sheriff that Anders was sleeping with half the women in the county, mostly married women, and he steals information from them. Was he blackmailing them too?"

Again, Lang shrugged. "I don't know. Stealing isn't right."

"Neither is spying on people," Mike snapped, then calmed. "I guess the sheriff talked to Anders and later your dogs were . . ."

"Poisoned," Mr. Lang said.

"But that wasn't the end of it," Mike said, "because afterward you put up traps all over this place. If you'd put them up beforehand, your dogs wouldn't have died."

Mr. Lang nodded, then said quietly, "I think he did it on purpose."

"What do you mean?" Mike asked.

"I think Anders wanted me to see him, wanted me to go to a Frazier. He *wanted* to kill my dogs." There was a catch in the old man's throat.

"That would mean that the real target was *you*," Mike said. "You're well known for greeting guests with a shotgun, so is there anything around *here* that Anders wants?"

Again, there was that flicker in the old man's eyes.

"What are you hiding?" Mike asked quickly, but Lang said nothing.

"Any Civil War silver?" Sara asked into the silence. "More of this china?"

"No," Lang said. "It's not mine any way. Belongs to . . ." He looked at Mike, his eyes full of love. "Prudie's grandson."

"All this makes you even more of a target," Sara said softly to Mike, with fear in her voice. "If what Greg wants is here, when he finds out you own this place, he'll . . . he'll . . ."

"Good!" Mike said. He reached into his shirt pocket, withdrew a photo, and handed it to Lang. It was the picture of Mitzi Vandlo, taken when she was a teenager, but it had been age progressed. "Have you ever seen this woman?"

Lang barely glanced at it. "No."

"Look at it again."

Reluctantly, Lang took the picture, studied it, then gave it back to Mike. "No."

"You're sure?"

"I remember faces. Never seen her before."

Mike put the photo away. "This weekend is the fair. I want you to snoop around, spy on people, and tell me everything you see."

"Dirty people in this town," Lang said primly. "Always in bed together."

"The things you get up to in private are just as bad," Mike said as he looked at his watch. "I want you to tear down every trap you've set around here. Don't leave one of them. And burn the Mary Jane."

"I think it would be better if you buried it," Sara said, "or it might be like in that movie *Saving Grace*. We don't want Colin dancing around in the nude."

Mike looked at her as though she were crazy, but Mr. Lang gave an expression almost like a smile.

Sara didn't say anything, but she knew he'd seen the obscure movie. He might not have TV but, somewhere, he had a DVD player. Wonder if he's seen *Mad Men*? she thought. And he'd probably love *Dexter*.

"We need to go," Mike said as he stood up and looked down at Lang. "Remember to tell me everything." He put his hand on Sara's lower back and escorted her to the door. Lang went out with them, but he stopped by the dogs. Sara didn't think she was supposed to see that Mike slipped Mr. Lang some folded hundred-dollar bills, about five of them, and again told him to get rid of the traps.

After Mike opened the car door for Sara, he went to his trunk. It had half a dozen fifty-pound bags of dog food inside. "I'd put them away for you," he called to Lang, "but not until the traps are gone. Do it today."

Sara watched Mr. Lang nod, then Mike pulled out of the drive. "You weren't afraid of visiting him at all, were you?"

"Why would I be afraid?"

She stared at his profile until he smiled.

"Sara, my dear, I've seen how you love to take care of people, so I let you take care of me."

For a moment, she couldn't say anything. When Mike had been saying he didn't want to visit Mr. Lang, he had been completely convincing—but he'd been lying. She suddenly saw how he'd been able to work undercover for so many years. "Did you find out what you need to know?"

"Not a word of it, but he made me think about some things. From the time Vandlo was a kid, he was trained in reading people's faces. All he had to do was see the way your eyes got dreamy whenever that rotting old farm was mentioned and of course he'd start saying he was going to buy it for you. You know, Sara, I'm beginning to think that it might be true that Vandlo wanted that old farm just to please you."

"No," she said softly. "That would imply that he loved me, but he never came close."

"Really stupid man." Mike reached over to take her hand.

This time, she knew he was lying—and distracting her from Mr. Lang. He'd found out a lot but he didn't want to tell her what it was.

"So how about we get take-out sandwiches, go home, and eat them off each other's bellies before we go to the fair?"

"I don't think I've ever heard a better plan," Sara said, smiling.

But on the drive home, his cell rang, he said a few words, then hung up. "Stefan Vandlo has been released."

# 24

B Y THE TIME they'd bought sandwiches, driven back to Edilean Manor, and Mike had made a pitcher of green tea—he refused to drink carbonated beverages—their minds were on things other than bellies. All Sara could think was, This is it. Now it was just a matter of time before the "action" would start. Over the next few days she and Mike would have little time to be alone. He'd told her that at least a dozen agents would be coming to Edilean for the fair. They'd all be undercover, so any couple or groups of flirting males and females could actually be well-armed law enforcement people.

The sober news had taken away their original eating plan. They both had the same sandwiches: lean meat and lots of vegetables. Sara'd given up her tuna salad that was drowning in mayonnaise.

"I think I should go over some things with you," Mike said from across the table. He reiterated that at the fair they would act like a normal couple, lots of hand holding, teasing, laughing together. The idea was to shock the townspeople and set them to talking. It was to be a buildup to when Stefan Vandlo arrived and Sara told him—and the town—that she and Mike were married.

When he saw that what he was saying was scaring Sara, he tried to entertain her with a story from the dossiers he'd read. It was said that when Mitzi's husband found out that he'd been tricked into marrying an ugly woman, he couldn't consummate the marriage. But his young wife still got pregnant, and her old husband was too proud to say that he'd never touched the girl. When the boy was born and said to resemble a handsome young man who was a master pickpocket, no one mentioned it, but six days after the baby's birth, the young man was found dead. It was years later, when the husband said he was leaving everything to his stupid and cruel son with his first wife, that Mitzi's husband was found at the bottom of a staircase with holes smashed into his head.

When Mike finished the story, he again talked of using the games at the fair to draw attention to himself—and that made Sara think about what would happen when it was all over.

When they take Greg and his mother away in handcuffs, Mike will leave with them and I'll never see him again, she thought.

She did her best to calm down. It wasn't as though he'd lied to her. From the first he'd told her he was marrying her for the case. He'd even told her that after it was done they could divorce. And since the wedding, he certainly hadn't said he loved her. And he hadn't—

"Sara?"

"Sorry, my mind was wandering."

"You want some more tea?"

She held up her empty glass, and he filled it. "Last time" kept going through her head. A few days from now it would be like they'd never met. Their whirlwind relationship would be finished and they'd go back to the way they had been. She had a vision of herself alone in her little apartment, a hundred dresses on her lap. Maybe she'd take some refresher courses and try to get a job as a conservationist in Williamsburg.

She looked across the table at Mike. When they'd come in, he'd removed his clean white shirt and his shoes and socks. Now all he had on was his perfectly pressed black trousers and the belt with the little gold buckle. She'd ironed his trousers that morning and she'd chosen that belt when they were in Fort Lauderdale. His whiskers were very black and she knew he hadn't shaved before they went to see Mr. Lang because he'd been too busy making love to her. As for Sara, she'd removed her dress and was wearing her favorite blue teddy.

She wanted to reach out and touch him, but she didn't. He was telling her about the cameras they'd installed in the fortune-telling tent, but she could tell that he was worried about something. She hoped it was the case and not what she feared, that he was thinking about how to let her down easily when he told her she was just another victim that he'd had to rescue.

"Can you remember all that?" Mike asked.

She hadn't been listening, but then she'd heard it all before. "Tell no one we're married. That's to be dropped on Greg when I see him."

"And?"

"Be sure and get him into the open. To get the ultimate effect, I'm to shock him by telling him that just before our wedding I ran off with another man."

Mike raised an eyebrow at her sarcastic tone. "I hear his wife had a face-lift and she's looking good."

"That's nice," Sara said as she cleared the table.

"Your mother texted me that I'm to go to her house early tomorrow to get dressed."

Sara had her back to him as she stood at the kitchen sink. "In your kilt. Nearly all the men from Edilean will be wearing them, even my father and he hates dressing up. Luke will—"

Before she could finish her sentence, she was crying. Instantly, Mike had her in his arms. She buried her face in the warm skin of his shoulder and the tears kept coming.

Picking her up, he carried her into the bedroom, where he put her on the bed and stretched out beside her, his arms around her.

"I don't know what's wrong with me," she said.

He handed her a tissue and stroked her hair. "It's all right to be frightened. I wish you didn't have to do this, but we need to surprise Vandlo, and only you can do that. From the second you've told him that his plan has been foiled, we'll tail him so close that he—"

"It's not that," she said. She ran her hand across his bare chest, her fingers in the dark hair. Would they ever be together like this again? Who was going to make her go to the gym? Who was going to hold her when she cried? And make her laugh?

"Then what is it?" Mike asked. "You can tell me."

But she couldn't tell him. Her pride and her fear of yet another rejection wouldn't allow her to tell him what was bothering her.

They lay together in silence for a while. Sara knew they should get up and start getting ready for the fair. Mike would have to put on a kilt, and she knew that would cause a lot of laughter. And Sara had some long-skirted, medieval-looking dresses she wore, and of course Luke would have saved one of his wildflower circlets for her hair. She looked forward to it all, but right now she couldn't bear to separate from Mike.

Lifting her left hand up, he looked at her rings.

Sara turned onto her back, her body pressed against his. She could feel the fabric of his trousers against her bare legs. Again "the last time" rang in her head.

"They look good on you," he said.

"They're the most beautiful rings in the world."

"Everything was such a rush when I chose the diamond ring that I wasn't sure I was getting the right one."

"My mother didn't help you?"

"No. She stood by the computer and hovered over me like a bird of prey. I don't think anyone's ever made me as nervous as your mother does."

"Me either."

"When I said I wanted *this* ring, she kissed me on the cheek. I think maybe there were tears in her eyes."

"She knew I'd like it, that's why. Kim makes some modern rings that I don't care for."

"I saw those, but I couldn't see you wearing one of them. Do the rings fit? Will you have trouble getting them off?"

Sara's fingers curled up and she put her hand under the small of her back. "I'm not removing them. Ever."

He turned to look at her. "You have to. If the people of Edilean see the rings before Stefan gets there, they'll talk. Mitzi will hear, and she might call her son and warn him. As much as we want to, we can't tap into those throwaway phones they use."

"I guess you'll just have to figure out a way to keep my rings from showing because I am *not* removing them." She said this in her fiercest voice, letting him know that no matter how much he tried, he wasn't going to win.

But Mike didn't protest. Instead, he just lay there beside her, his arm under her shoulders.

"I, uh . . . I wanted to talk to you about something," he said at last.

Here it comes, Sara thought, and her body went rigid.

"As soon as this case is done, meaning that the Vandlos are taken away, I have to go back to Fort Lauderdale. I have three other cases pending, and I need to take care of them. The Vandlos aren't really my problem. I was just asked to help out because I have a sister here and . . ." He trailed off.

"And what?" she asked in a whisper.

"I was pretty angry that they burned down my apartment, but it worked out well, didn't it? That place the captain got me is nice, isn't it?"

"It's beautiful."

"A bit big though," he said.

"Quite large," she answered.

He was silent for a moment, and she almost didn't breathe.

"Sara," he said at last, "I know your life is here in this town and all your friends and relatives are here, but—"

"So are yours."

"My what?"

"All your relatives are here. And you and Luke seem to be hitting it off. And I think you'll like Ramsey."

"Yeah," he said, "but that isn't what I meant. I can live anywhere. But you've only lived here in this little town, so leaving it might be too much for you."

Slowly, it was dawning on her what he was saying. "You think I couldn't bear to get away from my mother who thinks it's her duty to tell me how to live? That I can't be away from snooping relatives who click their tongues at me because they thought the man I dated for four years ran off and left me? Get away from their pity because I was swept up by a man nobody can stand? Is that what you're asking me?"

She could feel his smile.

"Actually, that's exactly what I was asking. I know we don't know each other very well, but we've hardly ever argued and we seem to agree on most things."

"Except for food and the right to lie down for three straight hours to watch TV without doing even one form of exercise. And—"

When Mike laughed, Sara moved her hand to his flat, hard stomach. She could feel the ridges of muscle there.

Moving onto his side, he propped his head on his hand. "But we do agree on the fundamentals."

"Such as that you think I should do exactly what you tell me to every minute of the day?" she asked innocently.

"I was thinking of important things, like music."

"You like opera and I like—" She broke off because he kissed her, and her arms went around his neck.

He pulled away to look at her. "You want to go back to Fort Lauderdale with me and see if we can make this marriage work?"

"Yes," she said. "I'd like that very much."

He kissed her again, but in a way he'd never kissed her before. From the first moment they'd come together, there'd been great passion between them. They'd had sex on every conceivable surface, and in every position that Sara's flexible body and Mike's muscle could come up with.

But this kiss was different. There was something in it besides passion. There was a yearning, a longing for a great deal more than they'd given each other before. For all that Sara was surrounded by people who knew her, and for all of Mike's frequent conquests, essentially, they were alone. They clung to each other.

Mike moved back from the tender kiss. His body was half on top of hers and his hands smoothed her hair back as he looked at her face as though memorizing her features.

Sara held her breath. Was he going to say those three little words that she so very much wanted to hear?

"You know, Sara . . ."

"Yes?" she whispered, her breath held in anticipation.

"I hate those dishes you picked out."

"What?"

He rolled off of her and onto his back. "Those dishes with the flowers on them, I can't stand them."

She moved half on top of him. "Those dishes are Villeroy and Boch and they're great." She was kissing his neck.

Mike unbuckled his trousers. "I don't care what they are. I still don't like them."

"You better get used to them because I'm going to register that pattern and everyone in Edilean will give us place settings."

He held her away for a moment. "We'll get wedding gifts?"

"Sure, of course. Everyone in town will—"

"In *this* town? That'll get us what? Four gifts?" He slid the straps of her teddy down her arms.

"Very funny! Did you forget that the Fraziers are your relatives? I'll get Mrs. Frazier to throw a reception for us at their house. They'll invite the governor." Mike's mouth was on her breast. "And of course we're both related to the McDowells, and they're rich. I'll get the Fraziers and the McDowells to compete as to who can give us the most."

Mike stopped kissing to look at her. "I had no idea you were so mercenary."

She gave an evil little laugh. "I want every person who's said 'poor Sara' to *pay!*"

"You are truly wicked," he said, smiling.

"You ain't seen nothin' yet, baby," she said as her lips moved much lower on his body.

Mike didn't reply.

An hour later, Mike said she'd kept him too busy to get his work done. And her mother had left him four text messages asking him where he was and saying he had to go to her house to get dressed.

"Maybe I should show up like this," he said as he headed toward the shower. He was naked.

"You may think you'd scare my mother, but far from it. You'd end up being the one with the red face."

"Speaking of red body parts, I don't really have to wear—"

"There's no way you'll get out of putting on a kilt, so don't even try. I'll meet you at the fairgrounds in a little while. I'm going to go see Joce."

"Sure you don't want to join me in the shower?"

"You're postponing the inevitable." She wanted the time to dress properly and to think about her future—her new life.

"You're dying to tell your friend that you managed to tie a ball and chain around me, aren't you?"

"You're free to run back to the life you had. Oh! Wait! You didn't *have* a life."

Mike grinned. "Go. I'll see you at the fair. I'll be wearing a skirt. Half naked."

Laughing, Sara left the apartment.

Joce's eyes widened when she saw her friend. "Sara! What's wrong with your neck? You look like you were burned."

She put her hand up to her throat. "It's nothing."

"But that's not 'nothing.' Did you show that rash to your father?"

"Are you crazy?"

"Ah," Joce said slowly. "It's whisker burn, isn't it?"

Sara didn't answer.

"How far does it extend?"

Sara raised her eyebrows in a way that made Joce laugh. "You have to tell Tess."

Sara looked at her in disbelief. "Tell Mike's sister that I'm having a great time in bed with her brother? I don't think so. But . . ."

"But what?" Joce asked.

"Mike asked me to go to Fort Lauderdale to live with him. We're to see if our marriage will work." Sara held out her left hand to show her ring.

"I'm telling Tess," Joce said as she admired the three-diamond engagement ring. "She'll be as glad for you as I am." She picked up her phone. "We'll have to tell Tess in a way that'll make her laugh. Rams told Luke the hormones are getting to her and she's crying a lot."

"*Tess* is crying?"

"Yes. Wait until you're—Okay, too soon for that, but we must tell her about you and Mike."

Sara typed, handed the phone to Joce, who read it and said, "Perfect." She pushed Send.

In Venice, Tess's cell buzzed and she picked it up just before Rams made a flying leap for it.

"If it's that brother of yours and he makes you cry again, I'll—"

"It's Sara." Tess read the text and burst into tears.

"I'm going to kill him," Rams said as he snatched the little machine from his wife.

"Good cry. Good news," Tess sobbed. "Hormones."

"Yeah, I know. They're six hundred times normal." He was pushing buttons to bring up Sara's message. "Damnation!" he muttered. "I'm going to have to talk to my cousin about sending porno over the airwaves."

Tess blew her nose. "You're a prude. Give that back to me."

Grimacing, he handed her the phone.

"I'm going to get Joce to tell me the details. Oh! But I wish we could go home." Again, she looked at Sara's text message.

YOUR BROTHER PUT WHISKER BURNS ALL OVER MY BODY.
DIDN'T MISS A SPOT. HE ASKED ME TO GO TO FORT LAUDER-
DALE TO LIVE WITH HIM. SARA.

Sara spent over an hour with Joce, helping her memorize her lines for her role as a fortune-teller. Luke had ordered a copy of a fortune-telling book published in 1891 that explained how fortunes had been told for centuries by people without any psychic ability.

"Okay," Sara said, "let's go over it again," even though she knew Joce had it down pat.

"To an unmarried woman, I say, 'You are often lonely, but at the same time, you enjoy your time alone.' To a married woman, I say, 'You often feel that your husband doesn't understand you.'" Joce glanced down again. "An older man gets, 'You were once unfairly punished for a good deed you did someone.'" She looked at Sara. "Do you think that's universal enough that every old man will think it's true?"

"I don't know. Tell me what you think after you've told a hundred fortunes."

Joce looked back at her cards. "Mike told me to tell every woman over thirty this one. 'Something you've been planning for a long time is about to come true.' And Luke saw on TV that if you say, 'You are one person to the world and another one in private,' everyone will agree with you."

"That's true for me, what about you?"

"Sure, of course. Don't you think you should go make yourself pretty? It's getting late. Will . . . will Greg be there?"

"I don't know. I know he's been released, but Mike won't tell me where he is, so I don't know how long it'll take him to get here. Mike wants me to be surprised when Greg shows up."

"A surprise is when you're told you're carrying two babies instead of one. Seeing a man who wants to kill you is your brakes failing on a mountain road. That is not what I'd term a 'surprise.'" She paused. "Sara . . ."

"I know. I can't think about any of this or I'll get scared. Mike will be there, and he's going to talk to the Fraziers and . . ." She looked back at Joce. "It'll be all right. You want to go over the cards again?"

"No, I think I have it. Some of these things that are said to people make me sick." She picked up a card. "The book said that older, unmarried women are the most likely to go to fortune-tellers because they're desperate in their attempt to find a good man. It says the woman is frequently lonely and bitter, and the clue that this woman will pay for help is her use of sarcasm."

"Did they work hard to figure that one out?" Sara said, and they laughed.

Waving, she left the room. As she reached the back door, she looked up and saw Mr. Lang's old truck drive in, and the back looked to be full. "Uh, Joce," she called. "I sort of volunteered the use of your kitchen to Mr. Lang and I said you'd chop things for him."

"You did what?!" Joce yelled, but Sara had already slipped out the door.

# 25

WHEN MIKE GOT in his car, he had every intention of going to Ellie's to get dressed, but he kept thinking about Lang's house. Earlier, while Sara and Lang had been rambling on about cookies, he was looking at the room with an eye to bringing it up to a livable code. But something hadn't been right. He hadn't seen anything wrong or out of place or even odd—but he'd felt it. Of course Lang was lying about most everything he'd said, but that seemed to be his MO. As far as Mike could tell, the old man didn't seem to know how to tell the truth—or all of it, anyway. It was no wonder Lang thought Mike was his relative, Mike thought. They had a lot in common.

Whatever Mike had seen that morning was still haunting him, so he was going back to the farm to have a closer look.

As he pulled up next to the old house, he realized that it was because of Sara that he could make this impromptu visit. It had been her idea to replace Lang's dogs, so the animals knew Mike. Had

Lang adopted dogs on his own, Mike probably wouldn't have been able to walk onto the property as easily. Also, Sara got rid of Lang for the afternoon. Poor Joce.

It took Mike only twenty minutes inside the house to find what he was looking for. Electricity, he thought. Who could have imagined that electrical cords and lightbulbs would bring the downfall of criminals?

When Mike found what so many people had been looking for, he was so jubilant he wanted to call Sara and tell her—but he couldn't. It was better that she didn't know what was going on. Instead, he called Luke. From the background noise, he was at the fairgrounds. "Are you busy?"

"Everyone in this town is asking me to do so many things that I'm ready to take a pistol to them," Luke said in exasperation. "The answer is no, I'm not busy at all."

"I need your help," Mike said, "and I've solved the case."

"Did you find Mitzi or did you figure out what they want?"

"I have what they're after. Could you meet me at Merlin's Farm with your truck ASAP?"

"Ten minutes too long?"

"Yeah. Cut it shorter." He could hear Luke beginning to run as he held the phone to his ear. "If I call Sara's mother, will she help me or lecture me about some damned skirt I'm supposed to put on?"

"She'll do whatever's needed to protect her daughter. Want me to call her for you?"

"Naw." Mike could hear Luke starting his truck. "I now have a mother-in-law, and I think I should learn to deal with her."

"Good luck on that," Luke said as he snapped his phone shut. Six minutes later, after Mike had called Ellie and said he couldn't be there right now but to please not tell Sara, Luke skidded into the driveway of Merlin's Farm. The dogs went crazy barking, but Mike told them to sit and stay, and they obeyed.

"Let me show you what I found," Mike said and led the way into the house to the treasure trove in the secret closet.

A few minutes later he called Tess to find out the details about Sara's rights of ownership of the paintings he'd found. She turned the phone over to Ramsey, for him to explain.

Under the terms of her Aunt Lissie's will, all the paintings were owned by Sara. "I leave all CAY's paintings to my dear niece," the will said. At the time the will was written, there'd been only one watercolor, the funny one with the purple ducks. But it was Ramsey's father, Benjamin, who'd added the word "all" when he drew up the will. He'd said he wanted to be covered in case more showed up.

"Since you now own the house," Rams said to Mike, "there might be a case for you to sue her for ownership." When Mike didn't bother to reply to that, Ramsey laughed in an approving way. "You didn't ask, but legally, the rest of the things in the closet belong to you."

"Everything will be given to the descendants of the owners," Mike said quickly.

"Good," Rams said softly. "Let me know when it's safe for us to go home. Tess and I miss everyone. And, by the way, I heard you and Sara are staying together. Congratulations."

Again, that old feeling of hating everyone knowing his business went through Mike, especially since he'd never met this man. "Thanks," he managed to say.

"And I guess you won't be needing any financial help with restoring Merlin's Farm."

Even though Rams said it in the tone of a joke, Mike frowned. He wouldn't have accepted help, but he was now realizing that he'd married an heiress. And a rich woman could do better than a cop who hadn't even gone to college. "No, I won't need any help," Mike said and clicked off.

Two hours later, he and Luke drove away with the back of his pickup and Mike's car filled. They went to the storage place where Mike had a unit. It didn't take long to push his meager belongings to the back—Tess had rented him a big place in the hope that he'd fill it. The men began unloading the vehicles, and when they'd finished, they were both sweaty and dirty.

"Cover for me with Sara, will you?" Mike asked. "She thinks I'm at her mother's house. I have to make some calls so I can piece all this together."

"What about Vandlo?" Luke asked.

"He won't be here until tomorrow. I'm told every hour where he is, but when he does get here, he won't find what he's looking for."

"Except for Sara. I'm concerned that he'll be *very* angry to find his plans destroyed."

"That's an understatement, but I'm working to arrange it so he takes his rage out on me."

"And if he doesn't?" Luke asked.

"Sara doesn't know this, but tomorrow after she makes contact with Vandlo and tells him she married someone else, she'll be put in a van and taken away. If Vandlo wants revenge, I'll be the only one there." Luke still looked skeptical. "You have to trust me. I've been doing this for a while now and I can assure you that Sara is very valuable to me."

"The whole town knows that. The gossip is that when you look at her—"

"Leave me *some* pride," Mike said as he pulled the door to the storage unit down and locked it. "Let's get out of here."

"I think you should get to the fair as soon as you can. On opening night about five hundred people show up, and I don't like Sara being unprotected."

"She isn't and she won't be," Mike said. After Luke drove away, Mike parked his car a mile from the storage place, stood under a tree, and started pushing buttons on his phone.

Mike had always believed that there was a connection between his grandmother, Merlin's Farm, and the Vandlos, but he'd never been able to see what it was. By finding what Mitzi was after, Mike now had an idea of how the alliance could have been made.

He called the retirement home in Ohio where his grandmother had spent the last years of her life, where she'd died, and asked to speak to the head of nursing. He was put through right away. After he gave his credentials and told her some about the investigation, it didn't take long to find the person he was seeking. The large nose made Mitzi easily identifiable. As Mike suspected, she'd worked there, using the assumed name of Hazel Smith, and the nurse was eager to talk about her.

"I don't want to speak ill of anyone, but Hazel was a horrible woman," the nurse said. "After she left, the employees started swapping tales, and we found out what she'd done. She'd tell one person one thing and someone else another. While she was here, we had nothing but chaos. The problem was that none of us knew who was causing it. On the surface, Hazel seemed to be the most caring person we'd ever had here, and I was caught like everyone else was. Hazel came to me one day and said she'd seen my best nurse stealing from a patient who'd just died. She cried while she told me and I'm ashamed to say that I believed every word. Because of her, I fired an excellent caretaker."

"If it helps any," Mike said, "the woman you know as Hazel Smith has made many people believe her. Would you tell me everything you can remember about the week or so just before my grandmother died?"

"I guess you want to know about the night Prudence went hysterical."

"Yes." Mike's heart was beating hard. "Please tell me everything about that." He couldn't rush this, as he needed the woman to confide in him, so he had to let her talk at her own pace.

"Well, first of all, Prudence wasn't . . . I'm sorry to say this, Mr. Newland, but she wasn't liked."

"Do you mean she cleared a room when she entered?"

"Yes, I'm afraid so. She used to rather often tell us a story about having been raped. Perhaps you've heard it?"

"Every week I had the misfortune of being near her, I had to listen to it. And with every retelling the violence and horror increased. By the end, I think she was saying that Alex McDowell had used a hammer to crush her legs."

"Yes, we found that too," the nurse said. "But did you know that we have a resident therapist? Your grandmother loved to go to him, and I shouldn't tell you this, but when her story changed each week, he did some investigating into old newspaper accounts of the incident. For one thing, the rape didn't happen when she said it did. It was at night, not during the day, and she was returning from a party where she'd been drinking. Did you know that?"

"No," Mike said quietly. "I didn't." He was disgusted with himself that he'd never thought to look at old records. But then, his grandmother's so-called rape was something he'd never wanted to hear another word about.

"The psychiatrist thought it was possible that Pru was more than a little drunk when it happened, and that there was a possibility that she welcomed the young man. Later, when the man she said had attacked her wouldn't marry her, and even denied that he'd so much as touched her . . . Well, the doctor thought that perhaps Pru had come to embellish the event so dramatically that maybe Mr. McDowell actually was innocent."

Mike knew the nurse's words sounded true and he wanted to

hear more, but now was not the time. "But that night when she went hysterical, did she say anything different?"

"Yes, she did. On that night, nearly all the residents were in the living room watching TV, the same as always, when Pru started screaming. We never did succeed in teaching your grandmother that there were times when other people's needs were just as important as hers."

Mike snorted. "A lesson no one could teach her. What was my grandmother shouting?"

"That she'd seen the paintings they were showing on TV."

He knew that he and Luke had just moved those paintings from where they'd been stored at Merlin's Farm. "What was the show?"

"*Lost Treasures*. Do you watch it?"

Mike's life didn't leave much time for TV, but it seemed pompous to say that. "I'm afraid I don't," he said. "What's it about?"

"Valuable things that have disappeared. Our residents love it, and we watch it every Thursday night. In that episode, they showed some old paintings of tropical plants in Florida, and said they were very, very valuable. It's hard to remember the details because five minutes after they came on the screen, Pru jumped up and started screeching at the top of her lungs."

"What exactly, as best as you can remember, did Grans say?"

"Something about a boy . . . Bruce . . . Langley?"

"Brewster Lang," Mike said.

"Yes! That's it. I'm sorry to say this, but we'd had a lot of trouble with your grandmother snooping through people's belongings. And she loved to spy on others. We had to be careful to lock every door."

"I know that well," Mike said softly.

"Yes, I imagine you would." The nurse's voice was sympathetic. "Anyway, Pru said that just before the rape she'd seen the paintings they were showing on TV in this boy's house. She'd been looking in the windows—spying, but she didn't say that—and saw him with the artwork spread all around. I think she said he saw her watching him. Is that possible?"

Mike imagined the evening. His grandmother had been an angry young woman with too much booze inside her and she was looking through Lang's windows. Spying was something that he knew she loved to do, and as a child he'd learned to keep his curtains closed and the doors bolted.

That night, Lang had looked up, seen her watching him, and had probably followed her outside. Maybe Pru was trying to run away on her bicycle and maybe Lang threw stones at the spokes. Or maybe she was so drunk she crashed. She'd always liked gin. As for Lang, he may have thought Pru had come to see him, as she often did. And it was possible that since it was night, he thought she had at last realized he was closer to being a man and not the boy she'd always thought he was.

When her bike went down, Pru may have hit her head. That, mixed with the drink, would have made her fuzzy about reality. She saw a kilt such as Alex McDowell, the man she believed she loved, wore, and one thing led to another. She probably welcomed the man with enthusiasm.

No wonder Lang celebrated that day every year, Mike thought, and he wondered how Lang felt when, later, Pru had demanded that Alex marry her.

"Mr. Newland?" the nurse asked, "are you there?"

"Yes. What happened after my grandmother went hysterical?"

"We had to give her a sedative to get her to bed. That would have been the end of it if it hadn't been for Hazel."

"My guess is that she was very interested in what my grandmother had said."

"Extremely. She had the late shift and everyone was talking

about it. Hazel asked everyone what had caused Pru to go crazy. No detail was too small for her. She said a most curious thing, something that I've never forgotten."

"And what was that?"

"She said that old people knew many secrets, and if they were old enough, they'd forget what was supposed to be kept secret."

"I think maybe you were being told the reason why Hazel was there," Mike said, thinking that it might be why Mitzi had taken on a job at an upscale retirement home. When she'd fled, hundreds of police and Federal agents were searching for her, so she'd needed to lay low for a while. She must have been wary of restarting her usual scams on grieving women. After all, some of them had betrayed her.

So Mitzi had taken a job at a retirement home full of patients with relatives who paid a lot for the care they received. Maybe Mitzi had only been looking for jewelry, but she'd hit a gold mine with Prudence Walker.

"After that night, Hazel and Prudence were best friends," the nurse said. "For over a week, Hazel neglected all our other residents to spend time with Pru. I should have stopped it but things were so quiet here that I didn't. I still didn't realize it was Hazel causing the turmoil. I thought the peace was due to Pru staying in her room, so I was glad to spare Hazel's work for that calm."

"What did they do?" Mike asked.

"Talked. Pru's door was kept closed, but we heard them chattering away endlessly. I know they read all the letters from your sister because we had to get the box out of storage."

"Did Hazel say what they were talking about?"

"No, not really. Oh! Yes, I remember. One time at lunch she said that she found some little town fascinating. It had an unusual name."

"Edilean, Virginia."

"Yes! That's it," the nurse said.

Mike figured that Hazel/Mitzi had read the letters to learn about Sara who, through her aunt's will, owned the lost paintings. At the time the will was written, there'd only been the small watercolor of the purple ducks that hung on Sara's wall. Mike wanted to kick himself for not paying attention when Sara told him that Stefan wanted that painting. At the time, Mike had been so enamored of Sara that he'd overlooked a clue that was right in front of him.

"And my grandmother died a few days after the incident with the TV?"

"Yes," the nurse said. "She died in her sleep, and the next day a tearful Hazel quit. She said she couldn't bear seeing the people she loved die."

Mike wasn't sure—not yet anyway—but he thought Mitzi had probably murdered his grandmother. After Mitzi had obtained all the information she needed from Prudence, she got rid of her so she couldn't tell anyone what had gone on between them.

"Would you e-mail me a copy of Hazel's employee photo?" Mike asked. "I'd like to see it."

"Certainly, Mr. Newland," the nurse said. "And please keep me informed of what happens."

He told her he would, gave her his e-mail address, then hung up.

Next, Mike called Tess and asked her to start the paperwork of exhuming their grandmother's body. They needed physical proof that she'd been murdered. "And do you have any of the letters Grans sent you?"

"All of them. I thought that someday you might want to see them."

"Not me, but if the letters mention a nurse named Hazel, the AG will be very interested."

If it could be proven that Hazel Smith was Mitzi Vandlo, and if the body showed evidence of foul play, it meant that she could be tried for murder. At last, Mizelli Vandlo would be charged with something more onerous than fraud.

Minutes later, the nursing home e-mailed Hazel's security photo to Mike's phone. Curious, he studied the picture, noting the big nose and the small, lipless mouth. Mitzi wasn't any better-looking now than she had been back in 1973 when she'd conned Marko Vandlo into making her his third wife. While it was interesting to see an older photo of the woman, he didn't remember ever having seen her in Edilean. As he stared at the picture, he wondered what she'd look like if she finally had a nose job.

He called Captain Erickson and quickly told him what he'd discovered and asked that the IT guys work on Mitzi's photo. "I want to see what she'd look like if she had about half of that nose cut off. Maybe we're seeing her every day and don't realize it."

"We'll get right on it, and, Mike, good work."

"Think it's good enough to get me a desk job? My wife wants me to stay home."

Mike could almost see the captain smiling. "Yeah, I think we can arrange that. Along with a promotion and a pay raise."

Mike groaned. "Just don't put me in charge of the rookies."

"That's exactly what I was thinking of doing. I'll send the photo as soon as the guys get it done." He hung up.

Mike got in his car and drove straight to the fairgrounds without bothering to shower and change. He'd been gone too long, so he knew Sara would start asking questions—and she'd see too much.

"Poker face, Newland," he said as he checked his mirrors, but no one was following him.

It was hours after Mike left the apartment that Sara made her way through the crowded fairgrounds and walked into her mother's tent. In front were long tables covered with produce and food the people who made up Armstrong's Organic Foods had spent weeks preparing. This year Sara hadn't helped, but next year she would. Maybe by the next fair she'd be expecting or would have a newborn in her arms. She and Mike hadn't talked about children, but then, they hadn't talked about much of anything serious—except the case.

She brought herself out of her reverie to look around. Her mother and two sisters were inside the tent, all of them wearing the medieval costumes Sara had made for them in previous years. Sara's had a dark green velvet bodice and a plaid skirt that was said to be the old McTern tartan. Her sisters wore blue and burgundy, and her mother's costume was in shades of brown and yellow. "The colors of the earth," she'd told her daughter when Sara made it.

The inside of the tent was full of boxes and baskets of fruit. Coolers of cooked food were stacked high. Her mother said that even though it was a fair she refused to serve unhealthy food.

"She just rolls the fruit in batter, deep fries it, then coats it with sugar," her doctor-father said. "Perfectly healthy."

Sara thought she needed to send her father to Joce for a tarot card reading so he could hear what sarcasm *really* meant.

Sara was still standing by the tent entrance when her mother, a crate of cantaloupes in her arms, saw her. She smiled, but that expression turned to a smirk when she saw the faint redness on her daughter's neck. Sara had covered it with foundation and powder, but the red still showed.

Ellie instantly knew what it was. "Ah, whisker burn. That takes me back. I remember the time your father and I—"

"Mother, please!" Sara said.

Laughing, Ellie left the tent.

"Wait until you have your first kid," her sister Jennifer said. "You'll be totally grossed out by the stories she tells you."

"The sex sagas are my downfall," Sara's other sister, Taylor, said.

"Dad delivering you on a mountaintop didn't do you in?" Jennifer asked.

"No. It was the details about Mom and Dad's Scarlet Nights in Mexico. Even Gene turned red at that one."

Sara was blinking at her sisters. For the first time ever, they were talking to her as though she were, well, like she was a grown-up woman.

Jennifer had a box of fruit pies in her hands, and she seemed to understand Sara's puzzlement. "Didn't you realize that Mother considers you a virgin until you're married? That's why she's not told *you* any of her sex stories." She left the tent.

Taylor had three boxes of cookies. "You're lucky to have evaded her spicy little tales for this long." She followed her sister out.

Sara stood looking after her two sisters in shock. She was still standing there when Mike came in.

"Your mother sent me in here to get a couple bags of potatoes. And why the hell are your relatives asking me so many questions about my beard? I meant to shave, but—" Pausing, he looked at her. "Are you okay?"

"My sisters were *nice* to me."

"Sisters are supposed to be nice."

"Not mine."

Mike picked up a fifty-pound bag, slung it over his left shoulder, then squatted down to get a second bag. When he had one over each shoulder, he walked back to Sara. "So what did they say to you?"

"They said my mother is going to tell me sex stories."

"I know I didn't grow up here, but, Sara, isn't that a little . . ."

She came back to the present and looked at him. He looked great! He wasn't in a kilt as she'd thought he'd be but was wearing a T-shirt and jeans. But it looked as though her mother had been working him hard, because his shirt was drenched in sweat and it clung tightly to his body. She could count his abs.

In the next moment she realized that every other female there could also do the arithmetic. "I think I'll get you a clean, fresh shirt."

Mike's eyes told her he knew exactly what she was thinking. "A shirt that's twice as big as this one?"

"I was thinking three times."

"Gimme a kiss."

She turned her head to maneuver through the bags, but Sara's mother called, "Mike! Where're those potatoes?"

"Add a mother-in-law to the list of relatives I now have," he mumbled as he left the tent.

"Think of our nice, quiet apartment in Fort Lauderdale," she called after him.

"Yeah, there we'll only have crooks living upstairs."

And a baby or two downstairs? she wondered.

For the rest of the evening, Ellie kept her daughter so busy that Sara saw little of Mike. When she did catch a glimpse of him, he was on his phone, so they couldn't have talked anyway. Plus, he spent so much time with Luke that Sara thought that if she were a different person she might have been jealous.

She saw Ariel once, chomping away on a big caramel apple. When she saw Mike walk past in his clinging T-shirt, Ariel's mouth fell open so far a sticky piece of fruit fell down the front of her gown. If she'd been wearing something Sara had made, she would have helped her clean it, but Ariel had ordered her medieval-style dress from a place in New York. Sara'd been told the sleeve seams had ripped out twice.

When Ariel looked up again, Sara was smiling, and she hurried forward to hook her arm around Mike's. Maybe she wouldn't change his shirt after all.

"What are you up to?" Mike asked.

"Girl stuff. So where's Greg now?"

"He just left a filling station. Bought some Twinkies."

"Is that your ultimate condemnation? What state's he in now?" she added quickly.

"What kind of underwear do you have on under that thing?"

"None whatever. Why don't you point out who in this crowd is with you and who are just tourists?"

"Did you see Lang snooping around Joce's tent?"

"Are you ever going to directly answer one of my questions?" she asked.

"Not if I can get out of it."

"Want me to introduce you to your cousins the Fraziers?"

"Tomorrow I'm to fight them with broadswords, so I'll meet them then. I already know two of them. How many more are there?"

"The big three. Colin is the oldest, then Pere, that's for Peregrine—the same name as his father—and Lanny, which is for Lancaster."

"I'm glad I wasn't named by their parents."

"They're old family names. The Fraziers stick to them."

"Sara!" her mother called, and she groaned.

"More work to do. See you tonight?"

"Yeah." He kissed her cheek. "I have some calls to make so I might be late."

He started to turn away but she saw a glint in his eyes that made her catch his arm. She studied his face. "What's happened? You're excited about something."

"Nothing. It's just the anticipation of tomorrow."

"No. There's something else. You look . . . happy."

"Of course I'm happy. Beautiful day, gorgeous girl, good food thanks to your mother, and—"

"There's something else in your eyes. And I think I saw the same look on Luke's face. What are you two up to?"

"Little girls who ask questions don't get surprises."

"Are you trying to make me believe you and Luke are planning a surprise party for me?"

"Sara, I need to go."

She kept hold of his arm. "I want to know what's made you happy."

"You have! And that's all I'm going to say. Now go! If your mother sees me she'll make me move the porta potties."

"No wonder you and my father get along so well. You should get him to show you the places where he hides from my mother. Okay, go, but tonight I mean to get to the bottom of this."

Mike raised an eyebrow. "I mean to get right down to the bottom of everything."

Sara grinned. "Okay, keep your secrets . . . for now."

He kissed her cheek again, then hurried off.

Mike didn't get back to the apartment until midnight. Sara was sitting in the living room in the big chair, sewing on her lap, and sound asleep. He didn't want to wake her, so he went into the bathroom and took a long shower. When he was clean, he went back to the living room and scooped up Sara, sewing and all. She snuggled against him, only half awake.

He put her on the bed and picked up what she'd been sewing. It was a triangle-shaped piece of translucent black silk with little disks of gold-colored metal sewn along the top. "What is this?"

Sara rolled onto her back. "A veil for Joce. She said that people, even strangers, were asking more about when the babies are due than were listening to her readings. We thought that maybe if she put a veil over her face she'd look more mysterious."

Mike stretched out beside her. "Like Mitzi," he murmured.

"I did think of her."

"To hide her big nose and no lips."

"Joce is too pretty to want to cover anything, but I think it'll help keep her identity a secret. So are you ready to tell me what you and Luke have been up to today?"

When he didn't answer, she looked at him, and saw that he was asleep. She turned out the light, pulled the cover over both of them, and snuggled into his arms.

# 26

MIKE WAS DOING his best to stay calm, but it wasn't easy. He'd been told that Stefan Vandlo was still three hours away, taking his time, sitting in restaurants, flirting with waitresses, and boring the men who were trailing him. "He has a couple of bodyguards with him, so watch out," one of the agents told Mike when they stood in line for lemonade. "And one guy was his cell mate in prison, and he looks like he's been in a lot of fights."

As Mike sipped his drink, he looked around to see who could help him if he needed it. He could easily spot the men who'd done some training, but their problem was that they thought that if they built up their biceps and spent thirty minutes on a treadmill they were ready for anything. He didn't see one man who could actually move his body in a way that would be needed if there really were a fight.

This morning at six he'd been awakened by his mother-in-law pounding on the bedroom door. Sleepily, he said, "I guess she knows the way to open your front door."

"Of every house in town," Sara said tiredly. The day before had been a long one, and she'd have liked nothing more than to spend a few hours in bed with Mike.

"You two need to get dressed," Ellie called through the door. "Mike, you can't run around in Levi's for a second day in a row. You must put on your kilt."

"But Luke—"

Sara knew what he was going to say. "Luke was in jeans yesterday because he was setting up a booth. You'd better do what my mother says or she'll be in here." She was referring to the fact that Mike hadn't bothered to put on any clothes after last night's shower.

Grumbling, Mike pulled on a pair of trousers and left the room.

"Aren't you a sight for the morning," Ellie said, looking at his bare chest.

Mike closed the bedroom door and Sara snuggled back under the covers. She'd thought that she'd be nervous about meeting Greg today, but she wasn't. She knew her confrontation with him was going to send him into a rage. In the past, she'd been afraid of his temper. She hadn't realized that then, but she had been. In fact, she'd done a lot of things she didn't want to just to keep him from getting angry—and to keep him from hurting her with his many little put-downs.

Why hadn't she stood up to him? she wondered. Why hadn't she told him she wouldn't be spoken to like that? But she knew that at the time it had all been so gradual, and with the huge amount of work he'd given her to do, she hadn't had time to think about what was going on. Every time she protested what he was saying or doing, he would tell her *she* was the problem. "This is why you've never made money, Sara," Greg used to say. "This is why you live in your cousin's house and don't have a place of your own." At the time, his words had made her want to try harder, but now she couldn't understand why she didn't tell him what he could do with his complaints.

There was one thing she was very glad for and that was that she'd let Tess oversee her finances. She'd never told anyone, but Greg had repeatedly tried to get her to sign papers giving him power of attorney over everything she owned. "It's for your own good," he'd said, his tone implying she didn't know much about anything. "You know I love you and that I want only the best for you. I'm just afraid that if anything happened to me you'd be left with nothing." "How does my giving you all I own now leave me with nothing if you died?" Sara'd asked, as she was genuinely confused. "See what I mean?" Greg said. "You don't understand even the most basic things about finance." But Sara hadn't signed anything because she knew she'd have to face Tess.

Her mother's voice brought her back to the present. "And you, missy," she heard her mother say with a tap on the door, "unless you want me to come in there and dress you, I suggest you get up now."

"So much for being treated like an adult," Sara murmured as she got her clothes and went to the bathroom.

When she came out, still only partially dressed, she caught a glimpse of plaid in the living room and went to see it. Her mother had helped Mike dress in the full regalia of a Scotsman. It wasn't the dress kilt that he'd wear on the last day, but the one he'd have on when he competed in the games. His big shirt had gathered sleeves, and the kilt reached to his knees. He had on thick Scottish brogues with woolen socks that went over his muscular calves. He was gorgeous! He looked like something out of a storybook about conflicts of honor. She could almost hear the bagpipes and smell the heather.

"Oh, my," Sara said.

"Yeah," Mike said with a grimace. "Girl's clothes."

Sara looked at her mother, and they smiled at each other. There was nothing on earth more masculine than a man in the ancient Scottish costume.

Mike was looking at Sara in the long mirror that Ellie had set against the wall, and he read what was on her face.

"There's no time for that," Ellie said. "You two'll have to wait until tonight."

"Since when did you ever wait for what you want?" Mike asked his mother-in-law.

Ellie laughed. "Not often. Sara! Go put on your skirt. I'll give him back to you after the first battle. If the Fraziers haven't mutilated him, that is."

"Hmph!" Sara said. "My Mike will pulverize them." With her nose in the air, she went back to the bedroom.

Mike was looking after her and smiling until he saw Ellie glaring at him in the mirror.

"You hurt her and—"

"I know," Mike said. "I've already been warned. You won't mind that she lives with me in Fort Lauderdale for a few years until we move back here?"

"All I want is for my girls to be happy." Bending, she pulled on the hem of his kilt. "Everything will go all right today, won't it?"

"As soon as Sara sees Anders and tells him she's married, she'll be taken away from here until they're all in custody."

Ellie nodded as she adjusted Mike's shirt, and he was quiet because he could see that she had more to say. "About the marriage . . . I know you did it for the case, but—"

Mike smiled at her. "That was just an excuse. There've been a lot of women I could have saved by marrying them, but I didn't. Stop worrying. Concern yourself about what those giant cousins of mine are going to do to me today."

"Now *that* I'm not worried about," Ellie said as she turned away, but then she went back and hugged Mike. "Thank you. It was horrible to have to stand by and see my daughter so unhappy after the way Brian treated her. I understood why she took up with a jerk like Greg Anders, but I still didn't like it."

Mike said nothing. Later, as he bandaged Sara's hand to hide her wedding rings, he thought that if Ellie knew the truth about Brian Tolworthy and what had been done to him and why, she'd probably kidnap her own daughter and hide her away somewhere safe. That's just what Mike wanted to do, but he knew that as long as the Vandlos were out there, Sara would never be out of danger. Mitzi was well known for taking revenge, and if only her son were in custody, she would go after Sara for destroying what had taken them a long time to put into motion.

Today, the main goal for all of them was to catch Mitzi Vandlo.

When Mike got to the fairgrounds, his curiosity about the Fraziers came into play. Size didn't always make the best fighters. Luke had told him the basics of the mock sword fight he was to perform with the Fraziers today, but Mike wasn't interested in that. What he wanted to know was how the Fraziers felt about Sara. She spoke of them with affection, but then she sounded that way about everyone in Edilean. Even while she complained about her sisters, you could hear the love in her voice.

The way she talks to me, Mike thought and couldn't help his smile.

Minutes before, he'd reminded Sara that she wanted to tell Colin Frazier what she thought about his not telling her that Greg Anders was having affairs. Mike wanted to see how the oldest Frazier son reacted to being bawled out by a woman half his size.

Surreptitiously, Mike made his way around the fairgrounds as he followed Sara. Twice, he gave a slight nod to men he knew were there undercover. When Sara reached Colin, Mike stepped into the shadows.

He had to admit that it was amusing to watch Sara talking to Colin. As she talked to the huge young man, her head was so far back it was almost touching her spinal column. Colin kept his eyes on her and seemed to be giving her his total attention. But when he glanced to the side and saw a wooden crate beside one of the rides, he took Sara's arm and led her there. From the way she didn't stop talking as she stepped up on the crate, Mike thought it was something they'd done many times before.

Two rides over from them was a Ferris wheel; Colin was facing it, and Sara had her back to it. Mike heard a yell and saw a red snow cone dropping down from the sky, and it looked like it was going to hit Sara. Mike started to leave his hiding place, but then Colin put his hands on Sara's waist and moved her to the right, her feet not touching the ground. The snow cone splattered on the ground, inches from where she'd been standing, then Colin set her back on the crate and kept listening.

Grinning, Mike started to move away. He'd seen what he'd wanted to: Sara was being protected. But before he could move, Colin looked straight into Mike's eyes. He'd known all along that Mike was there and watching.

There was a question on Colin's face, asking if he'd passed the test. Mike gave a nod, then slipped away into the crowd. If he was to have cousins, he could do worse. The fight that was to take place in about an hour was going to be more interesting than he'd originally thought.

Sara was sitting on the bleachers, wedged between three women from her church. Two benches below her, Ariel was sitting beside her youngest brother, Shamus, and Luke was making his way toward Sara.

Below, on the large open field was Mike, looking so very handsome in his kilt and voluminous shirt. He was holding what Sara knew was a broadsword, a heavy weapon that weighed about thirty-five pounds. From the way he was letting the tip of it lie in the dirt, it seemed to be almost too much for him.

Circling him, and wearing kilts that Sara had made for them last year, were three of the giant Fraziers. Sara knew that the idea was to re-create some battle where the single, lone soldier had given up his life for his clan, but right now she didn't like that story. Every year the Fraziers participated in this, and she knew that they loved the boos and hisses aimed at them. This afternoon they'd redeem themselves as they played valiant warriors who won against the enemy, but this game was meant to put tears in people's eyes, to remind them of what the Scots had gone through in their history.

Luke got the ladies to scoot over so he could sit by Sara. "Scared?" he asked as he stuck his hand in her popcorn. "They won't hurt him."

Ariel heard what Luke said and turned to look up at Sara. "He'll be fine. My brothers decided that Pere and Lanny will back away and let Colin have him alone. I made Colin promise to be gentle." She was acting as though she was telling this in confidence to Sara, but Ariel's voice could be heard six benches away.

"My hope is that Mike doesn't hurt your brothers," Sara said just as loudly as she stuffed her mouth with popcorn.

Around them was muffled laughter from the townspeople, who were well aware of the lifelong animosity between the two young women.

If there was one thing the Fraziers had in common, it was that when they raised their voices, they could be heard, and that was demonstrated on the field.

"So you're our cousin," Colin bellowed, his voice sounding menacing. "You don't look like us."

"The angels must have *liked* my mother," Mike said back. His voice wasn't as loud as theirs, but the natural throatiness of it made the hairs on the back of Sara's neck stand up—and it made her remember last night when he'd awakened her with kisses. Unfortunately, Mike's deep voice seemed to have had the same effect on other females, as some teenage girls started squealing.

"I do believe he has a smart mouth on him," Pere said. He was a year younger than Colin's thirty, and as handsome as his brothers.

"Smart anything must mean I'm not related to the Fraziers." Mike's words made the crowd cheer. For the townspeople, it was great to hear someone challenge that rich family.

The circle of big men was drawing in closer around Mike.

"Should we call our young brother Shamus for this job?" Lanny shouted. "Methinks this old man but needs a boy to take him down."

Lanny made a halfhearted strike at Mike with his sword, teasing him, but Mike reacted in an instant. He lifted the heavy blade as though it weighed nothing and swung it in a circle above his head. Lanny and Pere stepped back, but Colin went forward. In one move, Mike blocked Colin's sword hand with his left forearm and hit the other two weapons with his so that they flew down the field.

When the motion stopped, Colin was left standing holding his sword, while his younger brothers were empty-handed.

The crowd was stunned into silence. They froze in place, hands on the way to their mouths, drinks poised midair. Mothers stopped warning their children; men stopped watching the girls; and the kids just stared. Sara was the first to recover. She stood up and began clapping. When the slight sound didn't rouse the crowd, she started cheering. Luke stood up beside her and added his voice to hers. An instant later, the people reacted with a roar as they came to their feet.

In the center of the field, Mike didn't show that he'd heard a sound. His eyes were on Colin, and he backed up to keep the younger men in his side view. When the crowd calmed and sat down, the two younger men stepped closer as they attempted to pick up their swords, but Mike grabbed one and threw it. It arced to the right, over the top of a tall stack of barrels to land on the other side, the blade going so deep into the earth that it gave a loud thwang sound.

This time, Sara didn't need to lead the cheering as people again came to their feet and started shouting.

Mike had two of the heavy swords and he moved in a circle, both of them raised above his head.

When Pere stepped closer, Mike lunged and came so close to slashing him about the neck, that the crowd drew in its breath. From the other side of the fair, people heard the shouts and started running. The roustabout who ran the Tilt-A-Whirl put the hand-brake on and left the long line of waiting customers. When they protested, he yelled, "Follow me." He passed a bunch of teenage boys and shouted, "Cage fight." They nearly trampled people as they started running.

On the field, Pere threw up his hands in surrender, then bowed to Mike. If he said anything, no one heard it over the noise of the crowd.

Lanny waited, then turned and also bowed to the audience in surrender. He was booed and hissed at loudly.

Only Mike and Colin were left, and neither of them looked as though he was going to give up. Mike had the two swords, but when the crowd calmed down, he smiled at Colin. "I wouldn't want to beat you unfairly, cousin," he said loudly as he threw the sword across the barrels where it landed within inches of the other one. The cheer that went up could be heard a mile away.

"Isn't he wonderful?" Sara breathed to Luke as she held on to his arm.

He clasped her hand and smiled down at her fondly. "Mike is

quite the hero, so cool he sweats ice cubes. But remember that Colin is no wimp. Mike'll have to work to beat him."

The men bent and began circling each other. Colin was the first to make a move as he pushed his sword forward, as though to stab Mike in the chest. But Mike made a leap and hit Colin in the chest with his foot, stunning the larger man so that he staggered backward. Mike landed on his feet, then circled around, sword raised.

After taking a moment to get his breath back, Colin stood up straight and said, "You're no more bother than a mosquito." At that a bunch of boys at the far end of the bleachers took Colin's side and started cheering, "Frazier! Frazier!"

Sara started a chant of "Mike! Mike!" and her side of the bleachers took it up. Except for Ariel and Shamus, of course, who stayed seated, but when people blocked their view, Shamus stood up and tapped the man in front of him on the shoulder. The man, an outsider, looked at the sheer size of Shamus, and sat down. Soon there was a path of seated people that allowed Ariel and Shamus to see the field while retaining their seats.

When Colin made a lunge at Mike, he twisted out of the way, but the sleeve of Mike's shirt caught on the sword, tearing it from shoulder to wrist. Big pieces of fabric dangled dangerously. Without losing concentration, Mike grabbed the hanging cloth and pulled. It ripped to the waist and he slipped what was left of it over his head.

When the sight of Mike, bare chested and in a kilt, sent the crowd nearly into a frenzy, he made a run at Colin, who jumped back, but not before Mike's sword went flashing through the air. The crowd drew in its breath in shock. This was a local fair, but Mike seemed to be playing it for real. In the last dash, had he cut Colin?

Colin stood still, looking down at his chest as though expecting blood to spurt, but then he saw something the crowd didn't.

Smiling, he stepped back, raised his arms, and turned in a circle. As though in slow motion, Colin's shirt began to fall away. Mike had deftly sliced it but hadn't so much as made a mark on his cousin's skin. When the shirt hung on Colin in big pieces, he pulled it off so that he too was bare from the waist up.

Girls started cheering at the sight of Colin's muscular torso, and Sara laughed.

"Looks like Colin's been working out," Luke said, watching through the pathway of seated viewers.

In the next second the men again started moving around each other and the battle began for real—or certainly too real for Sara's taste. Mike was faster and certainly better trained, but fighting Colin was like battling a rock. Mike ran over the tops of the barrels and at one point he hit Colin's shoulders with both his feet. Any swipe that Colin made with his sword, Mike easily eluded. Twice he jumped over the sword as it threatened to hit him in the stomach.

"I don't like this," Sara whispered, and Luke put his arm around her. "Don't let him get hurt." She buried her face in Luke's shoulder.

"Don't you realize that they're playing? There's no danger to either of them, and certainly not to Mike. All three of the Fraziers could go at Mike and they'd never catch him."

"Are you sure?"

"Absolutely. You should watch this. Colin is about to wear out, but Mike could go on all day. What kind of training has he had?"

"I don't know. Tess said something about China and Brazil." Sara handed Luke her BlackBerry. "Call Tess and ask her."

"And miss this fight? Ha! Come on, let's go down closer to the fence."

She followed Luke, and he lifted her down from the fifth bleacher.

She stood by the fence that was the boundary of the playing field and did her best to watch the fight, but it was difficult. Every slash Colin made with his big sword, Mike dodged. But now that they were closer, she could see that it was true that Mike was having a good time—and he looked like he wanted to continue all day.

But he glanced at the fence and saw Sara staring at him, on the verge of tears of concern, and he nodded at her. For her sake, he would end it. In the next second, he spun around to the back of Colin, leaped upward to plant a foot on the man's upper back, while at the same time lashing out at Colin's calves with the flat side of his broadsword. Colin lost his balance and hit the ground with a pow! of force. Mike put his foot on Colin's back and his sword at his neck.

The crowd started cheering hysterically. The underdog had won!

When Mike removed his foot, Colin got up, spitting mud out of his mouth. Mike held his arm out to Sara, and she went running to him. He swooped her up and spun her around—and the crowd's shouts were deafening.

When Mike kissed her, the outsiders laughed and shouted, but the people of Edilean stared in shock. Wasn't Sara supposed to be getting married in a few days? To another man?

"I think they've all seen us now," Sara said, but she clung to Mike, her cheek against his bare, sweaty chest.

"That's the idea."

"And it's why you married me," she said.

"That and a few Scarlet Nights of our own," he said as he looked into her eyes.

"Get a room!" someone from the crowd shouted, and everyone started laughing. Reluctantly, Mike set Sara down.

She ran to Luke at the fence while Mike and Colin took their bows. Colin made everyone laugh when he grabbed Mike from behind and lifted him off the ground. Then, parodying what Mike and Sara had just done, Colin swung Mike into his arms and pretended to try to kiss him.

Mike did a flip and ended up standing on top of Colin's shoulders, where he grabbed Mike's ankles and held him. Colin started a drunken dance about the ring while Mike worked to keep his balance. When Colin stopped, Mike jumped down and hit the ground rolling. At the applause of the crowd, Mike took a bow and Colin chased him, his lips made into a kiss as they ran into the tent at the back of the arena.

"My goodness," Mrs. Frazier said, looking at the two of them, shirtless and dirty and laughing.

Mike had never seen her before, but he recognized her from the tarot cards. She had on a gown of such richness that it would have done a medieval queen proud. Mike put one leg behind the other and bowed low to her. "Your royal highness."

Mr. Frazier, dressed as a prosperous merchant, stepped forward. "I think he understands who you really are, my dear."

Colin, from behind Mike, said, "He's little, but can I keep him, Ma?" He made Mike sound like a puppy.

"Beware the deadliness of the scorpion's sting," Mike growled.

"Beware the cousin's foot," Colin shot back.

Mr. Frazier stepped between them and held out his hand to Mike. "I hear your grandmother was my biological mother's sister. Sorry, but I never knew either one of them, but . . ." He didn't seem to know what else to say.

"Oh, Grinny," Mrs. Frazier said, "there'll be time for that later." She turned to Colin and obviously disapproved of his shirtless state. "You will find a clean shirt in the trailer." She looked at Mike. "And I suggest that you also put something on."

"Yes, ma'am," both men said in unison, then they ran out of the tent and back into the ring, where they immediately started punching each other.

"Want to get something to drink?" Colin asked.

"Wish I could but I have some things I need to do."

"Yeah, the whole town saw you with Sara." Colin lowered his voice. "Listen, I know some of the reasons why you're here, but not all of the story. If you need any help, let me know."

"Watch out for her, that's all I ask," Mike said as he left the arena to go back to Ellie's tent. As he knew she would be, Sara was waiting there for him with a clean shirt.

Minutes later, Mike got a text message.

HEY KID. HEARD U GOT MY INVITE TO JOIN ME. WHATEVER

UR DOING ITS WORKING. VANDLO PEELED OUT IN A RAGE.

Smiling, Mike tossed his phone in the air and caught it.

"What was that about?" Sara asked as she smoothed his shirt down.

Grabbing her about the waist, Mike swung her around.

"What's made you so happy? Last night and now this. What's going on?"

"Instinct, babe," he said, laughing. "It hasn't failed me yet."

Sara was waiting for an answer to her question.

"Let's just say that I was concerned that someone had betrayed me, but I couldn't make myself believe it."

"And he . . . or she . . . didn't betray you?"

"Naw. So where's Kim's little sister? Anna, was it? We need to rehearse before the show starts."

Sara's sister Taylor entered the tent. "I talked to Anna and she wants nothing to do with you. She saw your fight and she said, and I quote, 'He's too old and I don't like his beard.'"

Mike put Sara down and kissed her neck. "It wouldn't be the first time I've had to persuade a woman to like me."

"Now why do I doubt that you've had much practice at that?" Taylor asked, and Mike smiled at her.

"Stop flirting with my sister and go find Anna."

"Yeah," Taylor said, "or my husband will beat you up." Her husband was an overworked doctor who never had time to go to a gym.

"I'll win this game, and it'll be the last one," he said softly to Sara. "After it's done, I'll come back and put the wires on you, so stay around here and don't leave. Got it?"

"Yes," she said and took a deep breath. She knew he was telling her that Greg was on his way, which meant that the big blowout with him was going to happen soon. Her fear was that she'd be so angry when she saw him that she'd blurt out the truth about his mother and the investigation, and she'd ruin everything.

"You'll do fine," Mike said. "And don't worry about saying too much. I've seen what a great liar you can be."

"Is that supposed to make me feel better?"

He pulled her into his arms and after a quick glance to see that Taylor had her back turned, he kissed her. "When this is done I promise to make you feel a lot better."

She nodded, but she was still worried.

He kissed the middle of her forehead, and left the tent.

"Sara," Taylor said, "Luke told me that Mike's thinking about opening some sort of gym. Can I sign up Gene now?"

As Sara laughed she realized that she was at last beginning to bond with her sisters.

# 27

Sara wanted to see her husband in a jump rope contest, especially with a spitfire of a girl like Anna Aldredge, so she rushed to finish the chores her mother had given her. While she was out front unloading apple pies, she heard a lot of praise from people who'd seen Mike in the fight with Colin. Teenage boys were kicking at one another and making people laugh when they fell on the ground.

How very much she wanted to tell them that Mike was her husband!

Ellie stopped beside her and whispered, "It won't be long before we can give out advertising for Mike's gym. And are you ready to take on remodeling that run-down old farm?"

Sara smiled; her mother knew just how to cheer her up. She loved thinking of her future with Mike.

"He moved the prize car off the stand," a kid yelled. "He and some kid are going to give a jump rope show up on the platform."

There was no doubt who "he" was, and Sara untied her apron. Every year the Fraziers donated a car to be awarded to the overall winner of the games. Now it seemed that Mike'd had the vehicle removed so he and Anna could put on a performance. It wasn't something Sara wanted to miss.

But her father stopped her. "Sara, could I see you for a moment?"

He had on what her family called his "doctor face." For the most part, Henry Shaw was an easygoing man, content to let his wife and energetic two older daughters run his life, but when his medical abilities were needed, his whole personality changed. He became the man in charge.

Without hesitation, she went to him. "What's wrong?"

"It's Joce."

Instantly, Sara started toward the fortune-telling tent next to them, but Dr. Shaw caught her arm.

"She's all right, but she's overexerted herself. Luke and I are taking her home for a few hours so she can rest. Sara, I know you want to see Mike, but could you fill in for her? There's a long line outside Joce's tent, and the idea of letting people down is stressing her out. She said that you're the only one who knows what to do to take over for her."

"Of course," Sara said. "I'll do whatever she needs." She consoled herself with the thought that she'd be staying near her mother's tent, just as Mike had told her to do.

"Joce had Luke get her some clothes so she changed. Would you mind putting on that . . ." He waved his hand to mean the gaudy costume Joce had been wearing.

"Sure. Just give me a few minutes." As she went into the little curtained-off room at the back of the fortune-telling tent, Sara wondered how much Mike had told her parents on the night he'd arranged their marriage.

It didn't take Sara long to slip Joce's big, flowing robe on over her own costume and put on Tess's hoop earrings. At least with impersonating Joce, Sara could remove the bandage covering her wedding rings. On impulse, Sara asked her father to help her put a pillow over her flat stomach. With the veil and her heavy black eyeliner, Sara hoped no one would notice the change in fortune-tellers.

As Dr. Shaw tied the pillow in place, he said, "I hope that boy you married makes this real. I like grandkids. Uh, Sara, do you think I'm too old to join Mike's gym?"

She kissed his cheek. "Dad, in my eyes, you'll never be too old for anything."

Smiling, he fastened the veil around her face. With the red turban over her hair and her marriage rings finally exposed, it was difficult to tell her from Jocelyn.

"Go to it," Dr. Shaw said, and as he opened the flap to go outside, she saw a quick movement at the back. In other circumstances she wouldn't have noticed, but now she knew it was Brewster Lang lurking about.

As soon as her father was out of sight, Sara said quietly, "Everyone loves your cookies, Mr. Lang." She went inside and seated herself at the low chair. In front of her was a little round table that Shamus had decorated with astrological signs and iridescent stars, with another chair on the other side.

In front of the tent was one of the high school girls who'd volunteered to help at the fair, and Sara told her to start letting customers in.

An hour later, she wanted to scream that she needed a nap too. The townspeople had known it was Joce doing the fortune-telling. Maybe it was because they knew she was a newcomer to town or maybe it was the veil, but for some reason, the people poured out their hearts—and they took what Sara said in reply very seriously. From the first "reading" she'd found herself playing the role of counselor.

"Should I leave him?" one woman asked. Sara knew the woman and wanted to yell, "Yes!" Instead, in as mystical a way as she could manage, she referred her to a counselor in Williamsburg who worked with abused women.

"Is my husband having an affair?" Sara assured the woman, who was notoriously jealous, that he wasn't. Her husband had a belly bigger than Joce's, and no one made passes at him.

"Will I meet someone?" Sara liked the question from this woman because she'd seen Mr. Peterson looking at her in church. Sara told her that if she didn't immediately buy four new tires at Peterson's Wheels she'd have a wreck—and also, Arthur Peterson had a spiritual message for her so she needed to talk to him personally. The woman left in a hurry, and Sara hoped she was on her way to the garage.

Sara told two teenage girls to stop smoking in secret and to wear longer skirts. They went away laughing hilariously.

The worst part of the job was hearing crowds in the distance as they cheered at the games. She wondered what Mike was doing now. She'd never seen him jump rope. How good was he? That was, of course, a rhetorical question as there didn't seem to be a sport that Mike wasn't brilliant at.

Smiling, Sara wondered if their children would inherit his talents. She'd like a boy who was a martial arts expert. On the other hand, she hoped she didn't get a daughter who thought tree climbing was an art form. How would Sara relate to her?

"Oh, dear, I seem to have interrupted some serious daydreaming."

She looked up to see Mrs. Myers hobbling into the tent. She was a widow in her eighties who lived in a tiny apartment on the outskirts of town and regularly attended church. She hadn't been in Edilean long, but it was said that she'd lived there as a child and had returned when her husband died a few years ago. The poor woman walked with two canes, and even that was difficult. At church, she was always in the first five of any list of people needing charity.

As Mrs. Myers sat down, Sara shuffled the tarot cards, being careful not to bend them. "And what questions can I answer for you today?" Please, she thought, don't ask me how long you have to live.

"Oh, the usual, dear. When am I going to meet a man?"

Sara tried not to laugh, but when she saw the twinkle in the woman's eyes, she couldn't help but smile from behind the semitransparent veil. "How about a nice, healthy retired businessman?"

"I'd rather have a horseman, lean and dark, a man who will carry me across the fields on his black stallion and make love to me in the moonlight."

Sara's mouth dropped open. "I rather like that idea myself."

Mrs. Myers was squinting as she looked at the tarot cards. "So what does it say about me in there?"

Sara didn't know enough about the woman to come up with a fake fortune that fit her. But she did know she wasn't rich. "Money," Sara said firmly as she put down three cards. "I see a fortune in your future."

"Do you? And what card would that be?"

Sara wasn't sure what each card meant, but it made sense that coins meant money. She pointed to the one that had Greg scowling and surrounded by six women's faces on gold coins. "This one."

Mrs. Myers opened her handbag—so old it had cracks in the leather—and removed her reading glasses. As she opened them, she said, "I once wore a veil very much like the one you have on."

"Did you?" Sara said, smiling. "And did it get you what you wanted?"

"It got me a big, handsome husband," Mrs. Myers said as she put on her glasses. "He was a little old, maybe, but still in working order."

"Then it was worth it," Sara said, but her heart was pounding. A veil that got her a husband? A handsome young man who made love in the moonlight? Could he have been Greg's father? Was it possible that this woman was the notorious Mitzi Vandlo? She was much older than fifty-three, but when Sara looked at the woman's hands, she saw that they were mostly unlined and younger than her face. No one had suggested that Mitzi might disguise herself by looking older, and also, this woman didn't have the big nose that was prominent in her only photo.

Sara realized that if Mrs. Myers had told anyone else her story about a veil getting her a husband, it would have been a good joke. It was only because of what Mike had told her that Sara could recognize the woman.

Sara's first thought was that she wished she had a buzzer to push with her foot. She'd not asked Mike about the cameras in the fortune-telling tent, and now she wished she had. Was someone monitoring them or were they just making a recording that would be looked at later? If she made a gesture toward a camera, would it be seen by an agent?

Stay calm, she told herself as she quickly hid the card with Greg's face on it and spread others out on the little table. She reassured herself that if Mitzi had seen Sara and Mike together, it was all right because right now she was protected by the fact that everyone thought she was Joce, not Sara. This was good, because for all she knew, Mrs. Myers's old handbag contained a gun. To reassert her identity, she let her rings flash. Joce was a married woman.

Mrs. Myers was looking at the cards through her reading glasses, and her eyes were wide. "Where did you get that deck?" The woman's voice was breathless, as though she was seeing something wonderful.

The doubt of her being Mitzi Vandlo fled. "Beautiful, aren't they?" Sara said rather loudly. "There are only six sets in the world. My husband's publishing house printed them. They were going to use them for publicity for one of his books, but they were too expensive to produce, so these are the only decks that will ever be printed."

Mrs. Myers bent over to study the cards on the little table. "Do I recognize some of the faces?"

"Oh, yes. Shamus Frazier drew them all, and he surprised us by making portraits." Sara picked up the Judgment card with her mother's face on it. She was wearing a red dress, with a big handkerchief over her head, and gold earrings. "That's Mrs. Shaw, my friend Sara's mother." As surreptitiously as she could, Sara slipped a card with Stefan's face on it under the stack. She thought it was better not to let the woman see Stefan as a thoroughly unpleasant-looking man. "But I seem to be telling you all about my life, when I'm supposed to be talking about yours."

In spite of everything she could do, Sara felt panic rising inside of her. What should she do? Stay in the tent, be a psychic and wait, or run to Mike? But she knew that leaving was impossible. This woman had been eluding law authorities all her life, so she'd never stay there and wait to be captured.

Sara decided to do her best to keep the woman interested so she'd stay as long as possible and give someone time to come and . . . What? Arrest her? Sara tried to remember everything Mike had told her about Mitzi, but it wasn't easy, as her heart was in her throat.

"Let me see. Ah, yes." She looked at the woman. "Do you want to hear the truth of what I see in the cards, or are you like the others and just want sugarcoated candy?"

Mrs. Myers—Mitzi—blinked at her. "The truth," she said.

"All right. The veil you wore led to an unhappy marriage, and you've been a widow for a very long time." She looked up at the woman, her eyes full of apology. "I'm sorry, Mrs. Myers, I'm just telling you what I see. It doesn't seem that your husband was a nice man."

When the woman said nothing, just kept staring at Sara, she almost chickened out. She tapped a card. "But you've had love in your life with another man. He was young and very handsome." Sara smiled as sweetly as she could. "Was your description of moonlight rides from your own past?"

The woman said nothing.

Sara looked back at the cards. "But something happened to your young man. His future is cloudy."

The woman leaned forward a bit, as though she were intrigued.

"But wait. There's another love in your life. There's a child. A boy? A girl?" She looked to the woman for an answer.

Mitzi leaned back against the chair and Sara was afraid she was losing interest. "You're the fortune-teller, dear, not me."

Sara looked back down. "This child is very desirable to the opposite sex and you're glad of that, but it also causes you many problems."

Again, the woman was silent.

"Ah. Here. This card." She touched one. "It seems that you have a goal in life. You want something because it will give you . . ." She frowned a bit, as though concentrating. "Peace. Freedom. Yes, whatever it is that you want, if you find it, you will be given the peace you so greatly desire."

"You are such a clever young woman," Mrs. Myers said, then began to cough. "Excuse me." She coughed some more. "The hazards of getting older. I hate to trouble you, dear, but could you possibly run next door and get me some water?"

She wants to steal a deck of cards, Sara thought as she stood up, her eyes blinking rapidly as she tried to think of what to do. "Find Mike" was the first thought in her mind, but how did she do that without leaving this woman? What if she slipped a deck or two into her purse then ran out? Maybe she'd never be found again—and it would be Sara's fault that she was lost.

"Certainly," Sara said as she went through the curtain at the back of the tent. She stuck her head outside. "Mr. Lang!" she hissed. "I need you." The man didn't appear. Sara stepped inside and looked through the curtain to see Mrs. Myers just sitting there, giving Sara time to leave.

She looked up at the seam where the fabric walls joined the tent. There was a line of braid along the ridge, and she figured that the camera lenses were hidden in it. She raised her fist and turned around, then made another swirl and used both arms to gesture that someone was to come and help her.

She glanced back into the main part of the tent and Mrs. Myers was still sitting there, her glasses on the end of her nose. She'd picked up the deck that Sara had been using and was going over them. Sara drew in her breath. In the next second she was going to see Greg's face and she was going to know what was going on.

"Where's Mike?"

Startled, Sara turned around to see Ariel standing in the back opening of the tent.

"Mike?" Sara asked.

"Yeah, the guy you hang on to like he's about to drown. He's disappeared. I saw him walking around with some stranger, a really gorgeous guy. The way that man moved made me . . . But anyway, now we can't find Mike, and the next battles are about to start. Think he's afraid of a rematch with my brothers?"

Sara peeped through the curtain again, and Mrs. Myers was dropping three decks of cards into her bag. Since it looked like no one was going to show up to save her, Sara knew she had to act instantly or Mitzi Vandlo was going to get away. If she escaped, everything that had been set up to catch the woman would come to nothing.

Ariel was in the costume of a rich medieval woman. A piece of white silk was attached to her little velvet cap and extended down across her neck.

Reaching out, Sara gave a strong yank and pulled it off.

"What the hell do you think you're doing?"

"I'm catching a criminal," Sara said and looked through the curtain. Mrs. Myers was getting up. In another minute she'd be outside. Sara threw back the curtain, made a running leap, and landed on the woman, knocking her to the ground.

"Have you lost your mind?" Ariel asked from behind her.

Sara was lying full on top of the woman and she was working hard to shove the cloth from Ariel's headdress into Mitzi's mouth before she could cry out. "She's a thief and probably a murderer," Sara said as she wrestled with her. "And if Mike is missing, then she's—Ow!" The woman had tried to bite her. Sara straddled her, holding her down. "If Mike isn't here, his disappearance has to do with her son."

Ariel was watching Sara sitting on top of what seemed to be an old woman, but from the strength of the struggle, she wasn't that old. "Is Anders her son?" Ariel asked, her eyes wide in shock.

"Yes! The man that you knew was bed hopping with half the town, but you didn't even warn me about, is her son. And they're both wanted by everyone, police, FBI, Secret Service. They are major criminals."

Ariel didn't look as though she could comprehend all she was hearing. "You wouldn't have believed me if I'd told you about Greg."

Sara was sitting on the woman, who was bucking and trying to reach Sara with her hands and nails. "Are you going to stand there and watch or could you possibly help me? I need something to tie her up with."

Hanging in the corner was a long rope of red and purple with a big tassel on the end. Ariel snatched it down, and with it came about two yards of braid. As Ariel tied the woman's hands behind her, she said, "Did you know there's a camera up there?"

"This whole tent is supposed to be set up with surveillance cameras, but no one seems to be watching them. Tell me what you know about Mike."

"He's here on a case, isn't he? Colin told me—"

"I don't want to hear what your big-mouthed brother blabbed. What happened to Mike?"

"He finished showing off with Anna and—Did you see him lift that kid over his head? She went stiff as a board and Mike—"

Mrs. Myers was bucking hard under Sara. "I've been too busy catching murderers to see my own husband do anything!" Sara said in frustration.

Ariel halted in tying. "Husband? If he's here on a case, did he *marry* you to protect you from Anders?"

"Get that look off your face! Mike is mine, and I'm keeping him." Under her, Mrs. Myers had gone dead still.

"I think you've killed her," Ariel said.

"No, she's just upset that I didn't marry her son. Aren't you, Mitzi?"

The woman on the ground made some unpleasant sounds through the muffling of the cloth in her mouth.

"We have to get her out of here without anyone seeing her." Sara was pulling the pillow out from under her robe. There was no more need for the disguise.

"I'll go get Colin and—"

"No!" Sara said. "You can't tell anyone. Your brother will want to put her in jail."

"Of course he will. What else should be done with her?"

"If Mike isn't here, then it means he's been taken. His life could be in danger, and I'm going to trade this horrible old woman for him."

Mitzi Vandlo turned her head to look up at Sara.

"Oh," Ariel said, her eyebrows raised high.

"Yeah, oh. Go out there and tell that girl that Mrs. Myers has been taken ill and I have to help her to . . . I don't know. Make something up. Then go out the back and tell Mr. Lang to come in here, and—"

"Brewster Lang? I thought you were afraid of him."

"I don't want to know how you know that. Get him in here and tell him he has to be a fortune-teller."

"Brewster Lang tell fortunes? Are you crazy?"

"Ariel, this is no time for your negativity."

For a moment Ariel just looked at Sara sitting on top of the old woman. Sara's veil was hanging by one edge, and with the bright colors of the costume, she didn't look like the sweet, never-did-any-thing-wrong girl that Ariel had disliked all her life.

"Okay," Ariel said at last, and she took only half a minute to tell the high school girl in the front that there would be a delay. It took her just two minutes to find Mr. Lang, and when they came in, Ariel had her hand firmly on his shoulder.

Mr. Lang stopped trying to twist away from Ariel's tight grip when he was confronted with the extraordinary sight of Sara sitting on top of old Mrs. Myers. His small eyes lit up, and his tiny grin appeared. For the first time, he looked at Sara with respect and he tapped his nose. He'd seen the woman in the photo Mike had shown him.

"Yes, I think she had about four inches of it cut off," Sara said, and at that comment Mitzi tried to throw back her leg so her heel would hit Sara. But she wasn't fast enough for Mr. Lang as he kicked out and struck the woman's ankle. Sara heard her groan. "Help me get her up. I'm going to put this costume on her and cover her mouth with the veil."

"Someone has to tell me what's going on," Ariel said.

"Stole my paintings is what she did," Mr. Lang mumbled as he looked at the woman tied up on the rug.

Both Sara and Ariel turned to look at him.

"What are you talking about?" Sara asked as she began to remove the big robe and was glad she'd left her smaller costume on under it.

When Mr. Lang hesitated, Ariel said, "I'll set my brothers on you if you don't tell us what you've done."

"Nothing. All I did was find them when I was a boy. That man that lived there, the college professor, he never saw them. I made sure of that. I nailed the room shut."

"What room?" Ariel asked.

"Is there a secret room in Merlin's Farm?" Sara asked softly, and when Mr. Lang didn't reply, she said, "By the fireplace. That's why that fireplace is off center. It conceals a hidden door. Did Mike figure it out?"

Mr. Lang's old face nearly melted. "*He* took them? I saw him looking, but I didn't think he'd know. He's a smart boy. I'm glad he's mine."

"You're related to Mike?" Ariel asked, her eyes wide. "How did that happen?"

"Never mind that now," Sara said. "Ariel, help me get her dressed in this. Mr. Lang, I want you to stay here and tell fortunes."

"I can't—"

"I can't wrestle people, but I'm doing it!" Sara snapped. "If you want my husband to continue letting you live at Merlin's Farm, then you have to help out. You understand me?"

Mr. Lang nodded.

"Wow, Sara, when did you grow a set?"

"Ariel, shut up and help me."

"Yes, ma'am," Ariel said as they pulled the flailing Mrs. Myers upright.

"What car do you have here?" Sara asked.

"None," Ariel answered. "My whole family came in a van."

"Must have been the size of a freight train," Sara muttered, and Mr. Lang gave his funny little laugh.

"Better than those toys you and Jocelyn like." She held Mitzi's head while Sara tied the veil over the bottom half of her face.

"You know," Sara said as she looked at the woman, "you do look better with half of your face covered. Is it true that your old husband was so horrified at the sight of you on your wedding night that he couldn't do it?"

Mitzi's eyes shot fire at Sara.

"She hates you," Ariel said. "Truly and deeply hates you."

"It's mutual."

Ariel took one arm and Sara the other, but when they tried to move her, the woman dug her feet into the carpet thrown over the ground. But they managed to haul her into the back room of the tent where the curtains hid them.

"Great. Now what do we do?" Ariel asked.

"I don't know, but we have to get her out of here and cause as little attention as possible."

"And how do you propose we do that?" Ariel asked.

"I, uh . . ." Sara had no answer. Again, she looked up at the roofline. Why wasn't anyone watching them and coming to help?!

Ariel dropped her arm from around the woman. "I suggest that I go get a car and bring it here."

"Great idea," Sara said. They put Mitzi on the floor, then Ariel ran outside. Sara turned to Mr. Lang. "Did you destroy those traps like Mike told you to?" When his eyes shifted to one side, she knew that he hadn't. "Not even one of them?" Mr. Lang looked down at his feet. "Good!" Sara said. "Now go in there and start telling fortunes."

He seemed about to protest but didn't. With a resigned look on his face, he went through to the front.

For several long minutes Sara stood over Mitzi and worried about all the things that could go wrong. What if Sara's father returned and came to the tent? How would she explain what she was doing? On the other hand, her father loved helping people, so he might want to be part of it. But she didn't want to involve him in whatever was going to happen. And, of course, there was every member of her church, plus all her relatives. How would she explain this to them?

Mitzi was sitting on a little rug that had been tossed on the ground, and she was glaring hard at Sara, as though she could forcibly put thoughts in her head.

Sara glared back. "You'd better hope nothing's wrong with Mike or I'll make you sorry you were ever born." Sara thought of taking the gag out of the woman's mouth and asking her questions, but she'd probably yell and people would come running. There was no way in the world that Sara would be able to explain what she was doing.

On the other side of the curtain she heard Mr. Lang's low voice and thought that she should have made an effort to dress him in a costume. But then, Mr. Lang was so odd-looking on his own, he didn't need any embellishment.

She peeped through the curtain and saw Carol Garrison sitting there, her eyes wide. No one in Edilean had been this close to the secretive old man since . . . Well, maybe not since 1941.

Sara didn't know Mrs. Garrison and was glad she didn't have to try to make up a fortune for her—but it was obvious that the snooping Mr. Lang knew all about her. He told her that her eldest daughter was sneaking out her bedroom window to meet a boy whose family had just moved here from Atlanta and that they smoked cigarettes together. Her younger daughter had stolen three dollars from her mother's purse, and her son liked to sing when he was alone and she should get him lessons. As for her husband, he really was working late at night because he wanted to buy a boat, which he'd already made a deposit on.

Mrs. Garrison sat there in silence, eyes wide, mouth open.

"That's it," Mr. Lang growled. "Go away. Send in the next one."

"What have I done?" Sara whispered aloud as she closed the curtain and looked back at Mitzi Vandlo. Again, her mind filled with the treachery of this woman. "I hope they put you away forever for what you did to Brian. He was a very sweet young man and he had a great future ahead of him."

The woman's eyes seemed to laugh, and Sara had an almost irresistible urge to hit her. Instead, she looked away. Where was Ariel? What was taking her so long? By now she could have borrowed her family's van or even taken the prize car. She could have—

She broke off because the back of the tent suddenly parted and in came about three feet of the back of a black car she recognized. It was Mike's precious BMW. He was safe! Sara nearly tripped over the bound-and-gagged woman as she ran outside to the driver's side.

Mike's windows were so dark that she didn't realize Ariel was driving until she flung open the door and got out.

"Where's Mike?" Sara's voice held fear.

"I've already told you all I know about him," Ariel said as she went into the tent, which now had part of a car inside it.

Sara followed her.

"I thought we'd put her in the trunk," Ariel said. "That okay with you?"

"Yes, but how did you get Mike's car? *Why* did you get his car?

"Was I supposed to steal somebody's Camry? Or maybe a Kia?" She grabbed one side of Mrs. Myers. "Get her other arm." She glared at the woman. "You hurt me in any way and I'll make you sorry."

Sara was still looking at Ariel, waiting for an answer.

"My dad's a dealer. I called Sue at the office, gave her the VIN number, and she popped the car open."

"And she was able to start it that way too?"

"No, I did that. A few wires and . . ." Ariel shrugged.

They were struggling with Mitzi, as she'd gone slack in their arms and she was quite heavy. It took all their strength to get her into the trunk and slam the lid.

"I'm driving," Ariel said.

When they were in the car and pulling out of the fairgrounds, Sara said, "Ariel, you're going to make some man a *great* husband."

Ariel didn't take offense. "The minute I find a man half as good as my brothers, I'm taking him. Can I assume we're going to Merlin's Farm?"

"I guess so, as whatever was in the secret room—paintings?—is what Stefan was after." Sara knew there was only one piece of art that someone had left her the rights to in a will, the CAY watercolor. Surely, that childish little picture couldn't be worth a lot of money.

Ariel was maneuvering Mike's car through the people of the fair, heading toward the road. When they reached the end of the grounds, a young man ran to move the barrier to let them through.

"Ah, the perks of being a Frazier," Sara said.

"If you start trying to make me believe you're jealous I'll stop right here. You nearly broke Lanny's heart in high school."

"I did what?" Sara put her hand on the dashboard to steady herself as Ariel was going much too fast. The old road followed K Creek, so it curved sharply.

"Nothing. You want to tell me what this is all about? What's so important that some detective *married* you to get it?" Ariel went around a thirty-mile-per-hour curve at sixty, then had to cut hard to the left to keep from ramming into a tree.

"Ariel! You're going to get us killed!"

"This car handles better than anything I've ever driven. I'm going to have Dad look at it. You know, don't you, that Mike has bulletproof glass in all the windows? I wonder what he's got stored in that false bottom in the trunk?"

At that, Ariel and Sara looked at each other with wide eyes. They didn't know what Mike had in the trunk, but they could guess. Weapons. And they had put Mitzi Vandlo in there with them. While it was true that she was tied up, if she got loose . . .

"Great," Sara said. "You *had* to get Mike's car, and now one of the most wanted criminals in the U.S. is locked away with a bunch of firearms. Good job, Ariel. Really smart."

"If you didn't want my help you shouldn't have asked me." They were at the entrance to the drive of Merlin's Farm, and when Ariel started to turn in, Sara halted her.

"Mr. Lang has set traps all over this place, and Mike told me about some of them. I want you to park the car in the orchard. If

Mitzi does get out, she'll have to make her way through traps that were set to catch her son."

Ariel followed Sara's directions and drove on the grass, snaking the car through the hedges, and stopped in the old orchard. "So now what?" she asked as she turned off the engine.

"I don't know. You have any ideas?"

"First of all, we should call Colin."

Sara looked at the clock on the dashboard. "Your whole family is at the games right now and they won't answer their phones."

"Then I guess it's just you and me."

As they got out of the car, Sara glanced toward the trunk. "You think we should . . . check on her?"

"And be greeted by gunfire? I don't think so." Ariel was looking around the orchard with half its trees missing. "This place gives me the creeps. I've always thought it was haunted."

"Mike and I are going to fix it up. Ariel, buck up your courage and let's go. And stay close to me or you may find yourself hit by an arrow."

The two women in their medieval dresses looked at home among the old buildings. Even though it was daylight, the women ran across the open lawn in a crouch and made their way toward the farmhouse. It wasn't until they got near the side entrance that they saw Greg's car.

Sara couldn't contain the fear that ran through her. Since she'd met him, Greg had had power over her. And even though the last two weeks had changed her life drastically, she still worried that he could rule her.

But she couldn't think about that now. Sara figured that if Greg—and she hoped Mike—were in the house they'd be in the big living room where the uneven fireplace would make a secret room possible.

Sara led them to the side of the house. Unfortunately, she could see in the window only if she stood on tiptoes. Stretching up, she peered inside, and what she saw made her heart pound. There were four men in the room. Greg/Stefan stood by the fireplace. Next to him was a man holding a gun that was aimed at Mike and the fourth man, both of whom were in the middle of the room. Mr. Lang's sparse furniture had been moved to the far edges so the floor was clear and a makeshift fighting ring had been created.

Mike and the other man were wearing only their trousers, no shirts, and their feet were bare. They were circling each other, but from the look of the blood on their faces, the fight had been going on for a long time.

The men were equally matched in size and weight, their bodies coated in muscle, with wide shoulders and tiny waists, and their back muscles flared out like the wings on a bat.

The other man struck out at Mike with his fist as though he were bareknuckle boxing, and Sara was glad to see Mike duck and dodge the blow. Then, in a flash, Mike bent and grabbed the man's leg and pulled hard. The man kept his balance for a few moments, but Mike butted his head into the man's stomach and he went down, with Mike on top of him.

The men were wrapped around each other, Mike on top, with the man's legs around Mike's back. Mike began punching at the man's head with his fists while the man pulled his legs down and gave a great push to Mike's stomach. Mike moved back, and in the next second they were again standing up and punching at each other.

Sara stepped down, her fist to her mouth to keep from screaming. She looked at Ariel. "Is that the man you saw at the fair? The one you were so hot for?"

Ariel shrugged.

"You are a worse judge of men than I am!"

"We have to call Colin," Ariel whispered.

"Mike would be dead by the time he got here." Sara looked at Ariel in her long skirt and silk top. "We need to distract them. What do you have on under there?"

Ariel gave a half smile of understanding and turned her back to Sara so she could untie her laces. "There's a little shop across from the New York Public Library, the big one, run by a tiny Frenchwoman. You can't believe the lingerie she carries. And it's all altered to fit you perfectly." Her voice was too fast as she worked to cover her fear.

"Really?" Sara asked. Her hands were shaking. "If you can . . . If you can get one of those men to follow you to the barn, there's a trap there." Sara tried to think of the objective and not about what could happen to Ariel if she got an armed man to follow her. She explained about the trap and the trip wire across the door, and she told her about the loft and Mike swinging down on the rope.

When Ariel's dress was loosened, she turned around and began pushing the heavy gown off her shoulders. "I'll be fine. Quit worrying about me." When the dress was puddled at her feet, Ariel was wearing a black silk corset with tiny red ribbons threaded through the top, and black panties that covered only half of her firm derriere. Her long legs were bare.

"I'm glad I don't wear the granny pants that you do."

"Ariel, why don't you try being nice? You might like it." Since Sara had made her own costume she'd fixed it so it was easy on and off. She'd concealed Velcro under the front seam of the gown, and now she quickly opened it. When she'd dressed that morning she'd thought of rewarding Mike for winning the games, so she'd put on some underwear he hadn't seen. Her white corset, white underpants, and the white stockings that reached midthigh were certainly a match for Ariel's outfit.

Ariel leaned back against the house. "So here we are, outfitted for a day at the Chicken Ranch, but now what do we do?"

In the next second, the question was answered for them when they heard shots in the distance.

Ariel and Sara looked at each other. "Mitzi," they said in unison. She had escaped her ties and found Mike's weapons.

"Go to the other side of the house," Sara said. "I'll let Greg see me."

Seconds later, the sound of the shots brought Greg and one of the bodyguards onto the porch. When Sara, in her white underwear, appeared at one side, both men looked at her in surprise.

On the opposite side there was a loud noise, like a big rock hitting the side of the house. The bodyguard went to see what it was, and there was Ariel, tall, slim, and in a black silk corset. He didn't even think to fire, just stood there looking at her.

Smiling seductively at him, Ariel took a step backward.

The man glanced at his boss, but Greg only had eyes for Sara. "It's a woman," the man said.

"Go after her," Greg growled. "This one is mine."

The bodyguard jumped off the porch and ran after Ariel.

Sara turned around and started running, but she couldn't outrun Greg. He caught her just as she reached the gravel yard in front of the old coach house.

She prepared herself for a blow, but it didn't come. When she looked at him his face had taken on an expression of great sadness and hurt. It was a look she knew well. He'd used it many times when talking about his former girlfriends—the ones who'd betrayed him and made him cautious of all women.

As Sara watched him, she was struck by how emotions could

change in an instant. A month ago, when Greg had looked at her with his sad, poor-me face, her heart had gone out to him. How could she possibly complain about anything he ever did? How could she add to the hurt he'd already experienced? Whatever she'd been about to question or complain about, she'd stopped. She didn't want it said about her that she'd ever hurt anyone— and she'd wanted to prove to Greg that not all women were as greedy, selfish, and manipulating as his previous girlfriends had been.

But now Sara saw that the feel-sorry-for-me look Greg was wearing wasn't real, and she wondered how she could ever have been so lacking in self-esteem that she had believed him.

What she wanted to do was tell him what she knew about him, but there was a gun stuck in his waistband, and she knew she couldn't do that. It was better to placate him, not make him angry.

Instead, she was going to do her best to use his giant ego against him. She willed the anger to leave her as she nearly fell against Greg, her arms around his torso. "Oh, Greg, my darling, it's been so awful while you were gone. You can't believe the lies people told me about you. But I didn't believe a word of them."

Her breath was held, waiting for him to believe her or . . . to shoot her. After what seemed like minutes, he put his arms around her.

"Sara," he said cautiously. "Why are you here and why don't you have on any clothes?"

"I was at the fair and Mr. Lang told me you were here."

"Lang?"

She pulled away to look at him. "Yes. Mr. Lang said you were here waiting for me and that you wanted to see me, so of course I came immediately. After I got here, I was at my car and I was changing out of my fair costume when I heard what sounded like gunshots. I was afraid Mr. Lang had his shotgun and he was after *you* so I came just as I was."

"Why did you run when I saw you?"

"You looked so angry at my dishabille."

"Your . . . ?"

She saw anger flash across his face and knew she'd made a mistake. He hated it when she used words he didn't know—and that look reminded her how she'd lived with his constantly changing moods. One second he'd be fine and the next he'd be in a rage—and it was *always* Sara's fault. All his bad moods—never the good ones—were, according to Greg, caused by Sara.

She pretended she hadn't seen his anger. "I've missed you so much," she said and made herself kiss his neck. "Did you miss me?" When you were with your wife? Or in jail? she wanted to ask.

"Sara, I don't have time for this right now." He pulled her arms from around his neck and stepped away, but she saw the flicker in his eyes. She had no idea if he knew about her marriage to Mike or not, but one thing was clear: He wanted sex. And she needed time. "There's an old summerhouse near here," she said softly. "Just behind those hedges."

"I . . ."

She began to back away from him. "Bet you can't catch me," she said in as enticing a manner as she could manage, then she took off running toward the summerhouse. But she'd seen the anger flit across Greg's eyes, and she knew that it wouldn't be long before he released his rage. As she ran, the image in her mind was of seeing Mr. Lang put the wire across the doorway of the old summerhouse and attaching the arrows just inside the entrance.

At the time, she'd visualized what would have happened if Mike or she had stepped into the pretty little building after the trap had been set. But Sara couldn't think of that as she ran across lawns, then around the tall hedge that protected the structure's privacy.

She headed straight into the building, jumping as she went through the doorway. At the other side she stood there with her back against the wall, and she could see Mr. Lang's four arrows affixed just inside the entrance. There was no way out.

Greg stopped outside the door. "Sara!" he ordered. "Come out here this minute."

"I'd rather you came to me," she whispered even though her heart was pounding in her ears.

When she disobeyed him, his wrath was released. "You little bitch!" he said as he lunged for her.

Everything happened at once. Greg drew his gun and took a step toward her—and she heard the click of the wire.

Greg saw her expression and knew something had happened. "Damn Lang and his traps!" he yelled as he pointed his gun at her. Instinctively, Sara dropped to the floor, her hands over her head.

Just as the gun went off, the arrows were released.

Stefan Vandlo, aka Greg Anders, aka several other names, was shot by four steel-tipped arrows—and he was silenced forever.

Sara was so horrified at what happened—at what she had caused—that she only managed to stand upright. Greg's blood was splattered on her face and clothes. To get out, she would have had to move Greg's body from where it was pinioned across the doorway, and she couldn't do that. She stayed where she was, her back against the summerhouse wall.

It took Mike quite a while to untangle himself from the agents who came to the call he made after they'd heard the shots. Within about four minutes the old farm was flooded with vehicles and men and they all had information to impart.

While they easily found Mitzi, Stefan eluded them. Emergency vehicles, including a helicopter, and many people were everywhere. The hunt for Stefan Vandlo was intense.

But Mike's only concern was Sara. He'd had to push his way through the crowd to get to Ariel. When she told him she and Sara had come together, he nearly panicked. He'd thought she was safe back at the fair.

Frantic, Mike began running. There was one place on Merlin's Farm that searchers could walk past and not see.

When Mike finally found Sara, she was at the back of the old summerhouse and Stefan Vandlo's lifeless body was strung across the doorway. Mr. Lang's arrows had pierced his body in four places, one of them being his heart.

Mike had no qualms as he pulled out the arrows and dropped the body to the ground. He went to Sara, took her into his arms, and held her tightly. "It's all right," he whispered. "You're safe now." He held her head on his shoulder so she couldn't see Stefan's body as EMTs carried it away. When it was clear, he led her outside, picked her up in his arms, and carried her back to the house. A fire truck and an ambulance were in the drive, a helicopter on the lawn.

Someone draped a blanket over Sara as Mike held her, and she saw Ariel leaning against the back of the fire truck. She had a fireman's coat over her shoulders, but her long, lean legs were bare, and at least a dozen men surrounded her. She gave a little salute to Sara as Mike carried her away.

He took her into the kitchen of the house and set her on the worn-out Formica countertop. After opening a couple of drawers, he found a stack of clean dish towels and wet one as he began to wipe at Sara's face. The cloths came away bloody. Greg's blood.

She touched the bruise by Mike's right eye, and there was a cut under the other one. He'd washed away most of the blood on his face, but she still remembered seeing it. Suddenly, she remembered how they got there. "Mitzi! We brought her here in your car but we heard gunshots! I think she—"

Mike kissed her gently. "It's all right. Mitzi got out, but she tripped on one of Lang's traps. We found her hanging from a tree in a net."

"She okay?" asked a voice at the door.

Sara turned to see the man Mike had been fighting with, the one who'd bloodied his face—the man who was working for Greg. "You did this to him," she half shouted. "I saw you hit him!" Her fists were clenched as though she meant to attack him.

"You're not her favorite person right now," Mike said. "Sara, my warrior princess, meet Frank Thiessen. I told you about him, and he's my oldest friend."

"Not so old," Frank said as he stepped toward Sara, his hand out to shake hers.

Sara didn't take his hand. She wasn't used to men who hit each other but were best friends.

"If it helps any, Mike's done worse to me. In fact, a couple of times, he's nearly killed me. I could show you some scars he's put on me . . ." Frank tapered off, as he could tell that Sara wasn't yet ready to see the humor in his words.

At Mike's nod, Frank left the kitchen. "Sara, baby, it's all right. Frank was working on another case when he heard someone mention the name 'Edilean.' He asked to be put on the Vandlo investigation because he knew my sister lived here. He went to prison for months so he'd have a good backstory when Stefan Vandlo was thrown in with him. And it was Frank who brought me into it. He worked hard to get info out of Stefan, but he wouldn't tell him anything. The best Frank could do was to make Stefan believe he needed a bodyguard."

"Was the other man I saw with Greg an agent too?"

"No," Mike said. "He was from Mitzi. I think she was fed up with the way her son messed up whatever she tried to do." Mike smoothed Sara's hair back. "Frank is the only person I told about Tess and Edilean. When Captain Erickson told me that info was out, I knew it was from Frank, and for a while I didn't know if I'd been betrayed or he was asking for my help."

"When I saw you two fighting—"

"We were trying to make everything take as long as possible in the hope that Mitzi would show up and she'd be caught. No one thought that you would be the one to catch her." He looked at her with such pride that Sara felt herself blushing. "When Frank contacted me at the fair we made a plan to put on a show to distract Vandlo for as long as we could."

"It wasn't a 'show.' You were really hurt." When she touched his face, she could see that he was trying not to wince.

"Frank and I trained together, and we've done a lot of cage fighting and—"

"Like you plan to do in the gym you want to open?"

"Exactly. How about if I demonstrate tonight? You and I can wrestle." Mike was grinning, but Sara wasn't. Too much bad had happened in the last few hours for her to smile.

Mike changed the subject. "Want to know how I found the hidden room? Lang ran a cord in there so he could have electric lights. When you and I visited him, and while you two were talking about cookies, I was looking around and I saw the cord disappear into the wall. But I didn't realize what I'd seen until the next day."

She caressed his cheek and looked at him with love. "You are smart, beautiful, and talented."

Mike laughed. "Then I must be a mirror image of you." He put his fingertips under her chin. "Sara, I'm sorry you were left alone to have to deal with what you did. The FBI kid they left in front of the tapes was told Joce left, so he assumed the fortune-telling tent would be empty. He went to watch Anna and me jump rope. If it makes you feel any better, he's now sporting two black eyes, one from me and one from Frank. I wanted to break his legs but Frank wouldn't let me." Mike shrugged. "Colin still thinks we should—"

He stopped when the door opened. A policewoman brought in Sara's long fair costume, and as she put it on the kitchen table, she looked at Sara in admiration. "You did a good job," she said, then left.

Mike smiled at Sara. "I haven't seen the tapes yet, but I hear you were great with Mitzi. I guess she was used to no one knowing about her, and since she didn't think you were her target victim, she blabbed to the wrong person. Whatever, the word is that you were magnificent."

"Not quite," Sara said, but she was pleased by his praise. "I think Mitzi was so excited about the tarot cards that she couldn't think straight, and I was scared to death. But I had help."

"Yeah, they talked to Ariel."

"What happened with her? That man was chasing her."

"When we heard the gunshots, Stefan and the other bodyguard ran out. Frank and I knew it was all over with. Mitzi would never show up if someone was shooting. Frank and I both called for help as we went after the others. Frank found the other bodyguard and brought him down."

"You mean he shot him?"

"Yes, but if Frank had arrived a minute later, I don't think Ariel would be alive." He hesitated. "But there was a problem."

When Mike's dimple showed, Sara looked at him in question.

"I guess you told Ariel that I swung out on a rope to keep you from running into the trip wire."

"What did she do?"

"After Frank shot Vandlo's bodyguard, Ariel tried to get away by swinging out on the rope. It was understandable, since she didn't know who Frank was, but he had a hard time catching her." Mike smiled. "But from what he told me, he liked it when he did latch on to her."

Sara could visualize the ensuing wrestle, with Ariel in her black underwear, fighting with all her might. Yes, she could imagine that Ariel would almost enjoy something like that.

"I do believe they like each other," Mike said as he leaned his head toward hers. "As for you . . . I think I've aged about ten years today. I was bombarded with Feds trying to talk to me and I wanted to know what had happened. If I'd even thought that you were here, I would have known just where to look." He touched her hair. "When I was told you were missing from the fairgrounds, I felt real panic. I got Ariel, and when she said you had come together . . . Sara, you shouldn't have—"

The look on her face stopped him. "All right, no lectures," he said. "I hate the danger you were in, but I'm really, really glad you caught Mitzi!" He put his hands on her shoulders. "And now, Sara, my love, as much as I like what you have on, I do *not* want other men seeing you wearing it. Let's get you dressed so you can go talk to some people, all right?"

When Sara caught his arm, he turned back to her in question.

"You called me your love."

Mike looked puzzled.

"You've not said that before." When he still didn't understand, she said, "*Love!* You've never said my name and *love* in the same sentence."

"You think I married you but I wasn't mad about you?"

"The case needed—"

Standing in front of her, he positioned her legs to either side of his hips. "There are lots of criminals, but I've never married anyone just to save her." He kissed her neck. "I love you." He kissed her cheek. "I love you more every day." He kissed her eyelids. "When I saw you standing in the back of that summerhouse behind Vandlo, with blood all over you, for a moment I didn't know if you were dead or alive, and I thought *I* was going to die."

"Me too," she said as she kissed him. "When I realized that old woman was Mitzi, I knew you were in danger and—"

"Shhhh," he said as he held her against him. "It's over now, and I have to go back to Fort Lauderdale on Monday. Think you can get packed by then? Except I don't know what I'll be driving."

"Your car . . . ?"

"Shot full of holes. What in the world possessed you to put Mitzi Vandlo in a car full of weapons? Couldn't you have stolen another vehicle?"

"Don't get mad at *me*. Ariel did it. Your beloved Ariel, who you go out on dates with even though you're a married man."

"I went out with her *before* I married you. And she—"

"I hate to break this up," Frank said from the doorway, "but everyone wants to see the woman who brought Mitzi down."

"I'll be there as soon as Sara gets dressed."

"Don't bother on our part," Frank said, then laughed at Mike's glare as he went outside.

"I take it the paintings hidden in Mr. Lang's secret room are signed by CAY."

"Yeah," Mike said. "Charles Albert Yates. Yesterday Luke and I hauled out a lot from that room." He lifted Sara off the counter. "There are about a hundred paintings, but there's much more. Everything in that room is old, and I have no idea what it is. There are wooden boxes full of letters and old diaries and clothes. The kilt and shirt Lang wore on that night in 1941, the ones I heard about for most of my childhood, were in there." Mike took a breath. "I don't understand why no one's found the room before now."

"Mr. Lang nailed the door shut," Sara said as Mike helped her into the long dress.

"So only *he* could see the contents. That makes sense."

"How did Mitzi find out about the paintings? And are they valuable?"

He was silent.

"Mike? What's wrong?"

"I sent photos of a couple of the paintings to the Feds in D.C. Sara, dear, you're a millionaire. Multi."

Her only thought was that now they could afford to renovate Merlin's Farm. And there'd be no worry about educating their children. And Mike could open the best gym there was. Smiling, she looked at him but saw that he was serious. "You're the only person on earth who could be unhappy about getting a lot of money."

"It's not my money. It's yours, and you could do a lot with it."

Sara had to work not to groan. Mike was letting her know that if she wanted to be released from her new marriage vows he'd let her go. "Think Tess can manage millions for *us*?"

"Sure," he said, and his dimple appeared.

She slipped her arm through his. "My mother has a list of people who want to join your gym."

"The question is whether or not we can get *you* out of bed to go."

"I—" she began but stopped when they stepped outside.

Besides the fire truck, ambulance, and the squad cars, it seemed that half of Edilean was there. And when they saw Sara, they began to applaud. She was sure that most of them had no idea what she'd done, but they'd been told enough that the town was proud of her.

She looked back at Mike.

"Go on," he said. "It's your moment. You're the hero." He gave her hand a squeeze. "No one will ever again feel sorry for Sara Shaw."

If she'd doubted her love for him, it would have dissolved in that moment. It was his work that had solved the case, but he was willing to step aside to give her the glory. "Newland," she said. "The name of the man I love."

Mike grinned. "Yeah, Mrs. Newland. My wife."

Turning, Sara went toward the people who were waiting to congratulate her—but she didn't let go of Mike's hand.

# Acknowledgment

I'D LIKE TO thank the person who made this book possible, my consultant, and most of all, my friend, Detective Charles J. Stack of the Economic Crimes Unit of the Fort Lauderdale Police Department.

Charlie, a former national champion of kickboxing and karate, and I work out together. In between pushing me to lift ever-heavier weights and hit that big bag with the gloves, he answered all my questions. Charlie instantly replied to all my many text messages, no matter where he was, in a courtroom or a meeting with the attorney general. He explained everything from FLPD retirement plans to the latest U.S. Supreme Court ruling to what the heck Muay Thai was.

He told me truly fascinating stories about his very dangerous undercover work. (AMC wants to do a documentary about one of them!) He read the scenes I'd written of the fights and about the real Mitzi's work, and did a great job of editing them.

His insights into how the minds of criminals such as the real "Vandlo" family work was brilliant—and spellbinding to hear. The magnitude of the crimes he works on and the absence of any public knowledge of these criminals horrified me.

I can never adequately express my gratitude to Charlie for his help, his intelligence, his kindness, and his never-ending patience.

Thank you, Charlie. You're a true hero.